The Man

from Nowhere

Originally published under the title 'And When the Music Stops'

THE MAN FROM NOWHERE

by

Gillian McRae

Norfolk: Sphinx House Publishing

Published by Sphinx House Publishing
Norfolk PE30 3QB

© Gillian McRae 2020

Chapter One

The siren sounded, loud over the incessant music, and immediately the men began to extinguish the lights strung along the tunnel. Overwhelmed by exhaustion, his shoulders and back throbbing with pain, Wilhelm put down his pick and rested his head against the rock face, uncertain whether he had the strength to drag himself back to his dwelling cave. But for once it wasn't the prospect of rest that was uppermost in his mind. Tonight he needed to be alone so that he could think. It was impossible here in the mine where the day was filled with hammering and voices, the drone of the air pumps and the music. Of course, there was always the music. Even in his cave there was always the music. And that was what he needed to think about.

This morning, as he worked by himself in a new tunnel, there had been a sudden loud crack followed by a rumble and instinctively he had crouched down, arms over his head, thinking the roof was about to fall. There was a crash to his left . . . then nothing. After a few moments he opened his eyes. As he got to his feet, shaking dust from his hair and beard, he saw to his amazement that there was now a gaping hole in the wall on which he had been working and, beyond it, a huge black cavern. In the dim light cast by his lantern he could see, hanging from its roof, pointed pillars of rock, like teeth in an enormous mouth. For a moment he stood staring in bewilderment but then, curiosity getting the better of him, he pushed his way through the hole and took a few steps into the cave.

It was as he picked his way across the uneven floor that he suddenly realised something was different. He could no longer hear the music. The shock of it made his legs buckle and he sank to his knees, shaking with fear. All his life he had been able to hear the music. And now, suddenly, it wasn't there. There was . . . nothing. An emptiness of sound. But with the fear came something else - a feeling he couldn't identify or define. It was a feeling that there might be . . . there could be . . . no, it was too elusive. Slowly he picked himself up and, staggering back to the hole in the wall, he pulled himself through. Hurriedly, not knowing why he did it, he piled some loose rocks up in front of the entrance to the cave so that it couldn't be seen, and continued with his work.

Now, at the end of the day, as he made his way along the tunnel leading from the mine to his dwelling cave, Wilhelm felt a need to remember exactly what he had seen and how he had felt. Reaching his cave, he put the lantern with its tallow candle down on the floor and sank onto the pile of rags in the corner, resting his head against the rock wall. The pain was almost unbearable tonight. He wasn't sure how much longer he could go on before he was Taken. He thought he would welcome it. It was over a thousand days since Eva had come to tell him that Lotte had fallen and broken her leg as she pulled a cartload of rocks. Eva had stayed with her until the Taker came and had held her hand while he put his cord around her neck and pulled it tight.

Since then Wilhelm had been very lonely. Once there had been four of them in the cave. But now the children were grown up and he hardly ever saw them. Konrad was working at the rock face and Marthe, having reached the age of four thousand days, was pulling the carts with the rest of the women. She was a strong girl and, if she continued to grow tall, They would probably take her for breeding and he would never see her again.

Wilhelm sighed and rolled his head, trying to ease the pain in neck and shoulders. He needed to think. Think about no music. Think about that feeling of - no, he couldn't remember what it was like. His eyelids drooped. But he didn't want to sleep just yet. He tried again. It was impossible. The music was lulling, lulling . . . He nodded briefly, then woke with a start. Somewhere between sleeping and waking had come the realisation that it was the music that was preventing him from thinking. He knew then that he would have to return to the cavern. How, he had no idea, was too tired to plan.

He looked at his food stock. There was very little left and it would be another three days before fresh supplies were given out. He could wait until the morning to eat. He took off his boots and, lying down on the rags, pulled the coarse blanket over him, blew out the candle and slept.

The next day as he hacked at the rock face, Wilhelm tried to devise a plan to return to the cavern. It would be easy enough to be at the far end of a tunnel when the siren sounded, somewhere that he could stay until after the lights had gone out and the other men had left. No one would know he was still there. After all, who would want to stay in the mine when he no longer had to? Sometimes men working by themselves in isolated passages would die during the course of their work and it could be many days before their bodies were found. Once or twice Wilhelm had found a body. As he had helped to throw it into the rubbish pit, he had felt a sort of envy of the man who had gone.

Crouching in the dark at the far end of the tunnel, some minutes after the siren, Wilhelm realised he still had no idea of what he would do when he reached the cavern. He couldn't now remember how he had felt in there, other than frightened, and fleetingly he wondered why he should choose to repeat the experience. But something extraordinary had happened there and he needed to define it, to find out what it was. He waited, listening to the sound of men retreating up the tunnels to their caves, then slowly, painfully, got up from his crouching position and, relighting his lantern, made his way to where he thought the cavern entrance to be.

At first he couldn't find it. He remembered that he had heaped stones in front of it but now there were several piles along the length of the tunnel, debris of the day's work. Slowly and with care he removed the heavy rocks until he could look behind them, then heaped them up once more, making sure they looked the same as before - although why he was being so cautious he couldn't say. The fourth pile proved to be the one he was looking for. He removed enough of the stones to allow him to squeeze through into the cavern then, as best he could, lifted them again to close the opening behind him.

Trembling with fatigue and apprehension, he turned and took a few steps forward. Once again, the absence of the music hit him like a hammer blow, even though he had been expecting it. He sat down on the rough floor, put his lantern beside him and, resting his head in his hands, started to think.

Strange thoughts began to fill his mind and, again, that feeling that he couldn't name. But he was overwhelmed by exhaustion and nothing was clear. Still, he had blocked the entrance and no one would know he was here. He had time. Putting his hand inside his shirt, he pulled out the things that he had kept hidden there during the day and placed them beside him. Then, blowing out the lantern, he lay down and slept.

How long he had slept he didn't know - longer than he had ever slept at one stretch before. When he woke he was momentarily disorientated. Thinking he was in his dwelling cave but hearing neither waking siren nor music, he was hit by a brief wave of fear before he remembered. Slowly he sat up. The cavern was completely dark but, even without seeing it, he could sense its vastness. There was an airiness that was never felt in the mines, but only in the larger caverns where the rocks were sorted and the supplies handed out. He could hear nothing from the tunnel. In the complete absence of sound that surrounded him, all he could hear was his own breathing. Feeling around beside him he found his lantern and his few possessions - his flint box, a spare candle, and all the food that he had - a few biscuits and a small piece of yellow food-cake. He could see no light coming through from the tunnel. The rocks which he had piled up at the entrance to the cavern appeared to have blocked it off completely. He lit his lantern. Beyond its small circle of yellow light he could see nothing except a pale glimmer where it reflected off one of the strange hanging stone teeth. The darkness didn't bother him, he was used to it, but now the lantern was somehow reassuring in its familiarity.

After his long sleep he was hungry. Breaking off a small piece of the food-cake he ate it slowly. He had drunk from the trough in the mine at the end of his shift and now he needed to pass water. Although he could hear no sounds coming from the tunnel, he could not risk being heard by someone who was working there. He would go further into the cave. He stood and picked up his things, finding that his long sleep had eased some of the pain in his shoulders and back. Quietly he made his way further into the cavern, then stopped and urinated on the stone floor. The sound of it was loud in his ears and for a moment he held his breath, wondering

4

whether he might be discovered. It struck him that already, almost without realising it, he had decided not to go back, had chosen to die here - with no pain in his back and no music in his ears and without the Taker's cord around his neck. But before he died, he needed to think. He sat down again. His mind was quite clear. He knew now, without any doubt, that the music suppressed thought. But why? Were They afraid of thought? He had never thought about Them before. They were just there. Although the Hundeiss had never seen them, They were a part of life. They supplied the food, the water, the clothes, the candles, the mining tools, and They used the rocks that the Hundeiss mined - although how and for what purpose Wilhelm didn't know, had never wondered. It dawned on him that They must also be responsible for the music. And now he had found a place where the music didn't exist. He wondered what else in this cavern could be different from the life he had known.

And then it struck him. That was it. The feeling - it was that things could be different. More than that - that they could be better. It had never occurred to him that things could be better. Things just were. But now the idea had taken hold he realised that it was entirely possible. A longer rest than the six hours allowed between the siren announcing the end of the day's work and sounding again to wake the Hundeiss to the new day. And more food. And clothes replaced more often, before the red and yellow cloth had been reduced to black rags.

Continuing to concentrate on the feeling, Wilhelm found he could define it now. It was a belief that things could get better and would get better. The strength of it took his breath away. He gazed out into the darkness beyond the glow of his lantern and wished that there were words for these things - for the feeling, for the absence of music, for the absence of sound. But how could there be when no one had ever experienced them? And then a thought - perhaps They had words for them. Perhaps They had experienced them. Wilhelm clapped his hands over his ears. His thoughts were taking him too far, too fast.

He took a deep breath and tried to calm his mind. Automatically his thoughts turned to Lotte. Since she had been Taken, his memory of her had become blurred and his sense of loss had been intensified by the knowledge that he would soon be unable to remember how she looked. But now, away from the music, he suddenly found that he could picture her face quite clearly, could see her in every detail, could hear the way she spoke his name. If he had needed any further reason not to return to the mines, this was it. To be able to die with a picture of Lotte in his mind . . . It was all he asked.

Wilhelm's mind stopped racing and he looked around him. Safe inside the circle of yellow light cast from his lantern, he hadn't paid the cavern much attention. Now he could see that his first impression of its size had been right. Even from where he was, twenty or more paces further in from the place where he had slept, he couldn't see the far wall. The lantern reflected on the pale surfaces of the tooth-like projections that hung from the roof and rose out of the cavern floor. But beyond them was total blackness.

Wilhelm tucked the flint box, the spare candle and the remaining food securely inside his shirt and stood up. He would go further into the cavern. He wanted to know how far away the wall was. Never before had he wanted to know anything. There had never been anything to know. But now he wanted to know about Them, he wanted to know about the music - and, before that, he wanted to know how far away the wall of the cavern was and what it looked like.

Holding the lantern in front of him, he moved slowly onwards. After a minute or two he turned and looked back. He could no longer see the wall through which he had come - wasn't even sure in which direction it was. But that didn't matter. He wasn't going back.

Passing close by one of the huge rock teeth, he put out his hand and touched it. Its surface was smooth and cold. Wilhelm held his lantern above his head and looked up. The tooth rose upwards, thick and strong, disappearing into the darkness. He couldn't see the roof.

The floor of the cavern was very uneven, with sudden sharp dips, and Wilhelm trod carefully, keeping his eyes fixed on his feet. Suddenly he stopped. He could hear a noise somewhere to his right. A slow, steady tapping, soft and high pitched. Turning, he saw three huge rock teeth hanging almost to the floor. Cautiously he moved towards them. Then stopped again. Water was dripping from the end of one of the teeth into a small pool beneath it.

Water. For the first time since waking, Wilhelm realised how dry his mouth was. Kneeling, he bent and used his hand to scoop the water into his mouth, then sat back on his heels and gazed at the stony tooth, wondering how it had come to be there, hanging in the darkness, dripping water. He had never before thought about the possibility of there being a place other than the one in which he lived - the music had made sure of that - but it seemed to him that if he had thought about it, he would have imagined the two places as identical, because how could things be different from what was? His head was beginning to spin again. Quickly he took his mind back to Lotte. Shutting his eyes, he could almost imagine that she was there with him, that they would die together in this huge cavern, would die quietly in each others' arms.

Wilhelm's thoughts slowed and his mind became calmer. After a moment or two he opened his eyes, raised his head and peered into the gloom. He was amazed by the size of the cavern. It was far wider and higher than even the sorting caves or the supply cavern. He had never dreamed that there could be so much space in one place.

Getting to his feet, he picked up the lantern. The candle was half burned but it would last several hours yet. And he had another inside his shirt. He walked slowly, trying to keep his mind focussed on what he was doing. Occasionally, his foot kicked a loose stone which rattled off into the darkness, the sound echoing loudly in his ears. This was unlike the floors of the tunnels that he was used to, floors that had been worn smooth over time by the tramp of the Hundeiss' feet on their way to and from the mines. This was a floor that looked as though it had never been walked on, as though his were the first feet ever to cross its surface. The thought made him shiver.

It was a long way to the far side of the cavern. And everywhere there were rock teeth, making it necessary for him constantly to change direction as he skirted round them. And then at last the light from his lantern reflected off something. He was there. He put out his hand and touched the wall. He didn't know what he had expected. It was only rock. Looking up, he thought that he could just see the roof of the cavern high above him.

He turned and leaned against the wall, peering back the way he had come, at the rock teeth disappearing into the darkness. Momentarily he wondered whether he had gone round in a circle, whether in fact he was close to the entrance back into the mine. It seemed as though he had walked a great distance but he might have been quite close to the wall several times and not seen it. Perhaps if he followed the wall round he would get an idea of the true size of the cavern. Suddenly it was very important to him to know that, when he died, as die he must, he was as far away from the mines and his dwelling cave, as far away from the music, the numbness in the mind and the pain in the body as it was possible to be. All that he wanted to carry from the mines was his lantern and his memories of Lotte. Raising his lantern, he turned to his right and, keeping close to the rock face, started to walk.

It was colder here than in the tunnels and in the dwelling caves. There were places in the mines, near the air pump outlets, where it was cold, but he could hear no sound of air pumps here. He could hear nothing except the sound of his feet on the rock floor.

The floor was sloping upwards now and Wilhelm put his right hand out against the rock face for support as he walked. Now he could see the roof of the cavern quite clearly if he lifted his lantern above his head. Suddenly he became aware that, to his left, there was another wall. He was no longer in a cavern but in a tunnel. Was he, perhaps, in an old shaft of the mine, one that was no longer in use, that had been shut off? But if that was the case, there would be signs of the rock face having been worked and there were none. If it wasn't a mine shaft, how had it got here, he wondered - and sharply stopped himself from thinking further, before the thoughts started his mind whirling again.

Trudging up the increasingly steep incline, Wilhelm's leg muscles started to ache. He wasn't used to walking such distances. Just ahead of

8

him, there was a small level area where he could rest. Sitting down, he leaned his back against the wall and peered at the tunnel ahead of him. There was a chance, of course, that it might lead him back to the mines. But there was also the chance that it might lead him to another cavern, as full of unimagined things as the first. He wanted to find out.

He was feeling hungry again. Reaching inside his shirt, he took out the remains of the food-cake and ate it slowly, following it up with one of the hard biscuits which, without water to help it down, made his jaw ache from the effort of chewing. Eventually he had swallowed it all and, getting to his feet, he picked up his lantern and continued along the tunnel.

✳ ✳ ✳

The tunnel went on and on. Every now and again it divided and, when it did, Wilhelm followed the wider pathway or, if the tunnels were of equal width, the one which seemed to slope more obviously upward. So far he hadn't had to choose between two that were identical. On one occasion the wider tunnel had led almost immediately to a dead end and he had retraced his steps and followed the other. It hadn't divided for some time now but, while it continued to slope upwards, almost imperceptibly it was becoming narrower. If he stretched out his arms, Wilhelm could touch both walls at the same time. It occurred to him that the tunnel might eventually narrow down to a dead end. If it did, there would be no point in going back - the other tunnels were probably all the same. He could do nothing but sit down where he was and wait for death.

At fairly regular intervals, he stopped to rest, his legs aching from the continuing gradient. By now he must be far higher than the mines and the dwelling caves and the cavern with the teeth. And it was getting colder. He didn't remember ever being this cold before.

Suddenly, the lantern spluttered and went out. Wilhelm stopped and leaned against the rock wall. He was loath to start using the other candle until he had to. Somehow it seemed that it would mark the beginning of the end. The tunnel had become very narrow and it might be possible for him to find his way by touch. He was having to move slowly anyway. The gradient wouldn't permit any speed, and he was getting tired. He put out

9

his right hand to feel the tunnel wall and trudged on.

It was easier than he had thought it would be. His left elbow, brushing the rock on the other side, told him that the tunnel was continuing to narrow. The roof, too, was getting lower and he was having to bend slightly to avoid banging his head. Suddenly he stopped and sniffed. He was near an air pump. He couldn't hear the familiar drone but, although only slight, the movement of the air was unmistakable. For a moment anxiety assailed him at the thought that somehow he had found his way back to the mines. Quickly, he reassured himself. It was impossible, having climbed for as long and as far as he had. But perhaps there were many places lying one on top of the other like the layers in a rock wall, and he had reached another place entirely. And, if he had, would this place be the same as his? Or maybe it would be better. The sudden thought that it might be worse stopped him in his tracks. But how could it be worse? He realised, now that there was no music to dull his mind, that it couldn't be much worse. In the place that he had left, he had been alone, without woman or children. There were days when there was nothing to eat. He had had little rest and continuous pain, and the music had stopped him from thinking. No, it couldn't be much worse than that. And he would only find out by going on.

The roof was now so low that he was almost having to bend double and his progress had become very slow. Before long, he decided that it might be better to crawl on hands and knees, pushing the darkened lantern in front of him. Trying it, he found that it was, indeed, easier although his ragged trousers gave little protection to his knees and shins as they scraped along the uneven surface. As the roof brushed his back, he bent his arms in order to bring his head and shoulders to a lower level, and his beard swept across the jagged floor which scratched his elbows and hands as he moved slowly forwards. Finally the tunnel became so small that he was lying almost flat and using his feet to push himself through. He would have to stop soon.

The air flow, however, was spurring him on. He wanted to go that little bit further, just that little bit more. He pushed - and found that he had wedged himself under a jagged piece of rock, which dug into his back, pinning him down. He could move neither forward nor back. So this was how it was going to end. So be it. He shut his eyes.

Time passed. Wilhelm was aware of the soreness of his arms and legs where the stones had scratched his skin. More intrusive, though, was the pain in his back which was steadily increasing from the pressure of the sharp rock. He wriggled, trying to get some relief and, as he did so, he thought that he felt the rock move slightly. Cautiously he wriggled again. This time he was sure that it had moved.

Immediately he felt his energy returning and, digging the toes of his boots into the floor to give him purchase, he pushed forward with all his remaining strength. He felt the stone give way and, in the same moment, knew that the tunnel was going to collapse on top of him. He gave one more frantic push - and with a great crash the tunnel fell in behind him. Wilhelm lay unmoving, his heart pounding, his breath coming in short bursts. Once his breathing had become more regular, he raised his head. He could sense that there was now much more space all around him. But as he started to pull himself to a sitting position he found that he couldn't move his right leg. Feeling inside his shirt, he took out the candle and the flint box. Carefully, he fixed the candle into the lantern and lit it. In the yellow light, he could see that his foot, encased in its stout boot, had been caught under the rock fall. Sitting up as best he could, he turned and removed the stones that were pinning it down. It felt bruised, but he didn't think the bones were broken.

Wilhelm drew his knees up to his chest and looked around. Once again, he was in a cavern. But there were no rock teeth here and, in the flickering candlelight, he could see the roof some way above him. For a moment or two he watched the flame, trying to judge the direction of the flow of air, then slowly got to his feet, testing his injured ankle to make sure that it would bear his weight. It was uncomfortable, but he could walk on it.

As he moved, he realised that the cavern was larger than he had at first thought, the roof sloping up sharply only a short way from where he had been sitting. Some distance ahead of him, in the blackness,

11

he was aware of a faint noise. Walking towards it, he suddenly saw, in the lantern's glow, a sheet of water falling down the rocky wall into a pool whose far end disappeared beneath some huge rocks. Holding up the lantern, Wilhelm could see the light reflected in the drops that splashed up from the surface of the pool. He stood and watched, wondering, for several minutes then, realising how dry his mouth was, he knelt and began to scoop water into his mouth. It was very cold. It seemed that the further he went, the colder everything became. He wondered how much colder it was possible for things to be.

Sitting back on his heels, Wilhelm peered into the darkness, trying to judge where the air flow was coming from. The way the candle was flickering suggested that the air pump was at the top of an outcrop that he could see rising like a series of uneven steps up the cavern wall. It looked as though it would be possible to climb it. But before he went any further he would have to rest again. He was very tired and all his muscles ached from dragging himself through the last stretch of the tunnel. His hands, elbows and knees were sore and his bruised ankle was throbbing. He got up and moved over to the outcrop, found a smooth section against which he could lean his back and sat. Blowing out the lantern, he placed it on the floor beside him. He shut his eyes but didn't sleep.

Wilhelm sat for a long time, gathering his strength and reviewing in his mind the extraordinary things he had seen. Eventually he felt ready to go on. He lit the lantern and stood up. Then, taking a deep breath, he started to climb.

It wasn't easy. None of the steps was flat and some were very narrow, while others were covered in small loose stones, and he had to place his feet carefully for fear of slipping. Several of the steps were too high simply to climb onto from the one below. With these, he had to lean forward across the higher step, put down the lantern, stretch his arms out to find a handhold and then, digging his feet into the vertical rock face, lever himself up. In his increasingly tired state he was moving more and more slowly, all his muscles aching as he worked his way towards the top. But in his mind the feeling that things could and would be better was still strong. Indeed, it seemed to have been strengthened by the fact that he had escaped from the narrow tunnel, that he hadn't been seriously injured in the rock fall, that he had found water and, most of all, that he was still climbing, climbing out of the mines. And beyond this cavern there could be something even better. He wanted to know.

He was nearing the top, and the movement of the air was becoming more noticeable, when he misjudged the height of one of the steps. He hadn't leaned far enough over onto it and, as he stretched forward, trying to get a handhold, his bruised foot, which he had raised and placed against the vertical rock face, slipped. For a moment he thought he was going to fall, to crash down onto the floor of the cavern, his bones broken, to die finally in pain, without knowing what lay still beyond him. He was seized by panic and, in his frantic haste to find something to hold on to, he knocked over the lantern. He heard the metallic thudding as it bounced down from step to step, coming to rest on the cavern floor far below him, leaving him in darkness.

Gasping from the exertion and shaking with relief that it was only the lantern that had fallen, Wilhelm clung with grim determination to the rock and steadied himself. There was no point, he knew, in climbing back down for the lantern, although the thought of leaving it behind saddened him more than he would have expected. Through the long journey out of the mines the lantern had been his companion. But he knew that if he tried to climb down in the darkness he would probably fall. And, even if he did manage to get down safely, he might not be able to find the lantern or the candle which, in any case, had probably been smashed to pieces. But, as his heart rate slowed to normal, he realised that there was an even better reason why he should just keep climbing. Not far above him, at the place where the air pump seemed to be, he could make out a faint glimmer of light.

Making sure he had a firm handhold, Wilhelm pulled himself up onto the next ledge and lay there for a few moments, breathing deeply. He was, he judged, about three quarters of the way up, although now that he no longer had the lantern, it was hard to tell. He raised himself onto his knees, then onto his feet, feeling carefully for the ledge above him, feeling for the best handholds. Taking a deep breath, he pulled himself up. He continued to climb, slowly and carefully and without mishap. The glimmer of light was getting closer. And there was no doubt that the movement of air was coming from the same direction as the light. Air pumps and light . . . was he coming to another place of mines and miners? But They must have air pumps and lights in Their place, too. Could he have reached Their place? He would know soon. And, if it was Their place, what would happen if They found him there? Would They send him back? Or would he be Taken? He could only find out by continuing upwards.

His shoulders and arms were aching fiercely from the exertion of pulling himself up, and he was getting very tired, but he was nearly there. As he pulled himself onto the final shelf, Wilhelm realised that it led directly into a small cave. He could see the light at the far end, feel the movement of the air. Relief at having got this far without injury swept over him and he found that he was shaking. He sat down on the rock floor, leaning forward over his knees, breathing deeply. But he didn't want to rest for too long now. Waiting only until the shaking and some of the pain in his arms had subsided, he got up and made his way towards the light.

He couldn't believe what he saw. After all this . . . after coming so far . . . to be able to see the light of this new place and yet to be able to go no further . . . he sank to his knees in despair. The entrance into the next cavern, to the place where the light shone, that entrance was about the width of his hand. There was no way in which he could get through it. Suddenly he was acutely aware of the pain in his muscles and joints, aware of his exhaustion . . . and now he would never know what lay beyond this cave, would never know what he might have found there. His shoulders slumped. And yet . . . perhaps if he looked through the opening, he might be able to see a little of what lay beyond. Even if he couldn't get there, to be able to see it would be something. Standing up, he moved a few paces towards the light and peered through the long, narrow crack. As he leaned forward, he put his hand against the wall of the cave - and jumped back, startled. That wall felt like no rock that he knew. In the pale light he could see that his hand was covered with tiny dark particles. And it felt damp.

14

Cautiously, he put his hand back on the wall. The whole surface felt damp and somehow . . . soft. He scraped at it with a finger and fragments fell away. His breath was coming faster now as he realised what this meant. He might be able to mine his way through, even without his tools. He might be able to claw away with his hands and remove enough of this strange, soft rock to allow him to squeeze through into the cavern beyond. Urgently, he began to scrape at the sides of the opening and slowly it became wider. There was something embedded in the rock - long and thin and hard - which bent as he pulled at it. It came away in his hand, bringing with it a large chunk of the rock. He was almost there. With renewed energy he scraped and pulled. He forced himself to continue until he was quite certain that he could get through. He didn't want to get stuck after all this. Eventually, the hole was large enough and he pushed himself out into the cavern beyond.

It was enormous. He could see no walls and there were no rock teeth, although he could make out various unidentifiable shapes some distance away. A large round lamp was hanging above him and hundreds of tiny lamps were dotted all across the roof.

Although the light wasn't as strong as he had been used to in the mines, it was still quite bright and he could see fairly clearly. He was on a steep slope, some distance above the cavern floor. But he was exhausted - had to rest before he could go on. Turning, he pushed his way back into the small cave, sank down onto the floor and was immediately asleep.

When Wilhelm woke, still aching from his exertions, everything was frighteningly strange. Even before he opened his eyes, he was aware that the light was much stronger than it had been when he went to sleep - stronger than it had ever been in the mines - and, somehow, of a different quality. The air, too, was different - although how he couldn't say - but, much to his relief, it now felt warmer. Raising his head, he opened his eyes a fraction and was dazzled by the brightness. He put his hands over his eyes, waited a minute or two, then tried again. By the third time of trying, it was easier. Pulling himself to his feet, he moved towards the hole in the

rock and stepped through into the next cavern, his eyes still half shut
against the glare. There was something wrong about the steep slope that lay
beyond. But what was it? Wilhelm was confused . . . he could see that it
was wrong, but he didn't know why. And then suddenly he realised . . . it
was the colour. It was a colour that he had never seen before. He stared,
bewildered. He could understand that there might exist physical objects he
had never seen - but colours? Apart from the colour of children's flesh
which blackened as they grew older, everything was red, yellow, brown,
grey, black or pale. How could there be another colour?

He turned his head cautiously, frightened of what else he might see.
The slope was strewn with small rocks and, bending, he became aware that
the surface on which they lay was made up of small spikes of differing
lengths and widths. Wilhelm brushed his hand across them tentatively, and
they bent easily beneath his fingers, then sprang up again. But even more
surprising was the fact that they felt wet. He looked round, trying to see
where the water had come from - he would have liked some to drink. But
there was no sign of its source. He was hungry, too, but all he had left was
biscuits, and it was too much of an effort to eat them dry.

As he became more used to the light, Wilhelm could see that he was in
a small recess between two rocky walls. Ahead of him on the cavern floor
were the shapes he had noticed earlier in the pale light. Even though it was
now so bright, he still couldn't identify them. Like the rock teeth, they
stretched up from the floor, but widened out half way up into irregular
shapes that seemed to be pierced by numerous holes. He wondered what
they could be and what their function was. Above them he could see the
pale grey roof of the cavern but it was too high for him to make out any
detail on it. Suddenly he realised that the lamps he had seen earlier had
been removed and he could no longer see where the light was coming from.
He supposed there must be lamps on the walls, but the rock face on either
side and the projections ahead of him blocked any view of the cavern
beyond.

There was only one way to find out more, and Wilhelm started to walk
down the slope. He was aware of faint noises which seemed to be coming

16

from far away, but he couldn't identify any of them. They were not the sounds of the mine - he could hear no hammering or voices or rumbling carts. And he could still see no walls. It worried him. He had spent his life in mines, in tunnels, in small caves. He wasn't used to such space.

As he drew nearer to the projections, Wilhelm could see that their upper sections were not, as he had thought, one block pierced by holes, but were made up of long pieces which seemed to have grown out of the broad bases like numerous fingers out of a hand. Inexplicably, there was something familiar about them. Tentatively, he reached up and pulled one of the long fingers down towards him. As he did so, it snapped and he found himself holding something he recognised. It was wood - the substance that formed the handles of the mining tools and was used in long poles to support the walls and roof of the mine tunnels. But the surfaces of these projections were much more irregular and rough than the wood which Wilhelm knew. And while the bases were much thicker than the poles that were used in the mine, the fingers were much thinner and, surely, wouldn't support anything. In any case, their tops ended way below the cavern roof. So why were they there? What were they used for? There was so much he didn't understand.

Pressing onward, Wilhelm soon reached a flat section of the cavern floor. A few more steps and he was in an open area, his view no longer masked by projections or rocky cleft.

It was even bigger than he had imagined. And still he could see no walls. The floor - covered mostly in the strange spikes - was uneven, rising and falling. But no part of it made contact with the roof and, in the distance, the highest parts of the floor prevented him from seeing any further. Wilhelm had no doubt, now, that this was Their place. The thought that he might meet Them face to face made him fearful. But what did they look like? He didn't even know if he would recognise them. Suddenly, like a candle being blown out, the precious feeling that things could and would get better deserted him and he was overcome by a sense of desolation such as he hadn't felt since Lotte had been Taken. Yes, he was seeing things no other Hundeiss had seen and was doing things no other

17

Hundeiss had done, but he understood none of it. And there was no one he could ask, no one with whom he could share his discoveries. He was totally alone. He sank down onto the cavern floor, realising that his legs were trembling. And yet there was nothing he could do. He couldn't go back. Even if he wanted to, he would never find his way. All he could do was to go on and try to regain the vanished feeling. And if this was, indeed, the place where They lived, he wouldn't be alone for long. Once They found him, he would be Taken and that would be an end of it. But he would have liked to have been able to tell someone about what he had seen.

Taking a deep breath, Wilhelm pulled himself to his feet and looked around. And then, to his left, he saw the four figures. They were completely covered in brown hair and each one was leaning forward, supporting itself on both arms and legs while its head bent low to the floor. They were speaking to each other in low droning voices, although Wilhelm couldn't make out the words. For a moment he hesitated. But there was nothing for it. They hadn't yet seen him but they would do so at any minute. Slowly he started to walk towards them.

As he got closer, one and then two of the figures lifted their heads and looked at him. They said nothing. Wilhelm didn't know what to do. His whole life until a day or so ago had been completely controlled by others. But now he had to make his own decisions. Should he stop or go on? Should he say something? He stood still. "I am Wilhelm," he said, his voice sounding strangely quiet in this huge cavern, away from the echoes of the mines and tunnels. "I am Wilhelm," he said again, raising his voice. The nearest one moved a few steps towards him and Wilhelm could see that what he had taken to be its arms were, in fact, two extra legs in the place the arms should be. He continued to stand there. Surely they would tell him what to do. But the one who had come towards him just stared at him out of huge dark brown eyes, then turned away and walked off in the opposite direction. The other three were paying him little attention and after a few moments they, too, turned and followed their companion.

Wilhelm was confused. Was he meant to follow them? Or were they not interested in him. And then a thought - suppose these beings weren't

18

Them. Perhaps they, like he and the rest of the Hundeiss, were controlled by Them, belonged to Them. There was no music here - but perhaps They had other methods of control. Everything was so different here.

He watched the beings move away. They hadn't told him to follow them. They paused some distance away, their attention seeming to be taken, once again, by the floor of the cavern. Perhaps they wouldn't tell Them that they had seen him. Perhaps he wasn't going to be Taken yet.

With that thought, Wilhelm made his decision and, turning to his right, walked away as quickly as he could. The cavern floor sloped gently upwards, then flattened out before starting to slope down again. Now he could see a long grey barrier just ahead of him which, as he approached it, he could see was made up of stones piled on top of each other to about the height of his waist. It stretched out across the cavern floor, cutting off the section in which he stood from the one towards which he was heading. Looking closely, Wilhelm saw that the stones had been piled carefully, fitting together, not haphazardly as in the mines. There were no mine workings to be seen, so these could not be rocks awaiting collection. It seemed as though someone had put them there simply to divide the cavern floor. But why?

Wilhelm climbed over the barrier and walked on. Wherever he looked, the floor was covered by the strange spiky material and, here and there, he could see groups of wooden projections, similar to those that he had passed earlier. When he had been walking for a little while, and had climbed over another two rock barriers, he looked back. There was no sign of the beings. He was getting warm and it seemed to him that the light was even brighter than before. It was starting to hurt his eyes again.

Coming over the top of another mound brought more of the cavern into view. There were still no walls in sight, nor any lamps. But now over to his left, surrounded by another of the stone barriers, he could see a huge block-like structure. It was several times wider than it was high and was pale with dark rectangles placed at intervals along it. It had a sort of lid, red in colour, with two small towers perched on top of it. Wilhelm climbed over the stone barrier and approached cautiously but with great curiosity.

Of all the things he had yet seen, it was, perhaps, the most puzzling because it was of such a regular shape.

It was then that he heard a sound, a movement, and from behind the block came one of Them. It was a curious mixture of the known and the unknown. It was wearing a pale shirt and, around its lower half, was wrapped a piece of black material. Its flesh was the colour of a young child and its hair was a pale grey. From its shape it appeared to be a woman - there was a bulge on the front of its chest that Wilhelm took to be breasts. But it was much larger than any Hundeiss woman, or indeed, any Hundeiss man - not taller but wider, with more flesh on it than anyone he had ever seen. As soon as it saw him it opened its mouth and shouted something Wilhelm didn't understand. He didn't know if he was being told to stand still or to come closer and he hesitated, fearful of what might happen if he didn't obey the command. The woman, if woman it was, shouted again and waved her arm at him. Clearly he was doing the wrong thing by standing. He started to move closer. She shouted again, louder, but this time it seemed that she wasn't addressing him. From round the corner of the block came another being, black, hairy, running on four legs. It raced towards Wilhelm shouting loudly and he could see that it had large pointed white teeth. He panicked and, not caring that it might be the wrong thing to do, but only wanting to get away, he turned and ran. Climbing over the stone barrier, he slipped, fell and struck his head. Instantly everything went black.

Chapter Two

Wilhelm's first feeling on regaining consciousness was one of fear. He was in a cart. Occasionally he had ridden down into a deep part of the mine in one of the empty rock carts and he recognised the sensation of movement. They must have thought he was dead and thrown him in here to take his body to the rubbish pit. His eyes snapped open in panic. He didn't recognise what he saw. The cart was large, but closed in, and very bright. The light hurt his eyes and he shut them again. He was lying flat on his back and something warm had been put over him. Raising his head slightly, he half opened his eyes and saw that it was red, the colour of blood. The movement sent a wave of pain through his head and neck and he remembered how he had fallen over the stone barrier. He shut his eyes quickly and rested back again, sensing as he did so that there was something soft under his head. The softness was comforting. But he knew that They must have had a reason for putting him in the cart. He remained fearful.

After a few minutes, he tried to open his eyes again. This time, the light wasn't as painful and he was able to see more clearly. Turning his eyes only, not moving his head, he looked around him and was shocked to find that one of Them, his flesh the colour of young children, was sitting next to him. Wilhelm could see no bulge of breasts so he supposed the being was a man, but he had no beard - no hair on his face at all - so he couldn't be sure. When the man saw that Wilhelm's eyes were open he said something which sounded gentle, but Wilhelm couldn't understand the words.

A slight jolt told Wilhelm that the cart had come to a halt. He heard a noise behind his head, saw the man get up and move to face him, and suddenly felt himself being lifted and carried out of the cart.

The next few minutes were a blur of impressions, of lights, of noise, of movement. Wilhelm's brain refused to function. He could comprehend none of it. Soon he found himself lying on a flat surface, raised above the ground, staring up at a roof not far above his head. He looked around him.

This cave was not like the ones he had known - the roof and walls were too flat and regular. But at least they were roof and walls. Here, at last, was something he recognised, something he understood.

The light was coming from a long thin lamp on the roof of the cave and, although it was bright, he found that he could now keep his eyes open without pain. There was a strange smell in his nostrils, sharp but not unpleasant. He wondered what it could be. His head was still aching badly.

Someone came over to him. It was a woman, with yellow hair and flesh the colour of a young child. She wore a pale shirt and trousers and held something rectangular and flat in one hand and a small thin tool in the other. She said something and Wilhelm realized that some of the words sounded familiar. He concentrated and found that he could recognise one or two of them, although the way the woman spoke them sounded strange.

".... seine Name? - your name?" she asked.

"Min Name?" Was that what she was asking him?

"Ja."

"Wilhelm."

The woman scratched with the tool on the flat rectangular object, then asked something he didn't understand. He shook his head. It made the pain worse.

"Verstuont niht - I don't understand," he said.

She repeated what she had said. Wilhelm still didn't know what it meant. He shut his eyes and said nothing. He felt the woman lift his arm, push up his ragged sleeve and wrap something around his upper arm. He turned his head and looked at it briefly. It looked like cloth and was a reassuring shade of grey. Closing his eyes, he rested his head back. The cloth round his arm was becoming tighter and tighter, almost painful and Wilhelm could feel something cold being pressed into the bend of his elbow. Then the pain stopped and the woman was taking the cloth away. He wished he knew what was happening. Or perhaps it was better not to know. Now she had picked up his hand and was holding him by the wrist. After a few moments she let go, then said something else, but Wilhelm wasn't listening. He heard her walk away.

She returned a little while later with a man who had no facial hair and who wore a long pale shirt, open at the front to reveal beneath it another pale shirt and grey trousers. Hanging down the front of his chest was a strip of red cloth. The colour caught Wilhelm's attention and, momentarily, he wondered whether it denoted what work the man did.

The man leaned over Wilhelm.

"Wilhelm?" he said.

"Ja."

He asked the question that the woman had asked earlier. Again Wilhelm said he didn't understand. The man looked strangely at him and, from a sort of fold on the front of his long shirt, he took a tool similar to the one with which the woman had been scratching. He held it up and a bright light shone into Wilhelm's left eye. Wilhelm let out a yell, screwed up his eyes and covered his face with his hands, trembling with fear and pain. The woman gently removed his hands from his face. Cautiously, Wilhelm opened his eyes. The man said something, again incomprehensible. He had put the tool away and, turning to the woman, he spoke to her at length. Then he walked away and Wilhelm and the woman were left alone together.

Wilhelm heard footsteps behind him and suddenly he was being moved. He hadn't realised he was lying on a cart. Was he going to be Taken now? He lay very still, his eyes shut. Shortly, the movement stopped and, opening his eyes again, he saw yet another man. Wilhelm wondered if he was a Taker. The Takers in the mines wore black trousers and black shirts that fitted closely to their chests and arms and curved up round their necks. But this man wore a long, loose garment that looked as though it was heavy. He lifted Wilhelm's head and Wilhelm took a deep breath as he waited for the knotted cord to be twisted round his neck. But it didn't come. The man put down a flat square of metal, and carefully moved Wilhelm's head to rest on it, saying something as he did so. Then he went away. Wilhelm stared up at the roof, not moving. After a few moments the man came back, took the metal square away, replaced it with another and

23

moved Wilhelm's head so that he was looking at the far wall. Once more the man went away, came back and removed the metal square. He said something and nodded. Then he smiled.

Wilhelm was horrified. Why was the man smiling? Men and women who lived together smiled at each other. But it was unheard of for a man to smile at another man. To the fear was added more confusion. The woman was there again now. Wilhelm shut his eyes, not daring to look at her in case she, too, smiled at him. He wouldn't know what to do. His mind was whirling. Then he felt the cart being moved again.

When it stopped, he opened his eyes and found that he was in the same place that he had been earlier. His mouth was feeling very dry and he licked his lips with the tip of his tongue. The woman was standing next to him and she said something. He recognised the word Wasser - water. He looked at her. Was it possible that she would show him where there was some water?

"Wasser," he repeated, nodding his head slightly, "Ja." She went away.

When she returned she was holding something in one hand. By the wall there was a flat ledge standing on long poles. The woman put the object onto the ledge and came over to Wilhelm. She moved something behind him and he felt the top of his body being pushed up so he was in a semi-sitting position. Picking the object up again, the woman held it out for Wilhelm to take. It was a container - and he could see right through it to the water within. He felt as though his head was going to burst, unable to cope with all the things that he was seeing. For a fleeting moment he wished himself back in the mines. But then he remembered the music. No, he wouldn't want to return to that. Cautiously he took the container, wondering how he was to get at the water. When he drank from the bucket in his cave or the trough in the mines, he would scoop the water out with his hand. But this container was too small to allow him to do that. After a moment's thought, he tipped it over very carefully and allowed some of the water to pour into his other hand. He drank, then repeated the exercise until all the water was gone. The woman took the empty container from him and went away.

24

Having drunk, Wilhelm felt better and, shutting his eyes, drifted into a light sleep. He was awakened by the woman tightening the cloth around his arm again. He didn't look at her. Then, once more, he was left alone. He could hear sounds coming from outside the place in which he lay - rattles, footsteps, voices - none of them making any sense. He was very tired, mentally as well as physically. The feeling that had spurred him on in his long walk through the caverns and tunnels - the feeling that it was possible for things to get better - had completely deserted him. He felt exhausted, indifferent to what happened to him now. He was in Their hands and although he hadn't yet been Taken, no doubt he soon would be.

Wilhelm continued to lie there, sometimes sleeping, sometimes just looking up at the roof which was comfortingly close after the vastness of the cavern through which he had so recently walked. From time to time the woman returned to tighten and loosen the cloth on his arm and to pick up his wrist and hold it. After what must have been two or three hours, she returned and said "Aufstehen Sie." He looked at her. She repeated it but it still didn't make any sense. She gestured to him and he thought he understood. Slowly he sat up, slid his feet down to the floor and stood up. He could see now that she had brought in a small three-sided cart. She pointed to it. "Sitzen Sie - sit down." He did as he was told. There was a small ledge on which he could put his feet. He rested back, hoping that they would Take him now. He was very tired. He had had enough.

The woman pushed the cart out into a bright tunnel with regular pale walls. Wilhelm kept his gaze fixed on the flat grey floor until, after a few moments, they turned out of the tunnel into a small rectangular cave. Looking around, he saw a ledge on the far side of the cave and, in the corner some pieces of metal, seemingly attached to the wall, with another hanging from the roof above them.

"Aufstehen Sie." The woman was giving him orders again. He stood up. She said something else but he didn't recognise the words. Again she gestured. She seemed to be telling him to take his clothes off. He pointed to his shirt and she nodded, so he pulled it over his head. He had forgotten about the biscuits and the flint box and they fell to the floor. Wilhelm scrabbled for them urgently, then realised that if he was going to be Taken, he no longer needed them. But their familiarity gave him a sense of reassurance in these strange surroundings. Clutching his possessions, he looked at the woman. She was holding out her hand. He wasn't going to be allowed to keep them. He handed them to her and she put them on the ledge next to some things that were already there. She motioned to his trousers and his boots. Bending, he undid his boots and removed them, then slid his trousers down and stepped out of them.

The woman moved over to the metal things on the wall and turned one of them. To Wilhelm's astonishment water started to pour out of the object which hung from the roof, disappearing down a small hole in the floor. It frightened him to think that water, which was so precious, was being lost but, looking at the woman, he could see she wasn't concerned. Again she gestured. It looked as though she was telling him to go and stand under the water. She gestured again and said something, then came up and pushed him gently towards the water. Apart from when he drank it from his hands, he had never had water on his body. What would it do to him? She pushed him again. He stepped towards the water and she nodded and handed him something. It was rectangular and pale. He didn't know what it was, so he just took it and held it. Then, taking a deep breath, he stepped under the water.

It was warm! He hadn't expected that. He looked up in disbelief and the water poured onto his face and into his beard. He looked down and saw that, where the water was running over his body it was turning black like the colour of his skin. The woman was saying something. "Waschen Sie sich." He didn't understand. "Waschen Sie sich," she repeated and made gestures of rubbing herself with her hands. Wilhelm copied the gesture. He had forgotten that he was holding the block that she had given him. Where he had rubbed his chest with it, there was a pale residue which the water then carried away. The woman nodded, so he did it again. And then the horror of it dawned on him. He could see that where he was rubbing, some of the blackness of his skin was disappearing. He wasn't being Taken. He was being turned into one of Them.

Instinctively, Wilhelm stepped out of the water, but the woman pushed him back, saying something as she did so. He stood there, watching the water taking away the colour of his skin. He wondered how it was that it could do this, could change him into one of Them, by being spread over him, while drinking it and scooping it up with his hands had never had this effect. It was only when the woman gestured to him and said "Waschen" once again that he realised that it must be the pale substance that he held in his hand that was responsible. Without thinking, he opened his hand and dropped the substance on the floor. The woman pointed and spoke. Wilhelm could tell that she wanted him to pick it up. Wearily he did so and began to rub himself with it again. Under her watchful eye, he continued to do this for some time, repeatedly rubbing his hair, beard, face and body, as his skin became paler and paler. Twice she beckoned him over to her, took the substance from him, rubbed it vigorously over his back, then pushed him into the water again. As he continued to rub himself, he realised that the piece of substance was gradually becoming smaller. He hoped that the woman wouldn't notice.

Eventually she seemed satisfied. Nodding at him, she said loudly "Genug - enough!" She turned the metal object on the wall and the water stopped. She took the piece of substance from him and moved to the ledge on which she had placed his flint box and biscuits. Lying next to them was some pale cloth of a type that Wilhelm had never seen before. The woman unfolded it and handed it to him. It was in the shape of a large rectangle. He didn't know what he was meant to do with it and stood there with it in his hand, water dripping from his hair and beard.

The woman said something, making rubbing movements with her arms. Tentatively Wilhelm rubbed himself with the material and found that it removed what water was left on his body and took some of it from his beard and hair. When his skin was dry, the woman handed him new clothes. They were pale with narrow bands of the colour that he couldn't name, the colour of the spiky material that covered the floor of the great cavern. The trousers were like those he was used to, with a tie-up around the waist, but the shirt was open at the front and down its right edge was a row of hard round objects while down the left edge was a row of holes. Wilhelm looked at these curiously. The woman shook her head and, coming over to him, inserted each of the objects into one of the holes, bringing the edges of the shirt together. Then she picked up a long shirt, which seemed to be made of the same material as the rectangle with which he had removed the water, and helped him put it on over the other clothes. He looked around for his boots but she pushed towards him two objects made of a soft brown material and helped him to put them on his feet. As she did so, she noticed the black bruises on his right ankle where the rock had pinned him down. She looked up at him and asked him something he didn't understand. He shook his head, lacking the energy even to try to work out what she had said. She looked again at the ankle, then stood up. And then she smiled at him.

Wilhelm didn't know what to do or to say. Did the smile mean that she was to be his woman? That they were to share a cave? Maybe the cave they were now in was to be theirs. She told him to sit and he eased himself back into the cart. From a fold on the front of her shirt she took a metal tool, pointed at one end and with two large circles at the other, then stood behind him and started gently to pull his hair. He could hear strange clicking noises. After a while she stopped and came round to face him. She took hold of his beard and now he could see what was happening. She was removing some of his beard. Each time she clicked the tool, some hair fell to the floor. When she had finished, she put away the tool, then picked up a rectangular object from the ledge. Bringing it over, she held it up in front of Wilhelm. In it he could see a man with pale skin and a short beard. He looked at him in horror, wondering how it was that he could be trapped in this small rectangle. He could only see his head and shoulders. He leaned forward to see the rest of the man's body and, as he did so, the man leaned forward as well. Wilhelm let out a yell and cringed back against the cart. Why was the woman showing him this? Was it a warning? Was she showing him what might happen to him? Was she showing him what would happen to him. What did she want him to do? Fearfully he looked up at her. Again she smiled at him, then put out a hand and patted his shoulder. Throughout his life, the music had prevented Wilhelm from thinking. Then for that short time during which he had made his way through the caverns and tunnels, everything had been different. He had been able to form questions and search for the answers and to consider with clarity what those answers meant. Now there were too many questions and no answers, nor any way of finding them, and he was too tired even to try to think. Wilhelm slumped forward and hid his face in his hands.

The woman had moved over to the entrance of the cave. After they had come in, she had closed it off by pushing a large rectangle which swung across into the opening. Now she pulled this back and started to push his cart out into the tunnel. So, they were not to share the cave. It was a question answered but, somehow, Wilhelm didn't have the strength to care.

They turned to the left and moved slowly up the tunnel. At the end of the tunnel, they entered a small cavern. Around its walls were openings leading to smaller caves in which he could see men dressed in the same sort of clothes as himself. In the centre of the cavern was a large block, behind which a woman, of similar appearance to the one who was pushing his cart, was sitting. They stopped next to the block and the two women spoke together for a few minutes, then the one who had pushed him here said "Auf wiedersehen, Wilhelm", turned and was gone.

Wilhelm felt bereft. Even though she had been one of Them, she had smiled at him and he had thought it possible that she was to be his woman. In time, she might have been able to explain this strange place to him. But now she had left him. He hadn't been allowed to keep his clothes, his boots, his flint box or his biscuits - those were all still in the cave where he had stood under the water. He had nothing left that was familiar to him.

The new woman said his name and he looked up. She was smiling. Wilhelm wanted to run. Why could no one explain anything to him? The woman spoke but it was a question, with words Wilhelm didn't understand. Why were they doing this? Surely they must know that the Hundeiss didn't speak their words. He shook his head.

She asked again.

"Ich verstuont niht!". He shouted it in frustration, then gasped at what he had done. But the woman simply nodded and scratched with a small thin tool on something that lay on the block in front of her. She asked another question. This time he just shook his head and she didn't ask again. She picked up a thin pale strip and fastened it round his left wrist, then pushed his cart into one of the caves. There were four large ledges standing on poles and covered with cloth. Beside each of them was a sturdy block of about the same height, which seemed to be made of wood. A beardless man with grey hair was lying on one of the ledges and the woman gesticulated to Wilhelm to get onto the one next to him. He clambered up, lay down on his back and gazed at the roof.

The light was very bright and seemed to be coming from a rectangular gap in the wall to his right. (Why, he wondered, were so many things in Their world rectangular?) He couldn't see any lamps and he couldn't see where the gap led to. He didn't really want to know. It seemed that the more answers he found, the more questions arose. Perhaps the thing to do was to stop asking questions.

The man next to him said something. Wilhelm turned his head and looked away again quickly, shocked by the appearance of his face which lay in folds, with deep creases beside the mouth and under the eyes. But he had noticed that the man was dressed like himself, with a pale strip around his left wrist. Was he, too, being transformed into one of Them? But he wasn't Hundeiss. Maybe there were other men who, like the Hundeiss, were controlled by Them, belonged to Them. Wilhelm wondered if they spoke the same words as the Hundeiss. He turned back to the man and said "I am Hundeiss. Who are you?" but he seemed not to understand. Wilhelm rolled onto his back and shut his eyes.

Footsteps approached and stopped next to where Wilhelm lay. He opened his eyes, feeling that perhaps he had been sleeping again, wondering why They were allowing him to sleep so much. A man stood, looking down at him. Wilhelm wondered whether he was the same man that he had seen earlier. There was a similarity about the face and clothes

30

but the strip of cloth around his neck was different, having patches of brown and black and yellow and - Wilhelm noticed with a sinking heart - one more colour that he couldn't name. And yet this colour wasn't quite as alien as that of the spiky covering of the cavern floor. This colour reminded him of something he had seen before. He turned his head away and tried to think. And then it came to him - grey. Not the grey of the metal mining tools but the grey of eyes. Of those few Hundeiss who had grey eyes, very occasionally one would have eyes whose colour was stronger than the others. That was what this colour reminded him of. He turned his head back and saw that he was right. This new colour wasn't totally strange. Somehow the thought was comforting. To give the colour a name - bright-grey, say - gave it familiarity. He wondered if it would work with the other colour. Suppose he called it . . . what? . . . spiky colour? cavern floor colour? . . . floorspike! He would call it floorspike. And it would be familiar and he would recognise it when he saw it and he would call it by its name. He had no doubt that They had another name for it, but that didn't seem to matter.

He realised that the man with the coloured strip of cloth was saying something to him. Wilhelm heard his own name but understood none of the rest. He looked into the man's face for a clue but there was none. Then the man turned and walked around the ledge on which Wilhelm lay and, as he did so, the two of them were enclosed by a huge piece of cloth which cut them off from everything else. Wilhelm stared at the cloth. It seemed to be hanging from a strip of metal which was itself attached to the roof of the cave, and it was covered in patches of different colours. He was aware of a great weariness in his body and his mind. He was being shown too much that he didn't understand, didn't want to understand. The words that They spoke sounded so familiar and yet he didn't know what they meant. He wished They would just leave him alone to die quietly. He had found out all he wanted to know. He doubted whether he had really ever needed to know about any of the things he had discovered as he made his way out of the mines. Perhaps he should have stayed in the mines and waited to be Taken.

31

The man was gesturing at Wilhelm's shirt. Wilhelm stared at him. The man leant over and pushed the hard round pieces through the holes so the shirt hung open. Then he started to prod Wilhelm's skin, with his hands and with various tools - a piece of metal attached to long smooth ropes that he put in his ears, a hammer with which he banged Wilhelm's knees and wrists, a stick with which he scratched the soles of Wilhelm's feet, a tool with a pointed protuberance that he pushed into Wilhelm's ears. Wilhelm said nothing and lay unresisting. He had ceased to care what they did to him. Eventually the man seemed to have finished. Leaving Wilhelm's shirt lying open, he turned and, with a sweep of his arm, pushed back the wall of cloth so that it hung beside Wilhelm's head. Then he walked away, stopping briefly to speak to a woman who was coming into the cave, pushing a metal cart. Taking something from the cart, the woman put it on the block next to Wilhelm. It was a container, identical to the one holding water that he had been given in the first cave. But this was empty. As he looked at it, the woman placed another, larger container full of water beside it.

Having put down the container, the woman helped Wilhelm to sit up and pushed a ledge, which was balanced on one side on metal poles, across his lap. Onto this she put something that she took from the cart. It was round and flat and on it were two mounds - one brown and one pale yellow - and a pile of small round things that were floorspike in colour. Next to it she put three metal objects that seemed to be tools of some sort. Wilhelm looked at it. What was he meant to do with it? He glanced over at the man next to him. He had been given something similar. Wilhelm watched to see what he would do. The man had picked up two of the tools and was using them to put some of the mound into his mouth. The woman looked over at Wilhelm. "*Essen* - eat." she said. This was food? It looked nothing like food. But perhaps here . . . He had nothing to lose, and he was hungry. Ignoring the tools, he picked up some of the brown stuff in his fingers and put it in his mouth. It was warm and it tasted better than anything he had ever eaten in his entire life. He found he had to chew it although it didn't hurt his jaw like the biscuits, but the pale food was soft and the round

32

things, although firm, were soft inside.

Wilhelm ate slowly, marvelling at the different tastes and the sensations in his mouth. He had been given a large amount. He wondered how long it had to last him. In the mines it would be almost two days' supply. When he had eaten about half, he stopped. Looking across at the other man, he saw that he had eaten all that he had been given. Wilhelm was surprised. He was feeling full now, fuller than he could ever remember feeling before, and he still had plenty of food for the next day. He licked his fingers. The man next to him was watching him and said something. Wilhelm looked over at him. The man picked up his metal tools and shook them at Wilhelm. Wilhelm looked away.

After a short time, the woman with the cart returned and took the flat food-holder from the other man. Then she came over to Wilhelm. "*Genug?* - enough?" she asked. Wilhelm nodded and, before he realised what was happening, she had taken his food-holder as well. Perhaps she was going to store it for him. But would she bring it back when he wanted it? He didn't know how to ask her. She put it on the lower level of the cart, then took a container off the top level and put it in front of him. It seemed to be made of the same material as the food-holder but was of a different shape, curving up at the sides, and it had something yellow in it, partly covered with a thin layer of red.

Once more Wilhelm looked over at the other man and saw him use his remaining metal tool to put the yellow stuff in his mouth. This food looked something like yellow food-cake and Wilhelm broke off a small piece and tasted it. It was much better than food-cake. Not only colours but tastes - tastes that he had never experienced before, that he didn't know existed. He was full of food but he went on eating until it was almost all gone, just to experience the taste of it. He had never in his life eaten such a large amount all at once and he could feel a discomfort in his abdomen. When the woman came to remove the food-holder, he made no protest.

Wilhelm sat back and shut his eyes. Having eaten, he felt much better, despite the sensation of pressure in his midriff. Suddenly he was aware that he needed to use the pit. He sat up and realised with horror that he didn't know where to find it. He swung his legs over the ledge on which he was lying and walked towards the entrance into the larger cave. The woman who had asked him questions when he arrived was no longer there but in her place there was another, bigger woman, wearing the same clothes. As he approached her, she looked round.

"I need to use the pit," he said.

She didn't understand.

"The pit," he said.

She shook her head and asked him something.

He rubbed his abdomen and gestured, trying to explain what he wanted. Then, suddenly, she nodded and stood up, beckoning to him. She led him down a short tunnel and showed him into a little cave, shutting him in there by swinging a rectangular block across the entrance. About a third of the cave was taken up by a structure which, on investigation, looked like a very large bucket. Clearly, though, it wasn't a bucket. It seemed to be attached to the floor and it was made of a pale substance, with a broad, flat, black rim. Was this the pit? It looked as though it was meant to be sat on. He pushed open the rectangular block. The woman was outside. He pointed to the bucket-like structure and gestured. She nodded impatiently and again swung the block across the entrance.

Wilhelm pulled down his trousers, sat down on the bucket and relieved himself. When he had finished and had put his trousers on again, he pushed open the block and stepped back into the tunnel where the woman was waiting. Pushing past him, she went into the little cave, then turned and spoke sharply, pushing down on a piece of metal above the bucket as she did so. There was a noise and suddenly water was pouring into the bucket. Wilhelm was horrified at the waste of water. Was she trying to tell him that he should have done that? The woman pointed to the pit, now empty, and said something. He just nodded and she seemed satisfied. She spoke again and pointed to a small pale structure that was jutting out from the wall of the tunnel just outside the little cave. Wilhelm looked at it. It seemed to be a container of some sort. There were metal knobs attached to it and a hole in the bottom which led into a tube that vanished into the wall. The woman turned one of the metal knobs and water began to pour from it into the container. All this water being lost . . . when water was so precious. Suddenly Wilhelm felt angry that They should have water to waste when the Hundeiss only ever had just enough. He looked at the woman. She was repeating what she had said. Wilhelm thought he heard the word "*waschen*" and remembered that the first woman had said this to him when he stood under the water with the piece of pale substance. He looked at the container and saw that, here too, there was a piece of that substance. But what was he expected to do now? Must he take his clothes off? Surely not - the container was far too small for him to get into, to stand or sit under the water.

The woman spoke again and he could tell from the tone of her voice that she was getting annoyed. She rubbed her hands together and said again "*Waschen sie.*" As Wilhelm stood there, still uncertain what to do, the woman seized his wrists and held his hands under the water, then took the piece of substance and handed it to him. He thought that he understood now what she wanted and cautiously rubbed the substance over his hands. She nodded but, when he continued to do what she had apparently told him, she snatched back the substance and, again, held his hands under the water. Then she turned the metal knob and the water stopped. She took something from a small box attached to the tunnel wall and handed it to Wilhelm. It was square and flat and pale and, as he took it, he realised that it was removing the water from his hands. He rubbed his hands with it and it became wet while his hands became dry. The woman took it from him and threw it into a bucket standing on the floor. Then she took him back into his cave.

Something had been put on the ledge where, earlier, the woman with the cart had put his food holder. It was a small container and in it was what seemed to be dark brown water. Wilhelm looked at it, puzzled. Then, glancing up, he saw the other man staring at him.

"*Kaffee,*" said the man curtly. Then, when Wilhelm frowned, "*Trinken sie.*"

So this was something to drink. The food that he had eaten and the sight of the water pouring away had made Wilhelm thirsty. He picked up the container and looked more closely at its contents. It smelled good. He couldn't remember ever being able to smell water before. Carefully, he tipped the container and poured a little of the liquid into his hand. It was very hot! Wilhelm yelped and dropped the container whose contents splashed down the front of his clothes. The woman who had taken him to the pit came running back into the cave and the man with the creases in his face spoke rapidly to her. She turned to Wilhelm and said something in a sharp tone. Wilhelm said nothing. The woman bent and picked up the container, then went away, returning a few minutes later with a fresh set of clothes. She waited while Wilhelm took off those he was wearing and put on those which she had brought. Then she inserted the round pieces into the holes to bring the edges together. She did it roughly and Wilhelm could tell that she was angry. When she had gone, he lay down again and stared at the ceiling.

He was still thirsty. Sitting up, he lifted the container of water that had been put on the block. It was quite heavy but it had a handle on its side which made it easy to hold. Opposite the handle was a notch in the rim. Carefully, so as not to spill any, Wilhelm tipped the container and poured some water into his hand. He was relieved to find that it was cold and he drank thankfully. Then he lay down and shut his eyes.

Time moved on. Images passed in front of Wilhelm's eyes, images of all that he had seen, but he no longer thought about their significance. He no longer cared. Strangely, he didn't feel threatened here, just isolated. He wondered if he could learn Their words so that he could understand what They were saying to him. And then They could explain . . . so many things . . It wouldn't be so bad if he could communicate with them . . .

He awoke with a jolt, realising that his bladder felt full. He stood up, moved to the wall of the cave and relieved himself. Suddenly the other man started to shout, loudly, insistently. The woman came running in again and, seeing what Wilhelm was doing, joined in the shouting. Wilhelm turned, having finished, and saw her anger. He didn't understand. What had he done wrong? She came over and pushed him roughly onto

36

the ledge on which he had been lying, shouting all the while. Then she turned and hurried out of the cave.

When she came back, she was with the man who wore the many-coloured strip of cloth and she was pushing the small cart in which Wilhelm had been made to sit earlier. She was still talking loudly, angrily. The man stood next to Wilhelm and spoke to him, then gestured and Wilhelm realised that he was meant to get into the cart. So that was it. He had done something wrong and he was, after all, going to be Taken. He stood up, moved over to the cart and sat down. The woman pushed him out, down the tunnel, then out into the great cavern, the cavern with spikes on its floor, the cavern with huge poles of wood that supported nothing, the cavern with living beings that were neither Hundeiss nor Them. He was pushed up a slope and into the large cart that had brought him here. The wall was shut behind him and the cart began to move.

They took him to a place which was very much like the one from which they had brought him. When he arrived, things were said to him, questions asked, and he ignored them all, not even trying to understand. He was taken into a small cave in which there was a man with a bright-grey strip of cloth dangling from his neck. He was sitting on something shaped like the cart in which Wilhelm had been pushed around, except without the wheels. There was another of these facing him and he told Wilhelm to sit on it. He began to ask questions and, like the women, scratched with a thin tool on a flat rectangular block. He spoke slowly and clearly and Wilhelm found he could understand a little of what he said.

"What is your name?"

"Wilhelm."

Then a question with words he didn't know. Wilhelm said nothing.

"Do you have another name?"

"No."

"Where do you live?"

"In the mine tunnels."

"The mine tunnels?"

"Yes."

"And how long have you lived there?"

"Always."

Then another question Wilhelm didn't understand. The man tried again. Once more Wilhelm shook his head.

"How old are you?"

"Nearly ten thousand days."

"What!" The man seemed surprised. Wilhelm repeated his age.

"How many years is that?"

Wilhelm shook his head. "Years?" he asked.

Again the man looked surprised. "Do you know what year this is?"

Then, when Wilhelm didn't answer, "Do you know what day this is?"

Wilhelm shook his head.

"Do you know who is the Chancellor?"

"What is chancellor?" If this man could communicate with him, perhaps he could explain things to him. But the man simply asked "Do you know where you are?"

"No."

Another question with strange words then, when Wilhelm didn't reply, "Do you have a woman?"

"No. Not now. She was Taken."

"Taken where?"

Wilhelm was puzzled. If this man was one of Them, surely he knew what Taken meant.

"Taken," Wilhelm repeated. "Her leg was broken and she was Taken."

The man nodded and scratched on his block.

"And do you have any children?"

"We were given two. They are working now."

"Do you work?"

"Of course."

"Where?"

"In the mines." Wilhelm couldn't understand why he should be asked such a question. Where else would he work. And then he realised. His skin was no longer black.

"I am Hundeiss," he said.

"Hundeiss?"

"Yes. I work in the mines."

There was a short pause, then the man asked "Do you ever hear voices?"

"Yes, when people talk." Wilhelm was getting more and more confused.

"Do you hear voices when there aren't any people there? Do you hear voices that tell you what to do - control you?"

"No." And then, again, a realisation. "I hear the music."

"The music?"

"Controlling."

"Ah."

✳ ✳ ✳

Wilhelm was taken back into the larger cave and told to lie on a ledge. Some time later, a woman came and stuck something sharp into his backside. After that he was left alone. Time passed. He noticed that the light coming in through the large rectangles in the walls changed, becoming dim and then going out, while lights were lit in the cave in which he lay. He was shown where the pit was and it was communicated to him in words and gestures that he must pass water in here, not on the floor of the cave. He was given more food, water, and more containers of the brown drink. A layer of soft cloth was put over him and he was told to sleep. When he woke, the lights on the other side of the rectangles had been put on again.

And so the days passed. Each day he was made to stand under the water and rub himself with a piece of the white substance, even though his skin was now as pale as Theirs. Each day he was given large amounts of food and drink. Each day a woman came and stuck something sharp into him. Sometimes a man came and spoke to him for a little time, asking questions, scratching at his block. Wilhelm found that he was starting to learn some of Their words. The thing on which he lay was a bed. The thing on which he sat was a chair. Occasionally Wilhelm spoke to the man in the

39

next bed. But mostly he just sat. He no longer had any pain in his neck or his back or his arms. But in one respect he could be back in the mines because, although there was no music here, he felt that he was no longer in control of his mind. He didn't know how They were doing it but they were stopping him from thinking clearly. He tried but his mind felt heavy. And so he just sat. And the days passed.

Chapter Three

"Good morning, Herr Doctor." The nurse in charge came hurrying towards Marcus Hellman as he pushed through the double doors leading to the ward.

"Good morning." He smiled at her, still a little embarrassed at the deference shown to him by the nursing staff and his junior colleagues. In the United States the relationships between different grades of staff were much less formal. He had enjoyed his eight years in New York and, for a time, had thought he would stay indefinitely. But, returning to Germany for ten days in order to enjoy the Millennium celebrations with his family, he suddenly realised that he wanted to come home. So here he was, just over a year later, newly appointed to a top specialist post at the comparatively young age of thirty eight.

"I'll tell Dr. Strauss you're here." The nurse disappeared down the corridor and Marcus went into his office, took off his coat and sat down. A moment or two later there was a knock on the door and a young woman came in, carrying a pile of folders.

"Good morning Dr. Hellman."

"Good morning Dr. Strauss." She was the youngest of the three junior doctors who worked with him and, although he had only been in this job for ten days, Marcus had already begun to wonder whether psychiatry was the right speciality for her. She was pleasant enough, hard working and quite bright but she was nervous. The patients seemed to sense that, and it made them uneasy and unwilling to confide in her.

He asked her to sit and she perched herself on the edge of a chair across the desk from him, balancing the folders on her lap. She started to give him a progress report on each of his patients, talking quickly as though she was worried about taking up his time. Marcus listened carefully, asking questions, making comments, deciding who he needed to see today. The patients on this ward suffered from a wide range of psychiatric problems and were in various stages of treatment and recovery. There were three young girls suffering from anorexia nervosa. all showing some signs of

41

improvement, but in whom progress would inevitably be slow. There were several patients suffering from clinical depression, including two who had been brought in after trying to commit suicide. One patient with schizophrenia was almost ready to go home, while three more were steadily getting better. Another two patients were being treated for severe agoraphobia and a third for a crippling obsessional neurosis. And then there was Wilhelm.

Marcus didn't know what to make of Wilhelm. His predecessor had admitted him some three months before and had diagnosed and treated him as a schizophrenic. But his condition didn't seem to be changing in any way - he was getting neither better nor worse - and Marcus, coming new to the case, had doubts about the diagnosis, although he would freely admit that he couldn't yet substitute another that was more appropriate.

Monica Strauss had left Wilhelm's notes till last, although whether by intention or by chance, Marcus couldn't tell. Opening the folder she glanced at the sheets of paper inside and said "Wilhelm's condition remains the same." Then, closing it again, she looked up at Marcus. He could see that she was waiting to be told which patient to bring in first.

"What do you think about the diagnosis?" he asked her.

"Which diagnosis, Herr Doctor?"

"Wilhelm's diagnosis . . . do you think he's suffering from schizophrenia?"

"Dr. Gerhardt made the diagnosis, Herr Doctor."

"Yes, I know. But do you think it's the correct diagnosis?"

She gazed at him uncertainly. "Yes . . . yes, of course."

"Explain to me why you think that. You know him better than I do. As far as I can see, he's been on quite heavy medication for nearly three months and he hasn't shown any signs of improvement."

"No, Herr Doctor. He hasn't responded to treatment."

"But he's not got any worse?"

"No, Herr Doctor."

Marcus wished she would stop calling him Herr Doctor in every sentence but thought that to ask her to do so would make her even more

42

nervous.

"So what makes you think he's schizophrenic?"

He was aware of the panic in her eyes.

"It's all right, Dr. Strauss," he reassured her, "I'm not testing you. But I want to know exactly why the diagnosis was made. So please . . ."

Monica Strauss opened the folder again and glanced at the notes. "He was admitted before I started working here, Herr Doctor, so I didn't see him at the time."

"No, I know that. But from his notes, you still think the diagnosis is correct?"

"Yes, Herr Doctor. He had a lot of classic signs. He's about the right age, he seemed apathetic, his behaviour was bizarre, his use of language was peculiar, his personal hygiene was dreadful and, when he was first admitted, he slept a lot. And he said his mind was being controlled."

Marcus nodded. Put like that, it did sound like a classic case of schizophrenia. But something wasn't right, he was sure of it. He ran his hand through his hair. He'd seen a lot of schizophrenics in the past few years and there was something about Wilhelm that just didn't seem to fit. He wished he could put his finger on it. Perhaps it was simply the fact that he hadn't responded to treatment in the way that one would expect.

"He's on clozapine, isn't he?" he asked.

"Yes, Herr Doctor. He was tried on risperidone first and then changed to clozapine."

Marcus nodded. Risperidone would have been his own choice for treating a newly-diagnosed schizophrenic. And, if that failed, clozapine seemed to produce some improvement in quite a number of patients who didn't respond to anything else. He would have expected one or other of these drugs to have had some effect. Why hadn't they? Was it because the treatment was inappropriate, because Wilhelm wasn't schizophrenic?

"Has there been any change at all in his condition since he's been in hospital?" he asked. "What about the apathy? How much can you get him to do?"

"He goes to the workshops every day, Herr Doctor. But when he's on

43

the ward he just sits and doesn't speak to anyone."

"And what about the bizarre behaviour? I've not seen any sign of that since I've been here. How does it manifest itself?"

"I haven't actually noticed anything very bizarre, Herr Doctor. But his language is still most peculiar."

Marcus nodded. He had spoken to Wilhelm on several occasions in the last ten days, but the conversation had been distinctly one-sided. For much of the time Wilhelm had sat, either shaking his head or saying "I don't understand". On the few occasions when he had attempted a reply, his peculiar pronunciation and his strange vocabulary had made most of his answers incomprehensible. At times he seemed almost to be speaking a different language, using words of which only he knew the meaning.

"And what about mind control?" Marcus continued. "Is he still hearing voices?"

"I don't think he ever heard voices, Herr Doctor. He described it as music."

"Music?"

"Yes, Herr Doctor."

Marcus shook his head. He had never before heard of anyone who thought he was being controlled by music.

"Leave me his notes, Dr. Strauss, and I'll have a look at them. Now we'd better see some of the others."

✳ ✳ ✳

Monica Strauss and the nurse in charge shepherded the last patient out of Marcus's office, shutting the door behind them. Marcus got up, stretched, and went over to his coffee maker. He poured a cup, then picked up Wilhelm's notes, moved over to the easy chair next to the window and sat down.

Opening the folder, he started to read the admission notes.

Wilhelm. Says he has no last name. Vagrant.
Address: Very hard to understand. Sounds as though he's saying he lives "in the mine tunnels".

Why, Marcus wondered, why no surname? And why, if he was a vagrant, would he give an address? And what did 'the mine tunnels' mean?

Schizophrenics, certainly, tended to have delusions but, in Marcus's experience, these were always based, however loosely, on something factual. They might think a neighbour was trying to poison them - but even if the poison was a fantasy, the neighbour existed. Or they might think that a particular shop was the entrance to Hell - and although there might be some doubt about Hell, the shop would be a reality. He read on.

Date of birth unknown. Says he is nearly ten thousand days old but doesn't know what that is in years (actually about 27).

This was truly bizarre. Why should Wilhelm give his age in days? And even if he thought it was important enough to have worked out the number of days, why couldn't he translate it back into years?

Transferred from City Hospital. Admitted via emergency department after head injury. Xrays show no fractures.

Nothing to say how the head injury had occurred. An example of sloppy clerking, thought Marcus. After all, if the injury had been sustained as the result of a fight, it might say something about whether Wilhelm was aggressive and might support the diagnosis of schizophrenia. If, on the other hand, Wilhelm had suddenly blacked out and hit his head, it might indicate some physical problem in his brain. He'd had no blackouts since being admitted to hospital, so the latter was unlikely, but it was still important to know.

Physical examination reveals nothing abnormal. In filthy state.

The filthy state, of course, might indicate schizophrenia. Schizophrenics frequently showed a deterioration in their personal hygiene. But the phrase might also mean that he had fallen in the mud when he was knocked out, or that his claim to live in a mine was correct. Perhaps he did live in a disused mine and the 'filth' was coal dust. And, of course, vagrants frequently were filthy just because they had no access to washing facilities. Marcus frowned. Such inadequate note-taking would not have been tolerated at the hospital in New York where he had been working for the past three years.

Transferred because of abnormal mental state and behaviour (urinated on ward floor, ate with fingers, poured coffee down himself).

Urinating on the ward floor, Marcus was prepared to admit, was abnormal. But eating with one's fingers? He did it himself sometimes. And as for pouring coffee down himself - had Wilhelm done this deliberately? Or was it an accident, the result of a tremor in his hands, perhaps? All this would need to be investigated. He hoped that, at this late date, someone in the medical ward would remember Wilhelm.

Unaware of current events (today's date, name of the Chancellor etc.). Doesn't know where he is.

That, of course, could be associated with schizophrenia - patients were sometimes unable to remember things. But, equally, it could have been caused by the head injury.

Says he had a wife but she was 'taken'. Whether he means by another man or that she died is uncertain although he qualifies it by saying 'her leg was broken' - suggests that he beat her up and broke her leg and she left him.

No, thought Marcus. It doesn't suggest anything of the sort. But it could be an example of the sort of inconsequential statements that schizophrenics sometimes made, hopping from subject to subject in so-called 'knight's move' thinking. He had a wife but she was 'taken'. What did 'taken' mean in Wilhelm's vocabulary? Why had no one tried to find out? Marcus sighed. Wilhelm had been unfortunate, coming into hospital under the care of an elderly psychiatrist who was on the point of retiring and a junior doctor who, evidently, was far from conscientious and jumped to conclusions.

Says he has two children. Actual phrase used is 'we were given two'. Possibly implies a religious trait or obsession. Says children are working which, given his age, must mean that wife was older than him and these were children by a former marriage.

A preoccupation with religion was certainly something seen in schizophrenia but, Marcus thought, the expression 'we were given two' was a fairly flimsy basis from which to draw such a conclusion. And, as far as he knew, Wilhelm had shown no further evidence of religious fervour while he had been in hospital.

Says he works 'in the mines' and is 'hundeiss', whatever that means.

Yes, one of Wilhelm's strange words. Again, that could tie in with a diagnosis of schizophrenia. But, although such a diagnosis would explain

46

the use of the words and unusual language structures, it wouldn't explain Wilhelm's bizarre pronunciation.

Says he hears music controlling him. Asked where the music comes from, says it comes from the walls. Who sends it? Says 'them'. Unable to state who 'they' are.

This was the only thing that truly suggested schizophrenia - the control by an outside force and the paranoia about 'them'. But control by music? In all his wide experience, Marcus had never come across a case like this. Auditory hallucinations were quite common among schizophrenics, but they were always in the form of voices. The voices might be perceived as being inside or outside the patient's head and they might be reassuring or, more frequently, threatening. But they were always voices - not music. And what sort of music? A full orchestra? A piano? A tin whistle? Well, he couldn't ask the doctor who had written the notes - he was Monica Strauss's predecessor and he had left for another job two months ago. So he would have to start from scratch and find out for himself. He turned to the next sheet of paper where, in Dr. Gerhardt's neat hand, was written Points of note: Fabrication, neologisms, controlled by external forces.

Diagnosis: schizophrenia. Rx risperidone.

So Wilhelm had been condemned to three months of heavy medication on a mental ward on the basis of a flimsy history. True, he exhibited a lack of touch with reality, a mild paranoia and a strange use of language - but was it enough? Marcus thought not. He read on through the scanty follow up notes which mainly consisted of the words 'no change'. When he came to the end, he shut the folder, finished his coffee and went in search of Monica Strauss.

✳ ✳ ✳

"Tell me what you've observed," Marcus said. Once again, Monica Strauss was sitting opposite him in his office. "There are several points in his admission notes that don't seem to have been followed up. For example . . ." he glanced down at the notes, "the bizarre behaviour - urinating on the ward floor, eating with his fingers and spilling coffee down himself. Has he done any of these while he's been on this ward?"

"He hasn't urinated on the floor, Herr Doctor. But he still eats with his fingers."

"And does he spill things? Is he particularly clumsy?"

"Not that I'm aware of, Herr Doctor."

"And I think you said that he slept a lot when he first came here."

"That's what I was told. But he doesn't now."

"But he still seems apathetic?"

"Yes . . ." She seemed uncertain. "He goes to the group activities with the other patients and there haven't been any complaints about him. But when he's on the ward he always sits by himself. He never talks to anyone, except occasionally to Oskar who's in the next bed. He never watches television or reads a newspaper or a book. . ."

"Can he read?"

"I don't know, Herr Doctor." She was surprised. Obviously, thought Marcus, that thought had never occurred to her.

"Has he ever been aggressive?"

"I don't think so, Herr Doctor. But he avoids the other patients as much as he can. And he avoids eye contact with the staff. He doesn't seem to like it if people smile at him."

Marcus had noticed that. When he had been introduced to Wilhelm, he had smiled as he said hello and had been surprised to see the patient flinch. Repeating the smile at the end of their short meeting, he had seen the flinch again. Since then he had tried to keep his expression serious when he was with Wilhelm, although why a smile should be frightening he couldn't imagine.

"Have you noticed any particular religious preoccupation? Does he talk about God? Does he seem to pray a lot?"

"I've never seen him pray, Herr Doctor. And it was really strange at Christmas - he didn't seem to understand the celebrations at all."

Marcus made a note. "I know he keeps himself to himself. But is he stubborn - does he refuse to do what the staff ask him to ?"

"No, not as far as I know."

"What about other signs of schizophrenia - adopting strange postures, sudden hostility, talking to someone who isn't there, laughing at things that aren't funny, excessive crying?"

"No . . . he doesn't seem to express emotions."

And suddenly Marcus knew what had been troubling him. The classic schizophrenic had a flat, almost reptile-like gaze, an expressionless face, a blunting of the emotions. But Wilhelm wasn't like that. He might not smile, he might be unresponsive, but his eyes were those of an intelligent man who, for whatever reason, was unable to communicate with those around him. Marcus had seen the same look in patients who had had strokes and were unable to speak. It was a sort of yearning. . . He took a deep breath, then smiled.

"Thank you very much, Dr. Strauss. That's been very helpful."

"Oh . . . right . . ." She was flustered again. "Thank you, Herr Doctor."

"Now, can you ring the emergency department at the City Hospital and see if anyone remembers Wilhelm?"

✶ ✶ ✶

As Marcus went back into his office to collect his coat, at the end of a long afternoon in the out patients' department, the 'phone on the desk started to ring. After a moment, in which he was tempted not to answer it, he picked up the receiver.

"Doctor Hellmann?" It was a woman's voice, brisk and efficient-sounding. "This is Nurse Frenzel in the emergency department. I believe you 'phoned for some information about Wilhelm."

"Yes. Thanks for ringing back. The thing is, I've just taken over Wilhelm's case and there's very little in his notes about how he came to be admitted. I was hoping that someone who was on duty at the time could fill me in."

"Well, I was on duty." The woman sounded doubtful. "But it's a long time ago. And he was something of a mystery."

"He still is," said Marcus drily. "But anything you can remember might help. Can I call in and speak to you - and have a look at his notes and Xrays? I could be there in about fifteen minutes."

"Yes, certainly. I'll go and have a look for his notes."

✶ ✶ ✶

49

When he arrived, Nurse Frenzel was with a patient. Marcus sat in the waiting area, glad of the opportunity to shut his eyes and do nothing for a few minutes.

"Doctor Hellman . . . I'm so sorry to have kept you waiting."

Marcus opened his eyes and looked up. He had expected someone older, more substantial. The woman who stood by his chair was late twenties, petite, with blonde hair cut in a bob and large grey eyes. They shook hands and she took him into the nurses' office and offered him coffee.

"I've found Wilhelm's notes," she said, handing over the thin folder. "I'm afraid there's not much in them."

Marcus took out the single sheet of paper and glanced through it.

Wilhelm. (Gives no last name).

Address: unknown (vagrant).

Date of birth: unknown

Circumstances of admission: Was chased off farmer's land by dog. Climbed over wall, fell and was concussed. Unconscious for about twenty minutes. Regained consciousness in ambulance.

On examination: Confused. Appears not to understand much of what is said to him. Strange accent. Seems to be speaking some form of dialect, but unrecognisable.

Neurologically nothing abnormal found. Cardiovascular system, respiratory system, abdomen all normal.

Blood pressure 120/80. Pulse 80.

Filthy!

Skull Xrays normal. No evidence of fracture.

Clean up and move to ward for observation.

Marcus returned the folder to the nurse. Well, he now knew the circumstances of the head injury but it didn't seem to help him at all, although the fact that Wilhelm had been unconscious for about twenty minutes might support a case for his present state being post-traumatic.

"Is there anything else you remember about him?" he asked the nurse.

"Well, yes." She hesitated and then went on, "There were some things that struck me as being strange - but they weren't written down."

She paused again and Marcus nodded at her encouragingly.

"Well, he seemed very confused. Of course, that might have been due

50

to the head injury. But usually patients who've been unconscious are reassured when they see a nurse and realise that someone's looking after them. He just seemed - well, as though he didn't understand what was going on. And when I smiled at him it seemed almost to frighten him. I'm sure I didn't imagine it." She sounded defensive.

"No, you didn't. He still reacts like that. You can see the panic in his eyes."

The nurse looked relieved. "I mentioned it to the doctor who examined him, but he didn't think it was important."

Marcus nodded. "It's certainly an indication of some problem going on in his mind. What else did you notice?"

"Well. . ." She spoke hesitantly. "I don't know if you've ever worked in emergency medicine, Dr. Hellman, but we get all sorts in here - ordinary people like you and me, children, old people, drunkards, vagrants - and we get to know them all - know their types, I mean - very well. The vagrants are usually filthy and we give them a shower and some fresh clothes and, if they're not being kept in, something to eat before we send them off.

Well, Wilhelm was absolutely black. And his beard and hair were terribly long - they looked as though they hadn't been cut for years. Actually, I cut them for him after he'd had a shower and, when I held up the mirror so he could see how much better he looked, he seemed frightened by his reflection. And before that, when I took him for his shower he seemed sort of, well, surprised by the water and he was very reluctant to go in. His clothes were like rags - no underwear or socks, just shirt, trousers and boots. Now that in itself is strange. Vagrants usually wear layer upon layer. And he got undressed without a murmur and usually you have a fair old tussle getting them to take their clothes off. And then, when I eventually got him under the shower, he didn't seem to know what to do. It was really strange . . . Once he started to wash, though, the dirt absolutely poured off him. And then I noticed that his arms and legs were badly scratched, as though he'd been fighting his way through brambles, and one of his ankles was very bruised. But it was when he got out of the shower that I realised that there was something very strange." She shook her head,

51

remembering it. "I did tell the doctor on duty but he didn't think it worth mentioning."

Marcus could hear the resentment in her voice.

"Doctor Hellman, I've been working here for seven years. I know what vagrants look like. And this man just wasn't a vagrant. Oh, yes, he was filthy and his hair was long and unkempt and his nails were broken. But his arms and shoulders were quite muscular and he had thick callouses on his hands, as though he regularly did hard manual labour. And when he got out of the shower, I could see that, apart from the scratches and the bruises, his skin was quite unblemished. And I have never, never seen a vagrant who hasn't been infested. And yet this man didn't have a single flea, a single louse, a single bite on his skin. I don't know how he got in that state, doctor, but I'd swear on the Bible that he wasn't a vagrant."

Marcus lay in the bath, drinking dry white wine and thinking. He often found that, in the matter of problem-solving, his mind worked best at the end of the day when he was relaxed. On the cork-seated stool, next to his towelling robe, was a small radio tuned to a broadcast of Wagner's Tannhauser. Marcus had been careful not to turn the volume up too high - having only recently moved into the apartment, he wasn't sure how thick the walls were and he didn't want to upset the neighbours - but, even so, the bathroom resonated and Marcus wallowed in hot water and music.

It was, he realised, the first time that he'd listened to an opera since his return to Germany. Last time . . . He let his mind drift back to that performance of Verdi's La Traviata at the Met - the last evening he'd spent with Julia. He sometimes wondered what might have happened if they'd met earlier, instead of two months before he was due to return to Germany to take up this new job. Would he have stayed on indefinitely? On balance, he thought not. Much as he liked the United States, he had been getting homesick for Germany. Whether Julia would have made up for that, he would never know. Sighing, Marcus finished his wine, leaned over the edge of the bath to set the empty glass on the floor, then rested his head back, shut his eyes and started to think about Wilhelm.

In the three days since his conversation with Nurse Frenzel, he had thought a lot about Wilhelm. What little she had been able to tell him about the case had only served to make it more puzzling. He had no doubt that she was right, that Wilhelm wasn't a vagrant. She had probably seen more vagrants during her time in the accident department than he would see in a lifetime. And from his first days on the wards Marcus had learned to trust experienced nurses when they expressed an opinion. But if Wilhelm wasn't a vagrant, what was he? Perhaps he had only recently become a vagrant. How quickly, Marcus wondered, did vagrants become infested with fleas and lice? The callouses and muscular development certainly suggested hard manual labour. Marcus had looked at Wilhelm's Xrays and had thought that he could see some arthritic changes in the neck bones. So he had ordered Xrays of Wilhelm's shoulders and spine and these had confirmed his initial impression - there were signs of wear and tear that one wouldn't expect to see in such a young man. It seemed that Wilhelm had, indeed, done hard manual work, for a prolonged period - and until fairly recently.

Marcus, who had never before lived in this part of Germany, had no idea where the nearest mines were. But if there were some nearby, and if a miner had gone missing from his job, surely the police would have been informed? And since Wilhelm came in to hospital with no identity, his admission would have been reported to the police. But no one had claimed him as an employee, a friend, a relative, a husband, a lover. Wilhelm had said that he was no longer married, although whether his wife was dead or just estranged from him wasn't clear. But what about the children? Well, if they were, as had been suggested in the admission notes, her children from a previous marriage, that might explain why they had made no effort to trace their missing father. A wave of sadness swept over Marcus, brought on partly by the beauty of Wagner's music and partly by the thought of Wilhelm, alone in the world, with no one who cared enough to find out what had happened to him.

Marcus loved psychiatry. It was all he had ever wanted to do. Physical medicine was interesting, certainly, but nowadays it relied so heavily on tests - blood tests, urine tests, Xrays, scans, biopsies - sometimes it seemed that all the doctor needed to do was to order enough tests and the diagnosis was made for him. But psychiatry . . . to get to the root of the problem in psychiatry needed good detective skills. There were no tests that would tell you that one patient's mental problems were due to the fact that she had been raped at the age of fourteen, or that another was suffering now because her favourite aunt died when she was six. The only way to get to the root of a psychiatric problem was to talk to the patient, to listen, to pick up clues and then to piece them together to make a diagnosis. Marcus loved doing that, loved it when he was able gently to coax information out of patients - often something they'd never told anybody else, or something they'd almost forgotten, but something that urgently needed to be aired if they were to get better. He loved putting together the pieces, as in a jigsaw, seeing the patient's life become a vivid picture, seeing where it had gone wrong and how he could help to set it right again. Psychiatry was very satisfying in that way. With modern medication and psychotherapy there were few patients who couldn't be helped at all and many who could be restored to perfect health.

But with Wilhelm the picture was far from vivid. Half the jigsaw, it seemed, was missing. And it was so difficult to talk to him. Marcus had considered the possibility that this difficulty in communication and the fact that Wilhelm seemed unable either to read or write might be due to a mental handicap. And yet he felt sure that this wasn't so. Since his discussion with Monica Strauss, Marcus had looked carefully at Wilhelm each time he talked to him and the expression in Wilhelm's eyes had convinced him that this was an intelligent man trapped . . . in what? Not in the mind of a schizophrenic, of that he was certain. Not, of course, that it would be unusual - young men and women who developed schizophrenia were frequently highly intelligent, but the schizophrenia masked the intelligence, the eyes became blank and expressionless, there wasn't that . . . that spark that he could see in Wilhelm, despite the medication. And although retardation would have to be ruled out, he was sure that Wilhelm's IQ wasn't below average. He hoped he would be proved right.

Because, for some reason, he wanted Wilhelm to be intelligent and strong and capable of living a normal life.

One thing that backed up his theory that Wilhelm's IQ was normal was the fact that, since his admission to hospital, he seemed to have picked up some additional vocabulary, although his ability to express himself still remained very limited. But why had his vocabulary been so poor in the first place? And why was his pronunciation so strange? Some of the staff had wondered whether he had some obscure regional accent but, when asked where he came from, Wilhelm just replied 'the mines'. And although he said he was 'Hundeiss', Marcus had been unable to find any reference to people who called themselves by that name.

Wilhelm's inability to communicate, of course, was half the problem. Psychiatry depended on communication, on finding out what the patient was thinking. If you couldn't do that, it reduced the whole process to something akin to a game of charades, assessing the patient simply through his actions and expressions. And it was all too easy to misinterpret these. It was interesting that Nurse Frenzel had noticed Wilhelm's fear of being smiled at. If one tried to imagine what could have caused this, one could come up with all manner of explanations, each more bizarre than the next, and probably none of them the right one. And his reaction to having a shower. She had said Wilhelm seemed astonished by the shower. Why? Even though he was filthy, he must have used a shower at some time in his life. He said he was a miner and mines were provided with showers for the men to use at the end of their shifts. So why astonishment? Unwillingness, yes, perhaps. Although Nurse Frenzel had said that he had undressed without any objection. And what was it that he had seen in the mirror that had frightened him? Then there was the business of urinating on the ward floor. He'd never done it since. Once he had been told where the toilets were, he had used them. So why not the first time? Why hadn't he asked where they were? The more Marcus thought about it, the more puzzling it all seemed to be.

The opera was coming to an end and the bath water was getting cold. Marcus heaved himself to his feet and reached across to pull the large white towel off the rail. Wrapping it round his waist, he stepped out of the bath and bent to let out the water. He dried himself quickly, put on his robe and cleaned his teeth. Picking up the glass and the radio, he went into the kitchen to deposit them both on the counter next to the sink. He switched off the radio, which was now relaying the thunderous applause greeting the final curtain at the opera house, turned off the lights and went into the bedroom.

Getting into bed, Marcus opened the novel lying on the bedside table and started to read. But he couldn't concentrate and, after five minutes, turned out the bedside lamp and lay down, his mind still buzzing. Normally with patients, he was content to take things slowly, allow the story to reveal itself at its own pace. But with Wilhelm he was impatient, not just because the man himself had been in hospital for three months without any change but because the whole thing was just - well, so strange.

He was pleased he'd made contact with Nurse Frenzel. It could be useful. Her friend Birgit had been on duty on the ward to which Wilhelm had been admitted. And although Birgit was now on maternity leave, Nurse Frenzel had offered to 'phone her to see if she could get any more information. Marcus had been pleased by her willingness to help, her understanding of how important it was to solve the puzzle. He shut his eyes and thought about Nurse Frenzel. She seemed to have the two qualities vital for a good nurse - efficiency and compassion. Added to which, he smiled to himself, she was extremely pretty. He hoped that she would come up with something that would give him a clue about how to proceed - and would also give him an excuse to see her again. Perhaps between them they could figure Wilhelm out. With that thought in his mind, he drifted off to sleep. But when he dreamed, it wasn't of Nurse Frenzel but of Wilhelm.

Marcus spent the next morning seeing out-patients. Two of them required more than their allotted time and the clinic over-ran by forty minutes. With scarcely time to eat a sandwich and drink a cup of coffee, he arrived at the afternoon's group therapy session only five minutes late. Wilhelm hadn't been invited to join the group, which was restricted to patients suffering from the so-called 'neurotic' disorders - depression, anxiety, anorexia, phobias - since the 'psychotics', who were understood to have lost touch with reality, didn't normally benefit from this form of therapy. While he was in the States, Marcus had met an English doctor who had neatly defined the difference between the two types of patients. The psychotic, he said, believes that two and two make five. The neurotic knows that two and two make four - but he worries about it. But, Marcus wondered, did Wilhelm believe that two and two made five - had he really lost touch with reality? Or was it a simple failure of communication that was making it appear so? Marcus still hadn't given up the idea that it might have been the initial head injury that had made Wilhelm behave in a strange manner when he'd regained consciousness. Certainly, there seemed to be no suggestion of anything particularly abnormal in his behaviour since he'd been on this ward.

Returning to his office after the hour-and-a-half therapy session, Marcus dealt with some post, made some 'phone calls, then took out a pen and started to jot down what he knew of Wilhelm's case, trying to find some clues, and to clarify what was fact and what was conjecture. According to Monica Strauss and the nursing staff, since Wilhelm had been on the psychiatric ward he had been a model patient. He never complained about taking his medication and always did exactly what the nurses asked him to - once he understood what that was. Sometimes gestures had to be used but this was becoming less necessary as time went on and his understanding improved. That, in itself, was odd. The only reason that Marcus could think of for someone having a severely restricted vocabulary was some form of learning disability. But that didn't tie in with the fact that, at the age of twenty seven, Wilhelm was starting to assimilate new words. Marcus shook his head and drew a large question mark next to the note he had just written.

Adding to the enigma had been the information proffered by Anna Braun, the senior occupational therapist, whom Marcus had gone to see the previous day. She was a tall, rather mannish woman with short grey hair, wire rimmed glasses and severely cut clothes but, underneath the severity, she was kind and intelligent, and the patients liked her. She offered Marcus coffee and asked what she could do to help him.

"I'd like to know your impressions of Wilhelm," he said.

Anna Braun thought for a moment. "A bit of an enigma." She looked at Marcus. "You think so too?"

Marcus nodded. "What puzzles you about him?" he asked.

"Quite a lot. When he first came here, the nurses thought he might have a problem with hand co-ordination because he'd never use cutlery - always insisted on eating with his fingers. But when I tested him, his manual dexterity was perfectly normal. And I've never been able to find out why he won't use cutlery. I asked him and he just shrugged. Then the other day one of the nurses told me that he's started to use a spoon - not a knife and fork, just a spoon. So what's brought that about . . .?" She shook her head.

Marcus nodded again and made a note. "Anything else?"

"Yes. I think he'd been here about three weeks when Dr. Gerhardt decided he was ready for some occupational therapy. And, as you know, we put patients who look as though they might be here long-term into 'work experience' therapies, so they can earn some pocket money. Well, Wilhelm's young and he's got a good physique, so I decided to try him out in the vegetable garden. We usually have about twenty patients working there and they all seem to enjoy it. Franz, who supervises them, has been with us for years and he's very good with the patients. Anyway, he took Wilhelm out and gave him a hoe and asked him to do some weeding. But, according to Franz, Wilhelm just stood there - it seems he had no idea what it was that was required of him, even though it had been explained very simply. And he seemed somehow bemused by his surroundings."

"In what way bemused?" asked Marcus.

"Well, he started to examine the plants - inspecting them very closely, feeling them between his fingers. But what really surprised Franz was Wilhelm's reaction to the weather. It was a rather dull day but suddenly the sun came out for a few minutes and it seemed almost to frighten him. Franz didn't know how else to describe it. In the end, it was obvious that

Wilhelm wasn't going to be of any practical use in the gardens and he was brought back indoors."

"Very strange," said Marcus.

"Yes," Anna Braun agreed. "Very. I mean, it's not unusual for us to have schizophrenics working in the gardens and they tend to cope quite well. No one's ever reacted like Wilhelm. Anyway, after that we tried him out in the workshops. We've got a variety of crafts going on - woodwork, metalwork, upholstery and so on - and the patients can choose what they want to do. Some of them become very skilled - a few have even set up successful businesses after leaving hospital. Well, Ernst, my deputy, took Wilhelm round and showed him what was available but it soon became clear that it was going to be impossible to teach him any of the crafts, not so much because he couldn't learn the mechanics of them but because he appeared not to understand why any of it was being done."

Marcus shook his head. "This seems to have been the problem all along," he said. "He'll do what he's told quite willingly but there's an awful lot of what he's told that he just doesn't seem to understand."

"And yet," Anna Braun continued, "I get the impression that his intelligence isn't below average. So why he should react like that is anybody's guess. Anyway, in the end we put him in the art room and let him dabble around with paints and clay. It turned out that he has quite a good eye for drawing - but the subjects he draws are very limited and his use of colour is very strange. He draws black faces - and I don't mean black as in African but black as in covered with soot. And if he draws figures, he always puts them in red and yellow clothes. He's quite industrious in the art room, but I'm told that when he goes back to the ward, he does nothing. The nursing staff haven't been able to get him interested in anything. He just sits."

Staring at his notes the following day, Marcus remembered Anna Braun's words and sighed. It seemed that no matter how much information he acquired on Wilhelm, none of it made much sense. He wondered whether he was missing something vital. But there was so little to go on. Unlike appendicitis or a stroke, mental illness didn't usually hit suddenly out of the blue. Most patients became ill over a period of time and, if they were incapable of telling the doctor about it when they were first admitted to hospital, there was usually a relative or friend who could provide the relevant information. But with Wilhelm there was nothing. He had appeared out of nowhere, fallen over a dry stone wall, knocked himself out, and arrived on their doorstep. And for the most part, since he had been in hospital he had been quiet and well behaved. Marcus had been over it all in his mind, time and time again. And now, getting it down on paper didn't seem to be helping. The jigsaw remained incomplete, the puzzle unsolved. Wilhelm did his day's work in the packing rooms and that was all. The rest of the time, he just sat. He didn't watch television. He didn't read. He didn't listen to the radio. He hardly spoke. He remained what he had been all along - docile, silent and mysterious.

Chapter Four

The following afternoon, Marcus paid a visit to one of the hospital's clinical psychologists and borrowed from him two puzzles designed to assess a patient's mental capacity. The first, often used for testing children, consisted of a box into which were cut holes of various shapes - a star, a square, a crescent, a circle, a triangle and some four or five others - together with matching plastic pieces which the patient had to push through the relevant holes into the box. The other was more sophisticated - the patient had to work out how to move a ball from one end of a series of tubes to the other, taking it through little doors that could only be released in a certain way, working out how to get it through a vertical tube with adjustable shelves and how to prevent it from running away into a cul de sac from which it couldn't be retrieved. Marcus laid the puzzles out, then asked one of the nurses to send Wilhelm into his office.

Wilhelm arrived and Marcus, speaking slowly and carefully, explained what he wanted him to do. Wilhelm looked at him quizzically, as if wondering about the purpose of this request, and then complied with it, completing the first puzzle in about ten seconds. Marcus couldn't help smiling. There was no doubt about Wilhelm's mental capacity. He didn't think he could have done the puzzle any faster himself. As Wilhelm looked up, Marcus hastily removed the smile from his face and nodded, saying "Good. Well done."

He leaned over to pick up the box, then opened it and tipped the shapes out onto his desk. Picking up the red triangle, he showed it to Wilhelm and asked him to name the colour.

"Red."

"And this?"

"Yellow."

"This one?"

"Bright-grey."

"Bright-grey?"

"Yes."

"What is this one?"

Wilhelm shook his head, apparently not knowing the word mauve.

"What is this?"

"Pale."

"And this?"

"I say floorspike."

"Floorspike?"

"Yes."

"That's your name for it?"

"Yes."

Marcus made a note, then looked up as there was a knock at the door. One of the nurses put her head around it.

"I'm sorry to disturb you, Dr. Hellman, but Nurse Frenzel would like a word with you. Shall I ask her to wait?"

"Is she on the 'phone?"

"No, she's come up to the ward."

"Oh, splendid." Marcus got up and said "Stay here please, Wilhelm. I'll be back in a minute."

Wilhelm nodded.

Nurse Frenzel was waiting in the corridor. She was out of uniform, dressed in a heavy-knit, pink polo necked sweater over a pair of jeans, and she was wearing subtle make up which emphasized her large grey eyes.

"I'm so sorry, Dr. Hellman," she began, as soon as she saw Marcus, "I didn't mean to disturb you but I've got that information you wanted, so I thought I'd call in on my way home."

"I appreciate it. And you've arrived at a very good time - I'm just doing some IQ tests on Wilhelm. Would you like to come in and join us?"

"Yes, I would. Thank you."

Marcus ushered her into the office. It was obvious that Wilhelm recognised her. His eyes widened in amazement and he seemed to shrink back slightly into his chair, as if he didn't know what to do.

"Wilhelm, you remember Nurse Frenzel, don't you? She looked after you when you first came into hospital."

"Hello Wilhelm." she moved over to where he sat. "How are you?" Marcus noticed that she didn't smile.

"Good."

That was something else that the nurses on the ward had remarked on. Wilhelm never said please or thank you, although the tone of his voice never had that surly quality usually employed by people who have no manners.

Nurse Frenzel sat down on the chair that Marcus offered her. "How's it going?" she asked.

"He did the shapes test in about ten seconds."

She laughed softly. "Good."

"I was just about to try him on this one."

"Gosh, that looks quite difficult."

"Well, we'll see."

Again Marcus explained as clearly as he could what he wanted Wilhelm to do. Wilhelm nodded and turned his attention to the puzzle. Carefully he worked out each stage, not making any mistakes, moving the ball along steadily and safely.

"Well . . ." said Marcus as Wilhelm completed the puzzle, "I don't think there's any doubt about that."

Nurse Frenzel shook her head. "The capacity is there," she said quietly. "Perhaps he just missed out on the schooling. Although if he can't read or write it would suggest that he missed out from a very early age."

She thought for a moment, then said "May I . . .?"

"Please."

She turned to Wilhelm and held up three fingers. "How many fingers, Wilhelm?"

"Three."

"And now?"

"Five."

"What is three plus five?" She held up first three fingers, then five, showing him the meaning of 'plus'.

"Eight."

"And seven plus five?"

"Twelve."

"And twelve plus twenty?"

"Thirty two."

"And seventeen plus twenty eight?"

"Forty five."

Nurse Frenzel looked over at Marcus, a surprised look on her face.

"Interesting," said Marcus. "Thank you, Wilhelm. You can go now."

"Go?" asked Wilhelm, pointing at the door.

"Yes. Thank you."

"What made you think of that?" asked Marcus once Wilhelm had left the room.

"I don't know. I just thought that if he could do puzzles he ought to be able to do mental arithmetic . . . But it doesn't follow. If he can't read and write, he shouldn't be able to do arithmetic . . ."

"Of course," said Marcus, "there are some forms of learning disability in which the patient has a peculiar facility for arithmetic while developing poorly in all other areas."

"I know it happens in the movies," said Nurse Frenzel, "But in real life?"

"Occasionally. . . . rarely."

"But in this case?"

"No," said Marcus slowly. "No, I don't think so."

He got up from his chair. "Coffee?" he asked.

"Thank you, Dr. Hellman."

"Call me Marcus."

For a moment Nurse Frenzel looked surprised. Then she smiled and said "And I'm Erika."

As Marcus took cups over to the coffee-maker, she went on "I've been trying to get Birgit on the 'phone since the other night, but she's been away. Anyway, she's back now and I've spoken to her and I asked her what she could remember about Wilhelm."

"And?" Marcus handed her a cup of coffee and sat down.

64

"Well, she went off duty soon after Wilhelm arrived on the ward, but she heard about him the next day from Helga who'd been on the later shift. Helga was in a fair old state and went on and on - apparently she was very angry because of the way he'd behaved. Birgit doesn't like her much - says she tends to be rather unsympathetic. In fact, Birgit reckons that it was due to Helga that Wilhelm was whipped out of there and onto a psychiatric ward in double quick time. Helga told Birgit that the chap in the next bed to Wilhelm was quite disgusted because not only did he wee on the floor but, when lunch was served, he ate everything with his fingers."

"He still does."

"But Birgit said that weeing on the floor was very odd because he knew where the lavatories were."

"Really? Is she sure?"

"Yes, he'd used them. Apparently after lunch he came out to the desk in a slightly agitated state and kept repeating something Helga didn't understand. And then he did a bit of miming and she realised that he wanted to pass a stool. So she showed him where the lavatories were."

"And he used the lavatory?"

"Yes. And she got very cross because he didn't flush it and she had to do it for him. But when she pressed the handle, he seemed quite shocked."

"Strange. . . I don't think he's had any problems using the lavatory on this ward. If he has, no one's reported it."

Erika sipped her coffee. "Have you found any clues in the notes?"

"Not really. I can't find anything to latch onto. Nothing that points to a specific diagnosis."

"But there are abnormalities?"

"Well, there's his vocabulary - you know how strange it is, and how limited."

Erika nodded. "When he was in the emergency department I had to communicate with him mainly by mime. He only seemed to understand the simplest of words."

"Yes, but the really odd thing is that he seems to have learned quite a few words since he's been in here. I mean, if he's capable of learning them,

65

why hasn't he learned them before? And some of them are very basic terms - things like bed and chair. And he's got his own words for other things. I asked him the colour of this piece just now," he held up the green star, "and he said 'floorspike'."

"Dr. Hellman . . sorry . . Marcus," Erika spoke thoughtfully, "I don't want to speak out of turn . . ."

"Go on - I need all the help I can get."

"Well, forget you're a psychiatrist. And forget that Wilhelm has been admitted as a psychiatric patient to a psychiatric ward. And just tell me what your conclusions would be if I told you that I'd met someone who spoke with a strange accent and who didn't speak much German but was learning more as time went on."

Marcus's jaw dropped. "He's a foreigner," he said. "Of course. But why has no one picked that up?"

"Well, for a start, although his accent is strange, it still sounds German - I mean, he doesn't sound as though he's a Frenchman or a Norwegian or whatever trying to speak German. And then, when he was brought in, we thought he was a vagrant. So we were already thinking that he was German and not an immigrant worker. And once we'd cleaned him up, he didn't look foreign. I mean, the Turks, for example, they're dark and rather swarthy. But Wilhelm's fair skinned and his hair's quite light brown. And, anyway, there aren't many immigrant workers in this part of the country. They tend to be in the industrial areas and the larger cities."

"Yes, that all makes sense. But if he was a foreigner, wouldn't he occasionally say something in his own language? I mean, when he speaks it just sounds as though he's speaking German with a peculiar accent and using some unidentifiable words. It doesn't sound like a different language. And he's got a German name."

"Maybe he's an illegal immigrant, perhaps a refugee - God knows there are enough of them around nowadays. So suppose he got into the country, having worked as a miner in wherever it is he's come from. And he can't get a job here and he's reduced to being a vagrant. And then he has the accident. He's adopted a German name to try to disguise the fact that he's

66

an illegal alien. And he won't give us his surname in case we trace him. And he tries to speak German all the time but every now and again a word from his own language slips in. Does it make sense?"

"It does indeed. Poor old Wilhelm - or whatever his name is. He's so scared of being sent back that he'd rather stay in a psychiatric hospital. Good grief. Well, in that case it's even more important for us to find out where it is he's come from. If he really is a refugee, he might be allowed to stay."

"Do you think he'll understand that you want to help him?"

"I don't know. I wish we could talk to him in his own language but . . . wait a minute. We've got a linguist on the ward."

"What, one of the doctors?"

"No, a patient. He's a student at the university. I'll ask him if he'll speak to Wilhelm. He might be able to recognise the language even if he doesn't speak it himself - Albanian or Croatian or whatever - and then we could get in an interpreter. And now I come to think of it, he's about the only person on the ward who Wilhelm ever talks to, so he might have picked something up already."

Marcus stood up. "No time like the present," he said. "Would you like to come with me?"

"Yes please."

They moved into the ward and through to the day room. Wilhelm was sitting in a corner by himself, staring into space. Oskar, the university student, was nearby, reading a book. Marcus and Erika went over and sat down next to him.

"Oskar," said Marcus, speaking softly so that Wilhelm couldn't hear, "this is Nurse Frenzel."

"How do you do." Oskar put down his book and smiled at her.

"We were wondering if you could help us."

"Yes?"

"You are the only person, I think, who Wilhelm talks to."

"His bed is next to mine. But he hardly speaks at all."

"Yes, I know. The thing is, you're a linguist, aren't you."

"A novice linguist. I'm only in my second year at university."

"But have you any idea of where Wilhelm comes from? Do you recognise his accent at all? And the odd words that he uses - the words that aren't German - have you any idea what language they are?"

Oskar shook his head. "No. I'm afraid not. I must admit I haven't thought about it very much. I did once ask Wilhelm where he came from because I wondered whether he was a foreigner, but he gave some very strange reply - I can't remember now what it was."

"Oh, well," said Marcus, "it was worth a try."

"Wait a minute," Oskar said. "It's Friday today. My tutor usually comes in on her way home on a Friday. She speaks about eight languages fluently and she's an expert on philology . . ."

"Philology?" asked Erika.

"The science of language. Comparisons between different languages. How languages developed - that sort of thing."

"Oh." Erika nodded.

"I could introduce her to Wilhelm, if you like, and see if she has any ideas."

"That'd be great," said Marcus. "But I'd like to speak to her first."

"Of course. I'll bring her in to see you when she arrives."

"You'll let me know what happens?" asked Erika as they left the day room.

"Certainly. After all, it was your clever idea . . . "

Erika laughed. "Well, let's hope it leads somewhere. I'll be very interested to hear. You can reach me at the emergency department - I'm on duty till two every day this week."

"It might be easier if I rang you at home," said Marcus casually. "I don't want to interrupt you when you're working."

"How thoughtful." He could see she was trying not to laugh. "I'll give you my 'phone number."

✶ ✶ ✶

Dr. Elisabeth Kramer, Oskar's tutor, linguist and expert on philology, wasn't what Marcus had expected. When Oskar had mentioned her,

Marcus had imagined a straight-backed, grey haired woman, bespectacled perhaps, grey-suited, flat-shoed, authoritative, stern and unsmiling. But the woman whom Oskar had just brought into his office was a tall, slim and supremely elegant blonde of around thirty, whose smile revealed white even teeth and drew attention to her warm brown eyes. She was perfectly groomed, beautifully made up and stylishly dressed. If Marcus had seen her and, not knowing who she was, had been asked to guess her occupation, he would, without hesitation, have placed her in the upper echelons of the fashion industry, perhaps the editor of a high class fashion magazine, with the latest styles at her fingertips.

"Please sit down," he said, trying not to stare. "You too, Oskar."

"Thank you." Dr. Kramer insinuated herself elegantly into the offered chair. Her voice had a gentle quality that was immediately endearing. "Oskar tells me you have a problem that you think I could help you with."

"That's right. We have a patient who was brought in some time ago after a head injury. And we're finding it very hard to communicate with him because his knowledge of German is limited, and we haven't been able to identify what language he speaks. In fact, we know next to nothing about him and it's making diagnosis very difficult."

Elisabeth Kramer nodded. "So you want me to try to find out what language he speaks?"

"Yes. We thought perhaps you might be able to recognise his accent or some of the non-German words he uses from time to time."

"I'll do my best." She smiled.

"Oh, one other thing. It sounds strange, I know, but can you try to avoid smiling at him. For some reason, it seems to worry him."

"That's awful! Poor man." The sympathy sounded completely genuine.

"Oskar," Marcus turned to the young man. "would you be kind enough to ask Wilhelm to come in here."

"Of course, Herr Doctor."

"One other thing," said Marcus as soon as Oskar had left the room. "This is strictly confidential but there's a small chance that Wilhelm's an illegal immigrant. If he is, we'll do everything we can to help him but I think he'll need reassurance if he's going to tell you anything about himself."

"I'll do what I can. "

"Of course, it may be a relief for him to find someone who speaks his own language. He's hardly said a word since he was brought in."

"So Oskar says." She shook her head, frowning slightly. Then, brightening, she said "Oskar seems to be getting on well."

"Yes, we're very pleased with him. He should be going home in a week or so. But we'll want to keep an eye on him in out patients - make sure that he doesn't start slipping back again."

His tutor nodded. "I think he understands now that working himself into the ground is counter-productive. But we'll keep a close eye on him as well . . . Now, tell me the name of the patient I'm going to meet."

"Wilhelm."

"Can I call him by his first name? It seems a little impertinent."

"He won't tell us his surname. It's possible that he's afraid we could trace where he came from if we knew it."

"Right. And you've no idea at all of where he comes from?"

"None whatsoever. But we wondered if he might be Eastern European - Rumanian or Croatian or something like that."

"Right. Well, the only Eastern European language that I'm fluent in is Russian but I know a little Hungarian and Polish and a few words of Rumanian, so we can see whether he responds to any of those."

As she was speaking, there was a knock on the door and Oskar ushered Wilhelm into the room.

Chapter Five

It was, thought Elisabeth, quite bizarre. When she had arrived at the hospital for her customary Friday evening visit to see Oskar, the last thing she had expected was to be asked to give an opinion on a patient. Oskar broached the subject by talking enthusiastically about Dr. Hellman, contrasting his youth and enthusiasm with the lately-departed Dr. Gerhardt whose place he had taken.

"You've seen him around, haven't you?" he asked Elisabeth. "Tall and dark - always looks as though his hair needs combing." Elisabeth smiled, thinking how typical it was that the fastidious Oskar should focus on his doctor's unruly hair. And, as she shook hands with the psychiatrist a few minutes later, she noticed with amusement that Oskar's description was entirely accurate. But she could see at once why Oskar liked him. His concern for his patients was obvious as he described the sad, silent man he wanted her to talk to. And when he mentioned the possibility that Wilhelm might come from somewhere in Eastern Europe, Elisabeth's mind filled with pictures she had seen all too often of refugees, forced from their homes, trudging along the road, not knowing where they could find safety. Well, perhaps she could now help one of them. She waited, with some slight apprehension, for Oskar to bring Wilhelm into the office.

Although during her visits to Oskar she had grown to recognise several of his fellow-patients, she couldn't remember having seen Wilhelm. She imagined someone small, downtrodden, elderly, and rather pathetic. When Oskar brought in a tall, muscular young man dressed in jeans and sweater, for a moment she didn't realise who he was. It was something of a shock to hear Marcus Hellman address him as Wilhelm. But her first idea that he would be pathetic wasn't so far off the mark. There was something - no, not pathetic - but intensely sad about him. When Oskar had become ill, she had been aware of it from his body language. He stooped, hung his head and was obviously devoid of energy. There was nothing of that about Wilhelm. He stood upright and looked her in the eye. But there was a sense of deep sadness, and in his eyes she thought that she could detect a

71

spark of fear.

Oskar had left the room, shutting the door behind him, and Marcus Hellman was introducing her to the patient. Wilhelm walked uncertainly to the vacant chair and sat down, his eyes fixed on Elisabeth.

"Hello Wilhelm," she said. "May I call you Wilhelm?"

He nodded.

"My name is Elisabeth."

He nodded again.

She didn't know quite how to start talking to him. She didn't want it to sound like an interrogation. And then there was Marcus's instruction not to smile. She didn't know how she could reassure Wilhelm that she meant no harm. If her first questions didn't pry too much - asked for information that the hospital staff already knew - perhaps that would prevent him from feeling threatened. She took a long, deep breath, then asked in Russian "How long have you been a patient in the hospital?" He didn't answer, so she phrased it another way - "Do you remember when you were first brought here?". Wilhelm sat and looked at her, saying nothing. It was clear that he didn't understand.

She tried translating the questions into Polish and then Hungarian, but the effect was the same. Changing to Rumanian and then Croatian, she altered the questions to match her limited knowledge of the languages. Having asked "Is the food nice here?" and having received no reply, she followed it with "Do you like to walk in the rain?". There was still no response. She remembered that there had been times, early on in his illness, when Oskar wouldn't respond to questions, when the effort of replying had just seemed too great for him to manage. But it was different with Wilhelm. She was sure that he didn't respond because he truly didn't understand what she was saying.

She didn't know what to do next. So far, Wilhelm hadn't said a single word. She hadn't even been able to hear this strange accent of his. Of course, that was it! He did know a little German. Perhaps she could get him to say a few words in that language. Speaking slowly and clearly, she asked him to tell her something about himself.

"My name is Wilhelm," he said after a moment's pause. "I am Hundeiss."

What Hundeiss was, Elisabeth had no idea, but she felt that it was too soon to ask him to explain.

"How old are you?"

"Nearly ten thousand days."

Elisabeth was surprised. "What is that in years?" she asked.

"What is years?"

Elisabeth paused for a moment, then asked "Where you live, do they measure time in days?"

"Yes, of course."

"And where do you live?"

"Now, here."

"And before?"

"Before, in the mines."

"And how did you get here from the mines?"

No reply.

Elisabeth racked her brains for a way to reassure him. How could she let him know that he was safe, that she was on his side, that she wanted to help him. And how could she do it without smiling?

"It's all right, Wilhelm. I'm your friend," she said and, almost without thinking about it, trying desperately to offer comfort, reached out and touched his hand. The second she had done it, she wondered whether she had done the wrong thing. Wilhelm seemed to flinch but, when he looked at her, the fear had gone from his eyes and had been replaced by a look which, although hard to interpret, might have been one of nascent trust. Still, remembering what Marcus Hellman had said about the possibility of Wilhelm being an illegal immigrant, Elisabeth thought he would need more reassurance than this if he were to be persuaded to tell her anything that might incriminate him.

"We won't repeat what you tell us to anyone," she assured him, hoping that he understood. "But we should like to know how you came here from the mines."

Instead of answering, Wilhelm looked at Marcus. Instinctively Elisabeth asked "Would you like Dr. Hellman to go out?", realising with embarrassment as she said it that it was an impertinence on her part. This was Marcus's room and Wilhelm was Marcus's patient. But when Wilhelm said yes, she was sure that she had done the right thing.

Marcus looked at her. "Are you sure?" he asked.

She nodded, then got up and walked with him to the door. "He's scared of something," she said softly. "He might just tell me if we're left alone."

"I'll be right outside the door if you need me. He's never been violent. There's no reason to think he'd hurt you."

"Of course he wouldn't!" Elisabeth was shocked at the very idea.

She went back inside. With Marcus Hellman out of the room, Wilhelm seemed to relax a little and Elisabeth asked him again how he had come from the mines to the hospital. Hesitantly, he started to answer, telling her about caverns and tunnels and floors covered with strange spikes. And, as he did so, Elisabeth became aware not of an accent, as such, but of certain inflections and constructions of speech which, to her annoyance, she couldn't identify, although there was a familiarity about them that intrigued her. Listening carefully, she tried to free her mind of preconceived ideas.

And suddenly it became clear, although for a few moments she couldn't believe what she was hearing. It took her back to the days when she was working for her Ph.D., writing a thesis on the development of the Germanic languages in which she had described how the language of the original Germanic tribes had transformed itself into Old High German and then, in the eleventh century, into Middle High German, the language of literature and poetry. And now Wilhelm seemed to be talking to her in that same language. After her first initial astonishment, she realised that it had to be a dialect. There were one or two places in which dialects survived that had a close affinity to the German language in its earlier forms, often mountainous areas, cut off by the terrain from surrounding communities. She had studied these dialects when she was writing her Ph.D. and now she dredged her memory for some vocabulary or form of grammar which would distinguish them from each other.

Carefully, she formed some questions in each of the dialects in turn but Wilhelm didn't react to any of them as she might expect someone to do when hearing his native language spoken after an interval of many weeks. Could there be, she wondered, a dialect that she hadn't come across when she was doing her research. Or maybe there was one that she had forgotten. Perhaps the best way forward would be to speak in Middle High German which, it seemed, was very similar to the language that Wilhelm spoke.

Choosing her words carefully, she rephrased the questions that she had asked in the dialects - and Wilhelm responded eagerly and without hesitation. Elisabeth was flummoxed. She knew of nowhere where a dialect had remained identical, or nearly identical, to Middle High German. And yet it seemed that there must be a speech island which was still using this form of the language. She was intrigued.

"Wilhelm," she began. "Please trust me. We really want to help you but we do need to know more about you."

She could see that Wilhelm looked puzzled. "Don't you understand?" she asked.

"What do you need to know?" asked Wilhelm. "You are one of Them. You must know."

"Who are they?" asked Elisabeth.

"You are not Them?"

"No. I don't think so."

After a moment Wilhelm said "We thought that there were just Hundeiss and Them. But everything is so different here." He lapsed into silence.

"Tell me about your home."

"Home?"

"Your house."

"I do not understand."

Elisabeth remembered what Marcus had said about Wilhelm's limited vocabulary. Even within the language that he spoke, it seemed, there were words with which he wasn't familiar. But home and house - surely these were words that he should know. She tried again.

"Tell me about the place where you used to live."

"I lived in cave number forty seven."

Extraordinary, thought Elisabeth, that he should know the word cave but not house or home. But presumably that was the word his people used for - what? - a house, a farm, a particular area? If there were other words used by these people in an anomalous way, their vocabulary might form the basis of an interesting research paper. But before she could investigate it, she would have to find out where it was that it was spoken.

"Is it a long way from cave forty seven to the hospital - to where you are now?" she asked.

"I think so. I came through long tunnels and many caverns. And there was no music."

"Music?"

"Yes. There was no music in the tunnels or in the caverns. And there is no music here."

"Do you like music?"

Wilhelm looked at her and didn't reply, shaking his head slightly as though trying to clear his mind.

"Did you have music in your cave?" Elisabeth asked.

"There is always music. In the caves and in the mines. It is the music that . . . I don't remember. In the tunnels and the caverns it was different. There was a . . . clearness. But here there is control but no music."

Elisabeth frowned. "What sort of control?" she asked.

"Of the mind."

"And in the caves and the mines . . . your mind is controlled?"

"Yes. By the music. Here I am controlled but not by music."

This must, Elisabeth thought, be the result of whatever medication Wilhelm was being given. But what was this music that had controlled Wilhelm's mind in the place he had come from? - and where was it that he had come from?

"Can you remember how many days it took you to get here?"

"No. Without work you cannot count the days. But I slept perhaps four times."

"Do you count only the days on which you work? What about Sunday? Holidays?"

"What is Sunday?"

"Sunday is . . . How many days in the week do you work?"

"What is week?"

"A week is seven days. Do you call it something else?"

Wilhelm shook his head.

"How many days do you work before you have a day off?" Elisabeth asked.

"I work every day. Until I come here. Here it is strange. I am allowed to sit and to rest and to sleep."

There was a look almost of wonder on his face. Elisabeth was appalled that anyone should think it extraordinary that he should be allowed to rest. And did Wilhelm really mean that he worked every day of his life without ever having a day off? Surely not.

"Where did you work before you came here?"

"In the mines."

"And did you live near the mines?"

"Yes. My cave was in the mine tunnels."

"You lived underground?"

"What is underground?"

Elisabeth was becoming truly confused by Wilhelm's limited vocabulary. Words which she would have expected him to know just weren't there. Surely, she thought, a miner should know the meaning of underground. She glanced at her watch and realised that they had been talking for more than ten minutes and that Marcus was still waiting outside. She had discovered what she had been asked to find out - the language that Wilhelm spoke. But that was now posing more problems, more puzzles that were begging to be solved. She would have to discuss it with Marcus.

"Wilhelm," she said, "we must stop talking now but I should like to come back and see you again."

"Yes. Come back." There was a strange expression in his eyes that she couldn't quite interpret.

"I'll talk to Dr. Hellman and arrange it. Stay there for a moment." She got up and went to the door. Marcus was leaning up against the wall outside the room, talking to one of the nurses. As Elisabeth came out, he broke off his conversation and came briskly towards her.

"Have you found out anything?" he asked.

"Yes, but it's not what I expected."

They went back into the office. Wilhelm looked up as they entered.

"Thank you, Wilhelm," Marcus said. "You'd better go now or you'll miss your evening meal."

Wilhelm stood up, keeping his eyes on Elisabeth.

"Thank you," he said. The words sounded awkward on his lips. Then he left the room.

"Good heavens," said Marcus. "You obviously made an impression on him. That's the first time he's said thank you since he's been here. Now, what have you found out."

"Well, we spoke in German and, although I couldn't place his accent, he started to use words that I recognised," Elisabeth explained, anxious for Marcus to understand her reasoning in coming to her extraordinary conclusion.

"So you know what language he speaks? Excellent!"

"Yes. But it's not as clear cut as that. You see, it's not an Eastern European language. It's German."

"A dialect?"

"Well, yes and no. It's certainly German but . . . well, it's a form of the language that was last spoken over six hundred years ago."

"What?" Marcus Hellman's face expressed his astonishment.

"I know," continued Elisabeth. "It's bizarre. I mean, there are speech pockets with dialects that haven't developed in the same way as modern German but I don't know anywhere where the people still speak an almost pure form of Middle High German. Added to which, I don't understand why Wilhelm's vocabulary is so limited - there are a lot of words that he doesn't seem to understand even in his own language. And I've still no idea where he comes from. It seems as though there are more puzzles to be solved than you imagined. But at least we now have a way of communicating with him."

Marcus nodded. "Of course, we still need someone who can interpret for us. I don't suppose you could . . . " he looked at her hopefully. "I'm afraid we couldn't pay you."

"I'd be delighted," said Elisabeth. "And don't worry about not being able to pay me. I'm so intrigued by the whole thing that I'd have been quite upset if you didn't want me to continue."

She remembered Wilhelm's comment about his mind being controlled and mentioned it. Marcus nodded.

"I'm really not sure that the drugs are doing him any good at all. To my mind the original diagnosis was made on very flimsy evidence. I think the next thing we need to do is wean him off all his medication and see what happens."

"How long will that take?"

"Two to three weeks. It's probably best if you put off trying any serious conversation until his mind's clearer. But if you could pop in from time to time - just to say hello and remind him who you are - that'd be great."

"Sure, I can do that. And in the meantime I'll do a little research. If I can locate this dialect pocket, at least we'll know where he comes from and you might be able to contact some of his friends or family."

"That, of course, would answer a lot of our problems. Well, we'll keep our fingers crossed, shall we?"

✶ ✶ ✶

Over the course of the next three weeks, while Wilhelm's medication was slowly reduced and Marcus watched him closely for any signs of abnormal behaviour, Elisabeth went in to the hospital six times. Each visit was brief. Wilhelm remained quiet, calm, unemotional, but Elisabeth had the impression that he was pleased by her arrival and reluctant to see her go. He started to talk more freely, telling her about his days in the hospital, his paintings and the food that he had eaten and, as he did so, she became increasingly aware of the limitations of his vocabulary.

On Elisabeth's third visit, while she was sitting with Wilhelm in the day room, Marcus came in with a young woman whom he introduced as Erika Frenzel, the nurse who had looked after Wilhelm in the emergency department. The two women shook hands, smiling at each other and, as they did so, Elisabeth was aware, out of the corner of her eye, of Wilhelm recoiling from them. She turned towards him and caught something that looked like panic in his eyes. Suspecting that he was finding so many visitors disturbing, she stood up and announced that she was going.

Marcus walked with her to the door. "He's doing well," he said. "No signs of any change in his personality or his behaviour. Give him another couple of weeks and we'll have him off the drugs altogether and then you can start work."

But as that day approached, Elisabeth found herself becoming more and more nervous about the prospect. Why, she couldn't say. She was used to dealing with people. She was, each year, personal tutor to six or seven students at the university; they consulted her not just about their work but also concerning problems with their accommodation and their finances and even, on occasion, their love lives. She had been the one who had told Oskar that he must see a doctor when he started to sink into depression. When, after weeks of persuasion, he did, it was she who had gone with him to his appointment and accompanied him on the journey into the hospital. She had been the one who had informed his parents, who lived several hundred miles away, and it was she who visited Oskar regularly once or twice a week and kept his family up to date on his progress. She felt responsible for her students, tried to help them when she could, and was rewarded by quite a number of them keeping in touch with her after they graduated.

So why should she be nervous about interviewing Wilhelm? She tried to analyse it. Well, of course, she would be speaking in Middle High German, but it was a form of the language with which she was very familiar, so that should pose no problems. Nor was it Wilhelm himself who made her nervous - he was in no way aggressive or intimidating, indeed far from it. No, reluctantly she had to admit to herself that what was causing her anxiety was the mystery in which the case was enshrouded. Despite some careful research, she had been unable to find any reference to a speech pocket with a dialect almost identical to the language of six hundred years ago. So where was it that Wilhelm came from, and what was he going to tell her about his previous life? She wasn't sure that she wanted to know. But, she told herself, she would have to go through with it. There just wasn't anyone else.

✳ ✳ ✳

"Would you like to use the desk?" asked Marcus as he ushered Elisabeth into his office for her interview with Wilhelm.

Elisabeth paused, then said "No, let's keep it as informal as possible."

She lowered herself into one of the easy chairs and was just taking a notebook and pen out of her bag when the door opened and Wilhelm came in.

Hesitantly, he said "Hello Elisabeth."

"Hello Wilhelm." Elisabeth still found that she had to remind herself not to smile. "We're going to have a longer talk today." She spoke in Middle High German. Wilhelm nodded and, prompted by Marcus, sat down opposite her.

"Dr. Hellman and I want to help you, Wilhelm," Elisabeth continued. "but we need to know more about you."

Still Wilhelm said nothing. Elisabeth looked at Marcus who asked "Do you want me to go?"

"Well . . . " said Elisabeth, "you probably won't understand very much . . . I am sorry, Marcus, I always seem to be throwing you out of your own office."

"That's all right. I can go and dictate some letters. I'll see you later."

Once Marcus had left the room, shutting the door behind him, Elisabeth turned back to Wilhelm.

"How are you feeling now that you're not taking the drugs?" she asked.

"Drugs?" Wilhelm frowned at the word.

"Medicine."

Wilhelm shook his head.

"Potions," Elisabeth tried. "Remedies . . ."

Wilhelm still looked blank. Elisabeth gave up.

"How are you?" she asked.

"Well."

"Do you feel any different from when we first met?"

Wilhelm nodded. "I can think. The control has gone."

"Good. Wilhelm, may I ask you some questions about yourself?"

Wilhelm nodded again.

"Where were you born?"

"Born?"

Elisabeth was puzzled. She was sure that she had used the right word. Maybe her pronunciation was faulty.

"Yes," she repeated, speaking as clearly as she could.   "Where were you born?"

Wilhelm shook his head. "What is born?"

"Where did you live when you were a baby?"

"Baby?"

"Small child."

"Cave forty seven."

"And that's where you lived as an adult, too?"

"Yes."

"When you were a child, who did you live with?"

"Ursula and Friedrich."

"Were they your parents?"

"Parents?"

"Mother and father."

Again Wilhelm shook his head. "They were my adults. They looked after me."

"And did you have brothers and sisters?"

"I don't know."

"Did your parents - your adults - have other children?"

"No."

"And when you grew up, did your adults still live with you?"

"No. They had been Taken."

"Taken? Taken where?"

"Taken."

"I'm sorry, Wilhelm, I don't understand."

For the first time since she had known him, Wilhelm's face showed emotion, although whether it was frustration or anger, or perhaps both, she couldn't tell.

"Taken . . . Taken . . . they were dead."

"Oh, I see. I'm sorry. They must have been quite young when they died."

"No." The emotion had subsided and a note of resignation had crept in. "Around ten thousand days."

Elisabeth frowned. Wasn't that the age that Wilhelm had said he was now? She must have remembered wrongly. Even so, ten thousand days didn't sound very much. She made a note. She could work it out later.

"Is that a common age to die at where you come from?"

Wilhelm shrugged. "Many are Taken earlier. If you are injured or if you can no longer work, you are Taken."

Elisabeth gasped. "You mean, they are killed?"

"We say Taken. A cord round the neck . . . it is quick."

Elisabeth sat silently, fighting down a wave of nausea. What sort of people were these who killed each other when they could no longer work? Her rational mind told her that Wilhelm was making it up - it sounded like the imaginings of a horror-story writer. But what could he have to gain by it? For the time being, she would have to take his bizarre story at face value. But she didn't want to ask the next question. Getting up from her chair, she went over to the desk on which there was a carafe of water. Slowly, she poured water into a glass and then sipped. The nausea subsided and she returned to her seat, glass in hand.

"Wilhelm," she asked. "who was it who killed - who took - Friedrich and Ursula when they could no longer work? Was it you?"

An expression of horror sprang onto Wilhelm's face. "No!" he shouted. "No! It was the Takers. It is always the Takers. I would not do such a thing. I loved them. They were my adults. . . they were my adults." His voice tailed off and for a moment Elisabeth thought that he was going to burst into tears.

"I'm sorry, Wilhelm," she said quickly. "Please forgive me. But, you see, where you come from, life is so different from the way it is here. The only way for me to find out is to ask questions."

Wilhelm nodded. "I can see it is different here. People are different. There are many people here who I think are older than me. If I had stayed in the mines, I would have been Taken soon."

Elisabeth was shocked by the matter of fact tone in which he said it. "Just because of your age?" she asked.

Wilhelm shook his head. "I could not have worked much longer. The pain had become too severe. It would have been good to rest."

Elisabeth felt tears spring to her eyes and she blinked rapidly to clear them. "What pain?" she asked softly.

"In my back and my shoulders. From the work in the mines. Now I have not worked for so long and the pain has almost gone. And here I can rest. That was never allowed before."

"But you must have been allowed some time to rest."

"Six hours for eating and sleeping. Then eighteen hours work."

"Good God! And this was every day?"

"Of course."

Elisabeth sat back in her chair, her mind whirling. Wilhelm clearly believed the story that he was telling her, but how could it possibly be true?

"Wilhelm," she said, "you do know that we'd never send you back there, don't you."

"I did not know. I wanted to know that, but I did not know."

Elisabeth looked at him and wondered how it could be that there were people enslaved in mines, presumably somewhere in Europe, and that no one knew about it.

"Wilhelm," she said, "if we're to help you, we've got to know where you came from. Where exactly are the mines?"

Wilhelm shook his head. "I do not know. I had never left them before."

"How were you kept there? Were there guards?"

"Guards?"

"People to stop you leaving?"

"No. There were the Takers and the Carriers. And Them. But we didn't see Them."

"Who were the Carriers?"

"They took away the rock that we mined and they brought things to the supply cave - food and water and clothes."

"Did they feed you well?"

"There was never enough food. Here I eat in a day what I would have eaten in three or four. There was enough water if you were careful. But it was precious. Here I am asked to stand under water to make my skin pale. Here it is not precious."

"And what was in the rock that you mined?"

"In it?"

"Yes, what were you mining it for? Was it coal?"

"It was just rock. We mined it and the women pulled the carts to the sorting caves and the Carriers took it away."

"And did no one ever rebel? Did no one ever try to leave the mines?"

"We did not know there was anywhere else to go."

Elisabeth tried to imagine a life spent underground unaware of the outside world, unaware of trees and birds and sunlight and flowers, and she felt cold inside.

"How many people work in the mines?" she asked.

"I do not know. About a hundred, a hundred and fifty. No more. There are eighty caves. Some people live alone, some live together."

"Did you live alone after your adults were Taken?"

"At first. And then with Lotte."

"Is she your wife?"

"She was my woman, yes."

"And do you have children?"

"We had two."

"Does Lotte work in the mines?"

"Everyone has to work. Lotte pulled the carts. And one day she fell. And her leg was broken. And she was Taken."

"Oh, Wilhelm, I'm so sorry." It seemed such an inadequate thing to say in the face of all that he had been through, but Wilhelm looked at her and nodded gently.

"She was a good woman," he said. "She looked after the children well."

"Did she have to work while she was pregnant?" Elisabeth asked.

"What is pregnant?"

"When she was expecting the children. . . When she was with child. . . Before the children were born."

"I don't understand."

"You obviously have a different word for it. How else can I put it?" Elisabeth thought for a moment. "When the children were growing inside her . . ." she broke off, seeing the horrified expression on Wilhelm's face. "What's the matter?" she asked.

"Children . . . growing . . . inside my Lotte . . . " he shook his head as though to brush off something unpleasant that had adhered to him.

"Wilhelm." Elisabeth came to a decision. "Do you trust me? Do you believe that I'd never do anything to hurt you?"

"Yes." Wilhelm didn't hesitate.

"You see, your life in the mines was so different from the way things are here that I just don't know what questions to ask you. So . . . will you just tell me about it?"

Wilhelm nodded. Elisabeth felt herself relax. "Thank you."

She got up out of her chair and walked over to the window. It was a fine spring day, the sun warm, the trees full of fresh new growth. Out in the hospital grounds people were walking slowly, enjoying the sweet air that held the promise of a good summer. She turned back to Wilhelm.

"Shall we go outside?" she asked. "We could walk for a little and talk as we go. Would you like that?"

86

"I . . ." Wilhelm hesitated.

"You'll be quite safe. I'll look after you. And you can tell me about the things here that you don't understand and I can explain."

Wilhelm stood up. "Yes. That would be good. After I left the mines there were many things that I didn't understand and I wanted to know. But when I came here, they started to control my mind and I couldn't think. But now my mind is clear again. And there is so much I want to know."

"Then let's go out," said Elisabeth, and she opened the door and led the way.

✳ ✳ ✳

They walked side by side in silence for a short time, then Wilhelm said "It frightens me."

"What does?"

"Everything. In the mines there was just the rock and the carts and the people . . . my people. You didn't need many words. Here it is all so different . . . and there is so much of it. And I don't know the name of anything. When my mind was controlled I didn't want to know, but now I do. It frightens me not to know the name of anything. When I first came into . . . this," he gestured around him "it was all so strange." He pointed to the grass. "I called that colour floorspike. Because it is the colour of the spikes on the floor."

"Don't your people have a word for it?"

"No. I had never seen that colour before I came out of the mines."

Elisabeth tried to imagine a world without green and again felt that cold feeling run down her spine.

"What colours do you know?"

"Black . . grey . . red . . yellow . . brown. . . And pale."

"Pale? Is that what we call white?" Elisabeth pointed at the uniform of a nurse who was pushing a patient along a path in a wheelchair.

"Yes - white."

"And the colour that you called floorspike, we call green."

"Green." Wilhelm repeated the word thoughtfully.

"And the spikes of green are called grass."

87

"Grass. It is good to be able to name things. It makes them feel less strange."

"Do you not know blue either?" asked Elisabeth.

Wilhelm shook his head.

"It's the colour of the sky."

"I do not know sky."

Elisabeth pointed. "That's the sky there, up above us."

Wilhelm looked. "Some of my people have eyes almost that colour but we do not have a name for it." He paused. "We do not say 'sky'. We call it the roof."

"Roof? Oh . . ." Elisabeth suddenly realised the implication of what he had said. "The sky isn't a roof, Wilhelm. We're outside."

"The roof is above it?" Wilhelm looked up. "It must be very high. I could never have imagined a cavern this big. And that lamp," he pointed at the sun, "It's so much brighter than anything we ever had in the mines. But why does it keep appearing and disappearing?"

"There's so much you need to learn, Wilhelm," Elisabeth said gently, "I think we must find someone who will teach you."

"That would be good," said Wilhelm and she thought she detected a note of enthusiasm in his voice.

They were approaching the rose garden. The bushes were just coming into bloom, in a variety of reds and yellows, pinks and white. Elisabeth thought again of Wilhelm's mines with their few sad, ill-lit colours and she felt cold, despite the warmth of the sun. The seat at the far end of the garden was vacant.

"Shall we go and sit down?" she asked. "And then you can tell me about the mines and it will be my turn to ask questions."

✳ ✳ ✳

For some minutes they sat in silence. Here, in the garden, Elisabeth felt more at ease, no longer feeling that she was playing the role of the interrogator, the inquisitor. Here she was just a friend, someone who would listen and who wanted to help. Away from the formal atmosphere of the hospital ward and the doctor's office they could have a conversation,

88

rather than an interview. She waited for Wilhelm to speak.

Eventually he said "It was all different there. I could never have thought that there was such a place as this." Again he lapsed into silence.

Then, "We knew only the mines and the tunnels and the caves. We say 'cave' but I think you say 'room'."

Elisabeth nodded but he wasn't looking at her, staring straight ahead, eyes unfocussed as he remembered.

"My cave, my room, was about the size of the room in which we met today. But it had very little in it. There were no chairs or beds - I didn't know chairs or beds until I came here. There was a shelf cut out of the rock wall and on that we kept food and needle and thread. And there were rags on the floor that we slept on. There was a bucket with water and a lamp and candles. That was all. . . . Here there is so much." He shook his head.

"In our caves and in the passageways there was no light except from the lamps we carried. But in the mines, there were lights along the tunnels which the Carriers fixed up. It was lighter in the mines than in the passageways and in the caves but it is so much lighter here. When I first came out into this cavern, this lamp," he pointed at the sun, "was pale. And then I went to sleep and when I woke everything was much brighter, but I couldn't see where the light was coming from. I thought there must be lamps in the walls but I couldn't see the walls either."

He broke off and looked at Elisabeth. "I don't understand why this lamp becomes pale at night."

"It's not the same . . . lamp," said Elisabeth. "This," she pointed, "is called the sun. What you see at night is called the moon. But actually, they're not lamps in the way that you think they are."

"The sun," repeated Wilhelm, "and the . . ."

"Moon," prompted Elisabeth.

"And the moon. But how are they different from lamps?"

Elisabeth felt she was getting in too deep. She struggled for a simple explanation that Wilhelm might understand. "Well, they give light in the same way. But they're not the sort of lamps that you have in the mines. That's why they're brighter." It was the best she could do. It would take a very good teacher to get Wilhelm to understand the true nature of the world in which he was now living.

"When I came into the cavern," said Wilhelm, seeming to accept the explanation. "the light hurt my eyes. But now I have become used to it even when it is as bright as this. Do you know why it changes from day to day?"

"Yes, I do," replied Elisabeth. "It's something we can talk about later on when you understand more about this place."

"That will be good. When I was first brought here I had so many questions and I could ask no one. They just shouted at me in words that I didn't understand. I have learned a lot of words now but it is still hard to talk to them."

"It will become easier," Elisabeth assured him.

"Yes. Everything else here is so good. I have enough food - and it is so good to eat. And there is no music."

"We have music," said Elisabeth, puzzled.

"No. I have heard what you call music. There is a box in the art room and what you call music comes out of it. But it is not the music that controls the mind and it can be stopped. In the mines and in the tunnels and in the caves there is always music. It surrounds us. We cannot stop it."

"What sort of music is it?" Elisabeth was intrigued, remembering Wilhelm's previous reference to the music, at their first meeting. "How does it differ from the music here?"

" Your music doesn't control."

"But what does your music sound like?"

"It is thin, high. You hear not so much with the ear but with the mind. And it is always there. I never knew that there could be somewhere with no music until I broke through the mine wall into a cavern. I stepped through the gap and suddenly I couldn't hear the music." Wilhelm stopped speaking and Elisabeth waited, saying nothing.

"I felt fear, great fear. And then I felt something else, something I had never felt before. It took time before I could understand what it was. But I had no name for it." He looked at Elisabeth. "Perhaps you have a name for it. If you do, it would mean it was real. It was very strong after I left the mines. Then when I was brought here and they started to control my mind again, the feeling was lost. But now my mind is clear and the feeling is slowly returning, so I must believe that it is real. But still it has no name."

Elisabeth looked at Wilhelm and saw in his eyes a look of desperation. "Tell me about it," she said.

"As I came through the tunnels and the caverns it was a feeling that things could get better, that there was something better. Now it is a feeling that I can understand what is happening here, that I will be able to talk to the people I meet. It is a feeling about the future, a feeling . . ." he tailed off, shaking his head.

Elisabeth smiled gently before she realised what she was doing, but it was all right - Wilhelm was no longer looking at her. "It has a name," she said. "We call it hope."

"Hope." Wilhelm repeated the word. "Hope. Yes. I have felt hope. And I am feeling hope again."

His vulnerability made Elisabeth want to cry, to put her arms round him and reassure him that everything would be all right, to comfort him as one might comfort a lost child. "You must never lose hope," she said. "now that you have found it."

"No," said Wilhelm. "Now that I know its name."

Two patients walked past them, making their way back from the vegetable gardens towards the main entrance of the hospital. Their clothes were stained with earth and they were talking about the relative merits of carrots and turnips. Wilhelm watched them go past, then, looking down at the jeans he was wearing, said "Where I come from we all wear the same clothes. We have a yellow shirt, red trousers. Every one thousand days we are given a new set. Then the old ones go with the other rags to sleep on. Very soon the clothes become black. My people are black, too. This," he looked down at his hands, "is not my colour. I am not the same colour as you. But when I came here, Erika made me stand under water and rub myself with something called soap and my colour came off. And now every day they make me do it again, even though I am now as pale as you."

Elisabeth gasped. This aspect of Wilhelm's terrible former life had not occurred to her. "You never washed in the mines?" she asked.

"No, never. In the mines water was precious. It was for drinking. And why would we want to rub our bodies with it?"

"Well, here water is not so precious. And everyone washes. It is to keep ourselves clean."

Wilhelm looked at her in amazement. "You wash?" he asked.

"Every day," said Elisabeth.

"You stand under water, like me?"

"Yes."

"But you are not Hundeiss."

"What is Hundeiss? It isn't a word that I know."

"It's the name of my people. We are all black-skinned, as I was when I came here. You are pale skinned."

"Wilhelm, the reason why you were black-skinned is because you had never washed. The blackness was from the mines. If I never washed, my skin would become darker and, if I worked in a mine, it would become black. But it wouldn't be my natural, my real colour. This is my real colour - and yours."

Wilhelm looked at her and suddenly gasped. "The children," he said. "Of course. The children."

"The children?" Elisabeth asked.

"When they first come to us, they are a different colour. They are the colour I am now, the colour you are. Then they become black. . . . it is because they do not wash."

Elisabeth nodded.

"When you say they come to you," she said, "what do you mean?"

"They are brought by the Carriers, to replace those people who have been Taken."

"But where do the Carriers bring them from?"

"From Them. It is something to do with breeding. They take young women for breeding, and then children come back. Does it not happen in the same way here?"

"Not quite. But what about the young women - can't you ask them when they come back?"

"They don't come back."

"I see. And is that the only way that children arrive in the mines?"

"Yes. How else?"

"And when they arrive, how big are they?"

Wilhelm looked at her, frowning. "They are the size of a small child," he said.

Elisabeth held her hands apart, demonstrating the size of a newborn baby. "That size?" she asked.

"No. How could a child be so small? They are . . ." he held his hand some two feet above the ground "about that size."

"And who takes care of them when they come?"

"They are given to people - to a man and woman. Then they work in the sorting caves until they are old enough to work in the mines."

"They go to work straight away?"

"Of course. Everyone has to work."

"And how old are they when they start working in the mines?"

"A man is three thousand five hundred days, a woman three thousand. The women pull the carts, the men break the rock."

"You told me that you had children."

Wilhelm nodded. "Lotte and I were given two, Konrad and Marthe. They were good children. I liked them."

"And are they still working in the mines."

"Unless they have been Taken, yes."

The sun was getting lower and a chill breeze was starting to ruffle the rose bushes. People who had been strolling in the gardens were beginning to make their way back into the hospital building. Elisabeth shivered, although whether from the drop in temperature or at the thought of small children working in the mines she wasn't sure.

"I think it's time you went back in," she said, standing up. "You don't want to miss your evening meal."

Wilhelm stood and walked with her back along the path. When they reached the hospital entrance he turned to face her.

"You will come back again?" he asked. There was an urgency in his voice and his eyes were anxious.

"Of course I will, Wilhelm. I'll see you again very soon."

"Good. Thank you Elisabeth."

Wilhelm turned and pushed through the glass doors into the entrance lobby and Elisabeth stood and watched until he had disappeared round the bend of the stairs.

Chapter Six

Elisabeth walked quickly along the sodden gravel path and into the main entrance of the hospital. Once inside, she lifted her head, which had been bowed against the wind, and removed her rain hat, feeling with disgust a trickle of cold water run down her neck. To her surprise, Wilhelm was in the entrance foyer, where Oskar used to sit. She hurried over, remembering as she did so not to smile.

"Wilhelm! Are you waiting for me?"

"Yes. Marcus told me you would come this afternoon."

"It's a horrid afternoon," said Elisabeth, looking back through the doors at the dark skies and pouring rain. "We can't sit outside today. Why don't we go and have some coffee?"

They turned and walked down a long corridor that led to the small cafeteria provided for the use of visitors and of people attending the out-patients department. Most of the clinics had ended for the day and the place was almost deserted. A mother with a young child sat at the only occupied table, finishing a snack.

"Sit down, Wilhelm," Elisabeth said, gesturing to the table furthest away from the child, who was talking loudly between mouthfuls. "I'll get some coffee."

She walked over to the counter and returned a few moments later with two cups of coffee and two slices of strudel.

Putting the tray down on the table, she took off her coat and hung it over the back of a chair where it dripped water onto the floor. She sat down and saw that Wilhelm was gazing at the accumulating puddle. Looking up, he turned an anxious face towards her.

"Why does water fall from the roof?" he asked.

Instinctively Elisabeth glanced up. The ceiling was intact.

"No," she said, "it's dripping off my coat." Then she realised what he meant. "Do you mean out there?" she asked, pointing through the window to where the rain still fell in a steady stream.

Wilhelm nodded.

"I'll try to explain," Elisabeth said slowly. "But I don't know if I can do it well enough for you to understand." She thought for a moment. Steam was rising from the coffee cups. She pointed. "Do you see this?" she asked. Wilhelm nodded. "Well, that's called water vapour. It's water in another form. And when enough water vapour gathers outside, it forms clouds - you've seen clouds in the sky?"

Wilhelm nodded.

"And when they get very big, the water vapour becomes water again and drops back down to earth. We call it rain."

"Why?"

"Why do we call it rain?"

"No, why does it go up and then come down again?"

"Well . . . because that's what it does. It just happens."

Wilhelm still looked puzzled. "Who decides when it will happen?"

"Nobody. It just happens."

Wilhelm shook his head. "Does no one try to stop it? All that water being wasted."

"Oh, it's not wasted. We must have rain. When it comes down it collects together and then we can use it for drinking and washing. And plants can't grow without rain. So without it we'd have nothing to drink and no food."

Wilhelm nodded, seeming satisfied. He turned his attention to the coffee and strudel that Elisabeth had put in front of him.

"What is this?" he asked.

"Strudel. I think you'll like it. It's pastry with apples and raisins and spice in it."

Wilhelm shook his head again. "I don't know these things. What are they?"

"Well, you know apples, don't you? You must have them on the ward? Round, green, this sort of size?" She formed a circle with her hands.

"Yes - but how are they in here?"

"They're sliced up and cooked."

"Cooked?"

"Eat it and tell me if you like it."

Wilhelm picked up the strudel and took a bite. His eyes widened. "It is very good."

Elisabeth drank some coffee, then asked "Did you - or Lotte - not cook food in your cave?"

"No. I don't think so."

"Well, what sort of food did you eat?"

"Foodcake and biscuits."

"What?"

"We had yellow foodcake and red foodcake. The Carriers brought them every ten days. The red foodcake went bad quickly so it was eaten first. Then we ate the yellow foodcake and the biscuits."

"And that was all you had to eat?"

"Yes."

"No vegetables? No fruit? . . . No, of course, you said you'd never seen anything green. Didn't you become ill?"

"If you became ill you were Taken."

"And you ate the food cold?"

"Yes. I had never had hot food until I came here. And there is so much of it - and it tastes so good."

So that, Elisabeth realised, was why, when she had first started to visit Wilhelm, one of his few topics of conversation had been the food that he had eaten.

"Where did the Carriers bring the food from?"

"I don't know. We went to the supply cavern and they gave it to us."

"What was it like, this foodcake?"

"It was a block, and we would break pieces off. My Lotte was very good at working out how much we could eat each day. She was good at many things, my Lotte. She sewed our clothes when they were torn. She rubbed my back and shoulders when I was in pain. She was a good woman." He looked at Elisabeth. "Even here I do not forget her."

"Of course not. She was your wife."

They drank coffee in silence for a few moments, then Elisabeth asked

"What sort of ceremony do your people have for a marriage?"

"I don't understand."

"When you and Lotte married . . ."

"What is married?"

Elisabeth frowned. Although she was getting used to Wilhelm's gaps in vocabulary, this was a word she would have expected him to know. She tried to think of a synonym that he might understand and failed. She would have to explain the word to him - but how do you define marriage in a sentence? She thought for a moment, then said "When a man and woman decide to live together for the rest of their lives and to have children together, they get married - they have what we call a ceremony and it, well . . . it ties them together."

"Ties them? With ropes?"

"No. I mean it joins them so that they belong to each other."

Wilhelm nodded.

"And here," Elisabeth continued, "you can either have a ceremony in a church or what we call a civil ceremony."

"What is a church?"

"It's a building in which people worship - show their love of - God."

"What is God?"

"You don't know about God?"

Wilhelm shook his head.

Elisabeth picked up her cup and drank some coffee, aware that Wilhelm was looking at her.

"I can't explain to you about God now," she said, feeling guilty that she was opting out. "Later we'll find someone who can teach you."

"Will you teach me, Elisabeth?" Wilhelm asked softly.

She raised her eyes to his. "I don't know that I can," she said.

"You are not coming to see me again?" Wilhelm's voice rose sharply, his eyes anxious.

"Of course I'll come to see you," Elisabeth hastened to reassure him. "But I don't think that I'm the best person to teach you."

Wilhelm nodded, visibly relaxing. "I have learned much since I have been here," he said.

"I know. You use a lot of our words now, as well as your own."

"It is good."

"Yes, it is good."

Wilhelm finished eating his strudel and licked his fingers. Elisabeth looked over to the far end of the cafeteria. The mother and child had gone, leaving a clutter of plates, cups, glasses and paper napkins. She and Wilhelm were of a similar age but sometimes their relationship felt like that of a mother and child. There was a warmth growing between them that was closer than that of friends or of teacher and pupil. And yet . . .

"Wilhelm," she began, "can I ask you something?"

"Of course."

"When I first met Marcus - when he asked me if I would talk to you because I knew your language - he told me that I mustn't smile at you."

Wilhelm looked down at his empty plate and said nothing.

"Why does it upset you, Wilhelm?"

"It is something between a man and his woman. A man smiles at his woman and a woman smiles at her man, yes, and also they smile at their children - but no one else."

"I see! So when the nurse - when Erika - smiled at you when you first came to the hospital . . ."

"I thought They wanted her to be my woman. And then the man smiled. And then the other woman . . . and I did not know. It frightened me. I could not understand."

"Oh, poor Wilhelm. How awful. But here smiling is just being friendly."

"I did not know."

"Of course not. How could you?" She paused. "Wilhelm," she said.

"Yes."

"You're my friend, aren't you?"

"Yes."

"But every time I see you I have to remember not to smile at you. And it's very difficult. Would it upset you if I smiled at you - now that you know that it just means friendship?"

Wilhelm looked at her. "It would not upset me if you smiled at me, Elisabeth."

"I'm so glad." She smiled with relief and slowly a small, shy answering smile appeared on Wilhelm's face.

"Well, that's a step in the right direction!" Erika sitting on the settee in Marcus's apartment, kicked off her shoes and tucked her feet under her. Marcus, pouring wine into three glasses, nodded his agreement.

"He's certainly coming out of his shell," Elisabeth said, taking the glass that he offered her. "But, even so, we're no nearer discovering where it is that he's come from. It seems so bizarre - a whole community of people kept underground in conditions of slavery, in this day and age. I mean, how did they get there and who's been enslaving them? And how come no one's found out about it?"

"I just wondered . . ." Erika started.

"Yes?" Marcus prompted, sitting down next to her on the settee. "Go on."

"Well, could it be something left over from the war? Could it be a concentration camp that was never discovered because it was underground?"

"Yes, but why would it still be carrying on? What would be the point. And who'd be running it?" Marcus shook his head. "And why would Wilhelm's people have been put in a camp in the first place? After all, the people that the Nazis wanted to do away with were those who were different, non-Aryan, non-German. If Wilhelm's speaking a language that was spoken in this country hundreds of years ago, there's no doubt that he and his people are German."

"Could they have been Jews, perhaps?" Erika asked tentatively. "Some Jewish families had lived here for centuries before the Nazis came to power."

"No." Marcus spoke with certainty. "The one thing that the Jews hung on to in the concentration camps was their religion. It was the only thing

100

they had left. But Wilhelm asked Elisabeth what God is. There's no way that Jews would have lost their faith so completely within a couple of generations that they wouldn't even know the name of God. But then, who knows? We've got so little to go on." He ran his hand through his already dishevelled hair.

"We really need to retrace Wilhelm's steps and find out how he got to that dry stone wall," said Elisabeth. "Perhaps I could take him out for a drive one day and see if he recognises anywhere."

"That's a good idea. Although it might be an idea to take a nurse with you. "

"I could go," Erika volunteered. "I'm free in the afternoons next week."

"Splendid. Well, fix it up between the two of you. I think Elisabeth's right - the only way of finding out where he came from is to see if he can physically retrace his steps."

"There are other puzzles, too, of course," said Elisabeth thoughtfully. "I mean, this business of the music that controls the mind. He described it as high and thin. I thought of a violin. But how can music control the mind?"

"I've been wondering . . ." Marcus began.

"Yes?" It was Erika's turn to prompt.

"Well, it did just occur to me that he might have come from some military establishment."

"Military establishment?" Elisabeth was confused. "What sort of military establishment keeps slaves in mines?"

"No, I don't mean that. I just wondered whether it could have been some sort of experiment in brainwashing."

"You mean none of what he's told us is true?" Erika asked.

"I've no doubt that he believes it's true. But could it just have been implanted there?"

"Do you know," Erika said slowly, "I think you might be on to something. After all, what is brainwashing but control of the mind. Do you think they could have used some sort of high pitched noise to help brainwash him?"

"I honestly don't know. I know very little about brainwashing. My experience is all to do with bringing people's minds out of abnormal states. But I suppose it's possible. I think the Chinese used constant noise to keep prisoners awake for days on end because the fatigue made their minds more susceptible to suggestion. Yes, it does seem possible."

"But if he's been brainwashed, could he be aware that his mind had been controlled and at the same time believe all the things he'd been told?" asked Elisabeth.

"Heaven knows," said Marcus. "But the mind can do curious things, so I wouldn't rule it out."

"Well, even if we accept it as a possibility, is there a military establishment near here?" asked Elisabeth. "And if there is, why didn't they look for him after he escaped?"

"I don't know of anywhere," Erika replied. "But presumably something like that would be very hush hush."

"Yes," said Marcus. "And that would probably explain why they didn't go searching for Wilhelm when he escaped. They'd hardly want him to be traced back to them. Or maybe, when they searched for him, they found out he was in hospital and realised they couldn't get him back without explaining who they were."

"Or maybe they wanted him to escape to see how he fared in the world," said Erika.

"That's not impossible." Marcus nodded. "It seems far fetched, but no more so than the suggestion that everything he's told us is true. But, just in case there is some super-secret military connection, you will be careful, won't you, when you take him out. Don't go exploring anywhere that looks as though it might be restricted. Just see if you can find that farm where he fell over the wall and then let him retrace his steps from there. Stay in the car if you can."

"Don't worry," Erika said. "We'll be fine. And remember, we'll have Wilhelm to look after us - he's a strong young man."

"Yes, not as strong as he might be. I'm concerned that he's not had any real exercise since he's been here. He's put on quite a bit of weight. Now he's becoming more communicative, I think I'll get the physiotherapist to give him some exercises to do in the gym."

"Be careful," Elisabeth advised. "He needs to know why you're doing it. You don't want him to think he's being forced back into some sort of physical slavery."

"No." Marcus smiled. "I'll tell the physio to be gentle with him."

"I'll explain it to Wilhelm," said Elisabeth. "Although I think you could converse quite easily with him now if you wanted to."

"Yes, I had a short chat with him the other day - the change in his vocabulary is quite dramatic. The nurses have commented on it too. You've been doing a fine job."

"I'm just happy to help. I feel so sorry for him."

"I wonder . . . " Marcus tapped a finger thoughtfully against his wineglass.

"What?" Erika asked.

"I just wonder whether it would help to find out what this music was like. I mean, if it was used for brainwashing, it might be useful to know what it sounded like. It might help to - to debrainwash him, or whatever the word is."

"How could we do that?" Elisabeth asked.

"What, find out about the music or debrainwash him?"

"Either."

"Well, the debrainwashing I've no idea. We'd have to get an expert in. But the music should be quite simple. I've got a friend who plays in an orchestra. I could ask him to make a tape of each of the high pitched instruments and we could see if Wilhelm recognises anything."

"Why not?" Elisabeth said. "It's worth a try."

"It's just such a shame that all this wasn't picked up on earlier." Erika sipped her wine. "To think that he's been sitting round drugged up to the eyeballs for three months. . ."

"Well, I can see why Dr. Gerhardt thought he was schizophrenic," said Marcus. "It was only because his condition hadn't changed during that time that I queried the diagnosis."

"I think you're being very charitable," said Erika, leaning over to kiss

Marcus's cheek. "The truth of the matter is that you're a much better psychiatrist than your predecessor."

"Well, of course," said Marcus, grinning broadly, "there's that, too!"

As they laughed, Elisabeth looked at her watch. "I must go," she said. "Someone's coming round to see me in about half an hour."

Marcus saw her to the door. "If you arrange your trip out with Erika, I'll let the ward staff know."

"Thanks, Marcus. And if you and Erika suddenly work out what this is all about before then - you will 'phone and let me know, won't you!"

✱ ✱ ✱

As she negotiated the heavy evening traffic, Elisabeth glanced at the clock on the dashboard and hoped that, when she got home, she wouldn't find Helmut already waiting on her doorstep. Although they had been lovers for almost as long as they had known each other, neither had a door key to the other's apartment. It was, she supposed, a way of stating their continued independence.

They had met the previous autumn, at a party given by one of Elisabeth's colleagues, and there had been instant physical attraction. Since then they had seen each other three or four times a week, except when Helmut was away on a business trips. She loved to be seen with him, aware of the impression that his imposing height, classic good looks and expensive clothes had on other women. He satisfied her intellectually, and he satisfied her in bed. There was no talk of love or of marriage and Elisabeth was content that it should be that way.

Five years ago it had been different. She had fallen deeply in love with a French professor who had been working in her department for a year, and she had believed that her love was returned. But then the time had come for him to return to his own university - and he had gone, without a word of regret or a wish to see her again, leaving her in the apartment that they had shared for over six months. She had felt deeply humiliated and it had left her with a mistrust of men and a fear of any deep emotional involvement. But she was thirty one years old now and the alternative seemed to be academic spinsterhood. There were several such women in her faculty - women with grey hair and greyer lives who had missed their chances, or never had any, and had compensated by devoting themselves to their work. She thought she would rather do that than risk the pain that might result from allowing herself to love someone as she had once loved Philippe. But, for the present, Helmut suited her needs perfectly. And, although it was not impossible that they might eventually marry, it was something that she didn't think about.

Again she glanced at the clock. Helmut's 'plane would have landed by now. She was looking forward to seeing him after his three weeks in Tokyo - three weeks in which she had become increasingly preoccupied with Wilhelm. She thought that perhaps she might discuss the case with Helmut and see whether his keen legal mind could come up with any answers to the puzzles that it presented. Although she tended to discuss only certain aspects of her work with him, she had told him about the initial encounter with Wilhelm and he had listened with interest as she talked about speech islands and the development of isolated dialects. However, he had made it clear early on in their relationship that, while he was interested in her academic work and her research, he had no desire to hear about what he called her 'social work'. He understood that as a member of the faculty she had to take responsibility for some of the students. But he had suggested that visiting Oskar in hospital was more than the university really required of her. And he had expressed surprise at Oskar's illness, wondering how someone "supposedly so intelligent could allow himself to suffer from depression." Elisabeth had said nothing. It was, she knew, hard for people who had neither experienced depression themselves nor seen it in someone close to them, to understand that it could no more be controlled by the patient than could pneumonia or appendicitis. Having had a cousin who had committed suicide in his twenties after several years in and out of mental wards, she knew all about it. But she was not going to discuss it with Helmut. It was something she felt deeply about, and such things she kept to herself.

To her relief, when she got home Helmut had not yet arrived. She hurried inside and had just taken off her coat when the buzzer on the entry-

105

phone sounded. Pressing the button, she heard him say "Elisabeth - it's me" and felt the familiar little flutter in her stomach at the sound of his voice.

A few seconds later he was at her front door.

"Darling." He bent to kiss her. "How are you, my sweet? The plane was on time for a change."

"I was worried that you might be early," said Elisabeth, removing her arms from round his neck and leading the way into the sitting room.

"Why? Would I have met another of your lovers shinning down the drainpipe?"

"No." Elisabeth turned and kissed him. "There's still only you."

"I'm glad to hear it." Helmut slumped into an armchair and watched as Elisabeth opened a bottle of wine.

"So what were you doing?" he asked.

"I was round at a friend's." She handed him a glass and sat down facing him.

"Anyone I know?"

"No. You remember I told you about that patient in the mental ward who I was asked to talk to?"

"The refugee?"

"Yes, except he may not be a refugee. We still haven't been able to find out where he comes from. The whole thing gets stranger by the minute. I've spent the last hour discussing it with his doctor and we still can't make any sense of it."

"Young sexy doctor?" asked Helmut with a smile and a raised eyebrow.

"Young sexy doctor and young sexy doctor's girlfriend, actually."

"That's all right then. I've missed you Elisabeth."

"Good." She smiled.

Helmut finished the wine in his glass and stood up, holding out his hand.

"Let's go to bed," he said.

✶ ✶ ✶

When Elisabeth woke the next morning, Helmut was still asleep. She got up carefully, so as not to disturb him and went into the kitchen to pour herself a glass of orange juice. By the time Helmut stirred, she had showered, dressed and made a pot of coffee. He came into the kitchen wearing the old towelling bathrobe that he kept at her apartment. It was, she reflected, probably the only old garment he possessed.

"Sorry I slept so long," he said, sitting down at the table.

"That's all right," said Elisabeth. "It's Saturday. You can stay in bed all day if you want to."

"No." Helmut ran his hand through his hair, reminding her of Marcus, "I need to get back home. I came straight here from the airport and there'll be messages and post to deal with."

"Can't you leave them until after the weekend?" asked Elisabeth, putting a cup of coffee and a basket of rolls in front of him.

"No." Helmut yawned. "Best to get it done. But I'll see you tonight. I'll book somewhere special for dinner."

After he'd gone, Elisabeth rang Erika and suggested that they take Wilhelm out on Wednesday afternoon.

"That suits me," Erika replied. "I'll find out where it was that the ambulance picked him up, and we can take it from there."

As the afternoon wore on, Elisabeth found that her mind was in two places, torn between the pleasant prospect of an evening with Helmut and her thoughts about Wilhelm. She was surprised at how concerned she had become for his welfare, almost as if he were her child. She had never before thought of herself in the role of a mother and wasn't entirely sure that it was one to which she was suited.

She tried to put Wilhelm and his problems out of her mind, but it wasn't easy and Helmut commented on her abstraction as, later that evening, they sat in one of the city's smartest restaurants.

"Sorry." Elisabeth shook her head, as if that would clear out extraneous thoughts. "I've got quite involved in this business at the hospital and it's all turning out to be rather strange."

"So you said. You still haven't found out where your foreign gentleman comes from?"

"No. It's most peculiar. I've tried to locate other speech pockets but I can't find any. And yet his dialect doesn't match any of those I know. And although he's learned quite a bit of vocabulary since he was brought into the hospital, he still can't tell us where he comes from."

"You mean he won't tell you."

"No, can't. He literally doesn't seem to know where it was."

"Has he lost his memory?"

"No, nothing like that. He remembers. But he doesn't know how he got here - I told you it was strange."

Elisabeth paused as the waiter arrived with their first course and she wondered momentarily what Wilhelm would make of this restaurant with its exquisitely presented food, its fine wines, its soft lighting and its subtle music . . . music, it kept coming back to music. Perhaps with Marcus's recordings they would get closer to a solution.

"Elisabeth?"

She realised that she'd been staring into space.

"I'm sorry, Helmut. I'm a bit tired."

Helmut raised an eyebrow. "You take on too much," he said. "I hope the hospital's paying you well for this work."

Elisabeth said nothing and they finished the first course in silence, broken only by short comments on the excellent food. When the plates had been removed, Helmut said "So what are these strange things the little foreigner's been telling you? Does he claim to have been picked up by a UFO and deposited on the hospital doorstep?"

"No." Elisabeth laughed. "Nothing like that. He was brought in after a head injury - he'd fallen over a stone wall. But when you ask him how he got there . . ." She tailed off, suddenly unwilling to tell Helmut the details of Wilhelm's journey, although why she couldn't say.

"Yes?" asked Helmut.

"Well, he just talks about walking for days. He didn't know where he was going so he can't give us any idea of the direction he came from."

"But he must know the name of the place where he lived before."

"Well, no . . ." Again Elisabeth hesitated. "He says that he and his

108

people were slaves. And somehow he managed to escape. He's told me about the conditions that he worked in and they were quite appalling. When he came here, he didn't even know the words for things as fundamental as chair and bed."

Helmut looked at her in amazement and then laughed. Elisabeth was indignant.

"It's not funny, Helmut."

"No, I don't suppose it is but obviously the man is demented."

"But that's just it - he isn't. He's perfectly sane."

"Oh, come on, Elisabeth! How can he be when he's been telling you all this rubbish?"

"I'm sorry, Helmut, but you've not seen him. Anyway, Marcus Hellman - his doctor - is convinced that he's not mentally ill."

"So what's he doing in a mental ward?"

"He was admitted under the previous psychiatrist, over three months ago. It was only when Marcus arrived that the diagnosis was questioned."

Helmut smiled at her. "I think all that proves, my darling, is that your Marcus Hellman isn't as good a psychiatrist as he obviously thinks he is. Anyway . . ." he went on before Elisabeth could say anything, "Let's not waste our first evening together in three weeks talking about miserable little foreigners who've lost their marbles." And he started to tell her about the complicated legal business that had taken him to Japan.

Elisabeth was disturbed. To her, Helmut was always most considerate and caring and she had tried to put out of her mind the scathing remarks he had made about Oskar's illness. But, she realised, Helmut saw her as an equal - attractive, intelligent, well-educated and with a good income - and, although she hated to admit it, she was aware that he had little time for those who were not possessed of these attributes. Even so, she was hurt by his lack of compassion and by his scornful dismissal of Marcus Hellman. She tried to listen to what he was saying but found it difficult. She wanted to get back at him, to defend her new friends and to break down his complacency but, as always, her unwillingness to show emotion held her back. When the waiter came with their main course, she took refuge in eating.

"It's a shame you couldn't have come with me to Tokyo," said Helmut as he refilled Elisabeth's wineglass. "You'd have enjoyed it. It's an interesting city."

Elisabeth smiled, glad that they were back onto safer ground.

"I brought you back a little something." Helmut reached into his pocket and took out a tiny parcel wrapped in a fine Japanese tissue paper.

"Thank you." Elisabeth took it carefully and unwrapped it. Inside was an exquisite antique ivory carving of a rat. "Oh!" she exclaimed. "It's a netsuke!" Some weeks previously, Helmut had taken her to an exhibition of Japanese art at the City Museum. She had fallen in love with the netsukes on display - beautiful miniature carvings in ivory and wood, originally used as toggles on the sashes of Japanese kimonos.

She stroked the tiny rat, admiring its finely carved whiskers and the way its slim tail curved around its body. "It's beautiful. Thank you."

"My pleasure." Helmut smiled warmly at her and Elisabeth relaxed again, feeling that the crisis had passed. For the rest of the evening they talked about travel and art and music, and by the time they got back to her apartment, Elisabeth had almost forgotten that they had come as close to an argument as they had ever been.

✶ ✶ ✶

Arriving at the hospital a few minutes late, Elisabeth found Erika and Wilhelm waiting for her inside the entrance. Apologising for her tardiness, she led the way back to the car park which was just inside the hospital gates and screened from the rest of the grounds by a tall bank of bushes. Elisabeth pointed to her car and said to Wilhelm. "We'll be travelling in this."

"Who pushes it?" he asked.

"No one. We all sit inside and . . . well, the car pushes itself."

"How?" Wilhelm was clearly puzzled.

"There's something inside that turns the wheels, but I can control which direction we go in and how fast we move and when we stop. You'll see."

110

Erika helped settle Wilhelm into the front seat, then got into the back. Elisabeth started the engine. As they moved out of the car park, Wilhelm said "It sounds like the air pumps."

"Air pumps?" asked Elisabeth.

"In the mines and the tunnels. We could always hear the air pumps. But I couldn't hear them when I came out of the mines and I can't hear them here either, but I suppose that's because the walls are such a long way away."

Elisabeth frowned, wondering how they would ever get Wilhelm to understand that he was no longer in a cavern, no longer underground.

As they approached the main road, Erika began to give directions.

"He was brought in from a farm a few kilometers north of the city," she said. "So if we turn left here we'll be heading in the right direction."

The route led them past shops and houses, a small park and a school. Wilhelm stared and said nothing. Eventually they reached the city outskirts and Erika directed Elisabeth down a road which led through increasingly rural scenery. Suddenly Wilhelm said "It was like this when I came out of the other cavern."

"Do you recognise where you are?" asked Elisabeth.

"No, but where I walked the floor was covered in . . grass."

"The farm isn't far from here," said Erika. "There should be a minor road off to the right a couple of kilometers further on."

Elisabeth found the road and turned the car into it, bumping along the uneven surface for two or three hundred meters until, coming over the brow of a small hill, they saw the farmhouse.

"Do you remember any of this, Wilhelm?" she asked.

"I remember the stones," he said. "I climbed over to get away from the one who was chasing me and I fell."

"Someone was chasing you?" asked Erika. "I didn't know that."

"Not like you or me. He was small, hairy, black. He ran on four legs."

"Oh, the dog!" Erika smiled.

"They are not people?"

"No. They're animals."

"What are animals?"

"Oh, Lord! Elisabeth," Erika appealed to her, "you explain. You're better at this than I am."

Elisabeth grimaced. "I'm not so sure. Well . . . animals are - well, they're living beings who aren't people. There are all sorts of them. There are dogs - like the one that chased you - and horses and cows and . . . well, hundreds of others. Perhaps one day we'll take you to the zoo - that's where they keep lots of different sorts of animals - and you can see them all."

Wilhelm was silent for a moment then said "I think I have seen other animals. When I came into this cavern, at first I saw no one. Then I saw four beings who I thought must be Them, because they were not like me. I approached them but they ignored me, so I walked on and it led me to this place."

"What were they like?" asked Elisabeth, bringing the car to a halt.

"They were large, brown, hairy. They had low voices."

"They sound like cows to me," said Elisabeth. "Well, that may give us a clue as to direction, as long as the cows haven't been moved to a different field. Now, look carefully Wilhelm and see if you can tell us which direction you came from."

Wilhelm looked. The farmhouse was surrounded on three sides by a low stone wall. He shook his head. "I fell over that," he pointed, "but I don't know which part of it."

They climbed out of the car and walked slowly along beside the wall. Suddenly Wilhelm said "Here. I remember I couldn't see the door the woman came out of but I could see that thing with clothes hanging from it. So I must have come from . . ." he turned around and pointed "over there."

"O.K." said Elisabeth. "Let's go for a little walk."

✳ ✳ ✳

"And he was sure, was he?" Marcus asked.

Erika nodded. "No doubt at all."

From the corridor outside Marcus's office came the sounds of the patients returning from their evening meal. Someone was talking loudly,

112

another laughed, then two or three others spoke. None of the voices was Wilhelm's.

"How far was it from the farm?" asked Marcus.

"Not very far. About a fifteen minute walk."

"And no sign of any restricted area?"

"No, nothing like that. Just fields and open countryside. And then it became hilly. And Wilhelm recognised a clump of trees down in a little valley."

"That was interesting, actually," said Elisabeth. "He said that, when he first saw them, he recognised them as being 'made of wood', as he put it, because in the mines they used wood for pit props. And because that was the only context he'd ever seen wood in, he assumed that the trees were some form of props. But then, of course, he couldn't work out what they were doing there because they didn't seem to be holding anything up."

Marcus laughed ruefully. "Good grief! How are we ever going to find someone who can teach him what's really going on? I mean, where do you start?"

Elisabeth shook her head. "And they won't just need the ability to teach, they'll need the patience to understand how much he doesn't know. I mean, I know he's learning a lot all the time but he's still putting the wrong interpretation on most of it. And he still hasn't grasped the significance of 'outside'."

"No . . . well, that's hardly surprising. So where did you go once you'd found the trees?"

"It led up into a sort of little gully," said Erika. "And Wilhelm said he'd come out at the top of it, so we clambered up and, sure enough, there was the entrance into the caves."

"You didn't go in, I hope," said Marcus.

There was silence.

"Oh, for heaven's sake. You didn't, did you? It could have been terribly dangerous."

"No it couldn't," said Erika. "I've done some caving and I know what's safe and what's not. I'd taken a torch with me and I went in very carefully."

"And was it as he'd described?"

Elisabeth smiled at Erika as Marcus's disapproval of her actions vanished before his enthusiasm to know what she had found.

"Exactly. You remember he said he climbed out of the large cavern up a series of ledges and they led into a smaller cave which opened into "this cavern", as he calls it. And he said he'd had to excavate the opening in order to get out, because it was very narrow. Well, when I went through, there was a little cave just inside the entrance and there were some piles of earth that looked as though they might have been the result of someone widening the opening. And the cave led onto a ledge which seemed to be at the top of a much larger cavern. I couldn't see the bottom, but I could just hear the sound of running water, and I remembered that Wilhelm said there was water pouring down one of the walls into a pool."

"So it does seem to be the way he came out." Marcus frowned. "But what do we do next."

"Go down and have a look at the cave, of course." Erika sounded surprised that he should need to ask such a question. "My brother Anton goes caving quite frequently with a couple of his friends but I'm sure they've never been in these caves."

"How will you explain that you found out about them?" Elisabeth asked.

"Oh, I'll probably say a patient was talking about them. Anton's not going to check up."

"But won't he think it odd when you ask him for a detailed description of the caves afterwards?" asked Elisabeth.

"I shan't need to." Erika grinned. "I'll go with them - and I'll take my camera."

"You?" Marcus looked shocked. "You're not going in there?"

"Why not? I've been caving before."

"No, it's too risky. Suppose you got hurt."

"No reason why I should. Caving's pretty safe as long as you're careful and don't do anything silly. And Anton and his friends are very experienced. They'll look after me."

"Hm. . . I think I'd better come too."

"But you've never been caving, have you?"

"No, but there has to be a first time for everything. And, anyway, I'd like to see these caves for myself."

"You just don't trust me, do you?"

"Of course I do. But I'd be happier if I was there to look after you."

"Well, if you're sure. I shouldn't think Anton will mind. He and his friends have taken beginners down with them before now. Do you want to come too, Elisabeth?"

"No thank you! Confined spaces and I don't get on together. You can tell me all about it when you get back!"

"I'll ring Anton this evening," said Erika. "We might be able to fix something up for the weekend."

"I still can't believe that we found the entrance so easily," said Elisabeth. "I thought that with all the trauma and the disorientation that must have occurred after Wilhelm came out, it was going to be really difficult. But he remembered all the landmarks and once we knew which direction to go in from the farmhouse, we had no problems at all."

"Of course," said Marcus, "the fact that you've found the entrance doesn't actually take us any nearer to knowing what's down there, or even where it is. It could be just underneath that cavern or it could be miles away."

"Well, Wilhelm said he walked for a long time through the tunnels and that they went up pretty steeply in places."

"Yes but he could have being going round in circles some of the time. Who knows? And what we do if we find the mines, I really have no idea. Somehow I don't think that barging in and leading everybody to freedom would work! And remember that Wilhelm said that the Hundeiss never saw the people who actually controlled the mines, only the Takers and the Carriers."

"Maybe they were the people in control," Erika suggested.

"No," Elisabeth said. "He seems pretty sure that there were others who were in ultimate control. But I suppose if you do get near the mines and

115

find that it's all as he says, you'll have to inform the police."

"And if we find that it's some sort of military instillation practising brainwashing, we'll just make a run for it and say nothing," said Erika.

"I've been doing a bit of investigating on that score," said Marcus. "And I think my picture of brainwashing owes rather more to Hollywood than to actual fact. I managed to find a book about it - hang on, I made some notes." He got up and scrabbled round in the papers on his desk then, not finding what he was looking for, started to rummage in one of the drawers. After a moment he pulled out a spiral bound notepad and flicked through it to find the page he wanted.

"Here we are." Marcus sat down again and looked at his notes. "Now admittedly this chap was writing in the 1960s but it was an in-depth study and I can't think that things have changed that dramatically since then. He describes the popular image of brainwashing as being 'an all-powerful, irresistible, unfathomable, and magical method of achieving total control over the human mind.' And then he says that it's not any of these."

"Oh," said Erika. "So what is it?"

"Well he's looking at it in the context of Communist China which used what it called 'thought reform'. And he says the power of the process lay in a combination of coercion with a sort of evangelism. And what they were doing was trying to alter what people believed in, rather than what they believed, if you see what I mean. They were trying to make them believe in Communism but a doctor, for example, wasn't made to believe that he wasn't a doctor, or a priest that he wasn't a priest."

"No," said Elisabeth slowly, "but then their goals may have been quite different. I mean, if Wilhelm has been brainwashed, who knows why it was done?"

"Oh, yes. I'm not saying that this rules out brainwashing, just that if Wilhelm has been brainwashed, it's rather different from what this chap's talking about. Anyway, a bit later on he talks about one of the people he met who'd gone through all this and he describes his eyes as showing a characteristic combination of fear and distance, which he says was known as "the thousand-mile stare". "

"Well," said Erika uncertainly, "the fear was there. But I don't know about the distance."

"And the fear was only in response to certain things," Elisabeth reminded her. "Such as smiling. And he's told us the reason for that."

"Right," said Marcus. "However, this chap does quote one case where the subject actually had delusions or hallucinations. He was a Roman Catholic priest and at one point while he was still in prison he thought that he'd been moved out of his cell and into a house. And then some time after that he thought that a priest he knew was in the cell next to him. And it was only after he was released over a year later that he discovered that this other priest had never been in prison at all."

"So," Elisabeth was thinking aloud, "if you kept someone underground and used brainwashing techniques . . . "

"It's possible, I suppose. But the problem is that, although you might get them to believe that they'd been slaves in a mine, I don't know that you could get them to forget everything that had gone before and believe that they'd always been there."

"What else does this man say?" asked Erika.

Marcus consulted his notes. "One of the people he interviewed had been coerced into making a confession, which he described as 'a novel' because each fabrication he came up with needed a lot more to support it. But he made the important point that his story became increasingly confused and contradictory. Now you can't say that about Wilhelm. Everything that he's told us seems to hang together perfectly - I mean it's totally incomprehensible but you can't find any contradictions in it, and he tells it the same every time."

The room was beginning to get dark and Erika got up and turned on the light. Marcus smiled his thanks, then turned back to his notes.

"Oh, yes, this was interesting. He talked about brainwashing being a form of death and rebirth, which links into the business of not forgetting what they were before. They didn't stop being priests and doctors but just became priests and doctors who were sympathetic to Chinese Communism. He says they suffered only a temporary, controlled, and partial "death"

117

because in order to send anything like a whole man out of prison, they had to resurrect a lot of the prisoner's former self."

"Which doesn't really relate to Wilhelm," said Elisabeth.

"No. In addition to which, Wilhelm hasn't been brainwashed into believing that he's done a lot of hard physical work. There's no doubt that he has done it - we've got the Xrays to prove it." Marcus put down the notebook and rubbed his eyes. "We seem to be getting nowhere pretty fast on this track. I think if we want to take it any further we need to consult an expert on the subject. But I suggest we leave that until we've investigated all the other angles. There's still the mystery of the music, but I've rung my friend Stephan and he's going to make a tape for me."

"Great," said Erika.

"Well, yes," said Marcus. "Except that, even if we can identify the instrument, I don't see where it's going to take us."

They sat in silence for a few moments.

"Well," said Elisabeth firmly, "we're doing everything we can and there's bound to come a point where it will all fall into place. . ." she faltered, ". . . isn't there?"

They laughed and Marcus said "Certainly there is." He looked at his watch. "But I don't think it's going to be today, so why don't we all go and get something to eat?"

Chapter Seven

Erika rang Elisabeth the next afternoon to tell her that the caving expedition had been arranged for Saturday.

"It's going to be fun. Are you quite sure you don't want to come with us?"

"Quite sure, thanks," Elisabeth replied. "Just thinking about it makes me feel claustrophobic! Is Marcus going?"

"Oh, yes. Mind you, I think he's a bit nervous, but he'll be all right."

"Anton didn't mind him tagging along, then?"

"No - he said as long as Marcus does what he's told . . . "

They both laughed.

"Anyway," Erika went on, "I'll 'phone you when we get back and tell you all about it."

"Thanks, I'll be waiting. Oh . . . well, that depends what time you 'phone because I'm going out on Saturday evening. When do you think you'll be back?"

"No idea. But it shouldn't be too late. I'll ring you as soon as I get in."

But when Helmut called for Elisabeth at 6.30. on Saturday evening, Erika still hadn't 'phoned. As they left the apartment, Elisabeth made sure that she turned on the answering machine.

Helmut took her to the theatre, to see a new and highly entertaining play which managed to take her mind off the caves and what Erika and Marcus might have found there. From the theatre, they went to a small restaurant on the outskirts of the city where the food was excellent. They discussed the play, the food, a book that they had both been reading and a new film which had the critics in uproar. Elisabeth didn't mention Wilhelm or the hospital or the caves. Helmut was at his most charming and the atmosphere between them was back to what it had always been, relaxed but with an ever-present awareness of the sexual chemistry which was such an important part of their relationship.   Elisabeth   was   relieved.   She wanted things to stay as they had been. She didn't find it difficult to keep her thoughts to herself and if that was what was necessary, well so be it.

Helmut was good for her self-confidence and she needed him. After Philippe had deserted her, her sense of self-worth had plummeted to zero and, although friends had tried to console her, she had felt herself to be unattractive, uninteresting, unimportant. Helmut had changed all that. He made it clear that he enjoyed being seen with her, relished her company and her conversation, and desired her physically. If the price of her continued self-confidence was that she must keep the different sections of her life separate, she would do so. And if it further meant that she must tolerate the occasional jibe from Helmut about people whom he considered to be inferior to himself, then she would turn a deaf ear and just hope that he didn't do it too often.

After dinner they returned to Helmut's apartment and made love. Whether it was from relief that their relationship was back to normal or the fact that she had been reminded how necessary he was to her well-being, Elisabeth felt her physical want of him was greater than ever and she threw herself into the love-making with such abandon that Helmut commented on the fact and teased her for being a wanton. She laughed with him, then clawed his back as he thrust deep inside her. It wasn't until much later, when she was asleep, that Wilhelm crept into her mind and she dreamed of huge echoing caves and endless tunnels and shattered lanterns.

They rose late the following morning and, after a light breakfast, drove out into the country where they lunched at a small inn. But by the time they were halfway through the meal, Elisabeth found she was becoming impatient to return home and learn what, if anything, Erika and Marcus had discovered. Masking her agitation as best she could, she was, however, greatly relieved when Helmut said he had an important 'phone call to make which might take some time. Pretending to have some work that she needed to do before the following day, she suggested that he take her home once they had finished lunch.

As they drove back into the city, it was all she could do to sit still as they neared her street. When the car pulled up outside her apartment block, she kissed Helmut and said goodbye. Then, aware that he was watching her, she walked slowly to the entrance, turned and waved, and

120

watched him drive away. Once his car had turned the corner, she ran in and up the stairs, fumbling with her key in the latch in her anxiety to get to her 'phone.

The light on the answering machine was flashing. She jabbed at the button and a woman's voice started to speak. So sure had she been that it would be Erika's that she didn't, for a moment, recognise it as that of her mother who had 'phoned to tell her that her cousin was getting married. The message was - or perhaps just seemed to be - a long one and Elisabeth shifted her weight from foot to foot, waiting for it to finish. Eventually there was a beep and, at last, she heard Erika's voice.

"Elisabeth it's Erika!" She sounded excited. "We've just got back and it's been a terrific day! We went down into the cave and it was exactly as Wilhelm said - the stepped outcrop and the pool with the water cascading into it. And you'll never guess what I found at the foot of the outcrop - Wilhelm's lantern. Do you remember - he said he dropped it as he was climbing out of the cavern? Anyway, I brought it back with me. And the cavern was huge, just as he said, and we found three tunnels leading out of it. But you remember Wilhelm said that the tunnel he came through collapsed just as he reached the cavern? So I went right round the walls - and I found it! Or, at least, it looked like what he described. I pointed it out to the boys and said the patient who'd told me about the caves had said that he'd gone through there and it went down a long way. And they thought I'd gone raving mad and said was that before or after the roof had collapsed? But, of course, there was no way we could explore it, even if we could have cleared all the rubble.

"So that was the end of that and we just spent the rest of the time exploring the cave and the other tunnels. But it was a great day. Oh, and Marcus has got the tape of the instruments and he's going to play it to Wilhelm tomorrow. I assume you're coming in to see Wilhelm as usual on Tuesday? If so, we can meet up then, because I finish work at about four, so I'll be coming over. And I can tell you more about the caving. . . oh, and Marcus was very good, even though it was his first time. I think he quite enjoyed it, too . . . Well, that's about it for now. You've got my number if

121

you want to ring me. Otherwise I'll see you on Tuesday. 'Bye." And again there was the beep signifying the end of a message.

Elisabeth's immediate instinct was to 'phone Erika back. But, she realised, Erika had told her all the really important news and would only be able to repeat what she had said. It wasn't long until Tuesday and, by then, Marcus too might have something new to report.

✳ ✳ ✳

Finishing her tutorial on the dot of four o'clock, Elisabeth wished her students good afternoon and hurried back to her office to collect her jacket. As she was making her way down the corridor towards the stairs, she heard her name being called and turned to see the head of the department coming towards her.

"I'm sorry, Herr Professor," she said, "I'm in rather a hurry this afternoon. Is it something urgent?"

"No, not at all." He smiled at her. He was a pleasant man in his fifties who had taken over the post when its previous incumbent had retired eighteen months previously. "I just wanted to have a chat about next term's timetable. Tomorrow will do if you have a few minutes to spare."

"Of course, Herr Professor. Thank you." Turning, Elisabeth almost ran towards the stairs.

As she drove out of the car park and towards the hospital, she realised that her stomach was churning with excitement. "This is ridiculous," she told herself. "Why am I getting in such a state?" But there was no doubt that the mystery of Wilhelm had got under her skin and she wasn't going to be satisfied until an answer was found.

Erika and Marcus were waiting for her in his office. As soon as Elisabeth had taken off her coat, Erika handed her a small pile of photographs. "The caves," she said. "I printed up the best ones."

Elisabeth sat down and leafed through them, with Erika leaning over her shoulder, explaining what each one showed. It was, as she had said, a huge cavern - even from the photographs that was apparent. Most of the pictures had one or more of the explorers in it, giving a sense of scale. Anton grinned at the camera in several of them looking, as far as Elisabeth could see, very like his sister. Two photos showed Marcus, rather self-conscious in his helmet and caving gear. There were pictures of the rock face and of the tunnels, of the small cave which led into the cavern and of the step-like wall below it, of the pool with its little waterfall and of the entrance to the narrow tunnel whose roof had collapsed. Elisabeth went through the pile twice and, on handing it back to Erika, realised that Marcus was standing beside her with something in his hands. It was the lantern. Crudely made, with no glass, and bent out of shape by its fall, there was still no doubt about what it was. Elisabeth took it from him, with great care, as though it were some precious object of great worth, and looked at it.

"It was exactly where you'd have expected it to be if he'd dropped it when he was climbing up that wall," said Erika.

"Have you shown it to Wilhelm?" asked Elisabeth.

"Yes," Marcus replied. "And he just took it and said 'my lantern'. I've only borrowed it to show you. He's been keeping it beside his bed."

Elisabeth turned it over in her hands. "It's so crude," she said. "And nothing on it to show where it was made."

"No. But it does confirm Wilhelm's story."

"It really doesn't help much, though, does it, if you can't get into the tunnel."

"No," said Erika. "But there's got to be another entrance to the mines, or how could the Carriers bring the Hundeiss their food and water? We'll just have to try to find out where it is, although I'm not sure how we go about it."

"Meanwhile," said Marcus, "we've got a little bit further on the music. Although that doesn't really help us much either. I'll play you what Stephan recorded and then tell you what Wilhelm said."

There was a cassette player on the desk and he pressed the play button. They heard first a single violin, playing arpeggios, getting higher and higher, then three violins playing together, repeating the same notes as before. Marcus turned the player off. "Wilhelm shook his head at both of those," he said. "But he said that his music was definitely played by a single instrument." He turned the tape on again and they heard the same

123

arpeggios repeated by one and then a duet of clarinets, followed by one and then two trumpets, a flute, a pair of flutes, a piccolo and, finally, a piano. Marcus turned the tape off. "The ones that came closest," he said, "were the flute and the piccolo but nothing matched it exactly."

"I remember Wilhelm saying that you hear the music with the mind rather than with the ear," said Elisabeth. "But I didn't really understand what he meant. Do you think it might have been something electronic?"

"What, you mean produced electronically?" asked Erika.

"Well, yes, possibly. Or perhaps they have something implanted into their brains that receives signals and translates them into music."

"Bit far fetched," said Marcus. "On the other hand, this whole thing's pretty far fetched. But I think an implant would almost certainly show up on Xray and you remember that Wilhelm had his head and neck Xrayed in the accident department. So I don't think it can be that. But of course you're right. It doesn't have to be what we understand as a musical instrument at all. It could be something like a dog whistle."

"Dog whistle?" Elisabeth asked, raising her eyebrows in surprise.

"Well, you know a dog whistle is too high for the human ear to hear. But suppose there's something that's too high to be heard but still somehow registers in the brain."

"Is that possible physiologically?" asked Erika dubiously.

Marcus thought for a moment, then laughed. "Actually, no, I don't think it is."

"But we haven't exhausted all high pitched instruments, have we?" asked Elisabeth. "I mean, we've only heard the orchestral instruments. There are lots of others - electric guitars - they can go quite high - and spinnets and lutes and recorders and pan pipes and even synthesizers."

"True," said Erika.

Marcus was looking thoughtful. "Hang on a minute," he said slowly. "We're forgetting about the mind control aspect. Now Mesmer used music as part of his ritual when he was hypnotising people. And although the various accounts I've read differ in the details, I seem to remember one of them describing some sort of machine where the 'music' was produced by water being run through glass pipes. Now that would be fairly high-pitched, I would imagine."

"Yes," Erika sounded quite excited. "I think you're onto something. Clever old you. Of course, we've talked about brainwashing which none of us knows anything about but we haven't thought about hypnosis. And yet we've all heard about people eating onions which they think are apples."

"It certainly seems plausible," said Elisabeth. "But would the effects of the hypnosis last so long. I mean, once the patient came out of the trance, how long would he continue to believe whatever he'd been told?"

Marcus grunted. "No, you're right, of course. The effects do wear off. Certainly, if you're using it therapeutically - to control chronic pain or to treat something like asthma or migraine - it needs to be repeated from time to time. Usually patients are taught to hypnotise themselves so they can reinforce the treatment. But there's no evidence that Wilhelm's hypnotising himself - and, anyway, no reason why he'd want to. So the effects of the original treatment, or experiment or whatever, should have worn off by now. And I have to admit that, although you can convince patients of all sorts of things while they're actually in a trance, there does seem to be a limit to what they'll believe once they've come out of it. . . . Damn, I thought we were going somewhere there."

There was silence for a few moments, then Erika said "The problem is that we keep coming up with answers that are plausible up to a point. But either they don't explain the whole thing or they don't hang together with other pieces of the puzzle. So we've got to be missing something. . . I wish I knew what it was."

"Well, we'll just have to keep plugging away and hope we find it. Meanwhile, we need to think about getting Wilhelm out of hospital."

"Out of hospital?" Elisabeth was concerned. "But where can he go?"

"We'll have to find him a place in a halfway house or a hostel. It's not ideal but he's not ill and, now he's off all his medication, I really can't justify keeping him in for much longer."

"But he doesn't know anything about the outside world. How on earth could he cope?" Erika sounded perturbed.

"Oh, we'll make sure he has plenty of help. It'll be a few weeks before we can actually discharge him, but we must begin to think about rehabilitating him. He needs to start getting out and about, seeing a bit of the world beyond these four walls."

"Elisabeth and I could take him out again," Erika suggested.

"We said we'd take him to the zoo," Elisabeth reminded her.

"That'd be great, if you could," said Marcus. "Actually, Elisabeth, I was going to ask you - Erika's on duty all weekend and an old school friend of mine has asked me to go and stay with him. But if I go, it means neither of us would be able to get in to see Wilhelm. So I wanted to make sure that you'd be able to come in and see him on either Saturday or Sunday before I accepted the invitation."

"Yes, that's no problem. I can come in on Saturday. In fact, I could take him to the zoo then if that'd be all right."

"Great." Marcus was pleased. "He'll enjoy that. Are you sure you can cope with him by yourself?"

"Oh, yes. He was fine when we took him out before. And if you think he's almost fit to leave hospital . . ."

"Excellent. Well, I'll ring Bernhard and tell him I can go. We haven't seen each other for about five years so there'll be a lot to catch up on. And can we three meet up again on Monday?"

Elisabeth and Erika nodded.

"Good," said Marcus. "I'll look forward to hearing about the trip to the zoo."

★ ★ ★

On Thursday evening, Helmut took Elisabeth to see the film that some critics had declared brilliant and others had found shocking.

"I can't see what all the fuss is about," said Elisabeth as they sat drinking coffee in Helmut's apartment at the end of the evening. "I've seen a lot better and a lot worse."

Helmut shrugged. "I sometimes think that critics live in another world."

"Anyway," Elisabeth continued, "I'm pleased we've seen it. Now we can talk about it with authority and give everybody our opinion."

Helmut laughed, then stretched out his long legs and yawned. "I'm tired," he said. "I've been working too hard."

"When do you ever not?" asked Elisabeth.

"True. Anyway, I shan't be working this weekend. I have a surprise for you. Do you remember me telling you about my friend Hans who owns a thirteenth century schloss? He's invited us to a party."

"How lovely!" said Elisabeth. A thought crossed her mind and she asked "How long will it take to get there?"

"Only half an hour or so. Why?"

"Oh, it's just that I have to meet someone on Saturday afternoon but I'll be through by five so that's not a problem."

Helmut shook his head. "No." he said. "We've been invited for the whole weekend, Friday night to Sunday afternoon."

"Oh, no. Oh, that's disappointing." Elisabeth made a face. "I'd have loved to go."

"And you will go," said Helmut a touch impatiently. "Just cancel your meeting. You don't usually work at the weekend. Tell them you'll see them on Monday."

"Well . . ." Elisabeth was torn between her desire to spend a weekend with Helmut in a thirteenth century schloss and her promise to see Wilhelm. For a moment she wondered whether she could just pop in to the hospital on Friday before she went, but her instincts told her that her disappointment at not being able to go with Helmut would be nothing compared to Wilhelm's disappointment if she had to cancel their outing. She shook her head. "No, I can't. I really can't. I am sorry."

"So am I," repeated Helmut firmly. "I've accepted the invitation. Hans is expecting us - both of us."

Elisabeth was a trifle piqued. "Well then he's going to be disappointed too. But you should have asked me before you accepted. You can't expect me just to fall in with your plans if you don't ask me first."

"There's usually no need," Helmut shrugged. "You've never been too busy to see me before."

"Oh, Helmut - don't put it like that. You know I always love seeing you. But I do sometimes have other things to do."

"Fine. Do your other things. But not this weekend. Hans is an important man. I don't want to upset him."

"It's hardly likely to upset him, surely. When you give a party, there's always a few people who can't come. Just tell him you didn't know I'd already arranged to do something on Saturday. Perhaps he'll ask us to come for the day on Sunday."

"I wouldn't dream of it. I'm not going to ask him to rearrange his plans. And I certainly don't intend to let him think that our relationship means so little to you that you only tell me what you're doing as an afterthought."

"Oh, Helmut!" Elisabeth was beginning to get exasperated. "You know that's not true."

"Then cancel whatever it is you're doing on Saturday and come with me."

Elisabeth shook her head. "I can't. Honestly I can't. I've promised to be somewhere else."

"For Heaven's sake, what is it that's so important?" Helmut demanded. Suddenly his eyes widened. "My God," he said, "it's that fucking foreigner."

Elisabeth was startled. She had never before seen Helmut so aggressive.

"It is, isn't it?" he persisted.

"I've arranged to see him, yes," Elisabeth said, aware of a note of defiance in her voice. "I've promised to take him to the zoo."

"Take him to the zoo!" Helmut sneered. "What, to visit his relatives? And what's he doing going out anyway. He's taking up a hospital bed that the German taxpayer's paying for. But he's fit enough to go out enjoying himself. Well, if he's fit enough to do that, he should be fit enough to be sent back where he came from."

"Helmut . . ." Elisabeth was appalled, "He was a slave there."

"So he says . . . And you believed him. Don't you realise that those sort of people will make up anything to get sympathy - slavery, mass extermination - it's all lies. Anyway, that's all he and his type are good for.

128

In fact, slavery's a bloody site too good for them, to my mind. If I had my way I'd exterminate the whole damn lot of them. Dirty, greedy, thieving - they're not people, they're untermenschen and we don't want them here in our country."

Slowly Elisabeth put down her coffee cup and stood up. She was shaking.

"Where are you off to?" asked Helmut.

"Home." Elisabeth could hear the tremor in her voice and didn't trust herself to say any more.

"Oh, for God's sake Elisabeth, don't be so childish. Forget about the zoo and come with me. The foreigner doesn't matter. He's nothing - a nobody."

"I had no idea you felt like that," Elisabeth said quietly. "No idea at all. Or maybe I've just been blinding myself. Maybe I just wanted to believe you weren't like that."

"Like what?"

"Capable of saying those things that you just said."

"Oh, Elisabeth. Stop being so naive. I'm proud of our country and I don't want it infested by scrounging foreigners. There's nothing wrong with being proud of being German."

"No," she agreed. "Nothing at all. But you can be proud of being German without believing that everyone else is inferior to you." She walked over to where she had put her coat and picked it up.

"Elisabeth . . ." Helmut's voice had a warning note in it. "You're not going."

"Yes I am. Goodbye Helmut."

"If you go now, that's it. Either you behave yourself and come with me this weekend or we're finished."

She turned to face him. "Goodbye Helmut," she said and walked out of the apartment.

✳ ✳ ✳

Elisabeth lay in bed, her mind going round and round. Wondering how she could have been so careless as to have allowed herself to get into such an argument, to end a relationship which had been so good for her. And the next second knowing that it was quite impossible for her to have remained Helmut's lover. And then trying to work out how it was possible that she had never seen any signs of his bigotry and prejudice in all the months that she had known him. And immediately being aware that the signs must have been there and that she had put on blinkers and ignored them for the sake of holding on to the relationship. And then feeling ashamed that she had sunk so low in her own estimation that she would turn a blind eye to traits that she abhorred just so that she might be taken out to the theatre and to restaurants by a handsome man and have her self-confidence boosted. And then thinking of Wilhelm . . . gentle, trusting Wilhelm. Wilhelm who seemed so grateful for everything that she and Erika and Marcus were doing for him. She couldn't have let him down. It would have been cruel. And yet what had she sacrificed just so that she wouldn't hurt him? Her relationship with Helmut had ended . . . and so on, round and round and round.

At about five o'clock she fell asleep and was woken two hours later by the alarm clock. Exhausted, she crawled out of bed, showered and dressed and got ready for work. She couldn't face breakfast. Having combed her hair and put on some make up, trying to hide the dark lines under her eyes and the pallor of her skin, she went into the little room that she used for storage and found a cardboard box. Taking it into the bedroom, she put into it all those things that Helmut had left at her apartment - his bathrobe, some shirts, socks and underpants, a pair of slippers, a razor and a hairbrush. She would ask her secretary to take it all round to his apartment after work. Heidi was a trustworthy young woman and she wouldn't ask any questions.

Elisabeth was at the front door before she remembered that she had two books that Helmut had lent her. One of them she hadn't finished reading. Never mind, she could get another copy. She took the cardboard box into the sitting room and added the books to its contents.

Turning, she suddenly saw, in pride of place in her display cabinet, the little ivory rat. Putting down the box she walked over and, as she raised her hand to open the glass door, she hesitated. She had grown very fond of that little rat. Then, shaking her head, she opened the cabinet and took it out. For a few moments she stood holding it, looking at its beautiful lines, at the delicacy of the carving, at the warm yellow of the antique ivory. She stroked its little head, turned it in her hand, then with her finger traced the fine line of its tail as it wrapped around its body. Would it really matter, she wondered, if she didn't return it along with Helmut's other things? After all, it had been a gift, not just something lent to her or left in the apartment. But a little voice in the back of her mind told her that she could never be entirely free of the memory of Helmut while she still had the netsuke. And she wanted to be free. She wanted to be able to forget completely about last night, about how she had been duped into believing that Helmut was the sort of man she wanted for a friend, for a lover. But it would be a wrench to have to give up the lovely little rat . . .

She sighed and, opening a drawer in the desk which stood beneath the window, took out some tissue paper. Carefully she wrapped the netsuke and dropped it in on top of everything else in the box. "A rat to a rat." she said. Then , picking up the box, she left the apartment.

✳ ✳ ✳

Looking out of the window on Saturday morning, Elisabeth realised that she had been hoping that it would rain so the trip to the zoo could be cancelled. Why, she wasn't sure. It wouldn't restore to her the weekend at the schloss nor the self-confidence that had come from her relationship with Helmut. But, even so, she would rather not have to spend the afternoon with Wilhelm. Her mind was too full of how the weekend might have been. She wasn't in the mood for playing the role of mother or maiden aunt taking a child to the zoo.

It was strange that she always thought of Wilhelm as a child. He was, she supposed, nearly the same age as herself. It was horrifying to think that someone could reach that age and know nothing of the world. She had been so fortunate in having parents who had instilled in her a love of books and art, music and theatre. And she had enjoyed sharing those things with Helmut. Pleasures were always enhanced if they were shared. Well, today she would be sharing an afternoon at the zoo with Wilhelm. She smiled ruefully. She would have to make the best of it.

The resolution was easier to make than to keep. During the course of the morning her thoughts kept returning to Helmut. She wondered how he had resolved the problem of her walking out on him. He wouldn't have allowed himself to lose face in the eyes of his friend. So she supposed that he would have gone to the house party. But how would he have explained her absence? Another thought - a more unpleasant one - struck her. Perhaps he hadn't. Perhaps he had just taken someone else. From the way that women always looked at him and hung on his every word, she knew that it wouldn't have been hard for him to acquire a new companion. Was it possible that within two days of breaking up with her, he could have found someone to fill her place, to share with him the weekend at the schloss, to share his bed, even? She hoped in her heart that it was unlikely but knew in her mind that it was all too probable. Even if he had gone alone to the schloss, it wouldn't be long before Helmut had some other woman as his constant companion, while she would have no one.

Some of the humiliation, the self-doubt, the anxiety, which she had thought she had at last overcome, was beginning to return. She shook her head. She must be firm with herself, remind herself that it was she who had ended the relationship. She should be proud of the stand that she had taken. And if she didn't find another man, so be it. She had a good job which she loved, she had friends, she had many interests. She could live without a man. But it would be hard.

✶ ✶ ✶

It was a few minutes after two when Elisabeth arrived at the hospital. Wilhelm was already downstairs, waiting for her. She thought he looked apprehensive but when she said hello and smiled at him, she received a flicker of a smile in return. In the car he was very quiet so that, after driving for some minutes, Elisabeth said "Are you all right, Wilhelm? We don't have to go to the zoo if you'd rather not."

"No. I want to go," Wilhelm replied.

"Well we don't have to stay all afternoon. Tell me when you've seen

132

enough and I'll take you back to the hospital."

"Thank you," said Wilhelm and lapsed once more into silence. Elisabeth concentrated on her navigation. She hadn't been to this zoo before. Indeed, she hadn't been to any zoo since she was a child. She remembered her parents taking her to the zoo in her home town. She smiled to herself as she recalled how she had wanted to see everything and, having done so, wanted to see it all again until, eventually, her exhausted parents had dragged her away while she begged for just one last look at the monkeys . . . or was it the elephants . . . she had forgotten which. She hoped that Wilhelm would enjoy the afternoon but was worried that he might find some of the animals rather frightening. It would, she thought, be best to avoid the elephants and the big cats to begin with and to show him the smaller animals first, the monkeys and the birds. Once she saw how he reacted to these she could decide what else they would look at.

She found her way without difficulty and was able to park the car only a hundred meters or so from the main entrance. They walked in silence towards the imposing wrought iron gates where Elisabeth bought two tickets and they went through a turnstile into the grounds. In front of them, wide paths wound round an open green space with flower beds and benches on which several sets of exhausted adults were sitting watching their children expend their seemingly endless energy by chasing each other around. Elisabeth spotted a wooden finger-board signpost a short distance away and they were walking towards it when suddenly Wilhelm stopped. She turned to see what was the matter. He was staring over towards his left.

"What is that?" he asked.

"What?" Elisabeth looked and was unable to see what it was that had caught his attention.

"That." He pointed.

He seemed to be pointing at a woman sitting on a bench, a baby buggy beside her.

"I can't see what you mean, Wilhelm."

"That . . . next to the woman."

"Oh, you mean that blue thing on wheels? It's a baby buggy. It's for pushing a baby round in, to save having to carry it."

"No. Not the blue thing. The thing that is in it."

"What?" Elisabeth was getting confused. "In the buggy? It's not a thing. It's a baby."

"Baby?"

"Yes, a baby. A young child."

"But it's so small."

"Well of course it is. It's probably only about six months old."

"But . . . but . . . I have never seen a child that small."

"What?" Suddenly Elisabeth remembered what Wilhelm had said about the children who were brought to the caves by the Carriers, children who were about two feet tall.

"All children are very small at first. In the caves you didn't see them when they were babies. You didn't see them until they had grown."

A boy of about seven ran over to the woman on the bench from the direction of the toilets. The woman stood up, took his hand and slowly began to walk towards the entrance, pushing the buggy. Wilhelm's eyes were fixed on them as they drew nearer. "Why does the baby not walk?" he asked.

"It hasn't learned to walk yet. Babies usually start to walk when they're about a year old - three hundred and sixty five days . . ."

Wilhelm nodded. "I know a year . . . three years are about a thousand days. But our children always walk."

"That's because they're older. Do they talk as well?"

"Yes, of course. Although not many words."

"Well that probably means that they're about two years old when they arrive in the caves."

Wilhelm looked puzzled. "So they would have been babies somewhere else?"

"Yes, they must have been."

"But where would they have been? Where would they have come from? Where they came from I must have come from too, but I don't

134

remember. . . "

"Try not to worry about it Wilhelm. You won't remember what happened when you were that young - very few people can."

"You can't?"

"No. My first memory is when I was about three."

Wilhelm nodded. "How old are you now?" he asked.

"I'm thirty one."

"Among my people you would be old."

"Yes. I'm very thankful that I'm not one of your people."

"So am I, Elisabeth."

"Well," Elisabeth said briskly, "shall we get on and see the animals?"

"Yes."

"I think we should start with the monkeys. They can be quite fun."

She turned to her left, resisting an impulse to take Wilhelm's hand, as though he were a child who might run off if not kept under control. A minute's walking brought them to the monkey house. Thinking that the noise inside might alarm Wilhelm, Elisabeth opted to walk round it and see whether any of the animals were in their outside enclosures. The first two were empty but when they came to the third there were three chimpanzees playing on a sort of climbing frame. Wilhelm looked at them open mouthed.

"They are not like the animals I have seen," he said.

"No. These are chimpanzees."

Wilhelm shook his head, his eyes glued to the antics of the chimps. "Why do they do these things?" he asked.

"That's the way that chimpanzees behave. It's natural for them."

Again Wilhelm shook his head. They stood and watched for a few minutes more, then Elisabeth said "Let's see what else there is."

Two enclosures further along, a family of baboons was sitting eating some fruit. And in the next was an orang-utan who looked at them out of deep set, intelligent eyes.

"These are all animals?" asked Wilhelm.

"Yes. And there are many more. All those that you've just seen are

135

apes."

"But you just said they were animals. And monkeys. And chim. . . "

"Chimpanzees."

"Chim - pan -zees," Wilhelm repeated carefully.

Elisabeth tried to explain as simply as she could, although she felt that she was fighting a losing battle. But, at the end, Wilhelm nodded. "There is so much to learn," he said, almost to himself.

"Would you like to see some birds?" asked Elisabeth.

"I know birds," said Wilhelm. "I have seen birds in the gardens at the hospital. They . . ." He thought for a moment. "They fly."

"Yes." Elisabeth nodded. "And just as there are lots of types of animals, there are lots of types of birds."

The birds were housed in a different part of the gardens and as they walked, Wilhelm continued to ask questions and to talk about what he had seen so far. When they reached the parrot house, once again they walked around rather than going inside. And suddenly, seeing Wilhelm's expression as he caught his first sight of the brilliantly coloured birds, Elisabeth was pleased that she had come.

"They are . . . they are . . . oh, Elisabeth, they're so beautiful." Wilhelm whispered the last word, in a tone of reverence.

Elisabeth smiled. "I didn't know you knew that word," she said.

Wilhelm looked at her questioningly.

"Beautiful," she said. "I didn't know you knew it."

"Oh yes," he said, "I have learned that word. I know what beauty is. And they are beautiful. . . and so are you."

Elisabeth was taken aback. "Thank you," she said, and lapsed into a mildly embarrassed silence.

For some thirty minutes they watched the birds, looking at parrots and parakeets, birds of paradise and humming birds, the large and the small, the colourful and the plain, the noisy and the silent. Elisabeth had always loved birds and was happy just to stand and watch them and to see Wilhelm's obvious pleasure. Eventually she said "I think there may be some other birds here that you would like to see."

"Yes?"

On their way from the monkeys to the parrots Elisabeth had noticed a sign pointing towards the penguins, so they retraced their steps a little way and shortly came upon the pool. Wilhelm gasped. "What are they?" he asked.

"They're called penguins."

"They are animals?"

"They're birds. But they don't fly. They swim."

"What is swim?"

"Oh . . . well it's what you do in water. To keep afloat."

"I don't understand."

"No. I'm not surprised," Elisabeth sighed. "I've explained it very badly. Just watch them and you'll see."

As she spoke, one of the penguins dived into the pool and disappeared from view, to come up a moment or two later at the far side.

"What are they doing? Are they washing?"

"No, they're swimming. Penguins don't wash."

"But you said everyone washes."

"People wash. And some animals wash by licking themselves with their tongues . . ." she laughed as Wilhelm made a face.

"So why do they swim?" Wilhelm returned to his original question.

"Because where they live naturally there is a lot of water."

"I don't understand. Do they not live here?"

"Yes, these penguins do. But penguins in general . . . oh, good grief! Look Wilhelm, I'm sorry but my head's spinning. I really do think that we must get Marcus to find you a teacher who can explain all this stuff to you. I find it very difficult."

"I'm sorry. I will not ask any more."

"No. . . it's not your fault. If you want to know something, ask. And I'll do my best to answer. But my answers might not always make sense to you."

To their left, three children came running up to the pool, talking noisily, pointing at the penguins and laughing. Wilhelm turned to look at them and the child nearest to him, a boy of about nine, looked up and smiled. To Elisabeth's amazement, Wilhelm smiled back. Turning to her, he asked "It is all right to smile?"

"Yes, of course."

"Good." And he turned his attention back to the penguins, the smile still on his face.

Ten minutes later, having watched the penguins slide and scramble on the rocks around their pool, and dive and swim in the water, Elisabeth suggested that they have some coffee before seeing anything else. She had noticed a little cafe near the entrance, where they could sit outside and watch the people come and go. They turned and walked slowly back.

Two young women came towards them, dressed less warmly than was appropriate for the still-cool spring day, in skimpy sun tops and shorts. As they passed they looked over at Elisabeth and Wilhelm, then giggled. Elisabeth was surprised. She had recognised the look on their faces - it was the sort of look that she had become used to seeing on the faces of other women when she was out with Helmut - a look of admiration mixed with envy. But why should they . . .? Slowly she turned her head and looked at Wilhelm. It was as though she were seeing him for the first time. She had always thought of him as a child and had never seen him as a man. Now, suddenly, she saw what those young women had seen - a tall, muscular young man with a strong, handsome face and dark expressive eyes, collar-length light brown hair and a neat beard, broad-shouldered beneath his close-fitting check shirt, his tight blue jeans emphasising his small round buttocks and powerful thighs. It was all she could do to keep walking. Wilhelm turned to her and said "Yes?" and she realised that she had been in the middle of saying something. She laughed awkwardly and made some excuse for her sudden lapse.

When they reached the cafe, she left Wilhelm sitting at a table outside, then went in to buy coffee and cake. As they sat in the spring sunshine, eating and drinking, Wilhelm talked but she found it hard to listen or to reply. She tried to keep her gaze fixed on the middle distance, willing herself not to stare at him. By the time they had finished their coffee she knew that she couldn't stay any longer at the zoo, that she had to get Wilhelm back to the hospital, that she had to get home and sort herself out. Searching round for an excuse, she said she was tired and asked Wilhelm whether he would mind seeing the rest of the zoo on another day.

"Of course not. I'm sorry you are tired."

"It's all right." Elisabeth was already feeling guilty for having lied. "We'll come back again soon." But, as she said it, she knew it was another lie.

✶ ✶ ✶

By Sunday Elisabeth had convinced herself that it was the suddenness of the realisation that had caused her extraordinary reaction. After all, her relationship with Wilhelm was primarily a professional one. And even though he might look like a man, his behaviour and his experience and his knowledge were still very much those of a child. Although his intelligence, she had to admit, seemed to be above the average. She wondered whether she should mention any of this to Marcus and Erika when she reported on the zoo trip, and decided against it.

She spent the day pottering about, cleaning the apartment, doing some washing, marking students' essays, speaking to her mother on the 'phone, writing letters. She ate her evening meal early, in front of the television. Shortly after eight o'clock she was sitting watching a film and nibbling some fruit when the 'phone rang. It was Erika, calling from Marcus's apartment.

"Marcus is insisting that you come over," she said. "Don't ask me what it's about. He's just back from his weekend and he's found something out and he's in such a state of excitement about it that he couldn't even ring you himself. But he says you've got to come over now because he's bursting to tell us and he won't tell me without you being here as well. So unless you're terribly busy, please come because I can't stand the suspense."

"Of course I'll come. I'll be over in about twenty minutes."

Elisabeth unplugged the television, put on a jacket, and ran out of the apartment, leaving her tray with its dirty plates and a half-eaten pear on the floor beside her chair.

Erika opened the door to her and took her jacket, ushering her into the sitting room where Marcus sat with a huge grin on his face. He stood up as she came in and offered her a glass of wine, which she accepted.

"Please . . ." begged Erika as he poured the wine. "Get on with it. Elisabeth's here now - so tell us!"

"Well. . ." Marcus settled back into his chair, the grin still in evidence. "I think I've found the link . . . the piece in the puzzle we've been looking for. Now, I grant you, it's bizarre - but then this whole thing has been bizarre from start to finish and I suppose it's fitting that the explanation should be something out of the ordinary. I must admit, when it first occurred to me, I couldn't believe it, but it all fits so well that I think it really must be the answer in the absence of anything else. Have you read Sherlock Holmes? He said when you've eliminated the impossible, then whatever remains, no matter how improbable, must be the truth."

"To hell with Sherlock Holmes!" exclaimed Erika. "Just tell us what you've found out."

"Well, you know I've been away for the weekend, visiting Bernhard?"

"Yes," Erika and Elisabeth chorused impatiently.

"Well we had a great weekend, catching up on all the news . . . He's a school teacher . ."

"For heaven's sake, Marcus," pleaded Erika, sitting bolt upright in her chair, "Get on with it!"

"OK, OK." Marcus was clearly enjoying himself. "Anyway, this morning Bernhard suggested we go into town to see the pageant. They put it on every Sunday between May and September. And suddenly, as we were watching it, I realised that there were elements that were familiar, and then things started falling into place. The high-pitched music that controlled the mind - well, that was the pipe. And the name, Hundeiss. There were a hundred and thirty children according to the legend - hundert dreissig - that could easily have been contracted over the centuries to Hundeiss. And their going into the mountain - and even the fact that Wilhelm's people wore red and yellow. It all fell into place." He sat back, the grin broader than ever.

"Marcus!" Erika shrieked. "What the hell are you talking about?"

140

"The pageant - it was all there . . ."

"What pageant? Where?"

"In Hameln. Bernhard lives in Hameln - I thought I'd told you. And the pageant tells the story of the Rattenfaenger - the Pied Piper who took one hundred and thirty children from the town and disappeared with them into the bowels of the earth in the thirteenth century. Their descendants must have been down there ever since. It all fits perfectly with everything Wilhelm's told us - the music, the name, the mines . . ."

For a moment or two there was silence. Then Elisabeth cried "I can't believe what I'm hearing. Don't you see - it's a hoax. An elaborate hoax." She could feel the rage welling up inside her but, above all, she was aware of a great feeling of hurt, of having been betrayed.

"No. . . " Erika was uncertain.

Elisabeth turned on her. "Of course it is. We've been had. He's been putting on the performance of his life - and laughing at us all the while. My God, he's been clever. All the facts, the language - even that lantern planted in the cave that he said he came out of. Well he's got his story for his newspaper article or the book he's writing . . . he'll be able to tell them what idiots we all were, pandering to him, talking, listening - taking him to the zoo . . ."

"No." Marcus was attempting to sound firm. "Let me explain . . ."

Elisabeth put down her wine glass and got up. She was shaking and she had a strange sense of deja vu. "There's nothing to explain. If you want to believe this load of rubbish that's up to you, although I would have thought you had more sense. But don't expect me to be involved. So you can tell Wilhelm - or whatever his name is - that I won't be round to visit him again. I've got better things to do." And picking up her jacket, she stormed out of the apartment.

141

Chapter Eight

When Marcus opened his front door in answer to Erika's ring, one glance at his face told her how worried he was. She put her arms around him and for a moment they stood holding each other in silence. Then, taking Marcus's face between her hands she kissed him lightly. "I've missed you," she said.

"I've missed you too. It's been a bad week."

Marcus turned and led the way into the sitting room.

"Still no word from her?" Erika asked as she sat down next to him on the settee.

"Not a thing. She's not answering her 'phone and I've lost count of the messages I've left on her answering machine"

"Is it possible that she's away?" asked Erika tentatively.

"Unlikely. It's almost the end of the semester so I imagine she must be up to her ears in student assessments."

"Maybe she's just been too busy to ring."

Marcus looked at her and shook his head. "I've even tried ringing her at the university. I got onto the department secretary but, when I said who I was, she said Elisabeth was in a meeting. So I left yet another message for her to 'phone me back urgently. . . That was two days ago."

"Perhaps she didn't get the message."

"I'm sure she did. I had the impression the secretary had been given specific instructions that I wasn't to be put through."

"Damn! And how's Wilhelm?"

"Totally wretched. We're back to square one. He just sits. He won't speak to anyone. He won't eat. I don't think he's sleeping. And I honestly don't know what to do - I feel so frustrated. He's not suffering from clinical depression - I can't treat it with medication - it's simply despair in reaction to something he doesn't understand. And how the hell do I explain it to him? I can't. His knowledge, his experience . . . they're far too limited for him to grasp what's happened. So he's reacting as an animal does when it's abandoned . . . he's just pining away."

"How can she do this!" Erika exploded. "How can she treat him so callously?"

Marcus put his arm round Erika's shoulders. "It's not entirely her fault," he said, gently. "She was very hurt. She really did believe it was a hoax."

"Well, that's ridiculous. And anyway, even if it was . . . we're as involved with it as she was and we haven't abandoned him."

"That's not strictly true, you know. I mean, yes, we're involved with him at a professional level - and we care about him. But there was a lot more going on between those two than met the eye - you know that. If it did turn out to be a hoax, all we'd lose would be a bit of pride. But for Elisabeth it'd be quite different. She'd be totally humiliated."

"Yes, I suppose you're right. But what can we *do*? We can't just leave it."

"I thought of going round to her apartment but she'd probably just shut the door in my face."

"What about if I went? She might be more willing to talk to me."

"Let's see how Wilhelm is over the next few days. He may pick up a bit now you're back."

"I felt awful about having to go away. I felt I was deserting both of you."

"No. It was important for you to do that course. If you'd turned down the place, it could have been a year before you got another chance. "

Erika nodded. "But I can't help feeling guilty. "

"You've no reason to."

"What did you say to Wilhelm?"

"I said you'd be back tomorrow. I tried to explain about your course and I think he understood."

"And what did you tell him about Elisabeth?"

"What could I tell him? The only time he speaks is to ask me where she is and when she's coming in and I have to say I don't know. I had to tell him that she might not be coming back."

"Oh, Lord, was that a sensible thing to do?"

"Well, I thought that it was better for him to know than to go on hoping and pining."

"What was it . . .?" Erika's voice drifted away.

"What was what?"

"Something Elisabeth said. I'm trying to remember . . . something about hope . . .something Wilhelm told her . . . " She frowned in concentration, then said "Of course. That was it. Wilhelm told her that when he came out of the mines, as soon as he got away from the music, he was aware of a feeling that he'd never experienced before. And it stayed with him until he came into hospital and was put onto medication. And then when you took him off the drugs it returned. And he described it to her - and it was hope. But he didn't know that it had a name because he'd never felt it before. Can you imagine that? To live your whole life totally devoid of hope? . . . And now she's deprived him of hope again. How could she do such a thing!"

"Well, of course, she wouldn't have if she still believed his story, but she's convinced herself that none of it's true."

"How could she possibly doubt it . . . particularly now!"

"Yes but she doesn't know what's been happening," Marcus reminded her gently. "I only wish I could think of a way of getting through to her. We'll just have to hope that something happens to change her mind. And meanwhile I'll keep on 'phoning and leaving messages."

✱ ✱ ✱

Standing in the deserted street, Erika wondered what to do. She had intended to go in and knock on Elisabeth's door and, when it was opened, make her listen to what she had to say, pushing into the apartment or putting her foot in the door if necessary. But the entrance to the building was locked and guarded by an entry-phone. Erika doubted very much whether, on learning who it was who had pressed the button, Elisabeth would let her into the building.

Still, she had to get in somehow. She had to confront Elisabeth face to face. Perhaps if she rang the bell to one of the other apartments she could persuade someone to let her in . . . She pressed a button at random and stood listening, her heart pounding. Nothing happened. Evidently there was no one at home. Erika waited a minute or so to be certain that she wasn't going to get an answer, then gathered her courage to try again. But, before she could do so, the door was opened from the inside by a man in white overalls, carrying a box of carpentry tools. He nodded to Erika and stood back to allow her to go into the building. She nodded her thanks and, hardly able to breathe for nerves, made her way up the stairs to Elisabeth's apartment.

By the time she got there she was trembling with apprehension. It wasn't going to be a pleasant encounter but she mustn't fail. She couldn't let Wilhelm down. She, at least, would stay loyal. She thought that her anger at Elisabeth's callousness would help her find the words she needed. Taking a deep breath, she banged on the door but there was no reply. Her immediate thought was that Elisabeth knew who it was and was refusing to answer. But commonsense told her that, as there was no spy hole in the door, this was impossible. Obviously Elisabeth wasn't yet back from the university. Well that was all right. She would wait. She would wait for as long as it took. Erika propped herself up against the wall and fixed her eyes on the stairs.

Fifteen minutes passed before she heard the street door opening and footsteps coming up to the first floor. When Elisabeth saw her she stopped and, for a moment, there was a look of anxiety on her face. Then she moved towards her front door and, in an expressionless voice, said "Hello Erika. What do you want?"

"I want you to come and see Wilhelm," Erika replied, trying to keep her voice steady.

"I'm afraid I've better things to do with my time." Elisabeth's tone was harsh.

She put her key in the lock and opened the door but before she could turn and shut it, Erika had pushed in after her.

Elisabeth rounded on her. "I don't think I invited you in, Erika."

Previously Erika hadn't really been aware of the difference in their height but now Elisabeth seemed to be towering over her. She had a strong urge to step back but stood her ground, refusing to be intimidated.

"I must talk to you," she said.

"There's nothing to be said. Please leave."

"There's everything to be said." Erika was aware that her voice was rising. "Wilhelm needs you."

"Oh, stop being so melodramatic. He doesn't need anybody. He's played his prank and he's got his result."

"It was no prank Elisabeth. Believe me."

"Oh, grow up, Erika. What else can it be but a hoax. The Pied Piper indeed . . . "

"I know. I know it's ridiculous and obviously we don't know all the story but please . . . ."

"Look Erika, I've had a tiring day and all I want to do is to sit down and relax, so I'd be grateful if you'd just leave."

"No."

"I beg your pardon!"

Erika stepped back so she was leaning against the open front door, pushing it against the wall. "I'm not going to leave until I've said what I've come to say," she said. "So either we go and sit down and talk like civilised human beings or we can argue here in your hallway with the door open so that all your neighbours can hear. The choice is yours."

Elisabeth glared at her. Then without a word she turned and walked into the sitting room. Erika shut the front door and followed her. Elisabeth gestured to her to sit down and they sat facing each other, bolt upright, on the edge of their chairs.

"Well?" Elisabeth's tone was impatient.

Erika took a deep breath and tried to speak calmly. "I don't want to argue with you Elisabeth. We've always got on so well before. But you must come with me to see Wilhelm."

"Don't tell me what to do, Erika. I've said that I'm not going to see him again and I mean it. I assume you want me to hear him explain why he did it - well, I'm not interested."

"No, Elisabeth, it's nothing like that . . . "

146

"Quite frankly, I don't really care what your reason is. Whatever you say, it's not going to change my mind."

"Please, Elisabeth . . . He's dying."

"What?" For a moment Elisabeth's face registered shock and distress and Erika thought that at last she had got through to her. But then her eyes became cold again and she said "Don't talk nonsense! It's no more than three weeks since I last saw him and he was fitter than either of us. I don't know why you should want to take part in his wretched hoax, Erika, but it's not very amusing."

"It's not a hoax." Erika fought on. "And nor is Wilhelm's story. Just think about it for a moment. Surely no one would risk being incarcerated in a mental ward for months on end just for a hoax. It's not as though we found out about this Pied Piper connection a week or two after Wilhelm had been admitted. If we had done, or even if we'd latched onto it from something that he'd told us, then I would have been suspicious as well. But after nearly four months . . . no."

"I'm sure he didn't intend to be there for four months." Elisabeth smiled disdainfully. "It must just have happened like that."

"But if he's that clever a hoaxer, surely he'd have found some way of giving us a hint. And what about the language - that can't be easy to learn and he was absolutely fluent."

"No, but I don't imagine he'd have learned it specially. He would have known the language and then planned the hoax."

"But how many people speak Middle High German really fluently? There can't be many - and I'd be willing to bet that you know most of them personally."

Elisabeth looked surprised, then said "Yes, I suppose I do."

"Then look at the way Wilhelm was admitted to hospital," Erika continued. "I've read the same stories that you have about journalists going into mental institutions as patients so they could compile undercover reports - and they all arrived at the hospital exhibiting a full range of mental symptoms to make absolutely certain they'd be admitted. But Wilhelm arrived after a head injury - a genuine head injury, which had knocked him

147

out. He was confused, yes, but not raving, so how could he have been sure he'd be admitted."

"I don't know. Maybe he hadn't worked that part out properly."

"Oh, Elisabeth," Erika chided her gently, "how can you possibly believe that he'd work the rest of the plan out to the last detail and not bother with the most important part?"

Elisabeth shook her head but said nothing.

"And what about his behaviour on the ward?" persisted Erika. "He sat by himself, hardly spoke to anyone for two months, submitted to medication. I understand your reaction, believe me - but none of those undercover journalists stayed in hospital more than a couple of weeks and they certainly didn't add to their difficulties by learning other languages to use while they were there."

"I know, but . . ."

"And then think of the coincidence," Erika went on relentlessly. "If Marcus hadn't gone to visit Bernhard for the weekend and if they hadn't decided to watch the pageant on Sunday morning, we still wouldn't have had a clue. There are too many 'if's' for it to be a hoax."

Again Elisabeth silently shook her head.

"And there's one other thing. You've got to know Wilhelm very well in recent weeks. Do you really believe that anyone could be that good an actor to carry this through."

"I don't know," Elisabeth burst out. "I don't understand any of it."

"No. We none of us do. But clearly it's not a simple hoax. It's all too ridiculous for words, I agree, but if it is a trick then Wilhelm's not in on it. He's as much a victim as we are. Maybe it is some form of brainwashing - who knows? We never did pursue that idea very far. But whatever the truth or non-truth of his story, Wilhelm believes it. And since he believes it, he sees us - the three of us - as his only friends. And he sees you - well, I think you know how he feels about you."

"How he feels . . ." Elisabeth shook her head.

Erika was surprised. She had thought Elisabeth was more perceptive than this. "Surely you're aware that he's in love with you?" she asked

148

gently.

Elisabeth stared at her, a look of confusion on her face. "In love . . . no . . ."

"That's why it's hit him so hard - you suddenly disappearing from his world."

"I didn't know." It was scarcely more than a whisper. "Perhaps I was a little too hasty." She looked down at her lap.

"Perhaps," said Erika.

For a moment there was silence then suddenly Elisabeth's head snapped up, a look of horror on her face. "But you said . . . you said he's dying. That wasn't true . . ." Erika could see that she was waiting to be told that this had been an exaggeration, a ploy to gain her attention.

"I'm sorry."

"But why? What happened? Surely something can be done?" There was an urgency in Elisabeth's voice that was close to panic.

"When you didn't come on the Tuesday for your usual visit, Wilhelm started to get anxious. He asked where you were and we had no answer to give him. Marcus tried 'phoning you, leaving messages - he tried everything he could think of to get in touch with you."

"I know." Elisabeth whispered the words.

"Then Wilhelm stopped eating, stopped talking. He didn't do anything except sit and gaze in front of him. I was away for five days - I had to go on a course - and Marcus thought that perhaps when I got back it would cheer Wilhelm up. But it didn't. It's you Wilhelm wants to see. Marcus had to tell him that he didn't think you'd be coming back. And then he stopped drinking too. So he had to be moved to a medical ward. He's on a drip but he's refused a naso-gastric tube and they can't force it on him. He's getting weaker and weaker. Marcus and I go in to see him two or three times every day but he's stopped responding to us. They don't think he can last very long. He's just lost all will to live. Marcus is at his wits' end." She stopped speaking and, looking over at Elisabeth, saw that she seemed to be gazing at an empty space in the middle of her display cabinet. There were tears rolling down her cheeks.

149

"I can't believe I did this to him . . ."

"You weren't to know," said Erika.

"Is it too late? Please tell me it's not too late."

"I don't know. I hope not. That's why I'm here."

"Thank you. Thank you, Erika. Oh, thank you . . ." And Elisabeth put her face in her hands and sobbed.

After a moment, Erika asked "Do you feel like going to see him now?"

Elisabeth raised her head, her face streaked with mascara. "Yes, yes, of course. Just give me a moment." She got up shakily and left the room. Five minutes later they were in Erika's car and heading towards the hospital.

✳ ✳ ✳

As they hurried down the corridor towards the door of the ward, Elisabeth suddenly stopped. Erika turned to face her. Elisabeth's eyes were wide with anxiety.

"What do I say to him?" she whispered.

"Don't worry," Erika reassured her. "You'll find the right words. And he'll be so pleased to see you."

As Elisabeth still hesitated, shaking her head, Erika put out her hand. "Come on," she said gently and, hand in hand, they walked onto the ward.

"He's down at the far end, near the nursing station," said Erika. "He looks dreadful, so be prepared. He's lost a lot of weight."

Elisabeth nodded, wiping her eyes with her free hand, and they walked slowly down to Wilhelm's bed. Sitting next to it, his head bowed, was Marcus. At the sound of their footsteps, he looked up and, jumping up out of his chair, came over to them and seized Elisabeth's hands.

"Elisabeth. Thank God!"

"How is he?" Erika asked.

"Much the same." Still holding one of Elisabeth's hands, he led her to the bedside. Erika could see the shock on her face as she registered Wilhelm's appearance - the thin haggard face, the grey pallor of his skin, the lank lustreless hair, the dull and unresponsive eyes. But suddenly, as Marcus bent to say "Wilhelm, Elisabeth's here," she saw a spark of life come into those eyes - a spark she hadn't seen for weeks - and the dry cracked lips moved to form the word "Elisabeth".

Elisabeth took a step forward, her eyes fixed on Wilhelm's face.

"Hello Wilhelm." Erika could hear the tremor in her voice. "I'm sorry I've been away for so long."

Slowly, painfully it seemed, Wilhelm shook his head and his mouth took on the suggestion of a smile as he repeated "Elisabeth".

Elisabeth sat down in the chair that Marcus had vacated and stretched out her hand to take one of Wilhelm's in hers.

Marcus said "We'll be back a little later," and, turning, walked with Erika out of the ward and into the corridor.

Once outside the ward, he turned to her. "How *did* you do it? I was praying that you'd get her to come back with you but I honestly didn't believe it was possible."

"I don't know," Erika answered. "I forced myself into her apartment - she wasn't at all happy about that. And then I just talked. I honestly can't remember what I said. I was just determined that I wasn't going to leave until I'd got through to her, even if it took all night. Something I said must have touched a nerve because suddenly she was in tears."

"Well done." Marcus put his arms round her and hugged her. "You're a very clever woman."

Erika shook her head. "No, not clever. Whatever I did was instinctive, not planned."

"Well, however you did it," said Marcus "it worked. That's all that matters. Now how about some coffee? I think you deserve it."

When they returned some fifteen minutes later, the junior doctor who had been looking after Wilhelm was sitting at the nursing station, doing some paperwork. Seeing them enter the ward, he came towards them, beaming.

"Amazing," he said. "Suddenly there seems to be hope. I take it that this is the woman who deserted him."

Marcus nodded.

"Well, let's just hope she doesn't do it again."

151

"I don't think she will," said Erika. "The circumstances were rather extraordinary."

"Yes," said the doctor drily. "So were the results. Anyway," he continued, "he should make a full recovery. What was it that made her come back?"

"Erika," said Marcus, and they walked on down the ward.

Wilhelm was propped up against a bank of pillows and Elisabeth was feeding him sips of clear broth from a spoon. He turned his head as they approached. Erika found herself unable to say anything and just stood there smiling broadly, feeling the anxiety of the past three weeks dropping away.

"Are you OK?" Marcus asked suddenly, putting an arm round her, and she realised that she had been swaying as the tension in her body dispersed. She sat down facing Elisabeth and watched as Wilhelm continued to take sips of the soup. When he had had enough, Elisabeth put down the bowl and the spoon on the bedside table and looked across the bed at the two of them.

"I think we'll leave you to have a rest now, Wilhelm," Marcus said. "But Erika and I will be in to see you tomorrow. . . "

"And so will I," said Elisabeth softly.

Wilhelm looked at her. "Thank you," he said. Then turning to Erika and Marcus, he repeated "Thank you," and again Erika thought she could see the ghost of a smile.

As they walked down the stairs to the ground floor, Erika said "Come back to my place. I'll make something to eat and we can talk."

"Oh, I don't think . . ." began Elisabeth.

"Please, Elisabeth," said Marcus. "We need to talk."

"Yes, yes, I suppose so. Yes, OK, thank you Erika."

Stepping outside into the warm evening sun, Erika realised it was a lovely day.

✱ ✱ ✱

They drove through the heavy rush hour traffic, Elisabeth sitting silently next to Erika, Marcus following in his own car. Erika said nothing.

She could see that Elisabeth was still close to tears and she wanted to allow her time to collect her thoughts.

When they arrived at her apartment, Erika headed for the kitchen while Marcus took Elisabeth into the sitting room. Hurriedly, Erika took some cold meat and cheese out of the fridge, made a salad and sliced some bread. Placing it all on a large tray, she carried it into the sitting room. Marcus had put a white cloth, cutlery and plates on the small dining table that stood in the corner by the window. Elisabeth was sitting in an armchair, staring straight ahead of her, hands clutching a damp tissue.

"Let's have something to eat," Erika said, briskly. "Marcus, will you open a bottle of wine, please?"

"Of course." Marcus disappeared into the kitchen.

"Elisabeth?"

Elisabeth turned her head slowly towards Erika as though uncertain that she had been addressing her. "Yes?"

"Would you like to come and eat?"

"I'm not really very hungry."

"Nevertheless, come and try. You need to eat something. You've had a shock."

"Of my own making." Elisabeth stared down at her hands.

"No. It wasn't of anybody's making. You must stop blaming yourself."

"Of course you must," said Marcus, returning to the room with a bottle in one hand and three glasses in the other. "Anyway, Wilhelm's going to be all right."

"But look what I've put him through. How could I do that?"

"Elisabeth," Marcus said firmly "you're not going to help anybody, least of all Wilhelm, if you continue to agonise over it. What's done is done. You can't undo the past. All you can do now is to be there for Wilhelm and help him get better - which he will. We all do the wrong thing at times and we all hurt people. It's part of being human."

"But I know what it feels like to be hurt like that," said Elisabeth. "And I can't bear the thought that I could do that to someone else."

"And that's why you're finding it hard to forgive yourself, isn't it?" said

153

Marcus gently. "Because you can't forgive the man who hurt you."

Elisabeth stared at him, her eyes full of pain. Then she nodded silently.

"And do you think Wilhelm will be unable to forgive you?"

"I don't know. I wouldn't blame him."

"You feel guilty for what you've done."

"Of course I do."

"And if the man who hurt you had been distraught when he found out what he'd done, would you have forgiven him?" asked Marcus.

Elisabeth gave a little sob, then nodded.

"So why do you think that Wilhelm will refuse to forgive you when you're so contrite. Is he really that unkind?"

"Unkind? No, of course not."

"But if Wilhelm forgives you, why can't you forgive yourself? You're treating yourself as though you're as uncaring as the man who hurt you - and you're not are you?"

"No!" There was shock and denial in Elisabeth's voice.

"Well, then . . . " Marcus smiled.

"Come and eat," said Erika who had finished laying out the food on the table.

They sat down on the elegant bentwood chairs that Erika's mother had bought for her when she moved into the apartment, and Marcus poured the wine. As they ate, Marcus and Erika talked about things unconnected with Wilhelm. Elisabeth said nothing but, Erika was pleased to see, ate most of what was on her plate and drank a glass of wine. When they were finished, Erika said "Go and sit comfortably. I'll make some coffee."

She cleared the remains of the meal onto the tray and took it through into the kitchen. When she returned with the coffee pot and cups, Elisabeth was sitting in an armchair, her head resting back, her eyes shut, and Marcus had kicked off his shoes and was lounging on the settee, gazing at the ceiling. Erika put the tray on the table, poured the coffee and handed round the cups. Sitting down next to Marcus, she asked "Well, where do we begin?"

"I think," said Marcus slowly, "that I ought to explain just why I was so

154

certain I'd found a clue to Wilhelm's origins. I'm afraid it was my enthusiasm as much as anything that upset Elisabeth."

Elisabeth looked at him and nodded. "It was so far fetched and yet you seemed convinced that you'd solved the mystery. And I couldn't understand how an intelligent man like you could believe such rubbish."

"It was my fault. If I'd worked up to it more slowly, explained how I came to those conclusions, allowed you to argue each point in turn, you might not have reacted the way you did. I'm sorry."

Erika took his hand and squeezed it.

"So," Marcus continued, "let me do what I should have done then. Let me tell you what happened that weekend that led me to say what I did."

He drank some coffee, then went on "On the Sunday morning, as I told you, Bernhard - who's a teacher - took me into Hameln to see the Rattenfaenger pageant. And while we were watching the children being lured away by the Piper, he made some joke about wishing he could find a pipe like that, that he could use to control his class. And suddenly it hit me that here was someone using music to control the mind. And not just any music but a high pitched music, just as Wilhelm had described."

Elisabeth nodded. "Yes, I can understand you associating the two things . . . but, Marcus, it's not enough to base an entire theory on. I mean, whoever was controlling the Hundeiss may well have got the idea from the Rattenfaenger legend but it doesn't mean that they were part of that legend."

"No, of course you're quite right. But the music was just the starting point. Once I'd started thinking along those lines, I remembered something else that had puzzled me - Wilhelm told us that the Hundeiss lived on three types of food, red foodcake, yellow foodcake and the hard brown biscuits. Now, obviously, the biscuits were to ensure that their teeth remained healthy. And although 'They' obviously think of the Hundeiss as dispensable and kill them off as soon as they're no longer fit to work, it's still in their own interests to make sure that they remain healthy as long as possible. So we can be sure that the foodcake contained all the essential nutrients the Hundeiss needed and the right balance of protein, carbohydrate and fat."

"Yes . . . but what's that got to do with the Rattenfaenger legend?"

"Well, it seemed strange to me that such a synthetic form of food would consistently be either red or yellow unless it had been dyed. And then I remembered that Wilhelm said that their clothes, when they got new ones, were also red and yellow. And I'd wondered why just those two colours? What possible significance could they have? Well, the Piper in the pageant wears a multicoloured coat but, as I was watching him lead the children down the street, I remembered that in Robert Browning's poem about the Pied Piper it's different - he describes the Piper as wearing a costume that's half red and half yellow."

"But Browning was an Englishman," said Elisabeth with a frown.

"Yes, but he got all the other details of the legend right, so maybe he heard a version of the story where the piper wore red and yellow."

"Mm . . ." Elisabeth was clearly unconvinced.

"Anyway, that started me thinking even harder. And then Bernhard said something about the number of children in the legend and, as he said it, I heard the 'hundert dreissig' as 'hundeiss'. So I asked him if he knew anything about how the legend had originated. And it seems that, although no one knows the exact details, it's generally accepted that it's based on a true event. Well, I was absolutely staggered, as you can imagine, but he knows quite a lot about folklore, so I had no reason to doubt him. His interest was sparked when he was a student and he went to a series of lectures given by a chap called Johann Schultz - you may know him, Elisabeth."

"Yes, I do. He's Professor of anthropology at the university. I met him at a party last year - when my head of department retired. A charming man."

"And also, so I understand, a great authority on folklore and mythology. And, according to Bernhard, Schultz believes that the vast majority of myths and legends were originally based on some actual event. Obviously, over the centuries they've been embellished, but Schultz reckons that he can often make a stab at working out what the original happening

156

was. So, of course, when I heard that, I thought that maybe we ought to investigate the Rattenfaenger legend and it might bring us to what actually happened to Wilhelm's people and why they've been living underground ever since."

There was a silence. Then Elisabeth said "Yes, I can see now why you thought there might be a link. But your friend was wrong about the Rattenfaenger legend . . . well, he was right about it being based on an actual event, but he was wrong to say that no one knows what really happened. It's been proved that it was an exodus of young people who were recruited to go and populate Brandenburg and parts of Poland."

"Proved? But how?" Erika asked, puzzled. "And how do you know about it?"

"I know because the work was done by a Professor of Linguistics, at Gottingen. He used a computer to compare the names of people and places in those regions with names from around Hameln. Because, as he pointed out, people tend to name new towns and villages after the places they've come from - like Perth in Australia, or London in Ontario. And he found that there were villages in those regions that had very similar names to villages near Hameln. And also that there were groups of people in Poland who had names that didn't seem to be Slavic but could have been derived from the name Hameln itself."

"Well," said Marcus, "it's quite suggestive but it's not proof, is it. I mean, why would all these people suddenly surge out of Hameln and go and settle miles away?"

"Because the land had just been liberated from the Danes, and the Church and the aristocracy were anxious to get people out there, so they sent men round the country persuading people to relocate."

"Oh," said Marcus.

"And that," continued Elisabeth, "is another reason why I knew you were talking nonsense - if you'll forgive me for saying so."

"I'll forgive you," said Marcus with a rueful smile. "But it does rather leave us back where we started. And yet, there are still these strange links between the Rattenfaenger legend and what Wilhelm has told us."

157

"Yes," said Elisabeth. "And that's what convinced me that it must be a hoax."

"But you don't still think that, do you?" asked Erika anxiously.

"No. At least not on the part of Wilhelm. When I saw him today . . . " Elisabeth lowered her head, "When I saw him today I knew that he couldn't have been a part of it. And I knew that I was wrong ever to have thought that he could have been. But if he wasn't a part of it, then he was a victim of it, as much as we were, although I don't understand how it's been done or by whom or most of all why. And I can't see how we're going to find out."

"Well, we might start by finding out a bit more about the Rattenfaenger legend," said Marcus. "In fact, I've already arranged to do so. I rang Johann Schultz last week and said that I was making a study of the legend and asked if Erika and I could have a few minutes of his time. We're going over to see him at his house tomorrow evening."

Elisabeth shook her head. "Honestly, Marcus, I don't know what else he'll be able to tell you. The relocation theory is very widely accepted now. And, if the whole thing is some sort of elaborate hoax, I don't see how knowing more about the legend is going to help. I think we've got to accept the fact that we may never know the truth about where Wilhelm has come from."

Marcus looked at her. "And that would satisfy you, would it?"

"No, of course not. I want to know the facts as much as you do. But I just don't think this is the right way of going about it. I don't see that it can lead anywhere."

"No, I understand that. But at the moment it's all we've got. And I think we owe it to Wilhelm to pursue every lead, don't you? After all, if it is a hoax, then he's the main victim and if we don't fight his battle, he's got no one."

Elisabeth nodded, thoughtfully. "You're right, of course. It's just . . ."

"You don't want Professor Schulz to think that we're crackpots."

Elisabeth smiled. "Exactly."

"Don't worry, Elisabeth. I'll be very tactful - he won't think we're the least bit odd."

***

The door was opened by a plump, grey haired woman who invited them into the house and showed them into a comfortably furnished study.

"My husband will be with you in a moment," she said. "He's just speaking to someone on the 'phone. Please make yourselves comfortable."

Left to themselves, Marcus, Erika and Elisabeth sat down and looked around them. From the way in which the chairs were arranged around the walls of the room, Erika suspected that the Professor must hold tutorials in his home. Against the left hand wall, next to the window was a large desk covered in papers and, beside it, a high backed swivel chair. The upper part of every wall held bookshelves, crammed with volumes on anthropology, mythology and comparative religion, together with dictionaries and other reference books, all of them looking as though they had been well-used.

It was a pleasant room, easy to be comfortable in, although Erika noticed that Elisabeth was sitting on the edge of her chair, with an anxious look on her face. It had not, she thought, been easy for Elisabeth, agreeing to come with them, risking the possibility of making a fool of herself in front of a senior colleague. Erika still hoped that Johann Schultz might be able to tell them something that would give them a clue but, having heard Elisabeth's account of the paper written the Professor at Gottingen, she had her doubts.

After a few moments, the door opened and a burly, bearded grey haired man came in, smiling broadly. "Dr. Hellman. I'm sorry to keep you waiting." They shook hands. Then Marcus said, "These are my friends, who are also interested in this research - Fraulein Frenzel and Dr. Kramer." Professor Schultz shook hands with the two young women saying "I know Dr. Kramer, I think. We met at Professor Bader's leaving party."

"Yes, we did. I didn't think you'd remember me."

"Oh, I have a good memory for faces."

The Professor moved over to the swivel chair and sat down. "Now then, how can I help you."

Marcus cleared his throat, betraying to Erika at least that he was a little nervous. But he gave no signs of anxiety as he started to explain that, on a

159

recent visit to Hameln, he had become fascinated by the legend of the Rattenfaenger and that a friend, who had been one of Professor Schultz's students some years ago, had suggested that the Professor was the person who could tell him more about it.

When Marcus had finished, the Professor said nothing for a few moments. Then he nodded and said "I see." There was a look on his face that Erika couldn't quite fathom - not quite puzzled, not quite sceptical. But she knew instinctively that he didn't believe what Marcus had told him.

Suddenly he seemed to come to a decision. "May I ask you something, Dr. Hellman?"

"Of course."

"Is there any reason why you don't want to tell me the full story? The real reason why you want to learn about the Rattenfaenger? . . . Forgive me. I don't want to seem rude. But clearly there's a lot more to it than you've told me. You're an intelligent man and, if you just wanted to learn more about the Rattenfaenger legend, you could have bought a book from any one of a dozen shops in Hameln. But, no, you come to ask a Professor of anthropology to tell you about it. And not only you, but you bring two friends. I don't want to pry if you have a genuine reason for not telling me, but it would be much easier for me if I knew exactly what it is that you're after."

"I'm sorry . . ." Marcus was embarrassed.

"No, there's no need to apologise. But it seems rather a waste of all our time if I don't know how best to help you."

"O.K." Marcus took a deep breath. "I suppose I didn't want to tell you because it's a very bizarre story and we really don't know whether we're on the right track at all - in fact, Elisabeth - Dr. Kramer - doesn't think we are. But either someone has played a very elaborate hoax on us and on a friend of ours - although we can't work out how or why - or else . . . well, or else we don't have a clue what's going on."

"I see. Or rather, I don't see. Would you like to tell me more? I can assure you I'm perfectly trustworthy. Nothing you tell me will go any further."

Marcus looked over at Elisabeth who bit her lip, then shrugged in acquiescence.

"It really is very bizarre . . ." Marcus began.

"Dr. Hellman, I'm an anthropologist and an expert on myths and legends - I'm used to hearing bizarre stories. And you'd be surprised how many of them have an element of truth."

"Yes, of course. Well, it started a few months ago . . ." With help from Erika and Elisabeth, Marcus told the Professor how Wilhelm had arrived at the hospital, about the language he spoke and the things that he had told them concerning his former life. Erika told him about her caving trip and Marcus finished with an account of his visit to Hameln. The only thing that wasn't mentioned was the way in which Elisabeth had walked out and how it had affected Wilhelm. When Marcus had finished he said "I told you it was bizarre."

The Professor nodded, stroking his beard. "Fascinating," he said. "Quite fascinating. I congratulate you for noticing the things that match up with the Rattenfaenger legend. But why are you so sure now that it's a hoax? And do you think that this young man . . . Wilhelm . . . is a part of the hoax?"

"No, no. We think he's a victim, too, although we don't know how it's been done. I actually thought that it might be a genuine link but Elisabeth's persuaded me that it's a hoax because apparently there's a Professor of Linguistics who's proved that the legend's based on a mass migration of people from Hameln to Brandenburg and Poland."

"Ah yes." Professor Schultz's eyes twinkled. "Professor Udolph and his computer. Well, you know not everyone thinks that he's come up with the definitive answer."

"Really?" asked Erika.

"It was a very good article," continued the Professor. "And in its way very plausible." He stood up and took a large map from one of the shelves, then unfolded it on the floor and directed his desk lamp onto it so that they could all see it clearly. It showed most of northern Europe.

Crouching down, he said "Professor Ulrich points out that there is a place called Beverungen near Hameln - here," he pointed to a spot in northern Germany, "and there are places with very similar names, Beveringen - here in Brandenburg," again he pointed, "and Beweringen - here, near Stargard in north west Poland. And he suggests, as you know, that Beveringen and Beweringen were founded by former residents of Beverungen - which might well be the case. And there is no doubt that there are a lot of people in those areas with names like Hamel and Hamelnikov. But . . " he looked around at them, smiling. "Can we be sure that the event that moved these people there is the same event that lies at the bottom of the Rattenfaenger legend? For example, there are villages and towns elsewhere with similar names - there are three in Belgium - Bevergem, Bevingen and Beveren." He pointed to each in turn. "And there's a Berwang in the Tyrol, and a Bevergen to the west of Hameln, near Osnabruck, and a Bernigen in Switzerland, and a Beuvrequen in northern France and even a Beverone in Italy - not as close matches, I grant you, but they all have a strong similarity. And there are people with names like Hamel all over the place, although I accept that it's unusual to find them in areas where most people have Slavic names."

The Professor sat back on his heels and looked around at them. Erika noticed that Elisabeth was listening keenly and had lost her look of apprehension.

"Now, then," the Professor continued, "let's take this a step further. Say we accept that these people did originally come from Beverungen - does that automatically connect them with the legend? Did you notice where Beverungen is?"

Without waiting for them to reply, he pointed again at the map. "It's here - over fifty kilometers south of Hameln."

He smiled and stood up, leaving the map open on the floor. Settling back into his chair, he said "Professor Udolph points out that the Bishops and Dukes of Pomerania and Brandenburg sent out so-called locators whose job it was to bribe people to settle in those areas that had been snatched back from the Danes after the Battle of Bornhoved in 1227. But if one of these locators encouraged the legendary one hundred and thirty

162

people from Hameln to move to one of these new settlements, why would they have named their villages after a place that was fifty kilometers from their home town? Remember, we're talking about the thirteenth century. The roads were poor and these people weren't nobility so they were more likely to walk than to ride. Now, if you were founding a new settlement, would you name it after a village two days' walk away from your native town? It seems unlikely to me. If they came from Hameln, why not call the place after Hameln? And if they did that, are we to assume that they ended up in Hameenlinna in Finland or Hammel in Denmark?"

He paused and looked round again at his audience. Erika found herself envying his students who had the opportunity to hear him speak regularly.

He nodded at her. "Interesting, isn't it? This is the wonderful thing about myths and legends - you can make all kinds of hypotheses but it's very rarely possible to prove anything, which makes for fascinating far-reaching debate."

"So what you're saying," said Elisabeth hesitantly, "is that Professor Udolph is right when he says that people from the Hameln area were recruited to move into Eastern Europe but that this doesn't necessarily mean they were the one hundred and thirty of the legend."

"Exactly. People were being recruited from all over Germany over a period of years. Hameln was a fair sized town by thirteenth century standards so it seems more than likely that people would have gone from there. But - and here we come to the second 'but' - if people were going from all over Germany, why is it only in Hameln that we have the impression of young people being snatched away in a large number and, even more significantly, on a particular date." He turned to Marcus. "Do you remember the date?"

Marcus shook his head.

"Well, it was June 26th 1284. And that in itself is interesting. It was nearly sixty years after the Battle of Bornhoved, so they wouldn't have been the first people to have moved to the east. The people of Hameln would have known about the slow exodus of people from Germany - rather like the exodus of the Irish going to America in the nineteenth century. And, certainly, families would have been saddened to lose their relatives when they went off to new lives. But it wouldn't be something that was unusual or horrifying. And I believe that it's almost always the unusual or the horrifying that's at the root of a legend. Otherwise why remember it? If your children go off to make a new life for themselves, just as the children of the next town and the next have done - why the shock? And why remember it happening on one particular day? Is it likely that a hundred and thirty would all have left on the same day? It seems far more probable to me that they would have gone in smaller groups - perhaps twenty or thirty at a time. Even today, with modern facilities, it's not easy for a group of over a hundred people to travel together. And these people would have had to travel a long distance, finding their food as they went. Could they expect to do that easily if there were so many of them? I don't think so."

There was a knock and Frau Schultz put her head round the door. "I'm sorry, Johann, am I interrupting?"

"No." The Professor got up out of his chair. "Perfect timing." He bent and, picking up the map, folded it and replaced it on the shelf.

Frau Schultz pushed open the door and came in carrying a tray with coffee and cake, which her husband took from her and offered round to his three guests. After she had gone, Marcus said "So you think that it may have been something more dramatic than simply an exodus of economic migrants that was at the root of the Rattenfaenger legend?"

"Certainly I do. Because, you see, that sort of migration doesn't explain the other legends. None of them is as well known as that of Hameln, but there are many similarities."

"Other legends?" Erika nearly choked over her coffee. "You mean that there are legends in other towns about the Rattenfaenger?"

"I do indeed. There's a book of folk tales from northern Germany that was published in the eighteen forties which tells of a man with a hurdy-gurdy who lured all the children out of a city in Brandenburg. Now that in itself is interesting, because Brandenburg is one of the places that Professor Ulrich says the Hameln emigrants were taken to. And like the Hameln

164

story, the Brandenburg children were led into an opening that appeared in a nearby hill and they were never seen again.

Then there's a similar story in a book of Prussian tales, which was published a few years later, in which over one thousand children from Efurt suddenly left the city dancing and singing and finished up in another town. In that story, the children didn't disappear and their parents were able to come to fetch them, but nobody knew how they had been lured away. It was said to have happened about twenty five years before the events in Hameln. Maybe it was a rehearsal - who knows?"

Erika realised she was sitting open mouthed, her cup of coffee forgotten. "Extraordinary," she croaked.

"Yes, quite extraordinary. Then there's a similar legend from England . ."

"England!" exclaimed Elisabeth.

"Actually from the Isle of Wight, which is just off the south coast of England. The story was published in the eighteen thirties in a book of legends of the island and it concerns a place called Newtown. It's very similar to the Hameln legend except that the children were led into a forest where they disappeared."

Elisabeth shook her head. "Could all these legends have been based on the original Hameln story?"

"They could . . . but I think it's unlikely. These aren't like modern urban myths. The point about those is that they always happened to a friend of a friend and could have occurred anywhere. But the Rattenfaenger legend - there are always local details given and, often, dates as well. And they're so widespread." He paused, smiling. "Not just Germany and England but also Morocco, and Turkey, and Spain."

His listeners gaped.

"Those legends aren't recorded in books as far as I know. But I've heard them in my travels from people who have assured me that the events happened locally and that the story has been handed down from generation to generation."

"Good grief." Marcus was the first to find his voice. "But . . . " he tailed

165

off.

"Precisely," said the Professor. "It opens up all kinds of questions. And it's possible that your friend Wilhelm may be able to help us answer some of them."

Chapter Nine

Elisabeth lay awake, staring at the ceiling. Her bedside clock said 1.27. She wanted to sleep, had tried imagining herself walking along a solitary beach, the sun warm on her hair, a soft breeze blowing, the gentle waves lapping at her feet. But she couldn't hold the image in her mind. She kept seeing Wilhelm as he had been three days ago when she visited him on the ward - haggard and near to death. She reminded herself that, already, he was much better and tried to conjure up the way that he had looked when she had gone in to the hospital after work that afternoon. He had been sitting in a chair, hair freshly washed and combed, happy to see her. But the first image kept coming back - of Wilhelm ill, of Wilhelm dying - because of what she had done. She couldn't help blaming herself, despite Marcus and Erika's constant reassurance. It was her fault. She should have realised, she should have known, she should have been more ready to listen, she shouldn't have jumped to conclusions.

She turned onto her left side, away from the clock that reminded her that the night was ticking away in sleeplessness, and curled her knees up. The foetal position. She remembered reading about it. When people wanted to protect themselves they instinctively resumed the position that they'd taken in the womb, knees drawn up, arms folded across the chest. Why, though, did she need to protect herself? No one else was blaming her. Wilhelm certainly wasn't. Could it be true, what Erika had said - that he was in love with her? Surely not. And yet, why else would he starve himself when she stopped visiting him. What other explanation could there be. But she hadn't known . . . hadn't realised. . . How could she have known? Erika and Marcus knew, though. And if she had known, would she have reacted differently, or would she have thought that, too, was a lie, that Wilhelm's supposed attachment to her was part of the hoax? She didn't know. She didn't know anything any more. All she knew was that he had nearly died. And if he had died it would have been her fault. And yet it was only she who was blaming herself. Marcus and Erika were being so supportive. And Wilhelm had been so pleased to see her each time she'd gone in, hadn't even mentioned her long absence or the reason for his present condition. And yet she felt so insecure.

Reluctantly she admitted to herself that it was her insecurity that was at the root of the problem, that had caused her to act as she had. Her first reaction to Marcus's revelation was fear that she had been betrayed. But why betrayed? The victim of a hoax might be made a fool of . . . but betrayed? She supposed that, if the hoax were perpetrated by a friend, it might be seen as betrayal. And certainly she thought of Wilhelm as a friend. She stared into the darkness, knowing that she wasn't being honest with herself, knowing that it went deeper than that. After Philippe she had built up a mental barrier to protect herself. She had thought she was safe but the revelation of Helmut's true character had shaken her and, coming on top of that, this had been just one thing too many.

Elisabeth took a deep breath, realising that she was now thinking of Wilhelm together with Philippe and Helmut, knowing she could no longer deceive herself. She must admit it . . . she was attracted to Wilhelm. And it was that attraction that had made the possibility of a hoax seem like a betrayal. But how had it happened? She had avoided emotional involvements for so long, trying to keep her life on an even keel. And now, to form such an unsuitable, such a ridiculous attachment. But she had been aware when it had happened, had rushed home from the zoo, unable to remain in Wilhelm's company while she wasn't in complete control of herself. She remembered all too well that sudden realisation of Wilhelm as a man, tall and handsome in his check shirt and his tight jeans, the little flutter in her stomach that she used to feel when she saw Helmut, the weakness in the knees at the sight of him.

She didn't know what she was going to do. She could not, she would not let Wilhelm down again. But they could never be more than friends. It was impossible. After all, they were literally from different worlds. What she was feeling was simply a physical reaction, nothing more. It wasn't love. It was just a natural reaction to a handsome young man. And yet, he was so much more than that. Yes, he may have had no education, have no knowledge of the world, but he was kind and gentle and . . . ohhhh . . . . She

168

wailed out loud, finding in the sound some relief from her pent up emotions.

She turned again, unable to get comfortable, wanting to see the clock once more. One thirty. This was absurd. No good could come of going over and over it in her mind. She would ask Marcus how to deal with it, how to explain to Wilhelm that they could only be friends. Marcus was a psychiatrist, he was used to dealing with people's emotional problems. He would advise her. Meanwhile she must get some sleep. She tried visualising the beach again... sun, white sand, soft breeze, gentle waves . . . Professor Schultz asking if he could meet Wilhelm. It had been natural, of course, following on from their discussion. But, as he said it, Elisabeth had gone cold, thinking that now he would have to learn how she had treated Wilhelm and how ill he had become as a result. And then Marcus, smiling, saying "He's a bit under the weather at the moment, so can we leave it for ten days or so? He should be better by then." And the Professor agreeing and arranging a date for the meeting. Elisabeth couldn't think why Marcus should protect her, but she was infinitely grateful that he had done so. Her shame at her own behaviour was deep enough, without other people knowing about it.

So Professor Schulz was to meet Wilhelm on Thursday of the following week. Elisabeth wondered what they would make of each other. Her original favourable impression of the Professor hadn't changed but, although she had been fascinated by the arguments that he had raised against Professor Udolph's paper, at the same time she was astonished that he truly believed there might be something more to the legend of the Rattenfaenger, the Pied Piper, than the paper had suggested. For some reason, his belief made her uneasy. Her life would have been so much simpler if she had never got involved in all this in the first place. And yet, she was pleased that she had met Marcus, and Erika . . . and Wilhelm. And on that thought, she fell asleep at last.

Walking onto the medical ward at five thirty on Thursday, Elisabeth was surprised to find that Wilhelm was nowhere to be seen. A nurse came over to her and asked "Are you looking for Wilhelm?" When Elisabeth nodded, she said "He's with Professor Schultz. They shouldn't be too long - they've been in there for over an hour. If you want to sit outside in the waiting area, you'll see them when they come out of the office."

Half an hour later, Elisabeth was just beginning to think that she might leave a message for Wilhelm and go home when the door of the doctor's office opened and Wilhelm came out, accompanied by Johann Schultz. At the sight of him, looking so much better, looking so much the way he did that day at the zoo, Elisabeth caught her breath, then got unsteadily to her feet, hoping that her reaction hadn't been obvious either to him or to the Professor. Seeing her, Wilhelm came over, smiling.

"Elisabeth . . . this is Johann. We have been talking - about the mines, about Them, about so many things . . ."

"Hello Wilhelm," Elisabeth said. "Yes, I know Professor Schultz." They shook hands.

"Profes . . .?" asked Wilhelm.

"Johann," said the Professor. "I realised that Wilhelm calls all of you by your first names, so I thought it would be easier if we were all on first name terms . . . if that's all right?"

"Of course," said Elisabeth.

"It's been a most interesting conversation," continued the Professor. "and I'd very much like to arrange another meeting with you and your friends to discuss what Wilhelm's told me. Will you 'phone me so we can fix a time?"

"With pleasure, Professor . . . Johann."

"Good. Well, I must go or Magdalena will wonder what's become of me. Goodbye Wilhelm. I hope we shall meet again soon." And he walked off down the corridor.

Wilhelm took Elisabeth into the day room. He was, she noticed, still rather thin, his face still a little drawn, the dark rings beneath his eyes not yet completely gone. But mentally he was fully recovered and, as he told her about his meeting with Johann Schultz, she realised that he must have told him in ninety minutes everything that it had taken her weeks to find

170

out. She found she was looking forward to hearing what Johann had made
of it all.

✱ ✱ ✱

Marcus and Erika were as anxious as Elisabeth to hear Johann's
conclusions and the following evening found them all once again at his
house. He greeted them with evident pleasure and ushered them into the
study.

"A very pleasant young man, your Wilhelm," said Johann once they
were seated. "We had a long conversation. His description of the mines
and the way in which his people are treated was extraordinary."

"I don't think he's making it up," said Marcus, leaning forward in his
chair. "Whether it's true or not, I'm sure Wilhelm believes it."

"Oh, I think it's true," replied Johann. "Which, of course, leads us on to
a very important point. . . If it is true and if there are other people down
there being treated in the same way that Wilhelm was, then the
responsibility is on us to find out where they are and who is holding them,
so that they can be released."

There was a moment's silence, then Erika asked "Do you think we
should call in the police?"

"No." Johann shook his head. "I'm afraid it's not that simple. But if we
accept that Wilhelm is telling the truth, then somewhere beneath us, deep
underground, there are people enslaved to masters of whom we know
nothing. To save the people, we must find the masters. And then, perhaps,
it will be time to call in the police, or even the army. You see, Wilhelm's
people may not be the only ones down there. There may be many tribes,
widely scattered. To find Wilhelm's mine would save only the Hundeiss,
not the others."

"Oh, but surely . . ." Elisabeth began, then tailed off. The others were
looking at her quizzically.

"Surely?" prompted Johann.

Elisabeth shook her head. "I'm afraid I'm just a natural sceptic. I find it
very hard to accept any of this."

"Splendid. You're an academic, that's just as it should be. Don't

171

believe anything until you have the proof. Quite right. But you trust Wilhelm, don't you? You don't think he's deliberately lying to you?"

Elisabeth felt herself blushing. "No," she said. "I believe that he believes it. I just can't bring myself to accept that it's the truth."

"Of course." Johann smiled. "Like any sane and normal person you take all these stories with a pinch of salt. Well, all I'll ask of you - of all three of you - is that you keep an open mind while I tell you some folk legends." Turning in his chair, he reached into the pile of papers on the desk and pulled out a folder from which he extracted some sheets of paper, apparently cut from magazines. "Have a look at these," he said, passing them to Marcus.

Marcus and Erika leafed through them, both looking slightly bemused, then handed them on to Elisabeth. Each sheet bore a reproduction of a painting, each from a different era - sixteenth, seventeenth, eighteenth and nineteenth centuries. The thing that they had in common was that they all depicted fairies. Elisabeth looked up, puzzled and faintly disturbed, feeling that asking her to believe in fairies wasn't something she would have expected from a professor of anthropology. Johann, she noticed, was smiling, watching their reactions.

"Fairies," he said. "Every nation, every culture has them under different names. In some places they are huge, in others tiny. They may be the same size as humans, and look very like them - do you know Shakespeare's *A Midsummer Night's Dream*?"

They all nodded.

"The fairies in that play are almost indistinguishable from humans - they appear in the same scenes as them, so we know that they're meant to be the same size. They are beautiful to look at, but they don't have beautiful characters. The huldre, or elves, of Scandinavian and Germanic legend are also very like human beings - distinguished only by the fact that they have cows' tails. And the huldre are interesting because, while some of them - the bergfolk - live in the mountains, the underjordiske live underground. And not only do they live underground but they have a nasty habit known as bergtagning which, literally, means 'taking into the mountain.'" He

172

paused and looked around. "Taking people into the mountain. Kidnapping them."

"Professor . . ." Elisabeth began.

"Johann," he corrected her.

"Sorry, Johann. You're surely not asking us to believe that Wilhelm's people were kidnapped by fairies."

"Not fairies as you understand them, of course not. But what is the truth behind fairies? Originally they weren't the charming little spirits that adorn children's story books. There was an evil side to them. So what was the origin of these evil beings who kidnapped people and took them into the mountain? Perhaps we should investigate that."

"I see." Elisabeth nodded. "But surely that was so long ago . . ."

"But if we believe that Wilhelm's people were originally kidnapped by the Rattenfaenger, then that, too, was a long time ago. And the other stories similar to those of Hameln - some of them seem to be quite ancient. So who were these beings - or people - who kidnapped children and took them down into the bowels of the earth to work for them? And why did they do it?"

He riffled through his file again, pulling out a single sheet which, once more, he passed to Marcus. "Do you know what that is?" he asked.

"No." Marcus shook his head. It looks like the earth but . . ."

"Precisely. 'But' . . ."

Erika and Elisabeth looked at the picture in turn. It was a black and white photograph, again from the pages of a magazine, and it seemed to show the earth pictured from outer space and taken from an angle somewhere above the north pole although there was a strange dark circular area over the pole itself.

"You've heard of hollow-earthers?" asked Johann.

"People who believe the earth is hollow?" asked Marcus. "Jules Verne wrote a novel about that - I remember reading it when I was young. About an expedition to the centre of the earth. But surely this can't be a real photograph?"

"Oh, it's a real photograph all right," smiled Johann. "But the hole that it seems to show isn't real, although believers in a hollow earth would tell you that it's the one photograph that managed to slip past the censors. Of course, since this was taken, there have been many many photographs taken from space and none of them shows a hole."

"So this is a fake?" asked Marcus.

"No, not a fake, a composite. It's made up from a series of photographs taken over a period of twenty four hours. That way, the whole of the globe was shown in daylight. But during the winter, the extreme north has no daylight, so it shows as a black circular patch - not a hole, just an area of darkness which contrasts strongly with the rest of the globe."

Erika looked at the picture thoughtfully. "You can see why people might think it's a hole." she said. "Particularly if it backs up their own pet theory."

"But does anybody, other than the odd crank, seriously believe that the earth is hollow?" asked Elisabeth.

"Oh yes," Johann smiled. "It's a belief that you'll find all around the world. Indeed, some people claim to know the location of several of the entrances leading to the centre of the earth."

"And is one of those in Germany?" asked Erika.

"No, not as far as I know. But that doesn't stop Germans from believing in it." He paused, then added "Hitler believed strongly in the hollow earth theory."

Marcus snorted. "Well Hitler believed in black magic."

"Precisely."

Something in the tone of his voice made Elisabeth look up sharply. Johann was no longer smiling.

"You're surely not suggesting . . ." she began.

"My dear friends," said Johann gently, "what I'm saying is that you may be getting involved in something which could lead you into great danger. You need to be warned, to know the risks that you may have to face. And if you wish to go no further, I will understand."

"And what about you?" asked Marcus. "Would you be content to take it no further?"

174

Johann shook his head. "No. This is something I must pursue for the sake of Wilhelm's people and for all those others who might be down there. Once before Germans stood aside and said nothing and did nothing and over six million people were slaughtered. Those few who did stand up to the tyrant were ruthlessly destroyed, but their work lived on and, ultimately, he too was destroyed."

There was a short silence, then Erika said "I'm with you, Professor."

"And me," said Marcus.

Elisabeth nodded. "Wilhelm is our friend. He relies on us. We can't let him down. But if it's as dangerous as you think it might be, then why not hand the whole thing over to the police? Let them investigate, find out who the people in control are."

Johann shook his head. "I'm afraid that, even with my reputation as an academic, they might dismiss me as a crank. The police aren't equipped to deal with cases like this. The powers of those we are seeking to overcome are very great."

"Powers?" asked Elisabeth in disbelief. "Are you saying that Wilhelm's captors have occult powers?"

"I have no doubt of it."

"No, I'm sorry . . . I can't go along with this." Elisabeth was shocked at the turn the conversation was taking. "Marcus," she turned to him, "surely you can't believe in this mumbo jumbo? You're a doctor!"

Marcus smiled. "Being a doctor doesn't mean that one has to deny the existence of everything that can't be proved scientifically, although I must admit I used to do just that. A doctor's training is based very firmly on what can be seen and felt and measured. But after I qualified I used to write the occasional article on medicine for a magazine - and then one day they asked me to do something on unorthodox therapies - healing, acupuncture and so on. Well, at first I didn't want to - didn't want to waste my time. And then I thought that, perhaps, if I turned it down, they might not ask me to write anything else. So I agreed. But my scientific mind told me I couldn't just condemn the therapies out of hand - I had to investigate them first . . . and then condemn them!"

175

Johann laughed. "And once you'd investigated them . . .?" he asked.

"Well, then, of course," said Marcus, "I found I couldn't condemn them. Because I'd actually seen them working. And the results were too consistent to be due to a placebo effect. So I had to concede that they were effective. But when I asked the therapists to explain how they achieved their results, they all talked about the manipulation of energies. And that left me in a quandary. Because although I was able to accept that the therapies worked, I couldn't accept the theory of how they worked. Finally, one delightful lady - an ex-nurse, very down to earth, very practical - said to me "But you can be a healer, too." And she showed me how I could become aware of those healing energies and how I could use them. And it was amazing - I could actually feel the energy in my hands and I could use it to treat patients. I still do occasionally - not for anything major, but to treat headaches, stomach upsets, that sort of thing. So I have no doubt that those energies exist even though they've never been measured in a laboratory. And if those energies exist, why not energies of good and evil?"

"I'm afraid I agree," Erika said apologetically to Elisabeth. "My grandmother was psychic, so I have no difficulty accepting that there are powers that we don't understand."

"I know it's hard for you, Elisabeth," said Johann. "and I'm not asking you to believe everything I say just because I say it. But if you can find it in your heart to trust me and to keep an open mind . . ."

Elisabeth looked at him, seeing the sincerity in his eyes, accepting his great wealth of knowledge accumulated over many years, realising that she had no reason not to trust him. And somehow what he had said made a kind of sense: there was a feeling that perhaps they were getting somewhere at last after so many dead ends. Eventually she nodded.

Johann smiled. "Good. Now, it's important that you protect yourselves as best you can." He took a key from his pocket and unlocked a drawer in his desk, then pulled out from it what seemed to be three necklaces. He held one up for them to see. On closer inspection it was a long gilt chain with several little symbols hanging from it, rather in the manner of a charm bracelet.

176

"I want each of you to wear one of these," he began. "The sacred symbols they bear will offer you protection." He handed a chain to each of them.

There was a gasp from Erika. "I'm not wearing a swastika!"

"The swastika," said Johann "wasn't invented by the Nazis. It was adopted by them because it was an Aryan symbol, coming originally from India and the lands to the north, but like so many things they adopted, the Nazis distorted it. The ancient swastika was a symbol of light and it was said to spin clockwise. The Nazi swastika spun counter-clockwise, making it a symbol of darkness. If you look carefully at these swastikas, you will see that they are engraved on one side and plain on the other, so that there is a clear distinction between the back and the front, and that they are clearly clockwise-spinning."

They examined the engraved faces of the little gold swastikas and Erika ran a finger over hers as if to reassure herself.

"The cross, of course," continued Johann, "needs no introduction. You will be aware of its power as a symbol, even if you aren't practising Christians. The six pointed star next to it is known as the star of David. But its Hebrew name is the mogan Dovid - the shield of David. And it can protect just as a shield can. You probably recognise the ankh which comes from ancient Egypt." He pointed to the T shaped symbol, surmounted by a loop, which always reminded Elisabeth of a baby's dummy.

"And what's this?" asked Marcus, fingering the fifth symbol, which was a curious dumb-bell shape.

"That is a vajra, or dorje. A double ended thunderbolt. It comes from Tibetan Buddhism which teaches that good and evil are just opposite sides of the same thing. That, in fact, there is no duality. It is only from our picking and choosing that duality arises."

Marcus and Erika looked blankly at Johann. Elisabeth frowned. "Are you saying that they believe that good and evil are the same thing?"

"No. In this world as we understand it there are indeed good and evil. But by resisting evil, by discriminating against it you can cause a greater dichotomy and can cause it to grow. And that is where the danger lies.

177

Because the alternative to resistance, as we in our unenlightened state understand it, must be to give in, to be seduced by darkness. The Buddhist teaching is to use the power of the darkness to overcome it, to turn it against itself, rather as in judo where you use your opponent's own weight and strength against him. It requires many years of practice to be able to do that, but that is why the vajra is the most powerful symbol of all. Now . . ." suddenly his tone became brisk, "I want you each to put on the chain and to promise never to take it off - not in the shower, not in the swimming pool, not on the tennis court, not in bed - until this thing is over, if it ever is." He fumbled under the collar of his shirt and pulled out part of a chain on which they could see an ankh and a cross. "You see, I already wear one. It will hide perfectly well beneath your clothes if you so wish."

Elisabeth's fingers felt oddly clumsy as she undid the catch on the chain and put it round her neck, watching her friends do the same. Marcus was frowning.

"I can understand that you want to take every precaution possible," he said, "but you don't honestly think . . . I mean, we're not really in danger, are we?"

"I don't know," replied Johann simply. "But it seems to me unlikely that the incarceration of Wilhelm and his people will have a rational explanation. I have, over the years, come in contact with those who practise the dark arts and I find that I can now sense . . . Well, let's just say that I have a feeling about this. I may be wrong. I hope I am. But I would be seriously negligent if I allowed you to become embroiled in this without warning you where it might lead and without offering you some form of protection. So just humour me and wear the chains, please. And now," he smiled round at them, his expression placid, as though they had been discussing some light hearted novel or amusing television programme, "I think Magdalena will have coffee ready."

Johann ushered them into the large sitting room whose unsophisticated style of furnishings gave an instant impression of comfort and security. Elisabeth, somewhat unnerved by what Johann had told them, felt herself relaxing. Magdalena was waiting for them with coffee and cake. As they entered, she jumped up from her chair and her eyes went to the chain which Elisabeth had not yet tucked inside her blouse. Elisabeth thought she saw anxiety in Magdalena's eyes as she turned to her husband and said "Is it all right? Have they . . . ?"

Johann nodded and Magdalena rushed forward to hug first Elisabeth, then Erika and finally Marcus, murmuring as she did so "Oh my dears, my dears. God bless you all."

Elisabeth smiled nervously. When she had met Magdalena on their previous visit, she had taken an instant liking to her, but her obvious relief that they were wearing the chains suggested that she shared her husband's strange beliefs. Once again, Elisabeth felt uneasy.

Johann asked them to sit and, as Magdalena served the coffee, he said "I asked Wilhelm's permission to tell my wife what he had told me. She knows what we have been discussing."

Magdalena cut slabs of cake and handed it round to her guests, then said in a matter of fact tone "My father was one of those who conspired against Hitler. He was betrayed and the Gestapo came for him. They tortured him to death. My mother was left with two small children - I was three, my sister was seven - and nowhere to go because they had boarded up our house. Johann's father and mine had been colleagues at the university and his family took us in and looked after us for the rest of the war. They didn't worry about their own safety, they just did what they believed to be right. Johann was brought up to do the same. He has been fighting evil for many years, but this, I think, will be the greatest challenge."

The phrase struck oddly on Elisabeth's ears and she wondered how an anthropologist could be said to be fighting evil or whether Magdalena was referring to some other, unknown, facet of the professor's life. A shiver ran down her spine although the room was warm, and she clutched her coffee cup, feeling its heat between her hands. She could not, would not allow herself to believe that the professor genuinely thought that black magic was a reality. Those who claimed to have been affected by such things were, she was sure, simply susceptible to suggestion. But there had been something in Johann's voice that had been very convincing. She was beginning to feel very confused, on the one hand wanting to hear no more about the subject, but on the other desiring more information. However, neither the professor nor his wife seemed about to elaborate on Magdalena's statement and Johann, turning to Marcus, asked how long he thought Wilhelm would need to remain in hospital.

"He's ready to leave now. Mentally he's fine and he's more or less recovered from his recent illness. The problem is finding somewhere suitable to send him. We can't just discharge him, because he's got nowhere to go. He might be able to get some very simple sort of manual job but he can't read or write and he has no idea of how to take care of himself. And he still thinks he's living in a cavern . . . he knows nothing about the world except the little that we've been able to teach him."

Johann nodded. "Magdalena and I have had an idea which may solve your problem." He drank some coffee then asked his wife "Will you tell them or shall I?"

"You, my dear."

"Very well. . . We thought that perhaps Wilhelm could come to live here. Our two daughters have left home now, so we've got plenty of room. And Magdalena retired last year so she's at home all day. Before that, she was a teacher and she'd be willing to take Wilhelm on as a pupil. She is very good with young children which, educationally speaking, is what Wilhelm is. She could teach him to read and possibly to write. She could help him to understand more about the world, and she could teach him basic skills such as shopping and cooking so that, eventually, he should be able to look after himself."

"That would be fantastic!" said Marcus. "But are you sure you want to take on such a responsibility? I really don't know how much he's capable of learning - although he does seem to be quite intelligent - but no matter how quickly he learns, he'll still need full time supervision for quite a while."

"Which we'd be happy to provide," said Magdalena, smiling.

Marcus frowned. "There are other problems, too. Obviously, Wilhelm hasn't got any papers so he can't get any benefits from the State and he won't be able to get a job until he knows a bit more, which means we'll need to find some funding to pay for his board and lodging and for your teaching - and I'm not sure how easy that will be. Although, in the last resort, the three of us could probably raise what's needed."

"That won't be necessary," said Magdalena, smiling as Erika and Elisabeth hurried to agree with Marcus. "Wilhelm will be coming here as our guest and if he succeeds in learning something, that will be our reward. Of course, we'll have to wait and see how much he's capable of, but it's quite possible for illiterate adults to learn to read if they're prepared to work at it."

"He's always struck me as being intelligent," said Elisabeth. "When I first met him, he could only speak Middle High German - and with a very limited vocabulary. But since then he's picked up an huge number of words and he now speaks modern colloquial German fairly fluently. And he wants to learn - he's always asking me questions. The problem is that I never seem to be able to answer them satisfactorily because I just don't know where to start - his basic knowledge of the world is so limited."

Magdalena nodded. "Yes, it will certainly be a challenge. But we can take our time. He can stay here as long as is necessary."

Elisabeth sank back into the deep overstuffed armchair and sipped her coffee. She could picture Wilhelm in this environment and she thought he would be happy here. He would have a family again. She was sure Johann and Magdalena would take good care of him. And she had no doubt that he would prove to be a willing student. But would he be able to understand what Magdalena needed to teach him or would the truth about the world in which he was now living be too strange for him to take it in? And if he was able to learn and to absorb and to accept, would it change him? For so long - until that trip to the zoo - she had thought of Wilhelm as a child and it had been, she was sure, that childlike quality which had first endeared him to her. But Wilhelm as a man was a different matter. She tried to imagine Wilhelm worldly wise, sophisticated, educated and didn't like what she pictured. Worldly wisdom and sophistication were epithets she associated with Helmut, and she didn't want Wilhelm to become like

Helmut. And yet, she could surely not begrudge Wilhelm a chance to become independent and to make a life for himself.

"Elisabeth?" She realised that she hadn't been listening to the conversation.

"Sorry, Marcus . . . What did you say?"

"You were miles away."

"I was just thinking about Wilhelm. I think he'll be very happy here."

"We're going to bring him over on Sunday afternoon," said Marcus. "Magdalena would like us to stay on for dinner. Will you be free then?"

"Oh, yes . . . thank you."

"Good," said Magdalena, picking up the coffee pot to refill their cups. "He's bound to feel a little strange at first but it'll be easier for him if you're all here for the first few hours while he's settling in. And I hope you'll feel free to come to visit him at any other time that you'd like to."

Marcus smiled and Elisabeth could see the relief in his face. "I can't thank you enough." he said. "I've been racking my brains over how we were going to discharge him. This is just what he needs - a chance to learn to stand on his own two feet in a supportive environment."

Johann nodded, his face serious. "He'll be safe here," he said.

Chapter Ten

Sitting next to Wilhelm in the back of the car, Elisabeth was worried. Although she liked Magdalena and Johann, although she knew that Wilhelm couldn't stay at the hospital for ever, although she knew that there was no alternative, she still couldn't help wondering whether the move was a good idea. Was it perhaps too soon after the recent . . . upheaval. Would it just exacerbate an insecurity to which she had contributed, if not caused in its entirety? Today, when Elisabeth went in to collect him, Wilhelm had been very subdued. He had said nothing at all since leaving the ward and was now sitting rigid, bolt upright, staring straight ahead. In the front of the car, Marcus and Erika were chatting in low voices. Erika turned in her seat to look back at them and asked "All right, Wilhelm?" He nodded.

"You'll like it there," she continued, smiling reassuringly. Again Wilhelm nodded. On his knees he held a small canvas holdall in which were packed all his possessions - some clothes from the hospital's second-hand store, a toothbrush, toothpaste and a comb - and his lantern. He had refused to allow Marcus to put the bag in the boot, and was clutching it as though it were a lifeline. Elisabeth rested her hand lightly on his arm and he turned towards her, his eyes troubled and afraid.

"They're good people," she said gently. "They'll look after you. And we'll visit you often. . . I promise."

Once again, a nod.

Marcus turned the car into Johann's road and parked. This time, when they rang the bell, both Magdalena and Johann came to the door. Magdalena held out her arms. "My dears, come in, come in. And Wilhelm . . . welcome to our home - to your home now. I so hope that you'll be happy here."

Johann held out his hand. "It's good to see you, Wilhelm."

"Thank you." It was scarcely more than a whisper. As they trooped into the sitting room, Johann said "I'll just show Wilhelm his room. Would you like to come with me, Wilhelm?"

Wilhelm looked round at Elisabeth, his expression anxious.

"May I come too?" she asked.

"Of course," said Johann. "Why not? Is that all right Wilhelm?"

Wilhelm nodded and the three of them climbed the wide staircase to the first floor. The bedroom was bright and airy, spotlessly clean and furnished in pastel shades. There were pictures on the walls and a handmade coverlet was spread over the large bed.

"The bathroom is next door," said Johann, taking Wilhelm to show him. "And this," he said, opening another door, "is where Magdalena and I sleep. If you ever need anything during the night - anything at all - just come and knock on our door. Now I must go and give Magdalena a hand. Come downstairs when you're ready."

Elisabeth helped Wilhelm to unpack his few clothes, putting his shirts on hangers in the wardrobe. The comb and the toothbrush were placed on the basin in the corner of the room. Wilhelm put the lantern on the bedside table then sat down on the edge of the bed, his hands between his knees, his shoulders drooping.

"Wilhelm," said Elisabeth.

He looked up at her, his expression blank.

"You do understand why you've come here, don't you?" she asked.

Wilhelm shook his head. Elisabeth sat down beside him. "But Marcus explained it to you."

"Yes, but . . . you tell me."

It was the voice of a frightened child.

"Of course," Elisabeth said. "Well, you know that the hospital is only for people who are ill or injured, and they have to go home again when they're better."

"Yes."

"And because there are always new people getting ill and being injured, there's no room for anyone to stay in hospital longer than is absolutely necessary. And because you're well now, it's time for you to leave the hospital. . . to make room for someone else who needs to be there."

"Yes."

"But because you didn't have a home to go back to, we had to find one

184

for you. And Johann and Magdalena said they would like to have you come and live with them here."

"Why couldn't I come to your home?"

"My home? Because . . . because that's just not possible."

"Why not?"

For a moment Elisabeth was flummoxed as to how to explain. Then she said "I live by myself and I'm out at work all day. But you need a family who will be able to look after you. And Magdalena is going to teach you all sorts of things that you need to know."

Wilhelm thought for a moment, then said "It will be as though they are my adults."

"Exactly."

"I see."

There was a pause, then Wilhelm said "I loved my adults."

"I know," said Elisabeth softly. "And you'll like living with Johann and Magdalena. I know you've only just met them, but they really do care about you."

"Do you not care about me, Elisabeth?" Wilhelm asked, turning to her. And with a shock she could see desolation in his eyes.

"Oh Wilhelm," her throat tightened as she spoke, "of course I care about you. And I'll come to visit you often. But you can't live with me. My apartment - where I live - is very small."

"My cave was small but four of us lived in it at one time."

"Yes, but things are very different here from the way they were in the mines. You know that. Here everyone has to have his or her own room to sleep in. And I don't have a spare room that you could have to yourself."

"That wouldn't matter."

"It would, Wilhelm. Just trust me."

"But Magdalena and Johann sleep in the same room - he showed me."

"Yes, but they're married . . . they're husband and wife."

Wilhelm just looked at her, saying nothing. Elisabeth had a feeling that she was getting into a situation she couldn't control. Standing up, she said "I think we'd better go downstairs. Magdalena will be getting the evening meal ready."

Still Wilhelm sat looking at her.

"Trust me, Wilhelm," she said. "Please trust me."

Nodding, he got up and together they went downstairs into the sitting room.

✶ ✶ ✶

Once they were all seated around the dining table, enjoying Magdalena's excellent casserole, Elisabeth started to feel better. Wilhelm was looking more relaxed, eating his meal with obvious enjoyment and speaking more readily when he was spoken to. Elisabeth, remembering that there had been a time when he ate everything with his fingers, was pleased to see that he could now manage a knife and fork with considerable dexterity. Throughout the meal, she noticed that Magdalena, sitting on his left hand side, was paying him special attention, ensuring that he had everything he wanted, chatting to him cheerfully. At the end of the meal, when they were drinking their coffee, Magdalena turned to Wilhelm and said "Elisabeth tells me that you ask her a lot of questions - that there are a lot of things about this world of ours that you don't understand."

Wilhelm nodded, a slight look of anxiety on his face.

"It's all right Wilhelm," Magdalena hastened to reassure him, "there's nothing wrong with asking questions. In fact, if you don't understand something, it's the sensible thing to do. Now, while you're here you can ask me as many questions as you like, and I'll do my best to answer them. And what Johann and I have arranged with Marcus is that you're going to stay here for as long as you want to and I'm going to try to teach you the things you need to know. Eventually, when you've learned it all, you may want to move away and have your own home. But that will be for you to decide and, until then, this is your home - for as long as you want."

Wilhelm smiled at her shyly and said "Thank you. It will be good to learn. I have so many questions."

Magdalena patted his hand. "Good," she said. "Now I know that Johann wants to talk to your friends for a little while, so would you like to come and help me wash the dishes? You'll see your friends again before they go home."

Wilhelm nodded. "I will do whatever you tell me to."

When she had led Wilhelm, carrying a tray full of plates, into the kitchen, Marcus said "He seems to be settling in quite well."

"We'll do our very best to make him comfortable," said Johann "and to ensure that he's safe."

Elisabeth felt a little frisson of fear, hearing again that tone in Johann's voice when he spoke of Wilhelm's safety. She shook herself mentally, telling herself that it was ridiculous, that there was no reason why Wilhelm should not be safe.

Johann was looking round at them, studying their faces. After a few moments he said "We're all here because we care about Wilhelm and his people. But we must be very careful. Nothing we talk about here must be repeated - to anyone at all. Not family, not friends, not colleagues . . no one. And, for the time being, it would be better if even Wilhelm didn't know about our suspicions and our investigations. I don't want to frighten him in any way. Let him build up his strength and learn what Magdalena has to teach him before we burden him with anything else."

"So what do you plan to do?" asked Marcus.

"For the time being, nothing. I want Wilhelm to become more settled. And there are things that you, too, need to learn. These days people think very little about good and evil. They acknowledge some deeds as good and others bad, but they pay no attention to the forces of good and evil themselves. And yet those forces are as strong as they have ever been and the struggle between them is undiminished. And in recent times, we have become aware of a growing strength on the dark side."

"We?" asked Marcus.

Johann smiled. "There are others with whom Magdalena and I work," he said. "Others who have sworn to try to keep the powers of evil at bay. For the present, you don't need to know who they are. Just know that they are there."

Elisabeth could hear Magdalena talking to Wilhelm in the kitchen, and the clatter of dishes as they washed up. It all sounded normal, natural - and

187

yet in here Johann was talking about dark forces and good and evil. And, looking at Marcus and Erika, it appeared that they had no qualms in believing what he was telling them. Not for the first time, she wondered what it was she was getting herself into.

Johann stood up and took a bottle of brandy and some glasses from the sideboard. He poured some for each of them. "We will take it slowly," he said. "We will meet from time to time and discuss those things that you need to know. And every Friday, if you're not working, you'll come to dinner and we'll not talk about any of it but will just be a group of friends eating together."

Although it was said with a smile, Elisabeth was aware that it was not an invitation but an order. And looking at him, she knew that she would do as he said, and she would come to his house when he told her to, and she would try to open her mind to his strange ideas. A shiver ran down her spine and she sipped her brandy, feeling its warmth in her throat, taking comfort in its reassuring familiarity.

When Magdalena and Wilhelm returned, Wilhelm was smiling broadly. "I have already learned something new," he said. "I can now wash and dry dishes."

They all laughed and Elisabeth, looking at Johann and his wife, suddenly knew without any doubt that Wilhelm would be happy here.

✳ ✳ ✳

As Elisabeth was looking for a file in the department office, the secretary said to her "Are you looking forward to the conference next week, Dr. Kramer?"

"The conference? That's not until July."

"But it is July, Dr. Kramer."

"What?" Elisabeth turned round, shocked. "I hadn't realised. So the conference is. . ."

"Next week. That's right."

Elisabeth grabbed the file, which she had just found, and rushed out of the door to her own office where she rang the hospital and asked to speak to Marcus. After about five minutes, during which time she became increasingly sure that she had been forgotten, he came to the 'phone.

"Hello? Elisabeth?"

"Marcus . . . thank heaven. Look, I've got to go to a conference next week."

"Yes?"

"And then I'm going on to my cousin's wedding."

"Yes?"

"And I don't know what to do."

"Sorry Elisabeth, I'm not with you."

"About Wilhelm. What do I do about Wilhelm?"

"But he's with the Schultzes now. Why should you have to do anything?"

"Because I'm going to be away for three weeks - a week for the conference and another fortnight at home with my family. He'll think I've deserted him again."

"No he won't." Marcus' voice came down the line strong and reassuring.

"But he did last time."

"Well . . ." Marcus was hesitant. "I hate to say it Elisabeth, but last time you had deserted him."

"But what shall I do? Should I not go, perhaps?"

"No, of course you must go. Just call round and see Wilhelm this evening and explain it to him. He'll understand. You've seen how well he's settled in with Johann and Magdalena. He's much less insecure than he was. If you tell him why you're going to be away and when you'll be back, I'm sure it'll be OK."

Marcus was right, of course, Elisabeth realised as she put down the 'phone. Wilhelm had been in his new home for two weeks now and she had visited him there three times - twice for coffee and once with Erika and Marcus for the Friday evening meal. And on each occasion Wilhelm had seemed just a little more confident than the time before. Picking up the 'phone again, she rang Magdalena and asked if she could drop in.

"Of course my dear." Magdalena was delighted. "You know you're always welcome."

Even so, Elisabeth was conscious of an underlying nervousness as she approached the house that evening. She parked her car, walked to the front door and rang the bell. After a moment or two, the door was opened by Wilhelm who smiled and said "Magdalena told me you were coming. It's good to see you."

Elisabeth followed him into the sitting room where Magdalena was working on a piece of embroidery and listening to a recording of Eine Kleine Nacht Musik. As they entered, she put down her work and smiled.

"Come in, my dear. Johann's had to go to a faculty meeting so it's just the three of us. Make yourself comfortable and I'll go and get some coffee." She heaved herself out of the chair and went out to the kitchen.

Elisabeth, finding herself unwilling to broach the subject of her forthcoming absence until Magdalena had returned, filled in the interval with small talk, asking Wilhelm how he was and what he had been doing.

"Mainly I have been asking questions and Magdalena has been answering them. She knows about many things. And she is very kind."

"Good. I'm very pleased."

"And she has been playing me music by . . ." he paused, trying to remember the name. "By . . . Mozart - is that right?"

Elisabeth nodded. "And do you like it?"

"It was not what I expected. The only music I had heard before, outside the mines, was what was played by the box . . . the radio . . . at the hospital."

Elisabeth smiled. "Yes, I imagine the music there was rather different."

"I didn't like that music much but this is beautiful. I had no idea that music could be beautiful or that there could be such variety."

"Oh, there are all sorts of music," Elisabeth said. "But I'm glad you like Mozart. He's a favourite of mine."

For a few moments they sat and listened to the recording, then Elisabeth asked "And what else have you been doing?"

"Magdalena has been explaining to me about books and reading and writing. It's wonderful - to be able to record your thoughts, to communicate

190

with others without speaking. But I'm finding it difficult to learn."

Elisabeth nodded. "People usually learn to read and write when they're children. It's much harder to do if you're an adult - but I'm sure you can."

"I want to. I keep practising. Magdalena has given me a book of my own . . ."

Wilhelm leaned forward and picked up a small square book that was lying by his chair. At first glance it looked like a child's picture book, but when he handed it to her, Elisabeth could see that it had been written specifically for illiterate adults who were in the first stages of learning to read.

"This is good," she said, flicking through it.

Magdalena came in carrying a tray and, getting up, Wilhelm took it from her and placed it on the coffee table.

"They're excellent, those little books," said Magdalena, seeing it in Elisabeth's hands. "There's a whole series of them, all designed for adults. Wilhelm's getting through that one very quickly. He'll soon be ready for the next one."

She sat down and started to pour coffee. Looking up she said "Wilhelm, dear, I've left the strudel and plates in the kitchen. Would you be kind enough to get them for me? And the forks and napkins?"

"Of course." Wilhelm jumped up again and disappeared out of the room.

"He's settling in so well," said Magdalena, lowering her voice. "Johann and I are very pleased with his progress. And he's such a lovely young man - so gentle and considerate. We're really enjoying having him here. He talks about you a lot."

She handed Elisabeth a cup of coffee and, when Wilhelm returned, a piece of strudel. Taking his coffee and plate from Magdalena's hands, Wilhelm said as he sat down "The first piece of strudel I ever ate was with Elisabeth in the hospital cafe. I thought it was wonderful but it was nothing like this. I haven't yet learned the word to describe how good Magdalena's strudel is!"

191

Elisabeth tasted hers, thought for a moment and said "Superlative."

"Super . . .?"

"Superlative - it means the best."

"Superlative," Wilhelm repeated. "Right."

As she drank her coffee, Elisabeth tried to think of a way to introduce the reason for her visit. But to her great relief Magdalena forestalled her by asking "Are you going away on holiday this summer, Elisabeth?"

Elisabeth looked at Wilhelm. Magdalena went on "I've explained about holidays to Wilhelm, so he knows that one or other of you may be away for a few weeks."

Wilhelm nodded.

With relief, Elisabeth said "I'm going away next week. I've got to go to a conference first and then I'm going to visit my family. I'd have told you earlier but I've been so busy recently that it's rather crept up on me. I'm going to be away for three weeks, I'm afraid. "

Again Wilhelm nodded.

"I'll come and see you as soon as I get back," she continued. "And I don't think Marcus or Erika will be away then, so they'll still be visiting you."

Wilhelm looked at her. "You will come back, won't you Elisabeth?"

"Oh Wilhelm," her voice shook slightly, "of course I will."

The conference was full of new and interesting material delivered by speakers from around the world but Elisabeth was finding it hard to concentrate. Usually at an event of this sort, she would hang on every word, mentally devouring all the information that was presented. But now her thoughts kept going back to Wilhelm, as she remembered the look on his face when he had asked her whether she would return, and his trusting acceptance when she had assured him that she would. Three times during the conference week she 'phoned Magdalena, just to check that Wilhelm was all right. He was still a little nervous of the 'phone but he spoke to her briefly and seemed reassured that she hadn't forgotten him. The paper which she was presenting, on the use of language in mediaeval German poetry, was scheduled for the penultimate day of the conference. Elisabeth felt that she hadn't prepared it as well as she might have done - recently her time had been taken up either with teaching or with Wilhelm and there had been very little left over for her academic work. However, her paper was well received, so she was feeling quite pleased with herself by the time she set off to see her parents.

She would have a whole week at home before the wedding. Her mother was planning a shopping trip for them both to buy new outfits, and there would be relatives to visit and old friends to catch up with. The Kramers still lived in the large house on the outskirts of the town where Elisabeth had grown up. Back in her old room, with its flowered curtains, bright cushions and shelves of books from her childhood, she relaxed and, for the first time in some weeks, slept soundly and well.

"You're looking better this morning." her mother said, as she appeared in the kitchen in her dressing gown on the morning after her arrival. "I thought you seemed very tired last night."

"Oh, the conference was pretty hectic and it's a fairly long drive."

Her mother looked at her, sizing her up. "Hmm. Is that all?"

"What do you mean, all?"

"I wondered if you had something on your mind?"

"No," Elisabeth lied. "I don't know why you should think that."

Her mother smiled. "Because I know you, darling. But never mind, if you don't want to tell me . . ."

"Mother!"

"Eat some breakfast and get dressed, and then we'll go out. We can do a bit of shopping, and then we're meeting your aunt Clara for lunch."

The days passed in a comfortable and relaxed way but Elisabeth was aware that her mother was still looking at her quizzically as if waiting for her to tell her what was on her mind. Remembering Johann's warning, Elisabeth said nothing but, even if the warning had not been given, how could she possibly have told her mother what had been happening, with its background of fairy stories and legends and its implications of black magic?

The day of the wedding arrived, warm and sunny, and Elisabeth looked at her image in the mirror with approval. She had bought a blue dress and a white jacket from one of the smartest - and most expensive - shops in the town, setting the outfit off with a white hat and very high heeled white sandals. Standing next to her parents in the packed church, she watched her cousin, a few years younger than herself, drift up the aisle in clouds of white tulle and was surprised to find herself experiencing a pang of envy. She shrugged it off and tried to concentrate on the service, listening to the familiar words, enjoying the heady scent of the flowers that decorated the church.

Having lived away from home for several years, Elisabeth found herself almost as much an object of interest at the reception as the bride and groom. Aunts, uncles and cousins all wanted to know how she was and what she was doing. And there was the inevitable "Not married yet?" from several older relatives. It had never worried Elisabeth in the past - she had always smiled and said "Not yet, but I'll let you know when it happens." For some reason, today the question was irritating her. She gave her usual reply but felt that they were seeing through her insincere smile. What had changed, she wondered?   Was it because, no longer in her twenties, she was older than the bride? Or was it because she wasn't in a relationship? She didn't know. She drank a glass of champagne and continued to smile when a short dumpy woman, a neighbour and old friend of her aunt's, accosted her with "Elisabeth!   I haven't seen you in a long time.   Not married yet?"

Elisabeth gave her standard reply. The woman snorted.

"I'm pleased my daughter isn't on the shelf!" she said.

Elisabeth forced herself to smile and, turning away, found her mother standing just behind her. As they walked over to the buffet together, her mother said in a quiet voice "The only reason her daughter got married when she was nineteen was because she was pregnant. Ignore her - she's only jealous of your success. However," she picked up a plate and started to help herself to cold meat, "if you are having man trouble I hope you'd feel you could confide in me."

"Oh mother . . ." Elisabeth put her arms round her and hugged her,

194

while her mother exclaimed "Careful darling, I don't want to get food all down my dress - I haven't dared tell your father how much I paid for this outfit!"

Elisabeth laughed and the unpleasant moment was over but she found herself wishing that the cause of her distraction was something as simple as man trouble.

✳ ✳ ✳

Once the wedding was over, Elisabeth found that she was suddenly very anxious to get home. Her parents were disappointed but understanding. "'Phone me tomorrow," said her mother, kissing her goodbye. As she drove away, Elisabeth felt rather guilty. She didn't see her parents very often, and knew they would have loved her to stay longer. She promised herself that she would go back to see them soon. But now she had other things on her mind.

In the past twelve days, since leaving the conference, Elisabeth hadn't spoken to Magdalena, not wanting to feel obliged to offer explanations to her parents about who she was 'phoning or why. They would, she knew, have respected her privacy but would have been curious and it had been easier just to tell Magdalena that she would be incommunicado during that period. Since she spent most of her life within easy reach of a telephone, she had always believed that she didn't need a mobile 'phone. The possibility that she might one day have welcomed the opportunity to make private calls from her parents house had never crossed her mind. As soon as she could, she pulled into a service station and rang Magdalena's number.

At first she thought that there was no one at home but, just as she was about to hang up, Magdalena answered. "Is Wilhelm all right?" asked Elisabeth after the initial greetings had been made.

"He's fine but he's missed talking to you."

"I'm coming back a few days earlier than I'd planned. May I come over and see you tonight?"

"Of course, my dear. We'll expect you for dinner. Marcus and Erika are both coming."

"Thank you. About seven then?"

"Splendid. I'll go and tell Wilhelm. He'll be so pleased."

It was actually a little after seven when Elisabeth arrived, the journey home having taken longer than she expected.

Marcus and Erika were already there and greeted her enthusiastically when she walked into the sitting room. "Where's Wilhelm?" she asked.

"In the kitchen with Magdalena," said Johann, who had opened the front door to her. "They won't be long."

Erika started to ask her about the conference and the wedding, being more interested in the latter than the former. Elisabeth was in the middle of describing the startlingly pink outfit worn by the bridegroom's mother when Wilhelm came in.

"Elisabeth," he smiled at her, "I'm so pleased you're back." And he held out his hand to shake hers. It was the first time he had done that and Elisabeth was slightly startled but, after a second's pause, offered her hand which was taken in a firm, warm grip.

"Dinner is ready," said Wilhelm, leading them into the dining room where Magdalena was waiting to dish up. They sat down to a meal of meatballs in a delicate lemon and caper sauce, served with noodles and a selection of perfectly cooked vegetables.

"This is delicious," said Elisabeth. "I'm pleased I got back in time!"

"Gorgeous," said Marcus. "I've been so busy this week that I've been existing mainly on sandwiches and food from the hospital canteen. This is a real treat."

Magdalena smiled and said "I'm pleased you're enjoying it so much. Wilhelm cooked it."

"What?" Elisabeth was astonished.

"Wilhelm cooked it," repeated Magdalena. "He's turning out to be an extremely good cook."

Wilhelm smiled. "When Magdalena first explained to me about cooking, I could hardly believe what I was hearing. For most of my life I've eaten just three types of food - the foodcakes and the biscuits - nothing else. I had no idea how it was made or what it was made from or who made it. I didn't even know that it was made - it was just brought to us and we ate it. So when I discovered in the hospital that there were different types of food - so many different types - it was . . . something wonderful."

"A revelation," prompted Magdalena.

Again Wilhelm nodded, repeating "A revelation. And then, when Magdalena told me that I could make food, that I could make it taste the way that I wanted it to, when she showed me her books with all the recipes in . . . She's a wonderful teacher. She's teaching me so much."

And, indeed, Elisabeth had noticed a subtle change in Wilhelm. There was an increase in confidence, his conversation flowing more readily and a smile frequently on his face. The nervous puppy was maturing into a handsome dog. And he was handsome, there was no denying it. Tall, muscular and with his hair and beard neatly trimmed, he seemed so much more at ease. It was clear, thought Elisabeth, that the Schultzes were providing him with more than just a home and the education he needed - they were giving him the sense of security which he had never before experienced.

With the coffee came a sumptuous chocolate gateau, also made by Wilhelm. "I've never been able to make a cake that good," said Erika, finishing the last mouthful on her plate.

"Nor me," agreed Elisabeth. "But then they always say that the best cooks are men."

The conversation turned to what men did better than women or women better than men, with much lively discussion and laughter. Elisabeth assumed that, after the meal, Johann would want to speak to Erika, Marcus and herself alone, but he made no move to do so, nor did he ask them to come to see him the following week, except for their individual visits to see Wilhelm.

As they left the house and walked to their cars, Marcus said to Elisabeth "What do you think of our Wilhelm, then? Magdalena's doing a fantastic job."

Elisabeth nodded. "Yes," she said. "He's growing up very fast."

Chapter Eleven

Over the next few weeks, much to Elisabeth's relief, there were no further secret discussions in Johann's study. She still continued to go for dinner on Friday evenings with the others and to call in once or twice a week, sometimes with Erika and Marcus, sometimes on her own, for coffee and a chat. Meanwhile, Wilhelm blossomed. Magdalena, was encouraging his natural flair for drawing and had been introducing him to painting with acrylics and with watercolours.

"Is there no end to your talents?" Erika asked him one evening, when the three of them were visiting. She was looking at a little watercolour sketch he had made of a vase of flowers.

Wilhelm smiled. "Magdalena has been telling me that there are people in this world who are unable to see and others who can't hear - that's how I've been most of my life, except in my case there was nothing to see and nothing to hear. To be able to use colours - to create something with them - and to listen to music - real music - is wonderful."

"We'll have him singing soon," said Johann, who had just come into the sitting room to join them. "Actually," he went on, "we thought we might take Wilhelm to the opera. I think he's ready for it."

"Wonderful idea," said Marcus, enthusiastically. "What were you thinking of seeing?"

"There's a production of *The Magic Flute* starting the week after next and since Wilhelm has already discovered that he likes Mozart, we thought he'd enjoy that."

"Lovely!" said Elisabeth. "Beautiful music, lots of colour and a story so silly that it really doesn't matter if you don't understand what it's meant to be about!"

"We thought you all might like to come with us," said Magdalena, looking up from her embroidery.

"Great!" said Marcus. "I haven't been to the opera since I got back from the States."

Diaries were produced and a date arranged some ten days ahead.

"I'll get the tickets," said Johann. "And we'll meet at the theatre."

✳ ✳ ✳

As Elisabeth dressed for their evening out, she realised that this would be the first opera she had seen since she had broken up with Helmut. It was strange - when that had happened she had been sure she would miss their regular outings to the theatre. But the intervening months had been so busy that she had hardly given it a thought. Now, however, she was looking forward to seeing *The Magic Flute* in the company of her new friends. She hoped Wilhelm would enjoy it.

She dressed carefully. Remembering how hot it could get in the opera house, she would have liked to have worn a low neck, but not wanting to display Johann's chain with its esoteric symbols, she settled on a lightweight black dress, high necked but sleeveless, with a narrow band of silver running diagonally down the front from its left shoulder to its knee-length hemline. Opting for simplicity, she wore no jewellery other than a pair of plain silver drop earrings, and completed her outfit with a bright red jacket in a silky material. Leaving the apartment, she realised to her surprise that she was feeling a little nervous.

The theatre foyer was crowded but, as she went in, she saw Johann and Magdalena waving at her. Wilhelm was nowhere to be seen and for a moment she was worried but then realised that he must be there. The whole object of the outing was to introduce Wilhelm to the opera. If he had been unable, or unwilling to go, the trip would surely have been cancelled. She made her way over to them.

"My dear, you look lovely," said Magdalena. "Erika and Marcus have just gone to get us programmes."

A voice said "Hello, Elisabeth." It was the young man who had been standing on Johann's left . . . it was Wilhelm! Elisabeth gaped, unable to speak, feeling her knees turn to jelly. Wilhelm had shaved off his beard, revealing an attractive mouth and a strong chin. He was dressed in a well-cut dark suit and looked no different from any of the sophisticated young men thronging the foyer, except for the fact that he was better looking than most of them.

"Wilhelm," croaked Elisabeth. "I'm sorry, I didn't recognise you."

Wilhelm laughed. It was a good sound and Elisabeth realised that it was the first time that she had heard it.

"Magdalena persuaded me to shave off my beard. She said it made me look too old."

"Whereas I," said Johann, "am so old that my beard can't make me look any older!" Magdalena tut-tutted and patted his arm.

"And the clothes," said Elisabeth, looking Wilhelm up and down, "they're great."

"Magdalena said I couldn't come to the opera in jeans, so we went shopping."

"He's so much easier to shop with than Johann," said Magdalena. "He didn't get bored and he took my advice!"

Marcus and Erika appeared with programmes and complimented Elisabeth on her appearance.

"Doesn't Wilhelm look great!" said Erika. "I nearly didn't recognise him."

They moved into the auditorium. It was clear that Magdalena had explained in detail to Wilhelm what to expect because he settled into his seat as though he had done it a hundred times before. Throughout the first act his eyes were glued to the stage and as the curtain came down for the interval he turned to Elisabeth, his eyes shining, and said "This is wonderful."

Johann leaned across and said "Shall we try to get a drink?"

They filed out of their seats into the crowd that was moving back into the foyer. Johann had taken their order and gone off to join the queue at the bar when a familiar voice said "Hello, Elisabeth."

Elisabeth turned. It was Helmut. Perfectly groomed and wearing a designer suit, he looked no different from when she had last seen him. Hanging on his arm was a tall flaxen haired woman with long scarlet finger nails.

"Hello Helmut," said Elisabeth, holding out her hand to shake his. "How are you?"

"I'm fine. And you? You're looking well."

"Yes, I am well, thank you."

"This is Eva," he said, indicating the woman on his arm. She nodded at Elisabeth but didn't smile.

"Won't you introduce me to your friends?" asked Helmut.

"Of course. Helmut Krohn . . .Magdalena Schultz . . ."

Helmut took her hand, bowing slightly. "Frau Schultz."

"Erika Frenzel . . ."

"Fraulein."

"Dr. Marcus Hellman . . ."

Helmut gave Marcus a long look then held out his hand saying, with just the suggestion of a sneer in his voice "Herr Doctor."

"And Wilhelm . . . Steiff." What made her say that, she didn't know but it had suddenly seemed very important that Wilhelm should have a surname. Why Steiff had popped into her mind she couldn't imagine. She didn't know anyone with that name and the only connection she could think of was the famous Steiff teddy bears. Perhaps she had been trying to capture the feeling of security she had always associated with teddy bears. Anyway, Helmut didn't seem to have noticed her hesitation. He nodded curtly to Wilhelm but didn't say anything or offer his hand.

At that moment Johann arrived with a tray of drinks and Elisabeth introduced him to Helmut. The two men looked at each other and Elisabeth saw an expression in Johann's eyes that she couldn't quite interpret. She thought for a moment that they must already know each other but she also had the impression of strong dislike on both sides. Both said a polite but cold "Good evening", then Helmut said "We must go and get a drink. Good to see you again Elisabeth . . . and your friends." Again there was that suggestion of a sneer in his voice. He turned away with Eva and Elisabeth took the drink that Johann was offering her. She wondered whether he would mention having met Helmut before but he said nothing and she didn't like to ask.

As she watched the second act of the opera, Elisabeth's mind kept going back to that meeting. Something about it had made her feel very uncomfortable. She supposed that Helmut would have realised who Marcus was - she had talked about him on several occasions before that final row and it seemed likely that Helmut's attitude to him then would explain his behaviour to him tonight. But why had there been that subtle clash with Johann? She was sure she hadn't imagined it. She didn't like mysteries. The thought made her smile, knowing what a mystery she had become wrapped up in. She sighed, leaned back in her seat and let the music sweep over her.

✳ ✳ ✳

The following week, Elisabeth received a 'phone call from Johann, summoning her to a meeting. Once again, just the four of them were closeted in the study. "Is Wilhelm not joining us?" asked Marcus.

"Not yet," Johann replied. "His education is progressing very well but I don't think he's quite ready yet. It shouldn't be long, though."

"It's horrifying," said Marcus, "that a man with such an able mind should have been condemned to illiteracy and slavery. I remember when I first tested his intelligence - I borrowed some puzzles from the clinical psychologist - and I was so pleased when he got them right and did them quickly. And it's such a joy to come here and see his paintings and hear him talk about the music he's been listening to and the things that he's learned from Magdalena."

"It's not been easy for him," said Johann. "You just see the results. You don't see the hours of work that he puts in, the frustration he experiences when he can't grasp something . . . He's so determined. It's quite remarkable. Magdalena and I went over to some friends the other night and when we got back, quite late, we found Wilhelm almost in tears because he'd been trying to read something that had several words he didn't know - and not only could he not work out what they meant but he didn't know how to pronounce them. So there was Magdalena at midnight explaining to Wilhelm how to use a dictionary. And the pleasure on his face - I think he was ready to stay up all night looking at it!"

"We do tend to take our education for granted," said Erika thoughtfully. "There must be millions of people in the world with good brains and little or no access to education. We're so lucky."

"Well I don't think there's any risk of Wilhelm forgetting how fortunate he is," said Johann. "His memories of his enslavement in the mines are all too clear. We had a long talk about it a few days ago and I asked him about the rock the Hundeiss mined. It could have been anything, of course, but the fact that they were kept as slaves suggests that the mining process had to be kept secret. And that, in turn, suggests that what was being mined was something more exotic than coal, say."

He got up and took down a book which had been squeezed onto one of the shelves, lying on top of other books already there. "It occurred to me," he said, settling back into his chair, "that although the light in the mines was very poor, Wilhelm spent eighteen hours a day staring at the rock face and the way it looked would be imprinted on his mind. So I borrowed this book from one of my colleagues who's a geologist." He laughed. "One of the advantages of specialising in something like myths and legends is that no one seems terribly surprised when you start asking questions about subjects that are seemingly unconnected with your own field of study. The book's got some very good colour pictures and I showed it to Wilhelm and asked him if anything looked familiar. He picked out this plate." Johann opened the book to where a bookmark had been inserted, then held it up vertically so that they could all see the picture. To Elisabeth it looked like any dark-coloured rock. "Do you know what that is?" he asked.

They all shook their heads.

"It's kimberlite. Does the name mean anything to you."

Again they shook their heads, then Erika said "Wait a minute - kimberlite - does that have anything to do with the Kimberley mines?"

Johann smiled. "Very good. And the Kimberley mines are famous for . . ."

"Diamonds," said Erika.

"Of course!" said Elisabeth. "But surely there aren't any diamond mines in Germany?"

"There's no record of any mines," said Johann, "But that doesn't mean there aren't any diamonds. I asked my colleague about that. It seems that all the diamonds that we have today were formed millions of years ago, more than a hundred miles below the surface of the earth, and they've gradually worked their way up. So one never knows where they're likely to be found, particularly if one is prepared to go deep enough."

Marcus frowned. "But surely, someone would be aware . . ."

Johann shook his head. "If you look at the history of diamond mining you'll see that until the eighteenth century practically all the world's diamonds came from India. Only after that were deposits found in Brazil. You know about the Kimberley mines, Erika, because they're quite famous but, in fact, none of the South African mines was discovered until the late nineteenth century. And, more recently, deposits have been found in Siberia and in western Canada - deposits that were previously completely unsuspected."

Marcus shook his head. "I had no idea. In that case, it could make sense . . . But, on the other hand, if Wilhelm's masters - 'They' as he calls them - if They were mining and selling diamonds, then people would surely be curious about where they came from. Someone would have latched onto the existence of German diamond mines by now."

"But you're assuming," said Johann, "that they're mining the diamonds to sell, to make themselves rich."

"What other reason could they have?" asked Erika.

"Well," said Johann, "here we start to get into mythology again. Diamonds have always been regarded as having special properties. In ancient times, kings wore them when they went into battle - not only were they a symbol of strength and courage, but they were thought to make the wearer invincible. The Romans believed that they could ward off evil. In the middle ages they were thought to have healing powers, to ward off phantoms, even to cause lawsuits to be judged in the wearer's favour. They protected houses from storms and people against poisoning . . . and alchemists were very interested in them because some of them believed that they were a vital ingredient in the manufacture of the philosopher's stone - even that they were that stone."

"The philosopher's stone?" asked Erika. "As in the Harry Potter book?"

Johann smiled. "Exactly so. The philosopher's stone has found a place in all sorts of fiction, because no one really knows what it is, so it can be adapted to fit all kinds of stories. It's like the Holy Grail - some say that was the cup that Christ drank from at the Last Supper and in which Joseph of Arimathea caught drops of his blood. Others give it a far more esoteric and subtle meaning. Some years ago some English writers decided that it was nothing more nor less than a royal blood line - sang real - the descendants of Jesus Christ. People have speculated on the philosopher's stone in the same way. In its most basic form it was said to be the catalyst that would enable base metal to be turned into gold. But on a more esoteric level it cured disease and conferred on its owner eternal youth. Now that's something that's worth having. Imagine - eternal youth. You could do whatever you wanted, knowing that you had all the time in the world."

"That's all very well but . . ." Elisabeth began.

Johann smiled. "Go on."

"Well, all right, suppose the people who originally set Wilhelm's ancestors to work believed that diamonds held the key to eternal youth. Surely by now they'd have realised that they were wrong - or rather their descendants would have realised it."

"That, of course," said Johann "is assuming that it didn't work."

"What?" Elisabeth was astonished. "Surely you're not suggesting that someone really has found the key to immortality?"

"I'm not suggesting anything. But do you have any proof that they haven't? All I'm asking you - all I have ever asked you - is that you keep an open mind. There are things in this world of which we know nothing. There are forces and powers which in our present state of knowledge are inexplicable, and yet they exist. Scientists propose theories regarding the origins of the universe, the speed of light, even the ability of water to remember what has been dissolved in it - but none of them knows, because then they would no longer be theories but proven facts. What do you think someone living in the middle ages would have made of electricity? or radio? or microwaves? He would probably have called them magic because that would have been the only way in which he could have understood

205

them. But that wouldn't mean that they didn't exist - we know that they do - only that he didn't understand them. And are we really arrogant enough to claim that we have discovered everything, know everything about everything? that there is nothing that we don't understand?"

He looked over at Elisabeth who shook her head.

"No," she said hesitantly, "if you put it like that, no, of course there must be things we haven't discovered yet. It's just that . . ."

"The terminology troubles you," Johann finished for her. "Don't worry - you're in good company. Many highly educated people have the same problem. For example, a lot of Western doctors have, in the past, dismissed acupuncture out of hand because they have taken its terminology literally. I was pleased to learn that you weren't among them, Marcus."

Marcus smiled. "No, but I can sympathise with their difficulties." He turned to face Elisabeth. "Acupuncturists," he went on, "believe that disease is due to a disruption of the vital force of the body, which they call Qi. Thousands of years ago, when the theory of acupuncture was first developed, it was said that one of the ways in which Qi could be disrupted was if the patient's body was invaded by certain environmental conditions, such as heat or dryness or damp. Of course, nowadays, acupuncturists don't believe that's literally true, but they still use the same terminology, and, naturally, that gives orthodox physicians the perfect opportunity to shout 'rubbish' at the tops of their voices."

"Exactly," said Johann. "The acupuncturists continue to use these terms because they're a useful template - a shorthand, if you like - on which to base diagnosis and treatment. But the sceptics never investigate far enough to find that out. We can get into all kinds of trouble if we just look at the words and fail to understand the context. Remember that words are of our own making. You're a linguist, Elisabeth - I don't have to tell you this. Words have developed over the centuries to describe the things that we do and the things that we know. The reason we don't have the right words to describe the things we haven't yet discovered or understood is precisely that - it's because we haven't yet discovered them or we don't yet understand them."

206

Elisabeth nodded. "You make it sound so plausible."

"But I don't want you to believe it just because I say so," said Johann. "All I ask is that you don't dismiss anything out of hand unless you have actual proof that it's wrong."

"I'll try."

"What we've got to remember," Johann continued, "is that, assuming we're right in believing that the Hundeiss are mining diamonds, those diamonds are being mined for a purpose. If the purpose isn't wealth, then it must be power. And in this country we're all too aware of where a quest for power can lead and how dangerous it can be. It's true, of course, that many people seek power because they think they can do good - they stand for office in elections and they seek to represent the people who vote for them. They're inspired by a vision of how the world can be made into a better place. But there are others who seek power simply for their own ends, because they want to control their fellow men, and they'll use any means that they can find to achieve those ends."

"Such as war," said Marcus.

"Such as war," agreed Johann. "And other things that many might consider worse. Did you know that many of the men who surrounded Hitler were involved in the occult? They formed lodges which were the antithesis of the Freemasonry lodges - that's one reason why they persecuted Freemasons. And Hitler was obsessed with the power of religious artefacts, which he believed he could annexe to his own ends."

"Oh, no . . ." pleaded Elisabeth.

"No?" asked Johann.

"We're back in fiction again. There was an American film - I saw it some years back - about a Nazi quest for the Ark of the Covenant. It was great fun, but surely . . ."

"No, that was indeed fiction," Johann reassured her. "although I agree with you that it was a most entertaining film. But as far as I know, the Ark wasn't one of the artefacts that Hitler sought. However, he was fascinated by the Grail legend which, of course, had interested Wagner as well." Johann paused, then turned to Elisabeth. "I know you're something of an authority on mediaeval German poetry, Elisabeth. So no doubt you know the poem on which Wagner based his Parsifal."

"Very well indeed," said Elisabeth. "It's by Wolfram von Eschenbach."

"Can you remember how von Eschenbach describes the Grail?"

Elisabeth thought. "Yes . . . there's a section in which he describes it as a stone which confers health and eternal youth. Oh, yes, I see the link with the philosopher's stone. But that's just the retelling of a legend. It's not factual."

"Perhaps. How do we know? What we do know is that it's a legend of great power. Even though Hitler hadn't seen the Grail, he believed that he could turn its power to his own use. Even more so did he believe that he could use the spear of Longinus."

"The spear of Longinus?" said Elisabeth. "As in the Spear of Destiny?"

"As in the Spear of Destiny." Johann nodded.

"What is it?" asked Erika.

"It's said to be the spear that was used to pierce Christ's side when he was hanging on the cross," said Elisabeth. She looked across at Johann. "Sorry, Johann . . . may I?"

"Of course. It comes within your field of expertise."

"Well . . . only just. But . . ." She turned back to Erika. "It belonged to Longinus, who was a centurion, and legend has it that he later became a Christian and was martyred. I think he became a minor Saint. Anyway, over the centuries, it became incorporated into the Grail legend and, by the time Wagner wrote Parsifal, the spear that von Eschenbach writes about in his version had become the spear of Longinus. But it's only a legend."

Johann said gently "Never use the word 'only' when describing a legend, Elisabeth. It could come back to haunt you."

Elisabeth smiled.

"There are two other important facts about the spear," Johann went on. "The first is that it is said to be capable of pure good and of pure evil. The second is that the person who owns the spear can rule the world. Legend says that it was used by the Saxon King Heinrich when he defeated the Magyars, and by Otto the Great in his victory over the Mongols at the Battle of Leck, even by Constantine at the Milvian Bridge. So it's little wonder that Hitler hungered for it when he saw it."

"Saw it?" asked Elisabeth, disbelief strong in her voice.

"In the Hofsburg Treasure House. A little spearhead, broken and held together by gold thread. Whether it's the genuine article or not, who knows? But the idea of all that power . . . It's said that Hitler was obsessed by the spear. Did you know that he and Himmler were planning to build a new city at Wewelsburg where Himmler had his stronghold? It would have been the centre of their new religion, based on a mixture of Aryan mythology and the occult. The hall of the castle at Wewelsburg was converted into a huge Arthurian dining hall, with a round table and coats of arms for each of Himmler's lieutenants. And the ground plan of the city was to be in the shape of the head of a spear pointing towards the north."

"This is all fascinating, Johann," said Marcus, "but is it leading anywhere? I'm afraid I'm getting rather confused."

Johann nodded. "I'm sorry. But these are things you need to know. I don't know what we may have to face in the future and you need to be able to understand the workings of the minds of those whom we are up against. Remember, we really don't know anything about them, except that they are probably more powerful than we could possibly imagine. They must have a base somewhere in this area but whether we can locate it from the little we know is anybody's guess. We've all listened to Wilhelm's story. We must try to think whether there's any vital information in it that we've missed. Anything that might give us a clue as to the location of the mines or the location of the control? You're good at making connections, Marcus. That piece of deduction you did over the Rattenfaenger was quite impressive."

"Yes." Marcus smiled ruefully. "Particularly as it was partly based on a false premise."

Johann looked puzzled. "What was that?"

"Well, you remember that I linked the red and yellow of the clothes that the Hundeiss are given and the food that they eat with the red and yellow of the Rattenfaenger's costume . . ."

"Ah!" Johann's eyes lit up. "I think I see what you're getting at. The traditional Rattenfaenger, so to speak, has a multicoloured costume. It's variations of the story that say he wore a hunting outfit which, of course, could be red and yellow. I wonder if that might lead us anywhere?"

"Well, actually, I wasn't thinking of a hunting outfit. The reason I linked the colours with the Rattenfaenger was because I remembered Robert Browning's poem The Pied Piper. He describes the costume as being red and yellow - but it occurred to me afterwards that he probably did that just to get it to rhyme with the word he uses for a man - 'fellow'."

"It could be, of course, but - correct me if I'm wrong Elisabeth - English has an enormous vocabulary, more than many other languages. It would seem that, for a word as common as 'man' there must be a good number of homonyms so Browning could easily have described a multicoloured garment and still found a rhyme if he'd wanted to."

Elisabeth nodded. "I should have thought so."

"Which suggests," said Johann, "that Browning had actually heard a version of the story in which the Rattenfaenger wore red and yellow. Interesting."

"But it doesn't get us any further, does it?" asked Erika.

"I'm not sure," mused Johann. "It all depends on where Browning got his information from in the first place." He looked around his crowded bookshelves. "No . . . I don't think I've got anything . . . just a moment . . ." And he got up and left the room, returning a minute or so later with a large volume in his hands. Sitting down again, he began to leaf through it. "This should help us. It's a reference work of Magdalena's - about English literature and writers. . . Ah, yes, here we are - Robert Browning . . . born 1812 . . . father worked at the Bank of England . . oh. Oh, that's a pity. It seems that his maternal grandparents were German. He probably heard the story from his mother."

"Where did she come from?" asked Marcus.

"It seems she was born in Scotland, so that doesn't help. It doesn't say where her parents came from."

He passed the book, still open at the Browning entry, to Marcus who scanned the page.

"Hang on a minute," said Marcus. "According to this he had his first poem published when he was twenty one, in 1833. But The Pied Piper wasn't written until 1844. If it had been something he'd heard in his childhood, why wait till he'd been writing for eleven years before using what is, let's face it, a highly entertaining story? Maybe he didn't hear it from his mother. Maybe he heard it somewhere in Germany . . . perhaps he visited relatives . . ."

"Does it say that he went to Germany?" asked Johann, leaning forward towards Marcus and the book.

"No . . . no. He made two trips to Italy in 1838 and 1844, but not to Germany."

"But he might well have passed through Germany," said Johann, a note of excitement in his voice. "Remember this was the early nineteenth century. You travelled by road in those days - no aeroplanes or long distance trains. So he might well have made a detour through Germany - as you say, to visit relatives - on his way."

Johann sat back in his chair, smiling broadly. "Well done, Marcus. Well done. If we can track down where Browning went, find out whether the local legend had the Rattenfaenger in red and yellow . . . and if it turns out to be somewhere near here . . . .it may be just the lead we're looking for." He looked round at them all and nodded. "Enough for one evening. Let's go and have some coffee."

✳ ✳ ✳

When Elisabeth arrived at Johann's for dinner on Friday night, she had the impression that Magdalena was anxious about something. Johann, on the other hand, seemed to be strangely elated, his eyes sparkling as he talked. But nothing he said gave any suggestion as to the reason. However, when they had finished eating and Magdalena had served coffee, Johann turned to Marcus and said "I've been doing some more research into Robert Browning. I consulted one of my colleagues who's a specialist in English literature and he told me that, although the Pied Piper poem wasn't published until 1844, Browning had finished it by 1842, only four years after his trip to Italy."

"Did your colleague know anything about that trip, about where he went?" asked Marcus.

"Yes, it seems that he went by ship, directly to Trieste."

"Oh . . ." Marcus was clearly disappointed.

"But," Johann continued, "he came back overland, from Verona, by way of Salzburg . . and Germany."

"Fantastic!" Marcus sat upright in his chair, his eyes bright with interest.

"It gets better," said Johann. "I discovered that Browning's grandfather - his mother's father - came from Hamburg. Now, that's - what? a hundred and fifty - certainly less than two hundred kilometres from Hameln. Which adds strength to your theory that Browning spent some time at least in the vicinity of Hameln and heard the story then. And then my colleague told me that there's a man in America who collects handwritten documents and who has in his possession a number of letters that Browning wrote to his father during that trip. I've been in contact with him and, although he won't allow the letters to be photocopied, he's said that if I'm prepared to go over to the States, I can study them there. So I'm off to California next week."

So that, thought Elisabeth, was the reason for his high spirits.

"I'm trying to persuade Magdalena to go with me," continued Johann. "She's got a sister in California - married to an American - who she hasn't seen for about five years. It seems a perfect opportunity."

"I don't really want to leave Wilhelm," said Magdalena. And that, thought Elisabeth, explained her anxiety.

"I've told Magdalena that I can manage by myself," said Wilhelm. "I know how to cook and to shop and to use the telephone. I even know how to use the washing machine."

"I think it would be good for Wilhelm," said Johann. "After all, one of the reasons for him coming here was so he could learn to fend for himself."

"I agree with you," said Marcus. "It's all part of the rehabilitation process. It'll be a good experience for him - and we'll all be around to make sure that nothing goes wrong."

Erika nodded. "Marcus is right, Magdalena. And one of us could come over every evening if it would make you feel happier."

"Well, I don't know . . . "

"Go, Magdalena," said Wilhelm. "It's a wonderful thing to have a sister and you should see her when you get the chance."

"That's settled," said Johann. "After all, we'll only be away for ten days. Wilhelm will be perfectly safe. Marcus and Erika and Elisabeth will see to that."

✶ ✶ ✶

"Elisabeth! How good to see you." Wilhelm smiled broadly and stood back from the open front door to allow her to enter.

"How are you getting on, Wilhelm?" she asked, as he led her into the sitting room. Magdalena and Johann had been gone for three days.

"Fine. Magdalena's 'phoned every night to make sure I'm all right - yesterday she rang while Marcus and Erika were here, so Marcus was able to persuade her that the house wasn't falling down and I wasn't starving and she didn't need to catch the first 'plane home! . . . Please, sit down."

He gestured to the settee and Elisabeth sat down at one end.

"Would you like some coffee?"

"That would be lovely. . . Would you like me to make it?"

"Elisabeth!" Wilhelm's smile was slightly reproachful. "I make very good coffee. . . I won't be long."

Elisabeth leaned back against the cushions. Some music was playing softly in the background and, after a few moments, she recognised it as the Bruch violin concerto, a piece of haunting beauty which was a favourite of her father's. She closed her eyes, opening them again when Wilhelm returned with the coffee pot, cups and milk jug neatly arranged on a tray. She allowed him to pour, then took her cup and tasted it.

"You're right, Wilhelm - you do make very good coffee."

Wilhelm settled himself at the far end of the settee and smiled at her. "Thank you for coming in."

"I wanted to make sure you were all right."

213

"I'm having no trouble at all looking after myself, but I do miss the company of Johann and Magdalena."

"You're fond of them."

"As though they were my own adults . . . parents."

Elisabeth nodded. "And what have you been doing while they've been away?"

"I've done some painting. And I've been out for walks. There's a little museum a few streets away and I've been there. And I've listened to a lot of music."

"It's wonderful that you can enjoy music so much after the music in the mines."

"Oh, that was so different. There was no beauty in it. It was . . .I don't know, even now with all these new words that I've learned, even now I can't describe it. We called it music but it wasn't really. It was . . . sound. That's all. Just sound. Whereas this . . . isn't it beautiful."

Elisabeth nodded and for a while they listened in silence. When the recording had finished, Elisabeth put down her coffee cup and sighed. "Lovely, lovely, lovely!" She caught sight of some books on the floor near Wilhelm's feet. "You've been reading too," she said.

"Magdalena left me a pile of books," Wilhelm smiled. "And a dictionary so that I could look up all the words I don't understand." He pulled a face. "There are still a lot of those!"

"But you're enjoying reading now, aren't you?"

"More than anything. Although it's still hard work sometimes. But I had no idea there was so much . . . And today - oh, today, Elisabeth, I found something wonderful. May I read it to you?"

"Of course."

Wilhelm bent and removed a small red cloth-bound book from the pile. He turned to Elisabeth, his eyes shining. "To be able to read is wonderful, but to find a poem - and about a bird - in my own language is beyond anything."

He opened the book and began to read:

214

"Ich zoch mire einen valken mere danne ein jar   do   ich   in
gezamete als ich in wolte han . . ."

Elisabeth sat spellbound, as Wilhelm spoke the words she knew so
well, Kurenberger's Falkenlied - the song of the falcon. A simple verse with
a deeper meaning, which Wilhelm, in his innocence, had failed to
appreciate - it was the thoughts of a woman whose lover, nurtured by her
for over a year, had flown to a new mistress. The lover was seen as a falcon,
flying high in the sky, with silken jesses on its feet and red-gold feathers.
The verse ended with the simple line "Got sende si zesamene die gerne
gelip wellen sin! - May God bring those together who want each other's
love!"

When Wilhelm reached the end, he looked up and smiled. "Isn't it
beautiful?"

Elisabeth felt tears in her eyes. This was a man who only months ago
couldn't even read his own name, and now he was reading poetry.
Impulsively, she leaned across and kissed him on the mouth.

To her chagrin, there was no response at all. Mortified she pulled
away, feeling herself blushing.

"I'm sorry, Wilhelm . . . forgive me." She turned her head away, unable
to look at him.

"What . . . why did you do that?"

"What?" she snapped, still too embarrassed to speak normally.

"Why did you do that?"

"What do you mean?" She didn't understand why Wilhelm was
making such a big thing of a kiss. It wasn't as though she had tried to
seduce him.

"Why did you do that?" Wilhelm asked again.

"Oh for heaven's sake, Wilhelm! I've said I'm sorry - I just did it on
impulse because I love the Falkenlied and I thought you read it so
beautifully. But I'm sorry. I won't do it again. I don't know what you're
making such a fuss about - it was only a kiss."

"A kiss! Oh . . ." She could hear the surprise in his voice. "I've seen
Johann kiss Magdalena - when he goes to work and when he comes home -

but it's not like that. And I thought it was just a way of saying goodbye or hello."

"Well, no. It can be, but it's also an expression of affection. But surely, Wilhelm, you and Lotte . . . you must have kissed."

"No."

"Not even when you . . ." She stopped, embarrassed.

"When we what?"

Elisabeth looked at Wilhelm, frowning, suddenly suspicious that he might be teasing her, but he looked perfectly serious and a little perplexed.

"When you made love," she said.

"I'm sorry, I don't . . ."

"Oh, for heaven's sake, Wilhelm, when you made love, when you had sex . . . you did have a physical relationship, I assume."

"Yes, of course."

"And you didn't kiss?"

"No. Sometimes we would just hold each other, but often Lotte would massage my shoulders and back to ease the pain and I would rub her legs to stop the cramp."

"Yes, but not while you were making love." Elisabeth's embarrassment was turning into exasperation.

"I don't understand what you mean."

"While you were making love, having sex, enjoying your physical relationship - you didn't just massage each other then."

"Yes . . . but we called it rubbing the muscles, not making love . . . you call it massage."

They sat staring at each other, Elisabeth seeing her own confusion reflected in Wilhelm's face. Why was Wilhelm being so obtuse? He must realise what she was talking about . . . Suddenly the truth hit her, a truth that she didn't want to know.

"Wilhelm," she asked tentatively, "when you and Lotte held each other and massaged each other - was that all the physical contact you had?"

"Yes. . . We didn't know about kisses. We just eased each other's pain."

So that was why Wilhelm hadn't understood when she had asked whether the women had to carry on working when they were pregnant. That was why the children were brought by the Carriers. The music which dulled their minds must also have affected their bodies, denying them even that most basic source of pleasure. Elisabeth felt sick and her mouth was dry.

"Oh Wilhelm," she whispered, "I'm so sorry."

"Why?"

She smiled at him weakly as she wondered how she could explain.

Taking a deep breath, she said "Here, in this world, there is more to a physical relationship than just holding or massaging. There's kissing and there's . . . well, there's more." Her face felt hot with embarrassment.

"Will you teach me, Elisabeth? Will you teach me to kiss?"

"Oh, Wilhelm . . ." Again she leaned across and kissed him gently. This time there was a timid response.

"Is that right?" he asked.

Elisabeth smiled. "There's no right or wrong way," she said. "Kissing should just come naturally - and be enjoyed." She lifted her hand to his face and stroked his cheek, thinking how good looking he was, particularly now that he had shaved off his beard. In a wave of overpowering sensation, she knew that she wanted him. She slid her hand round to the back of his neck and gently pulled him towards her. Their next kiss was more intense and Elisabeth's tongue probed into his mouth, playing the male role as her passion mounted.

Suddenly Wilhelm pulled away and, looking down at himself said in a worried tone "Something has happened."

Elisabeth followed his gaze to the bulge now pushing forward the front of his jeans and had a terrible desire to laugh. Controlling it, she said "Oh, Wilhelm, have you never . . . "

Wilhelm nodded, his face serious, as he said "It started happening a few weeks ago . . . sometimes in the morning when I wake . . . I don't know why."

Elisabeth laid her hand gently on the bulge, and said softly "It's perfectly normal."

"But why?"

For a moment Elisabeth looked at him then she stood up and held out her hand. "Come with me and I'll show you," she said.

In silence, she led Wilhelm up to his bedroom. She shut the door, turned on the bedside lamp which cast a soft pink light around the room, drew the curtains, then turned to face him. Putting her arms around his neck, she kissed him again. She felt his arms go round her and she sighed gently. She ran her hands through his hair, then started softly to stroke his neck. The top of his shirt was open and she kissed the V of flesh that it revealed, noticing that he, too, was wearing one of Johann's chains with its tiny amulets.

Then, slowly, she began to undo his shirt buttons, following each action with a kiss to the part that she had exposed. When it was completely undone, she unbuttoned the cuffs, pulled the shirt back from his shoulders and dropped it on the floor. She hadn't realised what a wonderful physique he had, powerfully muscled, perfectly proportioned. Her hands went to his belt and with shaking fingers she undid its buckle and the button on his waist band and then unzipped his jeans.

Bending slightly, she lowered her head and trailed her tongue up his bare chest, from his navel to his neck, then returned to his mouth for another kiss. Wilhelm was breathing fast, with little gasps as she aroused him still further, and she was aware of her own heart pounding and the rapid rise and fall of her chest. She slid her hands inside his underpants and pushed them and his jeans down to his ankles, lowering herself onto the floor as she did so, then helping him to step out of them and his socks and canvas shoes. Raising herself to her knees, she put out her tongue and gently licked the tip of his erection and was rewarded by a moan from deep in Wilhelm's throat.

"Pull back the covers and lie down on the bed, Wilhelm," she said, her voice croaking strangely.

He did so and she stood up and walked over to where he could see her clearly. Then slowly and carefully she took off her own clothes, climbed onto the bed and straddled him.

Wilhelm looked up at her in wonder and raised his hands to stroke her breasts. Elisabeth ran the fingers of her right hand lightly down his chest and abdomen then, raising herself slightly on her knees she guided him into her. Wilhelm gasped, his eyes widening. Elisabeth started to move slowly, keeping her eyes on his face. His hands were moving everywhere now, over her breasts, her back, her buttocks and thighs. For a short time she continued to move then, grasping him firmly between her thighs, she leaned forward on top of him and rolled them both over until she was lying on her back. Looking up at him, she whispered "Now it's your turn."

Wilhelm began to move, tentatively at first, then with a power and a strength and a passion that threatened to overwhelm her, but at the same time with such tenderness and concern for her well being that she wanted to cry. She, who had had a succession of sophisticated and practised lovers, had never known that it could be like this. As they climaxed together, she was aware of sensations she had never felt before. She was pouring with sweat, exhausted, sated . . . happy. Wilhelm collapsed on top of her, then with a slightly worried look asked "Is that . . .?"

"Yes, Wilhelm," she laughed, gasping to get enough air into her lungs, "that's meant to happen."

For a while they lay still, then Wilhelm rolled onto his back and sat up slightly. Looking down at himself he said "Oh, and it . . ."

Elisabeth smiled. "Yes. But it'll come up again - in similar circumstances." She pulled herself up to sit beside him, dragging the pillows up behind their backs.

Wilhelm smiled at her. "That was . . . I don't know that I can find the words. Are there words to describe it?"

Elisabeth shook her head. "I don't think so. Not when it's that good."

"And you, Elisabeth, did you also . . . was it as good for you as it was for me?"

Elisabeth tried not to laugh. It was, she thought, the first time that a man had asked her "How was it for you" not because he wanted to be congratulated on his performance but because he genuinely wanted to know that she had enjoyed it.

"It was wonderful," she assured him, kissing him gently on his neck.

Wilhelm looked thoughtful. "Is it always like that?" he asked.

For a moment Elisabeth hesitated, then said "Yes, I think it can be - with someone you love." As she said the word, she wondered how she had managed to conceal her love for Wilhelm from herself for such a long time. It seemed so obvious to her now.

"And can every woman . . . have such pleasure . . . with the man she loves?"

"I don't know. But I think it's likely."

Wilhelm sat looking at her for a few seconds then, to her horror, his face crumpled like that of a small child and he wailed "Oh, no. Oh, my Lotte. My poor, poor Lotte."

Long into the night Elisabeth sat holding Wilhelm as he sobbed, soothing him gently with her hands, while her tears ran silently down her cheeks and into his hair.

✶ ✶ ✶

It had been dawn before Elisabeth had at last fallen asleep and it was late in the morning when she woke. For a fleeting second she didn't know where she was, and then memories of the previous night came rushing back. She turned, but Wilhelm wasn't there. Slowly she sat up, her eyes feeling sore and puffy, her head aching. There was a bath towel on the rail by the basin. Getting out of bed, she picked it up and wrapped it round her. Having retrieved her discarded clothes, she went into the bathroom, had a hot shower and dressed, then returned to Wilhelm's room, where she cleaned her teeth using her finger and some borrowed toothpaste, and tidied her hair with his comb. The face that gazed back at her from the mirror was pale, devoid of makeup, the eyes red-rimmed. She looked, she thought, as bad as she felt.

She wondered whether she should make the bed and decided that Wilhelm would probably want to change the sheets, so she left it and went downstairs. He was in the kitchen, preparing breakfast.

"I heard you moving about," he said as she entered. "The coffee's ready and there's orange juice if you'd like some."

"Just coffee, thank you," said Elisabeth, sitting down at the table. She watched him as he moved around the kitchen, getting out cups, putting rolls and butter, cheese and sliced ham on the table in front of her. When he sat down, she didn't know what to say. There was really only one thing she wanted to say and she no longer knew whether it was appropriate. She sipped coffee, saying nothing.

"Elisabeth," Wilhelm began, breaking open a roll, "there's something I need to explain to you."

"Yes," she said, trying to smile.

Wilhelm looked down at the crumbs he was making on his plate, then raised his head and looked her full in the eyes. "Lotte," he said.

"Yes."

"She was my woman for . . ." he paused to work it out, "for ten years."

Elisabeth nodded.

"I loved her very much."

Elisabeth went cold. Suddenly, she couldn't look at Wilhelm. She lowered her head, her restless fingers playing with the napkin lying next to her plate.

"Elisabeth?"

What did he want her to say? For God's sake, all she wanted to say was that she loved him. And that wasn't what he wanted to hear.

"Yes, Wilhelm." She forced herself to look at him again and tried to smile. He mustn't know.

"When she was Taken - when she was killed, I was desolate, empty. Life never had very much meaning in that place, but without her . . ."

Again Elisabeth nodded.

"In the place that I come from, when a man and a woman pair, that's it. When one of them dies or is Taken, the other continues alone. There is no second chance. There is no time. Life is too short. My Lotte spent her life in hard work and pain. She was perhaps twenty five years old when she died. The only pleasure we had was in each other. And the pleasure that I gave you last night - she died, never knowing that. All I had to offer her was my love."

221

Elisabeth fought back the tears, saying nothing.

"Lotte was a good woman," Wilhelm continued. "A warm and loving woman. She wouldn't want me to grieve for ever. I shall never forget her and I shall never stop loving her memory." Suddenly he reached out and took Elisabeth's hand. "But here," he said, "It's different. Here life is good and long. And here I've met you and . . . Elisabeth, I love you."

Elisabeth gasped and stared at him, shaking with relief.

"Elisabeth?"

"Oh, Wilhelm . . ." Unable to contain her emotions any longer, she started to cry.

Hurriedly Wilhelm got up and came to kneel beside her chair, still holding her hand.

"Elisabeth, what's the matter. Have I said something wrong? I'm sorry . . . I didn't know."

Now she was laughing through her tears. "Oh, no, nothing wrong. Oh my darling, darling Wilhelm. I love you too . . . I love you so much."

Standing up, he pulled her to him and they embraced, holding each other close, murmuring words of love, while the coffee grew cold.

Chapter Twelve

Wilhelm awoke to find Elisabeth leaning over him, kissing him gently.

"Darling, I must go. I've got to be at a meeting in three quarters of an hour."

Wilhelm smiled at her, sleepily.

"I'll see you tonight." Her voice was soft, close to his ear.

Wilhelm nodded. "I love you," he said.

"I love you too. I must rush, though. I'll see you this evening." She kissed him once more and was gone.

Wilhelm lay back, listening to her footsteps on the stairs and the sound of the front door shutting, and started to think about the day ahead. He was looking forward to seeing Johann and Magdalena again but his pleasure was tempered by the knowledge that, once they had returned, Elisabeth would no longer be able to spend the night with him in their house.

Things in this world, he reflected, were so different from the ways that he was used to. When a Hundeiss man chose his woman and she moved into his cave, it was understood that they would stay together until one of them died or was Taken. After that first extraordinary night with Elisabeth, he had hoped that it meant that she was now his woman, that they would stay together for the rest of their lives. But he seemed to remember her telling him, a long time ago when he was still in the hospital, that in this world there was a ceremony that people went through if they wanted to stay together. He hadn't understood at the time, hadn't taken it in. And now he didn't like to ask her about it in case it was the wrong thing to do. Magdalena had a phrase - "walking on eggshells". Wilhelm smiled to himself, ruefully. Despite all that Magdalena had taught him in the past few months, there were so many things he still had to learn. But, for some reason he didn't quite understand, he didn't really want to talk to Magdalena about his relationship with Elisabeth. Perhaps he could ask Johann.

He closed his eyes and thought about Elisabeth, picturing her beautiful body, remembering the smell and the feel of her, missing her already. Turning, he looked at the clock which Magdalena had given him. Reading the time had been one of the first things she had taught him to do. He had been aware of the clocks in the hospital but had never understood what they were for. There, when it was time to wake up, the nurse would wake him. When it was time to eat, food was brought. When it was time to go to the art room, he would see the other patients going and would go with them.

The bedside clock said 8.30. Time to get up. Magdalena and Johann would be home at about midday, probably tired after their long journey. Magdalena had shown him on the globe where it was they were going. Wilhelm was still having difficulty accepting that he was now living on the outside of this huge world, that he wasn't surrounded by the safety of walls and roof. At times he felt very exposed.

Having showered and dressed, Wilhelm made his way downstairs and had a quick breakfast. Magdalena always put the radio on when she was having breakfast but he hadn't touched the set since she'd left. He didn't really like the radio - the way the voices seemed to come from nowhere reminded him of the music in the mines and, if the voices were talking about something that he didn't understand, it worried him.

He washed up carefully and tidied the kitchen, wanting everything to be perfect for Magdalena and Johann's return. He was pleased Elisabeth was coming back tonight, even if she wasn't going to stay. He missed her when she wasn't there and, remembering how he had lost Lotte, he couldn't help worrying about her safety. He knew it was foolish, that everything was different here, but he worried nonetheless.

He hadn't told Elisabeth that he worried about her. He didn't want to say the wrong thing, to risk upsetting her or alienating her in any way. She had left him once - why, he didn't know, but he supposed it must have been because of something that he had said or done - and she had come back. But he knew that if she left again, that would be the end. He had no desire to live, even in this beautiful world, without her.

Sometimes Wilhelm thought about the people that he had known in the mines - the men who had worked with him, and the children, Marthe and Konrad, whom he and Lotte had reared - and he wondered whether they were still alive and whether any of them had found the hole into the cavern through which he had escaped. And sometimes he was overwhelmed with a great sadness that they were still there and that he was unable to free them, and he felt that perhaps he shouldn't be here, having a life of pleasure, when they were still in the mines. He knew that there was nothing he could do by himself but it occurred to him that Johann might know how they could be rescued. This was something else he would like to talk to him about. Meanwhile, there were other things that he must do.

When he was sure that everything in the house was the way that Magdalena would like it, and that he had left nothing undone, Wilhelm allowed himself to sit down with a book. He was working his way through Magdalena's large library, reading everything, understanding some of it, loving all of it. The poetry, in particular, delighted him and he found that much of it stayed in his memory and he could repeat lines that had appealed to him. It had been an additional joy to find that poetry - and especially poetry written in his own language - was also something that Elisabeth loved. Over the past few evenings, they had read a lot of poetry together, until desire had overtaken them and they had retired to bed, leaving the books still open on the floor.

It was just after midday when Wilhelm heard the sound of a key in the front door. Jumping up, he went out into the hallway to find Magdalena coming into the house with Johann following her, carrying two large suitcases.

"Wilhelm!" Magdalena hurried forward and took his hands, holding him at arms' length to look at him. "You're looking well. Have you coped by yourself?"

Wilhelm reassured her and, having shaken hands with Johann, said "I've prepared lunch."

"Wonderful," said Johann. "All this travelling makes me hungry."

While they ate, Magdalena and Johann told Wilhelm about their journey and about Magdalena's sister and her family. Johann didn't mention the papers that he'd gone to see. Wilhelm knew that they contained information about whether somebody was in Germany many years ago but he didn't know who this person was or why it was so important that Johann had had to travel so far in order to find out.

When they had finished lunch, Johann invited Wilhelm into his study.

"I have things I need to tell you," he said, once they were seated.

"And I have things I want to ask you about," replied Wilhelm.

"Go ahead," said Johann, leaning back in his big chair next to the desk. "Let's deal with them first."

Wilhelm didn't know where to begin. He sat looking at his hands for a few moments then, lifting his head, said "There are two things."

"Yes?"

"My people. They are still in the mines . . . And I am here."

Johann nodded. "And you feel guilty about that"

"Guilty?"

"You feel you shouldn't be here if they're still down there."

"Yes."

"And, of course, you want to get them out."

"Yes." A spark of hope arose in Wilhelm's mind. Could Johann have already been thinking about this?

Johann sat and looked at Wilhelm for a few seconds as though he were deciding what to tell him. Then he said "It's not going to be easy to get them out, Wilhelm. For a start, we don't know exactly where they are. And even if we did, we couldn't just go down and bring them up to the surface. It might be possible to get one or two out without it being noticed, but not everyone. And the people in charge - They - are not going to give up their control easily. So we need to find a way of overcoming Them."

Wilhelm took in a sharp breath. He hadn't considered this. He had always believed Them to be all-powerful. And now Johann was suggesting that they must be overcome. "Can it be done?" he asked.

"I don't know. First of all we need to find out who They are and where They are. Until we know that, we can't do anything."

"I see." The hope was beginning to fade. Wilhelm's gaze returned to

226

his hands.

"But it's possible that we're a little nearer to finding out. Some of the things I learned in America may well help."

Wilhelm's head snapped up. "In America . . .?" he asked.

"About a hundred and fifty years ago, a man called Robert Browning wrote a poem which we think is about how your people were taken down into the tunnels . . ."

"A poem?" Wilhelm asked in amazement. "A poem about my people?"

"It describes how a hundred and thirty children were taken into a mountain hundreds of years ago. It's based on a story that's well known in Germany. Marcus thinks that those children were the first of your people to work in the mines."

"Marcus? Has he been thinking about my people, too?"

"Of course. We all have. We all want to get your people out of there."

Wilhelm was overwhelmed. "Thank you," he said.

Johann smiled. "We have been talking about it ever since you came here," he said. "And when I went to America, it was to see some letters that Robert Browning wrote. He didn't live in Germany so I wanted to know where he'd heard the story because I thought it might be important."

"You went all that way to find out . . . about my people . . . to help my people?"

Again Johann smiled. "It was the only way I could get to read the letters. But I've discovered something from them that might be of use to us and, when the others get here this evening, I'll tell you all about it."

Wilhelm sat back in his chair, his mind reeling. To find out about Them . . . to be able to overcome Them . . . He had no doubt now that Johann and Marcus could do it. And he would help them. Together they would rescue the Hundeiss.

"You said there were two things you wanted to ask me about." Johann broke into his thoughts.

"Yes. . ." Wilhelm paused as he wondered how to put into words what he wanted to know. "It's about Elisabeth."

Johann smiled but said nothing.

"We love each other . . . When you were away, she came here . . . and she kissed me . . . I had never been kissed before."

Johann looked puzzled. "Do the Hundeiss not kiss each other?"

Wilhelm shook his head, then said, "She taught me to make love too. It was wonderful."

"Taught you . . . Don't the Hundeiss make love?"

"No."

Johann nodded. "I must say I wondered about that when you told me about the women being taken for breeding . . . Wilhelm, do you understand about breeding - do you know what it means?"

"No. . . it was some special sort of work. They always took young healthy girls. But we never saw them again."

"And do you understand how babies - young children - are made?"

Wilhelm was puzzled. It seemed that the conversation had strayed a long way from the question that he wanted to ask Johann. "No," he said. "They were just brought to the mines by the Carriers."

"Magdalena will explain it to you," said Johann. "It's important that you know."

Wilhelm nodded, frowning.

"But you wanted to ask me something about Elisabeth, didn't you."

"Yes . . . When we had made love, I thought that meant that she was now my woman. But she has gone back to her own home. And I don't know what I have to do to make her my woman."

"When you say 'make her your woman', do you mean permanently?"

"Till the end of our lives."

Johann frowned. "Well," he said, "here, life is usually much longer than in the mines. It's not uncommon for someone to have a series of relationships - when one ends, they go on to the next. So a man can have relationships with several women without any of them being permanent."

"But what about you and Magdalena? You're permanent."

"Well, yes, Magdalena and I are married . . . but marriage is a very serious step to take, Wilhelm, and I don't think you're ready for it yet."

"Why not?"

"Because you still have a lot to learn about this world. And you have to establish yourself, find a job and a home of your own. Then, if you and Elisabeth are still together, that will be the time to ask her to marry you."

"And then she will be my woman."

"Possibly. But it's also possible that Elisabeth may say no."

"But she loves me. She said so."

"I'm sure she does. But some women don't want to get married. They value their freedom. If she were to say no, it wouldn't mean that she doesn't love you. And it wouldn't mean that she doesn't want to be with you."

"I don't want to lose her."

"I understand. Have you talked to her about it?"

Wilhelm shook his head.

"Why not?"

"I didn't know what to say . . . or if I would be doing the right thing."

"Of course. But if you and Elisabeth really love each other, then, for the moment, that's all that matters. Time enough to think about marriage when we've worked out how we're going to get your people to safety."

Wilhelm was in the kitchen with Magdalena when the door bell rang. He heard Johann go to answer it and then Elisabeth's voice in the hall. Suddenly he felt nervous. He didn't know how he should greet her in front of Johann and Magdalena. Should he give her the sort of kiss that was a greeting? Or should he kiss her as he had done when he had opened the door to her on the last few evenings - on the mouth? Magdalena, who was cutting up some vegetables, said "Ah, it's Elisabeth. You'd better go and say hello, Wilhelm."

Going out into the hall, he found Johann helping Elisabeth off with her jacket. She turned, smiling, and solved Wilhelm's problem for him by coming over and kissing him warmly, full on the mouth.

"Hello my darling," she said. Then, turning to Johann, "Things blossomed while you were away."

"Yes," Johann smiled. "Magdalena and I suspected that something of the sort was in the air."

"I'm helping Magdalena in the kitchen," said Wilhelm. "I'll be back soon. I'm pleased you're here, Elisabeth."

He made his escape into the kitchen, feeling uncomfortable in a way he had never previously experienced. His face felt hot and he hadn't wanted to look Johann in the eye. A few minutes later he was pleased to hear the sounds of Erika and Marcus arriving. For some reason, he didn't want to be in the room with just Elisabeth and Johann. He hadn't seen Marcus or Erika for several days and he wondered whether Elisabeth had told them about what had been happening between them but, when he entered the sitting room, they greeted him as normal and made no reference to it.

During dinner, Johann and Magdalena described some of the places that they had visited and told amusing stories about things that had happened during their stay in California. Wilhelm listened avidly, saying very little. He often wondered whether a time would come when he knew everything that he needed to about this world. It sometimes frightened him that there was so much to learn. Despite the tyranny of Them and the conditions under which his people lived in the mines, there had been a kind of safety there. Down there he had known what to do in every situation that might arise. He had known what to say and to whom. The only thing to fear in the mines and the tunnels was death, and sometimes that had seemed more to be welcomed than to be feared.

He had told Magdalena something of his worries and she had reassured him, complimenting him on how much he had already learned but saying that he should tell her if he felt they were going too fast. He had said he would - but what was too fast? Almost every time somebody spoke to him there was new information to be taken in. And there was still so much in his reading that he didn't understand. Sometimes he felt that he just wanted to shut himself away for a while and think, to allow the information to settle as one would allow the food to settle at the end of a meal. He looked up from his plate and saw Elisabeth smiling at him and immediately felt better. He smiled back. With Elisabeth beside him, he could do anything.

At the end of the meal they all went into the sitting room.

Elisabeth, seating herself next to Wilhelm on the settee, slipped her hand into his. He squeezed it gently, feeling reassured by the contact.

"You know," Johann said, "that I went to California to look at the letters that Robert Browning wrote from Germany in 1838. They're now in the possession of a man called Michael Woodhouse who was kind enough to let me read them and take notes. And because I wasn't sure whether my English was good enough to understand every word, he allowed Magdalena's sister to come with me to help translate them. They made very interesting reading."

"Did they mention the Rattenfaenger?" asked Marcus, sitting forward on his seat.

"Indeed they did. It seems that Browning had cousins, whom he'd never met, in Hamburg. And, as you suspected, Marcus, he took the opportunity to visit them. He was there for a week or so and, during that time, he met a man - it's not quite clear how from the letters, but it seems he was an acquaintance of one of the cousins, possibly someone with whom he'd been doing business. Anyway, this man invited Browning to visit him in his schloss before he left Germany, which he did. He stayed with him for four days and while he was there, he heard the story of the Rattenfaenger. He wrote to his father about it, describing it as 'fascinating' and wondering whether his mother - whose parents, of course, were German - had ever come across it. He said that he had been assured by his host that it was a true story and that it was correct in every detail."

"Did he mention the red and yellow?" asked Marcus eagerly.

"No, but we may assume that was one of the details he was told." He turned to Wilhelm. "Marcus picked up the point that, in this poem about the Rattenfaenger who lured the children away from the town of Hameln, the Rattenfaenger's clothes were described as being red and yellow. Elsewhere - and in Hameln itself - the legend describes him as wearing multicoloured clothes."

"The clothes the Hundeiss are given are red and yellow when they are new," said Wilhelm.

"Exactly," said Marcus. "And, you see, it wasn't unusual in the past for people who worked for the same master to wear what is known as a livery - the same clothes as each other - and very often that livery would be of a specific colour which had something to do with their master."

"So our master was the person in the legend."

"It's possible," said Johann.

"But Johann," Erika interrupted. "did you find out where the schloss was or the name of its owner?"

"I was coming to that." Johann smiled. "And the answer to both questions is yes. The man's name, interestingly enough, was Pfeiffer and the schloss was - and still is - only twenty kilometres from where we're sitting."

✶ ✶ ✶

The morning after Johann and Magdalena's return, Wilhelm woke feeling strangely ill at ease with himself. It wasn't just that he was missing Elisabeth, although that was certainly a large part of it. Holding her last night when they had said goodbye, he hadn't wanted to let her go. As he watched her walking away from the house with Erika and Marcus, who were holding hands, he had wished that he could go with them. When the door was shut, Magdalena took his hand in both of hers and said "She'll be back tomorrow, Wilhelm. I know it's hard to be parted, but she'll be back."

At one point during the night he woke and, rolling slightly, stretched out his arm for her before realising that she wasn't there. A sick, empty feeling arose in his stomach as he remembered those nights after Lotte had been Taken when he had woken alone and desolate. Urgently, he forced himself to remember that it was different now. He would see Elisabeth in the morning. As Magdalena had said, it was only a temporary parting. But once awake, his thoughts started to return to the events of the previous evening.

Johann had said that the schloss belonging to the man called Pfeiffer was only twenty kilometres away. This was where the poet, Browning, had learned about the Hundeiss and about the man - the Rattenfaenger - who had lured them away into the mountain, into the mines, into slavery.

Johann thought there might still be someone there, at the schloss, who knew about the Hundeiss . . . even, perhaps, someone who was responsible for their continued slavery. Wilhelm had jumped to his feet, wanting to go there at once, to demand to be told where his people were being held and by whom.

"We can't, Wilhelm," Johann had said softly. "Not yet. We're not ready."

"But we must! My people are in slavery to Them - and you say that They are at this schloss. We've got to free them. We can't just leave them now we know how to help them. We've got to get them out. We've got to save them." He looked round and saw sympathy on all their faces but no one jumped up to join him.

Johann shook his head. "We can't, Wilhelm," he repeated. "They're too powerful for us. We'd never be able to do it. We'd just lose our lives in the attempt."

"You're scared!" shouted Wilhelm. "You're just scared. Well I'm not scared. I know how much twenty kilometres is, and it's not very far. I walk about five kilometres most days. I can walk to the schloss, I can go by myself. I can rescue them. I'm not scared."

Suddenly he was aware that Marcus had moved over to stand beside him, putting a firm, but gentle hand on his shoulder. "I'm not scared," Marcus said. And looking into his eyes, Wilhelm knew that this was true.

"I'm not scared," Marcus repeated, "and if I thought there was even a chance that we could get your people out safely, then I'd come with you this minute. But we've got to trust Johann, and if he says we're not ready, we've got to believe him. Because, Wilhelm, when we do go - and we shall go, of that I have no doubt - but when we do, we've got to succeed. You know that. There's no point in our going and being killed without getting your people to safety. Because who would rescue them then? Who would even know that they were there? It would be just as though you'd never escaped. They'd have no hope at all."

Wilhelm took a deep breath, feeling the tension draining out of him, acknowledging the sense of Marcus's words. Wordlessly, he nodded.

"We shan't be idle, Wilhelm," said Johann. "Just because we're not going to the schloss yet, it doesn't mean that we shan't be doing anything. There's still a lot that we need to find out. And we have to prepare ourselves - mentally, spiritually and physically - for the rescue attempt."

"And we'll be working together," said Marcus, leading Wilhelm back to his chair. "We're all in this to the end. We shan't desert you."

Once Marcus and Wilhelm had sat down again, Johann said "We're only at the start of unravelling this mystery. It's many, many years since Browning visited Pfeiffer. We can't even be sure that the schloss is still owned by the Pfeiffer family. We've got to learn more about Pfeiffer himself and about the schloss before we can decide what we should do next."

Thinking this over in the early hours of the morning, Wilhelm realised that Marcus and Johann had been right in saying that they would have to wait. But he was aware of a growing impatience. Now there was the possibility that they might be able to get his people out of the mines, he wanted to be active, not just to sit and talk. He turned in his bed, restless and wide awake.

When he came down to breakfast, Magdalena looked at him sharply and asked "Didn't you sleep?"

"Not well," he admitted, seating himself at the kitchen table.

Magdalena sat down next to him. "Try not to worry, Wilhelm," she said, pouring him a cup of coffee. "I know how difficult it is for you being here in a world so different from anything you've known before. And I know how hard you've worked to learn everything I've been teaching you. And we all know how worried you are about the people you left behind. But try to be patient. As soon as the time is right, Johann will tell you. You can be sure of that."

Wilhelm nodded wishing that, just for once, Magdalena wouldn't try to soothe him with words. He loved her dearly, appreciated her kindness and her warmth and her wisdom, appreciated the time that she lavished on him, teaching and advising, but just occasionally he felt that he would like to be by himself to work things out in his own mind. When he had come to this house, timid, unable to read or write, knowing nothing about the world, she had taken him in as a mother would take a child. Sometimes he thought that she had forgotten that he wasn't, in fact, a child but a man. Recently he had started to look at Marcus and to long for the day when he, too, could be independent, making his own decisions, not reliant on anyone else. He shook his head. His lack of sleep was making him irritable.

"Now then," Magdalena continued, "You have something to eat and then we need to have a talk because Johann tells me there's something I ought to explain. Elisabeth's not coming till eleven, so we've plenty of time."

✶ ✶ ✶

It was amazing, thought Wilhelm, as he sat listening to a recording of *The Magic Flute* later that morning, how very clearly Magdalena explained such extraordinary, incredible things. He was finding it very hard to believe the latest thing that she had told him, and yet, she wouldn't lie, would have no reason to lie. Now he came to think about it, he was surprised that it had never occurred to him to wonder where children came from. But in the mines, his mind had been dulled by the music and, by the time he had broken out, he had become accustomed to children just appearing - being sent by Them. To think of them actually growing inside a woman . . . The idea had horrified him, but Magdalena had had two children and she said it was a wonderful experience. Two children of her own - and of Johann's. That was the marvellous part, that they were actually made up of her and Johann. So that something of each of them was carried on.   To think that such a glorious thing as making love could result in the creation of a child who was a part of the man and a part of the woman. How wonderful it would have been if he and Lotte could have had their own children. Oh, yes, they had Marthe and Konrad and they loved them and cared for them, but they weren't part of them. If they had been, he would have felt that he still had something left of his beloved Lotte. He shook his head. She had been in his mind a lot recently. He knew she wouldn't mind about Elisabeth. She would have liked Elisabeth.

Elisabeth was going to take him to an art gallery today, to see some paintings. He was looking forward to it. Up till now, he had only seen paintings in books. Elisabeth said they were much better when you looked at the real thing. The real thing . . . like having your own children. He kept coming back to that. Magdalena said that, although some people who weren't married had children, she thought that Elisabeth probably took something called 'the Pill' which would stop her from becoming pregnant. Many people used methods to prevent children being made until they were married - committed to each other for the rest of their lives. Wilhelm could understand that. Konrad and Marthe had gone from the cave by the time Lotte was Taken, but many children lost one of their adults before they were grown and it was very hard for them. Children needed two adults to care for them.

More than ever now, he wanted to marry Elisabeth, to stay with her for the rest of his life - and to have children with her, part her, part him. He wondered whether Magdalena's God would help him accomplish that. Magdalena had explained about God a little while ago. Wilhelm had thought he sounded something like Them - in control of everybody and of the world in which they lived. But Magdalena had said no, God wanted what was best for his people whereas They were just interested in themselves. She had told Wilhelm that you could ask God for things and sometimes he would give you what you wanted, but you shouldn't ask for selfish things. Asking for selfish things was wrong. Wilhelm wondered if it would be wrong to ask God to give him Elisabeth.

The door bell rang and he jumped up, rushed into the hall and opened the door with trembling hands, sweeping Elisabeth into his arms as soon as she stepped over the threshold.

"Hello, my darling," she said, when he allowed her to speak. She put up her hand and smoothed his hair. "I've missed you."

"I've missed you too."

"Are Johann and Magdalena in? I ought just to say hello."

"I think Magdalena's in the kitchen."

As he spoke, she came into the hall.

"Hello, Elisabeth. I heard the doorbell. Wilhelm tells me you're taking him to an art gallery."

"Yes. I'm afraid I'm inflicting all my enthusiasms on him!"

"Would you like to come back for dinner this evening or do you have other plans?"

"That's kind - thank you - but actually I thought we'd eat out somewhere."

"Well enjoy yourselves. Wilhelm's got a key, of course, so there's no rush to get back."

Sitting in the front of Elisabeth's car, Wilhelm couldn't take his eyes off her face. He knew that he mustn't touch her while she was driving - she had explained that she had to concentrate and that mistakes could be dangerous. He understood that, but her closeness made it almost unbearable.

The art gallery was a large red brick building, situated in an area of the town that Wilhelm hadn't seen before. Elisabeth took Wilhelm's hand and slowly they walked round looking at the pictures. Elisabeth knew a lot about painting and Wilhelm listened avidly, learning about oils and pastels, impressionism and surrealism, perspective and chiaroscuro. One room held nothing but portraits and Wilhelm, still holding Elisabeth's hand, looked at her and thought how he should like to draw her. Magdalena had taught him to paint flowers and the views from the windows, but he hadn't yet drawn any faces. He wouldn't even need Elisabeth to be there - she was so vivid in his mind.

They had lunch in the gallery's small restaurant, then returned to their tour of the rooms. When they had seen everything, Elisabeth looked at her watch. "It's three o'clock. Shall we go for a walk? It's a lovely afternoon."

They got back in the car and drove a little distance outside the town. Elisabeth parked and they made their way down a narrow track which led to the river. As they walked, still hand in hand, along the path that bordered it, Wilhelm thought he had never felt so happy - with the sun, and the birdsong, and the flowers, and Elisabeth. They walked for about an hour, then Elisabeth said "I thought we might go into town and have an early supper and then go back to my apartment." Realising the implication of what she was saying, Wilhelm felt a tingle of excitement. He turned to look at her and saw from her smile that she knew what he was thinking. "I love you," she said, and kissed him.

Over the next couple of months, a routine established itself in Wilhelm's life. The weekdays continued much as before, with tuition from Magdalena, painting, reading and walking during the day and visits from Elisabeth, Erika and Marcus in the evenings. On Friday night they all had dinner together, sometimes cooked by Magdalena, sometimes by Wilhelm. But every Saturday, Elisabeth would come for him around mid-morning and they would spend the whole weekend together. At first, he came home on Saturday night, reluctantly leaving Elisabeth's bed for his own. But one Thursday evening when Elisabeth had come over to visit, Magdalena said "You know, Elisabeth, it seems silly for you to have to bring Wilhelm all the way back here on a Saturday night if you're going out again on Sunday morning. Wouldn't it be easier if he stayed over at your apartment?" And so it was arranged.

And now, after months of Wilhelm talking to Elisabeth about himself, about the Hundeiss and the mines and the tunnels, about Lotte and the children, about his fears and anxieties and hopes, Elisabeth started to tell Wilhelm about herself. He knew, of course, about her parents and her family, he had seen the photographs of her cousin's wedding, and he knew something of her work. But now she began to confide in him, telling him about her hopes and fears, her ambitions and disappointments. And he sensed that, by doing so, she was putting her trust in him, and that it was something that she wouldn't do lightly. At first she just told him about her work at the university, about her students and her colleagues, her research and her responsibilities. But then she started to tell him stories of when she was a little girl and what she had dreamed of becoming - an opera singer, a writer, and finally, realising her talent, a linguist.

One Saturday night they went to a concert of early music in a hall near the university. Afterwards, they walked down the road to a small restaurant that Elisabeth knew. They were sitting looking at the menu when two girls walked past their table and said "Hello, Dr. Kramer."

Elisabeth looked up, smiled and said hello, then introduced them to Wilhelm as two of her final-year students. He stood up, shook hands and smiled, as Magdalena had taught him to do.

"We saw you at the concert," said one of the girls, "Did you enjoy it?" And for a few minutes they talked about the music.

Glancing over, a little later, to the girls' table, Wilhelm saw them looking at him and he smiled. They were both very pretty, one dark, one fair. The dark girl, in particular, would make a good model for drawing, with her fine features and her curly hair. Wilhelm had been doing a lot of drawing recently and Magdalena had shown some of his work to a friend of hers, a well known portrait-painter. Impressed by Wilhelm's talent, he had offered to tutor him in the basics of the craft so that he could apply for a place at art school as a mature student. After three sessions of tuition, Wilhelm was starting to look at everyone he met in terms of how he would draw them. He turned his head and saw that Elisabeth had noticed where he was looking and who he was smiling at. "What pretty girls you have for your students," he said.

The meal was good but Wilhelm had the impression that Elisabeth was tired. He wished he could drive a car so that she could just relax on the way home. It was something that he would have to learn in due course. As they approached the apartment, he was aware, as always on a Saturday night, of a feeling of excitement. When they had gone in and Elisabeth had shut the front door, he put his arms round her and kissed her neck. Elisabeth looked up at him and smiled but somehow the smile was only in her mouth and not her eyes. Wilhelm frowned. "What's the matter?"

"Nothing. Why should you think anything's the matter?"

"You look . . .well, tired."

"Oh." Elisabeth shook her head. "Sorry about that. It's been a fairly hard week. And at my age, when I'm tired it shows in my face."

"I wasn't complaining."

"No. No, of course not. . . But I am tired. I could do with a good night's sleep."

239

They went into the bedroom and Elisabeth started to undress, her back to Wilhelm. He was confused and a little troubled. "Elisabeth . . .? Have I done something wrong?"

She turned, smiling brightly, too brightly. "No, of course not. I'm just tired, as I said."

When they had both got into bed, Elisabeth lay on her back staring at the ceiling. Wilhelm was beginning to feel really worried. "Elisabeth . . . please, talk to me."

"What about?" Again that bright smile.

"About you. About what's troubling you. . . Elisabeth, I may have spent most of my life underground, unable to read or write, but I'm not stupid. I know there's something wrong. Speak to me."

"I'm just tired," she said again. "Goodnight Wilhelm." And she rolled onto her side away from him and turned out the light.

Wilhelm felt sick. He had lost Elisabeth and he didn't know why or how. If only she would tell him, he might be able to make it right . . . but she didn't want to tell him . . . she didn't want him to make it right. She didn't want him any more. He was engulfed in misery. He lay on his back in the dark, eyes open, staring up towards the ceiling. His mind went back over the evening's events. Try as he might, he couldn't work out what he could have done wrong. Maybe he hadn't done anything . . . maybe she had just tired of him. . . He remembered what Johann had told him about some people having a series of relationships - maybe that was it, maybe she had fallen in love with someone else. He wondered whether he should leave now and go back to Johann and Magdalena's. But it was late and he would have to walk and he wasn't sure that he could find the way. And yet it was unbearable, having to lie here beside her, knowing that he mustn't touch her, knowing that she no longer wanted him.

He felt a shudder beside him and turned his head. Elisabeth's shoulders were shaking gently. For a moment, he wondered why, and then he realised - she was crying. Forgetting his anxieties about touching her, forgetting her rejection of him, he seized her and pulled her round to face him. There were tears rolling down her cheeks.

"Elisabeth!" He was shouting in his frustration and desperation. "You must speak to me. If there's something wrong - and I can see that there is - then I want to share it with you. I want to make it better. Elisabeth, you're all that matters to me and, if something's hurting you, then it's hurting me. So please tell me what it is."

"I'm sorry," she whispered. "I'm sorry. Forgive me."

He held her close, kissing her face and her hair, relief flooding through him. "There's nothing to forgive. Just tell me what the problem is."

"You."

"Me?" Wilhelm was horrified.

Elisabeth nodded. "You're every woman's idea of the perfect man. You're handsome, tall, muscular, you dress well, you've got beautiful manners, you're talented, you're intelligent, you're kind . . ."

Wilhelm was totally perplexed. "I don't understand," he said.

"No, I don't expect you do." Elisabeth wiped her eyes. She smiled ruefully and sat up, pulling the sheet up to cover her. "I'm just being idiotic. But I get scared sometimes when I see what you've become."

"Why?" Nothing she was saying made any sense.

Elisabeth took a deep breath. "A few years ago," she said, "I had a relationship with a man whom I thought I loved. We lived together . . ."

Wilhelm felt his stomach muscles contract. "You lived with him?"

"Yes. For six months. . . I'm sorry, Wilhelm, it happens."

"I see."

"I thought he was going to marry me. . . But he went away. He left me. I thought I was going to die, the pain was so bad. I've been very careful since then. I've not allowed myself to get too close to anyone. I've had sexual relationships, but I haven't loved anyone. . . until now. And now I've fallen in love with you. And I love you more deeply than I could ever have believed possible. And when I saw how those students looked at you tonight and then you smiled at them and said how pretty they were . . . well, I suddenly realised that you could have any woman you wanted. And if you left me, I don't know what I'd do. If the pain was bad when Philippe left me, what would it be like if I lost you - I just couldn't bear it . . . So I thought if I started to shut down now, it might not hurt as much when you do leave me . . .Oh, I'm sorry, I'm sorry . . I shouldn't have said anything . . . " And she burst into tears again.

"Elisabeth . . ." Wilhelm shook his head, bewildered by her confession, "Elisabeth . . even if I could have any woman I wanted, there is only one woman that I want, and it's you. Surely you know that?"

"Now, perhaps . . ."

"No, not just now." Wilhelm lifted her head, forcing her to look at him. "Not just now. Forever. For the rest of our lives . . . I've wanted to say this for so long . . . Elisabeth, will you marry me?"

Elisabeth made a small choking noise, looking at Wilhelm and shaking her head. For a terrifying moment he thought she was going to refuse him, then she flung her arms round him, crying "Oh, my darling, of course I will - of course I will."

Chapter Thirteen

Unusually, Johann called them all together for a meeting on Sunday evening.

"Before you begin, Johann," said Elisabeth, "Wilhelm and I have something to tell you all."

"Oh, my dears!" exclaimed Magdalena. "You're engaged!"

Elisabeth nodded, laughing.

"Oh, I couldn't be more pleased." Magdalena clapped her hands.

Wilhelm saw Erika and Marcus grinning at each other.

"We wondered how long it would take you," said Marcus. "Erika said not till the new year but I said any time now. . . So she owes me a bottle of Cognac."

"Oh, really, Marcus!" Magdalena was pretending to be shocked. "Gambling on your friends' affections! Really!"

Marcus laughed. "Seriously, though, congratulations both of you. It's great news. And an inspiring example to all of us who are still unmarried . . ." He turned to Erika who was sitting beside him on the settee and lightly kissed the tip of her nose. She blushed.

Wilhelm noticed that Johann was sitting quietly, saying nothing. Magdalena had noticed it too.

"Johann," she said. "what's the matter? Aren't you pleased for them?"

Johann smiled. "I'm delighted. Although I had hoped it would be a little while before the two of you finally committed yourselves to each other. Of course, I had no doubt that you would . . . it's just the timing that could be a problem. You see, until this business of the Hundeiss and the Rattenfaenger and Pfeiffer is resolved, your love for each other and your commitment could be putting you in danger. So we need to be very careful. First of all, there's the question of where you live. Nowadays, it would be quite unremarkable, since you're engaged, for the two of you to live together."

Wilhelm smiled. He and Elisabeth had discussed it and had decided that, as long as it wouldn't upset Magdalena and Johann, he would move into her apartment.

Johann looked at Wilhelm and shook his head. "You have to stay here, Wilhelm. It's vitally important that you remain under this roof. You can continue to stay overnight with Elisabeth at the weekends for the time being but the rest of the time you must stay here where we can keep an eye on you."

Wilhelm was puzzled. "But surely," he asked, "if it's all right for me to stay overnight at the weekends why isn't it all right for me to stay there all the time? And what about after we're married? We'll have to live together then."

"Of course, but I hope you weren't thinking of getting married before we've resolved the problem of how we get your people out. It would be most inadvisable."

"We hadn't got that far yet," said Elisabeth. "Is there really a risk?"

Johann nodded. "There could be. But even if Wilhelm is only here some of the time, we will be able to protect him - and you - more effectively than if he moves out entirely. . . I'm sorry, Wilhelm. I know it seems hard, but it won't be for ever. . . Now, I think we should have a drink to celebrate the good news and then I'll tell you the results of my most recent investigations."

Johann got up and went into the kitchen, returning with a bottle of champagne and some glasses on a tray.

"Magdalena's had it in the fridge for a couple of weeks," he told Marcus with a smile. "You and Erika aren't the only ones who saw what was coming."

He opened the bottle and poured. When they each had a glass, Johann raised his and said "Elisabeth and Wilhelm - I wish you a long and happy life together. And may the Hundeiss soon be free."

"Thank you," said Wilhelm, sipping cautiously. He had tried wine once or twice but didn't like it very much. It was the only thing he and Elisabeth disagreed on. This, however, was rather nice. He sipped again.

"And now," said Johann, back in his armchair, a sheaf of handwritten notes and papers on his lap, "let's get down to business. It's taken rather longer than I had hoped because the university has been keeping me very busy recently, but I have been able to find some information about both the schloss and the mysterious Herr Pfeiffer." He picked up one of the sheets of paper. "The schloss was built in 1282. Significant, perhaps, when you remember that the Rattenfaenger appeared in Hameln only two years later, in 1284. It seems to have been inhabited continuously since then, and always by a Herr Pfeiffer, although the relationship between the occupants isn't clear. I haven't been able to find birth or death certificates for any of them so I don't know precisely how the schloss has been handed down through the family. All I can tell you is that from the day it was built, there seems to have been a Pfeiffer in residence."

Johann took a sip from his glass and picked up the next sheet of paper. "So, that doesn't take us much further. And very little seems to have been written about either the schloss or its inhabitants. Apparently the various Herr Pfeiffers have been fairly solitary individuals, not given to hospitality."

Erika giggled. "Sorry," she said, as they all looked at her. "I just had a vision of the horror movie type of castle inhabited by the local vampire and his faithful hunchbacked servant, and the townsfolk outside the gates holding flaming torches and baying for blood."

"That may be nearer the truth than you think," said Johann.

"Oh come on!" Elisabeth sounded exasperated. "We've had the black magic bit and now you're giving us vampires?"

Johann smiled. "No, it's all right Elisabeth, not vampires. But just think about that movie stereotype. The mysterious castle, the single inhabitant who no one knows very much about . . It's not just about vampires. It's about somebody who is carrying on an anti-social activity that he wants to keep hidden from the outside world."

"No," said Elisabeth. "It can just as easily be about a recluse, someone who prefers his own company, who likes reading better than conversation - there are all sorts of reasons why people shut themselves off."

"Indeed," Johann nodded. "But the Pfeiffers have shut themselves off for seven hundred years. A family of recluses would you say?" He smiled at her.

245

"Now you're making fun of me."

"No, I'm not. To suggest that Herr Pfeiffer is a recluse is a perfectly reasonable thing to say and could certainly be true if we were talking about one or two generations. But we've got to take this in context. The Pfeiffers have been a mystery to those outside the schloss for the best part of a millennium . . . It's a long time. What have they been doing all that time?"

There was silence as they considered his question.

"We do, however," said Johann, looking at his sheet of paper, "have the odd clue. Over the centuries, Herr Pfeiffer has occasionally opened his doors to visitors - we know that Robert Browning was one of them. Unfortunately Browning doesn't say very much about his host in his letters other than describing him as an interesting man, well versed in local legends, and apparently with no wife or family - certainly Browning didn't mention anyone else living at the schloss. And that's about all apart from one fact which may well be significant - Pfeiffer had a large collection of religious artefacts, many of which were mediaeval or even older."

"But surely that makes it less likely that he was interested in the occult, doesn't it?" asked Erika.

"Not necessarily. Remember, the Nazis sought religious treasures - and not just for their monetary value but for the power they gave. But, of course, it proves nothing one way or the other, it's just something to bear in mind." Johann paused and took a sip from his glass. "So," he continued, "having failed to find out much about Pfeiffer, I looked to see if I could find his connection with Browning's cousin. But there I drew a complete blank. I did discover one interesting piece of information, though. Browning's cousin was a diamond merchant."

"So there is a link!" said Marcus.

"It's possible. Although, once again, it doesn't take us very far. But I began to wonder whether anyone else of note - anyone who has left letters or diaries behind - might have visited the schloss. There has been a newspaper published in this town since 1714 and almost every edition has been preserved on microfilm. So I went to the newspaper offices and started to look through their archives to see if I could find any records of

246

people who had been invited to the schloss. I started with the present day and worked backwards but I didn't find any mention of the schloss at all until I got to 1931. And then there was just a paragraph at the bottom of an inside page, which stated that Professor Karl Haushofer would be giving a lecture at the university before going to visit Herr Pfeiffer at his schloss." Johann looked round at them. "Do you know about Haushofer?" he asked.

They shook their heads.

"Thank God, they're all too young," said Magdalena.

"Haushofer," said Johann, "founded the theory of geopolitics - the idea that the state is a living organism and that the politics and the geography of a country are inextricably linked. He'd been a successful soldier - I believe he reached the rank of Brigadier - but in 1921 he became professor of geography at Munich university. One of his students there was Rudolf Hess. You know about Hess, of course?"

They all nodded, except Wilhelm. "Has Magdalena told you about Hitler?" Johann asked him.

"Yes."

"Well Hess was Hitler's deputy in the Nazi party. Don't worry if you don't understand all of this, though. Take in what you can and Magdalena will explain the rest in detail tomorrow."

"Thank you."

"Hess," Johann continued "introduced Haushofer to Hitler and it was probably from Haushofer that Hitler got some of his ideas, particularly those that could be used to justify his plans to expand Germany. But Haushofer had another side to him. He was deeply interested in things of an esoteric nature. When he was a young man he had travelled widely and had, at one time or another, investigated eastern mysticism. It's said that he received initiations - or more correctly empowerments - from Tibetan lamas, presumably when he was in China or India, since I can't find any record of his ever having been in Tibet itself. Now, who these lamas were, we don't know. It's possible that they weren't Buddhists but practitioners of Bon, which is a form of spirit religion found in Tibet and which has a well-recognised dark side to it. If so, he may have seen the empowerments as

247

offering him a way to manipulate people and events to his own ends. However, it is also possible that he did receive genuine Buddhist empowerments.

"It's often said that Tibetan Buddhism can be dangerous because it's about power. But the training involved in Vajrayana - the path of the vajra - can't be undertaken without a teacher and empowerments are not given lightly. And once a student is on the path, there is no turning back. But, of course, it is possible for a practitioner to abuse or misuse the powers that the practice brings. In Tibetan mythology there are six hells, each more terrible than the next. And the deepest and blackest of all these is Vajra Hell, reserved for those who corrupt the training and use the powers they have gained to their own ends."

Johann shifted in his chair, stretching his legs out in front of him. "We don't know, of course," he went on, "what Haushofer's empowerments enabled him to do. But what we do know is that he founded an organisation called the Vril Society whose aim was to train its members to awaken the forces of vril. In eastern cultures vril is known as kundalini and is said to be a coiled serpent of energy which lives in each of us, at the base of the spine. Awakening the kundalini can be very dangerous because it has enormous power. To awaken it without having learned how to control it can result in immediate death."

Johann put down the sheet of paper he was holding and picked up another. "So," he said "we know that Haushofer, a friend of Hitler and a man who was deeply involved in the occult, went to stay with Pfeiffer. I continued to search back through the newspapers but for a long time there were no more references to the schloss. And then I came across something that may well be the link that I - and some associates of mine - have been seeking for many years. In the autumn of 1788 this town was host for one night to no less a person than Wolfgang Amadeus Mozart - who then went on to the schloss, where he stayed for two weeks."

"Mozart?" said Elisabeth. "What on earth was he doing there? He didn't have any connections with the occult . . . " She tailed off. "Did he?"

"I'm not aware of any books that say he did," said Johann cryptically.

248

He turned to Wilhelm. "How much do you know about Mozart?" he asked.

"Not a great deal. Just what I've read in the notes that come with the CDs."

Elisabeth laughed. "He reads everything he can lay his hands on these days. Don't you, my darling?" And she leaned over and kissed him lightly on the cheek.

"Well," Johann continued, still addressing Wilhelm, "you know that he died when he was still very young."

"I thought he was thirty five?"

"That is very young, Wilhelm," Johann said gently.

Wilhelm shook his head. "Sometimes I forget," he said.

"And did you know," Johann went on, "that over the years there have been suggestions that he was murdered?"

"No, I didn't know that."

"It has been suggested that he was killed by another composer who was jealous of his popularity - there was a film made about that some years ago. And it has also been suggested that he was killed because he wrote *The Magic Flute* and in it gave away the secrets of Freemasonry, an organisation of which he was a member."

Wilhelm nodded.

"These are just theories, though. The truth - and this is known to very few people and must on no account be told to anyone outside this room - the truth is that he was murdered. And he was murdered because he wrote *The Magic Flute*. But he wasn't murdered by the Freemasons. Mozart became bored with them soon after he joined them. He wanted something more . . . exciting. And he found what he was looking for in a society devoted to the practice of the occult. "However, for some reason - we have no idea what - after some years he became disenchanted with the occult and tried to break away. Of course, they wouldn't allow it. Terrified by what he had become involved in and fearful that others might be drawn in as he had been, Mozart sought for a way to warn them - and he wrote into *The Magic Flute* as broad hints as he dared to show how the dark side might be overcome. . . Oh yes, Mozart was murdered. But it was by the practitioners of the dark side, not by the Freemasons."

"Forgive me, Johann," said Elisabeth. "but if this is such a well kept secret, then how do you know all about it?"

Johann looked at her. "Trust me," he said. Wilhelm remembered when Elisabeth had said that to him on the day he'd come to live in this house, and he turned to her, taking her hand and squeezing it.

After a second or two, she nodded. "We've come this far," she said.

"Since we all saw *The Magic Flute* a little while ago," continued Johann, "I assume you remember the story. And I know Wilhelm's listened to the recording of it since then."

"I've listened to it many times," said Wilhelm. "In fact, I know it very well now. The music is quite beautiful."

"Yes - many people think that Mozart was the greatest composer who ever lived. Not only was his music superbly constructed but he was amazingly prolific, producing vast quantities of work in his short life. We don't know for certain, but that's possibly the reason why he turned to the occult - to enable him to work faster, to write symphonies and operas in a matter of weeks. Of course, strictly speaking, the *Flute* is not an opera but a singspiel - a musical play - because it has spoken dialogue. And so those who believe there's no truth in the theory that he was murdered for writing it put forward as an argument that his librettist - the man who wrote the words - lived on for another twenty or so years after the *Flute* was first produced. Like Mozart, the librettist, Schikaneder, was a Freemason and it is argued that the Freemasons would hardly have taken revenge on the man who wrote the music but left the man who wrote the words at liberty."

"But surely," said Erika "if, as you say, Mozart was murdered for dropping hints about combating the black arts or whatever, then Schikaneder would have been seen as equally responsible for that. So the same argument holds."

"A good point," said Johann. "The answer, we believe, is that the crucial information is not in the words but in the music itself. Have you heard of the Mozart Effect?"

"Yes," said Marcus. "There was a study done at the University of

California in the 1990s. They found that people scored better marks in an intelligence test if they listened to Mozart before taking it. And I read something recently about a British study to look at its effect on patients with epilepsy."

"Actually," said Johann, "the research started in France in the 1950s but it was the California study that brought it to the notice of the public. And it's not just intelligence and epilepsy that have been tested - it's suggested that listening to Mozart's music may be beneficial to children with dyslexia and with speech disorders, and even with autism. Mozart had a remarkable gift - an ability to create music that could affect the human mind at the deepest levels. And combined with his knowledge of the black arts, it was probably not difficult for him to put something into *The Magic Flute* which could be used by those who needed it. However, although the fellowship to which Magdalena and I belong believes that the words give a hint as to how the music can be used, our members have been trying to decipher the clues for two centuries without success. Mozart left no record - naturally - of the organisation to which he belonged. All we know is that he joined a Masonic Lodge in 1784, when he was 28, and his association with the occult society probably came a year or two later. The first performance of *The Magic Flute* was on September 30th 1791. Two days later he became ill and he died on December 5th. He left his great Requiem unfinished - some people say that he was writing it for himself, knowing that he would die. Maybe he did. Maybe *The Magic Flute* was his great sacrifice, his penance for dabbling in the black arts."

Johann paused, then looked at Marcus and said "We only have this link now because you associated the Hundeiss with Robert Browning's poem. And we only have it because you, Wilhelm, were brave enough to escape from the mines. We owe you both a great debt of gratitude. But we're going to ask more of you before this is over."

Wilhelm glanced towards his friends on whom the fate of his people depended and felt a shiver run down his spine.

Johann picked up his glass and drank the champagne that remained in it. "You know, of course," he went on "that there are many allusions to things of Masonic significance in the *Flute*. The number three, which is significant in Masonic circles, appears again and again - the three ladies, the three genii, the three temples, even the opera's home key of E flat, which has three flats. The inscriptions on the temples - Wisdom, Reason and Nature, the padlock with which Papageno is punished for lying, the references to earth, air, fire and water - all these things have particular meanings for Masons."

"Unfortunately, we are in the position of someone who has part of a jigsaw puzzle and no idea of what the finished picture should look like. For years, we've been aware of these associations with Freemasonry but it's got us nowhere. And meanwhile the practitioners of the dark arts have been working ceaselessly, increasing their strength. Because, although we've known what was being done, we've not known by whom or where, and so we've been powerless. When someone is intent on great evil, he'll make enormous efforts to conceal his activities from those who would try to stop him.

But now, in the light of what we've found out, it seems reasonable to suppose that the title of Mozart's opera links to the Rattenfaenger legend which, in turn, seems to link to the schloss and Herr Pfeiffer. And, following on from that, is it possible that there's a reference to the spear of Longinus in the first scene where the ladies use their spears to kill the serpent? The ladies are the servants of the evil Queen of the Night but they also use their spears to rescue Tamino who represents the forces of good. You will remember that tradition says the spear of Longinus can be used either for great evil or for great good. Some say that Hitler actually acquired it, that the one in the museum is simply a replica or a forgery. Maybe. Or maybe the real spear found its way into someone's private collection - perhaps into Herr Pfeiffer's private collection. We don't know. What we do know is that those to whom we are opposed didn't stop at Hitler's death. They've continued their work, and now they're growing strong again. And we shall have to stop them - if we can."

✳ ✳ ✳

In the week that followed it seemed to Wilhelm as though they were all waiting for something to happen. There was a tension in the air and he took refuge in the time he spent with Elisabeth. On the Sunday evening, a week after they had announced their engagement, she took him to a performance of Bach's *Christmas Oratorio* which was being given in the cathedral. The music lifted their spirits and it was in a buoyant mood that they left the church and walked back to Elisabeth's car. Having fastened her seat belt, Elisabeth turned the key in the ignition. Nothing happened. She tried again. Still nothing.

"Damn!" she said.

"Why won't it start?" asked Wilhelm.

"I've no idea. There are all sorts of things that can go wrong with a car and I don't know anything about any of them. We'll have to get a taxi home and I'll 'phone the garage in the morning and ask them to come and look at it."

They climbed out of the car again and Elisabeth was just locking the doors when a man whom Wilhelm felt he ought to recognise came towards them down the street and said "Hello, Elisabeth."

Elisabeth turned. "Hello, Helmut." Of course, Wilhelm remembered, they had met at the opera.

"Are you having trouble?" Helmut asked.

"My car won't start."

"Can I give you a lift?"

"That'd be very kind, but not if it's taking you out of your way. We ought to be able to get a taxi quite easily."

"Are you going to your apartment?"

"No, back to Wilhelm's house. It's near the university."

"Ah yes, Wilhelm." Helmut turned to look at him and Wilhelm said "Good evening." He didn't like Helmut very much although he couldn't say why, just a feeling. But this was a friend of Elisabeth's, so he would be polite for her sake.

"In that case, it's not out of my way at all." said Helmut. "My car's just up the road."

His car was large and impressive, shiny outside and leather seats

253

within. He held the front passenger door open for Elisabeth, while Wilhelm climbed into the back.

"I take it you were at the concert?" Helmut asked as he started the engine.

"Yes. We didn't see you there."

"No. Lucky I saw you when I did."

Elisabeth gave him directions, then they drove for a while in silence, which was broken by Helmut asking "Have you always lived here, Wilhelm?"

"Wilhelm comes from the south," Elisabeth said before he had time to think of a reply.

"Ah, I thought it wasn't a local accent. And did you enjoy the concert, Wilhelm?"

"Very much, thank you. It wasn't a work I'd heard before."

"Really? What a sheltered life you must have led."

Elisabeth interrupted him to give further directions and a few minutes later they were outside Magdalena's house. They all got out of the car, Wilhelm opening the door for Elisabeth. Helmut came round onto the pavement.

"Good to see you again, Elisabeth," he said, taking her hand and touching it to his lips. Continuing to hold it, he looked long and hard at her, then said "I shall see you again soon."

"Yes. . . " Elisabeth seemed a trifle flustered. "Well, thank you so much for the lift Helmut. Nice to see you." And taking Wilhelm's arm, she walked with him to the front door without looking back.

✶ ✶ ✶

Wilhelm woke from a deep sleep and turned awkwardly, aware of the hard stone floor under his back. His shoulders ached from the exertions of the previous day and his leg hurt where he had caught it on a sharp piece of rock. He didn't know what had woken him. It couldn't have been the siren - he could hear no sounds of other people moving about. All he could hear was the music. He thought he'd been dreaming but he couldn't remember what it had been about. He guessed that it was about Lotte. She filled his thoughts and he missed her more with every passing day. His mouth was dry. He remembered that he had a little water left from the day before. He would drink it and then perhaps he would be able to sleep again. He felt around beside him for his candle and flint box . . .

Wilhelm's outstretched arm sent his clock crashing to the floor and woke him up. He was sweating and his heart was pounding. He sat up in bed and with trembling fingers turned on the bedside light. It was all right . . . it had been a dream, nothing more . . . everything was as it should be . . . He relaxed slightly and rested his head back against the headboard. It was only then that he realised that he could still hear the music.

Panic stricken he banged his fists against his ears, as if to clear them. He could still hear it. He shook his head. It made no difference. Struggling out of bed, he staggered to the door, wrenched it open and crossed the landing.. Raising his fist, he pounded on Johann and Magdalena's door, realising that he was sobbing. He heard sounds inside the room, then the door opened, Magdalena standing there pulling a dressing gown round her, face pale and concerned.

"I can still hear the music," Wilhelm shouted. "I can still hear the music. Help me!"

Behind Magdalena, he saw Johann who came forward and took his arm. "It's all right Wilhelm. You're safe. Magdalena, can you get his dressing gown?"

Johann stood supporting Wilhelm while Magdalena fetched the blue towelling robe that Elisabeth had bought for him and helped him into it.

"We must go down to my study," said Johann. "Magdalena, I think we shall need a hot drink in twenty minutes or so - perhaps some herbal tea?"

"Of course."

They walked slowly down the stairs, Johann's arm around Wilhelm, still supporting him, Magdalena following behind. Reaching the hallway, she went into the kitchen and Johann guided Wilhelm into the study and shut the door.

"Sit down Wilhelm," he said.

Wilhelm collapsed into the nearest chair.

Johann sat down beside him and said gently "Tell me what happened."

As best he could, Wilhelm told him of the dream, of how he woke, and of the music still ringing in his ears.

"They're getting closer," said Johann. "Somehow they've found out that you're here. We shall have to act straight away. I shall be back in a minute."

Getting up, he left the room, and Wilhelm heard him climbing the stairs. Moments later, he returned carrying a tray on which was a candle in a small silver candlestick, a silver jug and bowl, a small glass jar containing something that looked like coarse salt, and a very thin brown stick standing upright in a tiny holder. Putting the tray down on the desk, Johann went to a small chest of drawers that stood against the wall by the door. He opened one of the drawers, took out a white cloth and spread it over the top of the chest, then laid out on it the items from the tray. Having lit the candle, he put his hands together and bowed. Finally he lit the top of the thin stick. A sweet aromatic smell filled Wilhelm's nostrils. Johann was bowing again. Then, holding his hands out, palm upwards, he began to chant. Wilhelm couldn't recognise any of the words, it wasn't German, but the sound was somehow comforting and it partly masked the music that continued to sound in his ears. Still chanting, Johann lifted the jug and poured water from it into the bowl, then sprinkled in some of the salt from the jar. When the chant ended, he plunged his hands into the water then, turning, he said "Stand up, Wilhelm."

Wilhelm did so. Johann began to chant again then, raising his wet hands, he pressed them against Wilhelm's ears. When the chanting came to an end, Wilhelm realised that he could no longer hear the music. His knees buckled in relief and he sank back into the chair. Once again Johann sat down beside him.

"Can you hear me clearly, Wilhelm?" he asked.

Wilhelm nodded.

"Can you still hear the music?"

Wilhelm shook his head.

"That should protect you for a while. But if you notice the music coming back, even slightly, you must tell me immediately."

Wilhelm nodded.

Johann got up, extinguished the candles, bowed deeply once more and returned to his seat.

"How did they find you?" he asked. "Do you have any idea?"

"No, none at all."

"Have you met anyone recently who has taken an interest in you - talked to you about your past - asked you questions?"

"No. . . only Elisabeth's friend."

"Elisabeth's friend?"

"Helmut."

"Helmut? Oh, yes, I remember Helmut. . . But that was some time ago - have you seen him again since we met at the opera?"

"Yes, Elisabeth and I met him last night. Her car wouldn't start after the concert and he gave us a lift back here."

"Did he indeed? In that case we need to act quickly. Go into the kitchen and have a hot drink with Magdalena. I have some 'phone calls to make."

★ ★ ★

Johann didn't leave the house the next day, 'phoning the university to say that he had a family crisis to deal with. Magdalena had insisted that Wilhelm stay in bed and rest. She left his door open and, several times each hour, popped in with anxious face, to ensure that he was all right. Wilhelm, concerned that she was having to bring his meals to him, tried to insist that he should get up, but she refused to allow it and, still feeling shaken and tired, he didn't argue. However, at five thirty Magdalena came in and said "Elisabeth and Erika and Marcus will be here soon, so you'd better get up and get dressed now." Wilhelm did as he was told, standing for ten minutes under a hot shower, enjoying the sensation of the water on his skin. He had just finished dressing when he heard the door bell, followed by the sound of their voices in the hall. He went downstairs and followed them into Johann's study. Elisabeth turned to face him. She looked pale and drawn and held him tightly saying "Are you all right, my darling?"

257

"Yes. I'm fine. Don't worry." Wilhelm felt his own anxiety ebbing away as he tried to comfort and reassure her. "Johann's got everything in hand."

They all sat down. Wilhelm could see that Marcus and Erika, too, were looking very subdued.

Johann looked at them for a few seconds, then took a deep breath and said "As you know, they seem to have found out where Wilhelm is and soon - sooner than I had hoped - we shall have to face them. There is one more thing that must be done, though, and it is something to which you must each consent, of your own free will."

Wilhelm saw that Erika was looking anxious.

"I have told you," Johann continued, "that Magdalena and I belong to a fellowship whose purpose is to fight the dark forces that we are encountering now, to preserve the world and its great secrets from those who would corrupt and destroy them. For you to be able truly to join us in this fight, it's necessary for you too to become members of that fellowship."

"What does it entail?" asked Marcus.

"You must undergo an initiation during which you will have to commit yourselves to fighting evil with all your strength for the rest of your lives. Like the vajra path, there's no going back on it, so it isn't a vow to be undertaken lightly."

"It's something I'd be proud to do," said Marcus softly. Elisabeth and Wilhelm nodded and Erika said "Of course."

"Good. I had no doubt that you would all agree. In fact I had been intending to broach the subject with you fairly soon and we'd actually been planning the initiation for a few weeks' time. But after the events of last night it must be done as soon as possible, so I've arranged it for tomorrow night. It's vital that between now and then you observe certain restrictions in your lifestyle. You must eat no meat or any animal products - your diet must be entirely vegetarian. And you must drink no alcohol whatsoever."

"What about other . . . abstinences?" asked Marcus.

"You mean sex?"

Wilhelm saw that Erika's face had gone pink.

"In the Tantric tradition," said Johann, "sex is seen as the unification of two parts of the whole. In the present circumstances, although casual sex would certainly be harmful, sex with the person you love, the person who is, so to speak, the other part of you, may strengthen you."

As Wilhelm reached for Elisabeth's hand, he saw that Marcus had taken Erika's and was holding it tightly. Johann turned to Elisabeth and asked "Did you bring an overnight case, Elisabeth?"

"Yes."

"Good. You will be safer here. Tomorrow all of you must tell your colleagues that you have a close relative who is very ill and that, while that situation lasts, you may need to leave work at a moment's notice. And you will arrange for someone to be available to cover for you should that be necessary. We will meet here tomorrow night at six o'clock. Have nothing to eat or drink, except water, after three in the afternoon. Elisabeth and Erika, you must remove all nail varnish and make up and you must wear no perfume. You will be asked to take off your wrist watches and all your jewellery - apart from your amulet necklaces - before the initiation, so you may prefer to leave them at home. Is that all clear?"

They all nodded.

"Now before we go in to have coffee with Magdalena," Johann went on, "there is something I need to know. Elisabeth . . . who is Helmut?"

Elisabeth looked startled. "Helmut?" she asked.

"We met at the opera," Johann reminded her.

"Helmut . . . Helmut is an old friend."

Johann said nothing but sat looking at her.

"Helmut . . . was my lover," whispered Elisabeth.

Wilhelm felt as though someone had hit him. Had he, he wondered, sensed that there was still some attraction between them - was that why he'd taken a dislike to Helmut? Elisabeth turned to him, looking distressed.

"I'm sorry, Wilhelm. I did tell you that I'd had other lovers."

"Yes."

"But I never loved him." Elisabeth lowered her voice. "And the sex was just sex, just physical pleasure. It was nothing like the way it is between you and me."

Wilhelm said nothing, wanting desperately to believe her. She took his hand between both of hers.

"Wilhelm, I've had other men. It's not uncommon in this world. But they meant very little, and that was in the past. You are my future. I'm committed to you now, for the rest of my life. There will never be any other man for me, I swear. . . I love you."

He looked into her eyes and knew that she was speaking the truth, and a great wave of relief swept over him. He smiled, said "I love you too," and kissed her.

"I'm sorry Johann," Elisabeth said, turning back to him. "Why do you want to know about Helmut?"

"Wilhelm tells me he gave you a lift home last night."

"Yes. My car broke down."

"Why would it do that, I wonder?"

"I've no idea. The garage sent a man out this morning to look at it and apparently it started first time."

Johann nodded. "I'm not surprised. So Helmut brought you to the door."

"Yes. But . . ."

"When did your relationship with Helmut end?"

"Sometime in the spring - six . . . perhaps eight months ago."

"And have you seen him since?"

"Only at the opera, when I was with you, and last night. But why do you want to know?"

Once again Johann ignored her question.

"Does he live in the city?"

"Yes, but he's away a lot. He's an international lawyer."

"And did you ever meet any of his friends or colleagues?"

"No. We met at a party, so we had one or two friends in common, but I never met any of his other friends although . . ."

"Yes?"

"Well, when we broke up it was because a friend of his had invited us to stay for the weekend and Helmut had accepted the invitation without asking me if I was free. As it happens, I'd arranged to do something else and I refused to change my plans." She smiled. "I'd said I'd take Wilhelm to the zoo."

"You gave him up. . . for me?" Wilhelm asked softly.

"It seems that way, my darling."

"So you never met this person? You'd never visited him before?" asked Johann.

"No. He was holding a house party. He lived in . . ." Elisabeth's voice tailed off.

"Lived in . . . ?"

"A schloss."

"Ah. And do you happen to know what his name was?"

"No. . . yes . . .no . . .I think it was Hans . . .I'm not sure. . . I don't think Helmut ever mentioned his surname."

"And do you know where the schloss was?"

"No. We never got that far."

Johann nodded, then said "Elisabeth, did you ever discuss Wilhelm with Helmut."

Elisabeth shook her head. "No. . .well, I did mention him. I told him about how I'd been roped in to try to find out what language Wilhelm spoke. But at that point we all still thought that Wilhelm must be a refugee or an illegal immigrant. I certainly didn't tell Helmut anything about the mines or the tunnels or the Hundeiss. Anyway he wasn't interested."

"No?"

"No. I'm afraid Helmut isn't interested in anybody whom he considers to be inferior to himself. His attitudes are very . . . right wing."

Johann scratched his beard and said "Well, I think we must put it down to bad luck that we ran into Helmut at the opera. Evidently he must have started putting two and two together then, although how he recognised Wilhelm as being Hundeiss, I really don't know."

"You think Helmut's involved in all this?" asked Elisabeth in a shocked voice.

261

"I have no doubt of it. And I'm quite sure that he arranged for your car to have problems and to be on hand to bring you home."

Elisabeth sat, shaking her head. "So it's my fault that Wilhelm had that terrible experience last night . . ."

"No!" Johann broke in sharply. "It was no one's fault. How could you possibly have known? It's imperative that no one blames him or herself for anything that has happened or may happen. Self blame and self doubt only weaken one's resistance. It's vital that we remain strong at all times. And now," he stood up, "we'll go and have some coffee and talk about something else."

Chapter Fourteen

Since Johann had said that it was permitted, Wilhelm had hoped that he and Elisabeth might make love that night. But Elisabeth was restless, anxious, ill at ease, so he just held her and they talked and, eventually, fell asleep. His sleep was filled with dreams, none of which he remembered when he woke, but the music didn't return. Elisabeth left for work at eight thirty and Wilhelm filled in his day as best he could with reading and drawing, although he found it hard to concentrate on either.

At quarter to six Elisabeth arrived back and went upstairs to remove her make up and nail varnish. She returned looking pale and tense. Ten minutes later the door bell heralded the arrival of Marcus and Erika. They went with Wilhelm and Elisabeth into the sitting room and perched nervously on the edge of their chairs. Nobody said anything. After a few moments, Johann came in and said "We won't all fit into our car. Elisabeth and Wilhelm, you come with us. Marcus, you and Erika can follow in your car."

They trooped outside, still in silence, and got into the two cars. Magdalena, seated in front, next to Johann, turned and smiled reassuringly to Wilhelm and Elisabeth, but said nothing. They drove through the heavy evening traffic, Johann keeping a careful eye on his rear view mirror to ensure that Marcus was still following him. Eventually they turned into a road lined with large late-nineteenth century houses, outside one of which Johann stopped the car. He led the way to the front door, waiting for Marcus and Erika to join them before ringing the bell. A middle aged woman in a long, plain grey dress opened the door and stood back to allow them to enter the spacious hallway. Wordlessly, she took their coats and hung them on a stand by the door. There were already several other coats hanging there.

Johann turned to them. "Marcus and Wilhelm, come with me. Erika and Elisabeth, go with Magdalena." He led the two men down a corridor and into what appeared to be a changing room. There were pegs along the wall and a shower in one corner. Hanging from two of the pegs were long robes made of a soft white material, and on a small table there was a pile of clean towels. Johann said "Get undressed, shower and then put on the robes. Wait here and I'll come back for you in a little while."

Left to themselves, Wilhelm and Marcus looked at each other nervously. Then Marcus said "Do you want to go first?"

Wilhelm undressed and got into the shower. There was a new bar of soap on the shelf and he washed thoroughly, finding the warmth of the water relaxing. Coming out, he took a towel and dried himself while Marcus showered. By the time Marcus had finished washing, Wilhelm had put on one of the robes and was using the towel to dry off his hair. The robes were floor length, with long sleeves and round necks and felt soft against the skin. When Johann came back, they were both ready. He, too, had changed into a white robe, with a gold cord tied around the waist.

"As there hasn't been time to prepare you for the initiation," he said, "I'll tell you the correct responses to the questions as they're asked. All you need to do is to repeat them, if you believe them to be true. On no account must you say anything that you don't sincerely believe. If you are uncertain, you must say so. If I don't prompt you with an answer, just say what is in your heart. Now, come with me." He left the room and they followed him, bare footed, to the end of the corridor and through a set of double doors.

The room they entered was not very large - perhaps twice the size of Magdalena's sitting room - but it gave the impression of space, being very high ceilinged and practically devoid of furniture. Long dark blue velvet curtains hung over the windows, contrasting with the stark white-painted walls. In the centre of the polished wooden floor was a small round table covered with a white cloth. On it stood a silver cross, two small silver pots, a large silver cup, a pair of scissors and a length of fine gold cord.

On the wall opposite the door hung a vajra and on the wall to the right, a star of David. Glancing to the left, Wilhelm saw an ankh. He assumed that, if he turned, he would see a swastika on the wall behind him. Elisabeth and Erika were already in there, standing facing the table, with Magdalena behind them. They, too, were wearing white robes,

Magdalena's having a blue cord around the waist. Wilhelm noticed that their hair was wet. Johann positioned him and Marcus to the right of Elisabeth and Erika, then moved round to stand behind them, saying "You must stay absolutely still. Don't move unless you're told to."

Wilhelm had to work hard to obey him; his nervousness was making him feel fidgety. He concentrated on breathing deeply, trying to calm himself. He was finding standing in one position very tiring and the light in the room, from the two huge chandeliers overhead, was very bright. He was aware of Johann behind him and of Marcus to his left. He wanted to turn his head to look at Elisabeth to make sure that she was all right but knew he mustn't. He was comforted by the fact that Magdalena was with her and would look after her.

With no warning, the lights went out and they were plunged into total darkness. No one made a sound. Suddenly Wilhelm was no longer sure that the others were in the room. He wanted to turn, to look, but knew that it would be impossible to see anything in the darkness although, paradoxically, he was sure that Johann would be able to see him if he moved even slightly. Deprived of sight, he was becoming more and more aware of his own body, of his heart beating and of his breathing, of the soft white robe touching his skin and of the sensation of the polished wood under his feet. The darkness was having a strange effect on him. He was no longer certain that he was facing in the same direction as before. He felt disorientated.

Suddenly a bright light hit him full in the face. With an effort, he stopped himself from putting up a hand to shield his eyes. Two people stood on the other side of the table, between him and the light. They appeared to be wearing hooded robes which, against the light, looked black. He couldn't see their faces. From their build he thought that one was a man and the other a woman.

Wilhelm felt Johann's hand on his shoulder, pushing him down, and he knelt, thankful for the change in position although the floor was hard under his scantily covered knees. The man and the woman each picked up one of the small silver pots and, one walking clockwise and the other anticlockwise, poured what looked like salt in a continuous line on the floor, until they and the table were surrounded by a complete circle about three metres in diameter.

The pots were replaced on the table and the man started to speak. "You stand at the edge of a place that is between the known and the unknown, between the everyday and the inexplicable, between the reassuring and the terrifying. You stand under the watchful eye of God in his many aspects - Yahweh the Father, Christ the Son, the Holy Spirit, Allah the All-merciful, Brahma the Creator, Vishnu the Preserver, Siva the Destroyer, Avalokitesvara the Compassionate, Manjusri the Master of Wisdom. You have now to make a choice before God whether to go on or to turn back. For it is not yet too late to turn back. But be warned, if you choose to go on, then you are embarking on a path from which there is no turning back, a path on which you must continue for the rest of your life, however long that may be. It is not a choice to be undertaken lightly. You must consider it carefully and know that it would be better for you to die now than to enter this circle with fear or with deceit in your heart."

As he finished speaking, the light went out, leaving them in darkness once more. Wilhelm was uncertain how long they remained kneeling there. He hadn't understood all the names of God but he understood the meaning of what had been said and he knew that for the sake of his people he must go on. He trusted Johann and Magdalena. They were good people. If they said this was the right thing to do, then he was unafraid.

Once more the light snapped on, and Wilhelm screwed up his eyes while he became accustomed to it. The man and the woman hadn't moved. "Have you considered?" asked the man. Johann gave no prompt, so Wilhelm said "Yes," and heard the others do the same.

"And will you go forward or go back?"

Again Johann remained silent, so Wilhelm said "I will go forward." To his left he heard Marcus' voice say strongly "I will go forward." Then Elisabeth and Erika together, "I will go forward."

"How do you come to this circle?" the woman asked, and this time Johann whispered "I come with perfect love and perfect trust." Wilhelm repeated it, in chorus with the others. The man and woman raised their right hands and Wilhelm could see that they held small golden daggers. They moved forward and each marked a line through the circle, so that a segment of it was cut off from the rest. Stepping over the segment, the man moved towards Erika and Elisabeth and the woman to Wilhelm and Marcus, lifting them to their feet and kissing them each in turn, on the mouth.

Together the man and woman said "Thus are all first brought into the circle. Let them be admitted." The woman took hold of Wilhelm's and Marcus's hands and drew them into the circle across the cut segment, followed by the man leading Elisabeth and Erika. Johann and Magdalena stepped in after them, then bent and smoothed the white line so that the circle was once more continuous.

"You must kneel and take the vows," said the woman.

"Repeat these words," said the man, when they were kneeling again. "And mean them in your heart, for God sees into your heart and knows whether you speak the truth or not. . . I will keep the secrets that are entrusted to me and will never divulge them. . . I will love and respect my brothers and sisters and do whatever I can to aid them. . . I will listen to those who have come into the circle before me and I will do all that is asked of me. . . I will be truthful, honest, humble and diligent. I will fight evil with all my strength."

After Wilhelm and the others had repeated the words, there was a short silence, then Johann whispered "I swear that I shall keep these vows. . . May the ground fall from beneath me . . . may the sea rise up over me . . . may the air not sustain me if I break this trust." In a chorus, they repeated the words, then the light went out again.

For a few moments nothing happened and then the man began to chant softly, a strange but somehow soothing music that sounded as though it were coming from deep within his chest, reassuring even though the words were incomprehensible. The woman joined in, followed by Johann and Magdalena. The sound rose and fell, resonating around the room, seemingly magnified by the darkness, demanding attention. Slowly, it grew louder until it sounded as though it were no longer being made by four people but by ten . . . twenty . . . a hundred. There was no room in Wilhelm's head for anything but the chant.

Then, just ahead of him in the darkness he thought he saw a pinprick of light. He watched it as it grew larger, spellbound by the fact that it had no obvious source but seemed to be hovering some inches from the floor at the centre of the circle. Slowly it spread to enclose the whole circle and its occupants, enveloping them in a bubble of pure white light. When the bubble was completely formed, the chanting suddenly stopped and there was an intense silence. Wilhelm looked at the light in wonder, seeing it shimmering and moving as though it were alive.

He could see the occupants of the circle more clearly now, although he still couldn't make out the faces under the hoods. The man lifted the great silver cup from the table and offered it to Elisabeth and Erika in turn. When they had drunk from it, the woman took it and handed it to Marcus and finally to Wilhelm. He sipped cautiously. The contents were sweet and pleasant and unlike anything he had ever tasted before. Taking the cup from him, the woman returned it to the man who placed it on the table and began to speak, his voice ringing out, clear and strong..

"He who dwells in the shelter of the Most High, who abides in the shadow of the Almighty, says of the Lord 'He is my refuge and my fortress, my God in whom I trust.' For he will deliver you from the fowler's snare and from the deadly pestilence. He will cover you with his pinions and you will find refuge under his wings."

Wilhelm listened entranced to the beautiful words, remembering the eagle that he had seen when Elisabeth took him to the zoo, imagining what it would feel like to be protected by the strength of those great wings, cushioned by the softness of the feathers.

". . . His truth shall be a shield and a buckler. You will not be afraid of the terror by night nor of the arrow that flies by day, nor of the pestilence that walks in darkness, nor of the destruction that ravages at noon. A thousand may fall at your side, and ten thousand at your right hand, but it will not come near you. You will only look with your eyes and see the retribution of the wicked."

Although Wilhelm didn't understand every word, the meaning was plain and he found the idea of such power both reassuring and terrifying. How, he wondered, could They possibly withstand it?

" . . .For the Lord is your refuge and the Most High is your dwelling place. No evil shall befall you nor any scourge come near your tent. For he will give his angels charge over you to guard you in all your ways. They will bear you up on their hands lest you strike your foot against a stone. You will tread on the lion and the adder, you will trample the young lion and the serpent under your foot. Because he has given his love to me I will deliver him. Because he knows my name, I will protect him. When he calls me, I will answer him. I will be with him in trouble. I will rescue and honour him. I will satisfy him with long life and let him see my salvation."

When he had finished speaking, the man took the cord from the table and told the initiates to stand. Slowly and carefully, he went to each in turn, then to Johann and Magdalena, tying the cord round the right wrist of each, so that each was bound to the others. Finally, he tied it to the woman's wrist and to his own, saying "Let us be joined in love and friendship. Let us work together for the good of all. May God in all his aspects protect us and give us strength." Then, taking the scissors from the table, he moved round, cutting the links so that each person was left with a bracelet of the cord. As he made the final cut, the white bubble burst and they were left in darkness once again.

It seemed only a matter of seconds before the central chandeliers came on, the light reflecting brightly off the white walls. The two figures had gone and there was no sign of the circle. Wilhelm looked down at the cord on his wrist to reassure himself that he hadn't imagined it all, then Magdalena was coming up and kissing him and Marcus, and Johann was kissing Elisabeth and Erika and everyone was smiling broadly.

Back in the changing room Wilhelm and Marcus took their time dressing. Johann put his head round the door and said "When you're ready, come in and meet our hosts and some of our friends. The room opposite the front door."

269

There were about twenty people in there, all in normal clothes, who welcomed them with enthusiastic applause. Magdalena, dressed once again in skirt and jumper, came over and took their arms, then walked them round the room, introducing them to people. Another outbreak of clapping told Wilhelm that Erika and Elisabeth had come in. He turned and saw that they were both smiling and looking relaxed. Johann was greeting them and starting to introduce them to his friends. They were all offered wine and cake and the general atmosphere was one of gaiety and celebration. But at the back of his mind, Wilhelm remained aware of why they were there and what had led them to this place and he wondered whether these people truly had the power to overcome the music and to set the Hundeiss free.

In the car on the way home, Wilhelm sat holding Elisabeth's hand, saying little. He was, he realised, exhausted and he sensed that she felt much the same. Looking back, he found that although every detail of the ceremony was still vivid in his mind, he couldn't remember the name or the face of anyone to whom he'd been introduced. When they reached the house, he and Elisabeth excused themselves immediately and went upstairs. Climbing into bed, Wilhelm turned out the light, put his arms round Elisabeth and instantly fell into a dreamless sleep.

✷ ✷ ✷

"The initiation," said Johann, as they all sat drinking coffee the following evening "is only the beginning. Having been given the empowerment, you now have to learn how to use it."

"How do we do that?" asked Erika.

"In normal circumstances, you'd go once a week to the fellowship's house - where you were last night - and you'd be able to take your time learning what you need to know. But these aren't normal circumstances, so I'm going to have to ask you to come here every evening for several weeks so that Magdalena and I can train you."

"What does the training consist of?" Marcus asked.

"We shall meditate and you will learn to use visualisation and the energy of crystals. We shall practise lifting ourselves up towards the Divine, becoming One with each other, finding the spiritual power within ourselves. You'll learn to open your eyes and your ears to what the universe is telling you. It will require both concentration and dedication, but I have no doubt that you can all do it."

"A few months ago," said Elisabeth quietly, "I should have been highly sceptical of all this. But after last night's experience . . . when we were encased in that white light, I felt . . . as though I had all the mysteries of the world at my fingertips . . . and so peaceful. I don't think I've ever felt so peaceful."

Johann nodded. "Last night you were in the hands of four people - Magdalena and myself and the two friends who conducted the ceremony - who have been practising these skills for many years. But the cords that were tied round your wrists will continue to link you to all of us – to all the fellowship and all our combined skills, which you can call upon if necessary. So it's important that you don't take the cords off. Eventually they'll fall off, but by then you will have started to develop your own skills and will have learned other ways in which you can communicate with us. And now, if you're all agreeable, I think we should make a start."

Johann led the way upstairs and into a room at the back of the house. During the months he had been living there, Wilhelm had noticed Johann and Magdalena going into and coming out of that room from time to time but had thought nothing of it, assuming that it was a quiet room where they went to read or to study. They left their shoes outside the door, at Johann's request, and stepped inside onto a soft lilac-coloured carpet. There were upright chairs around the walls and large cushions on the floor. A small table standing against one wall held a single large candle, a large silver bowl, a small vase of flowers and the sweet-scented sticks that Wilhelm now knew to be called incense. Heavy velvet curtains, the same colour as the carpet, were drawn across the single window, and on the walls hung the familiar symbols - cross, ankh, star of David, vajra and swastika.

"If you're not used to sitting cross-legged for long periods, sit on a chair," said Magdalena, sinking down onto one of the cushions. After a moment's thought, Elisabeth chose a chair while the others joined Magdalena on the floor. Johann lit the candle and the incense and bowed to each of the four walls in turn. "Let us begin . . ." he said.

As Johann had predicted, the work was hard, but within a few weeks the effects were becoming evident. The six of them seemed able now, in their meditation, to work together, to generate a tangible power. Even outside the meditation room, Wilhelm had started to feel as though he was constantly in touch with the others, and it seemed to him that, if he really tried hard enough, he could somehow tap into their thoughts, could communicate without needing words.

But now, for the first time, he was having problems. The evening's meditation had begun, as always, with an invocation to the Divine and the visualisation of a column of white light to which each of the participants was linked by golden rays. Suddenly Wilhelm was aware that his mind was veering off in other directions and that he had lost his link with the light and with the others. It was as if something was tugging at him, demanding attention. He tried to look into the corners of his mind, to see what it was that was causing the distraction, but he could find nothing. He had the impression of something lurking, just out of sight, refusing to be identified. At the same time, he was aware of Johann's presence, gently pulling him back to the meditation through the white light and he was beginning to feel an actual physical discomfort, as though he were subject to two strong forces trying to take him in opposite directions. In the end, he gave up and just sat quietly with eyes closed, visualising nothing, paying attention to his breathing as Johann had taught him. It was a relief when the period of meditation ended and, as he stood up and stretched his legs, he realised that he felt tired and edgy. Johann looked at him anxiously and, after they had left the meditation room, asked quietly "Are you all right, Wilhelm?"

Wilhelm shrugged. "I think so. I just couldn't concentrate."

Johann nodded. "It happens sometimes. Get a good night's sleep. It'll be easier tomorrow."

But, once in bed, it was Elisabeth who fell asleep quickly while Wilhelm lay gazing at the ceiling. The long training was making him impatient. He wanted to be active, to do something positive to free his people. In frustration, he imagined himself vanquishing Them and rescuing the Hundeiss single handed and, in this frame of mind, he eventually fell asleep, to dream of storming the mines and tunnels, the spear of Longinus in his hand.

At some time during the night he woke briefly. His wrist felt as though it was burning. Moving to rub the painful area, he realised that the cord tied round it was cutting into him. Half asleep, he tried to pull it off, then remembered. Easing the cord with his finger, he found that it wasn't tight. It must have been caught on something but, in his half asleep state, he was unable to work out what it could have been. He was aware of Elisabeth moving next to him and put out his arm towards her. In the darkness he heard her say softly "Go back to sleep Wilhelm," and, comforted, he did.

He woke with a jolt in the early morning, uncertain what had disturbed him. He looked at the clock. It was 6.30. Stretching across for Elisabeth, he was surprised to find that the bed was empty. She didn't usually get up until seven. Perhaps she had to go in to work early today. He closed his eyes again but didn't sleep. There was something . . . something . . . . He opened his eyes and looked once more at her pillow. In the dim morning light he could see that there was something lying there. He sat up and put on the bedside lamp.

With a shock he saw that Elisabeth had taken off her amulet necklace. For a moment he was worried but then he remembered that the catch had become loose - she had nearly lost it yesterday. She had probably taken it off while she had a shower. He reached for it, with the idea of mending the catch for her, and noticed that, nestling in the fold of the pillow, was what looked like a small yellowish-white ball. He picked it up. It was a tiny carving of a rat in a smooth substance that he had seen before in a museum. He tried to remember . . . Ivory. A rat carved in ivory. It was exquisite, its tiny claws and whiskers beautifully depicted and its long thin tail curving round its body. Strange that he'd never seen it before, that Elisabeth hadn't shown it to him. He wondered why she'd put it on her pillow.

Putting the rat down, Wilhelm took the necklace and looked at the clasp. It seemed to be working perfectly. He couldn't see why it had slipped the day before. But perhaps Elisabeth herself had mended it this morning. The clock showed ten to seven. Pushing back the covers, he picked up the necklace, put on his dressing gown and went out to the bathroom. It was empty. Padding down the stairs, he turned into the kitchen, saying "Elisabeth, you forgot your necklace." She wasn't there.

Puzzled, Wilhelm went into each of the ground floor rooms in turn. They were deserted. Elisabeth's coat and the case in which she carried her books and papers were in the hall. She couldn't have left the house but, nevertheless, he was starting to feel anxious. Where else could she be? Unless . . . he ran up the stairs to the meditation room, turning the handle quietly so as not to disturb her. She wasn't there.

Wilhelm's mouth was dry. He called "Elisabeth." Then, more loudly, "Elisabeth." Then, with increasing panic, "Elisabeth."

The door of Johann and Magdalena's room flew open and Johann came out, his expression reflecting Wilhelm's deepest fears.

"She's gone," Wilhelm managed to say. "And she's left . . ." He held up the necklace.

Johann pushed past him into the bedroom and Wilhelm saw him stop dead in his tracks at the sight of the little ivory rat. Then he turned and rushed down the stairs and out of the front door, with Wilhelm at his heels. Elisabeth's car was still where she had parked it the night before. Further along the road, something lay on the pavement. Johann picked it up and turned round, his face ashen. It was the cord that had been around Elisabeth's wrist. It had been cut with a sharp knife.

✳ ✳ ✳

The early sun shone into the sitting room, giving it an appearance of normality that was in strong contrast to the events of the night. Wilhelm sat on the settee, Magdalena beside him, holding his hand. He was shivering.

"They will do nothing until nightfall," said Johann. "We have time."
"But how . . .?" Wilhelm asked hoarsely. "How did they take her?

274

When I was sleeping in the same bed. How did they come and take her without my knowing? How did they come into the house and take her out without any of us knowing?"

"I'm not sure," said Johann thoughtfully. "but I think I can guess. Did you wake at all during the night?"

"Briefly. The cord was cutting into my wrist. Elisabeth told me to go to sleep again."

Johann nodded. "Yes, the cord - or rather, the power in it - was trying to warn you."

Wilhelm let out a short cry. "And I went to sleep again - I let them take her." He felt numb with the realisation.

"No," said Johann firmly. "It wasn't your fault. Their power was greater. There was nothing that you could have done."

"But if I'd woken up, seen what was happening . . ."

Johann shook his head. "You couldn't wake. When Elisabeth told you to sleep it wasn't a suggestion - it was an instruction from Them. It was as effective as a blow to the head - you were powerless to resist it."

"But how did they get into the house?" Wilhelm persisted.

"I don't think they did. I think they lured her out."

"How?"

"There's a method that I saw being used when I was investigating an occult practice called voodoo. If they want to influence another person they give him, or her, some trinket, something they will become fond of and treasure. And they use that as a link, a way of getting into that person's thoughts and controlling them. I think someone - probably Helmut - must have given Elisabeth the little ivory rat that you found on her pillow."

"But I've never seen it before. Surely if it was something she was fond of, she'd have shown it to me?"

"Possibly. Or possibly she returned it to Helmut when they parted and he found some way of getting it back to her. Maybe he slipped it into her pocket or her bag when he gave you a lift home. If he was clever, he could have tucked it under the lining where she wouldn't find it. Once it was in her possession, they could use it to influence her whenever they wanted to. .

275

You found concentration difficult last night when we were meditating."

"Yes. I could feel you pulling me back but there was something else pulling me away."

"I think that was Them, working through Elisabeth, making sure you had no strength to resist them when they took her away. They would have woken Elisabeth at some time during the night by putting a thought into her mind. She would have been ordered to take off her necklace and then they would have told her where to find the little ivory rat. Once she had put that with the necklace, she would have been called down to the street. They must have been waiting just outside the front door, ready to cut the cord from her wrist - her last defence."

"But what do they want her for? Why her? Why not me?" Wilhelm asked.

"I think," said Johann slowly, "that I may have been wrong. When you suddenly started to hear the music, I assumed that they had discovered who you were and were trying to get control over you again. But now, I'm beginning to wonder . . ."

"What?" asked Magdalena. It was the first word that she had uttered since they had entered the room.

Johann looked at her, anxiety clear in his eyes. "Elisabeth said that Helmut had plans to take her to the schloss . . . plans that she threw into disarray by refusing to go with him, by keeping her promise to Wilhelm. I'm only assuming that it was Herr Pfeiffer's schloss they were meant to go to . . . it seems an extraordinary coincidence, but it's does seem to fit with what we know. And we can have no doubt that, if Helmut was taking her there, then he's one of their number and he wanted her to join them. And clearly he hasn't given up his plan. He may also see this abduction of her as a way of getting his revenge on Wilhelm for taking Elisabeth away from him."

"But why, then, did Wilhelm hear the music?" Magdalena asked.

"Did either you or Elisabeth tell Helmut that you lived with us, Wilhelm? Or is it likely that he thought that this was your house?"

Wilhelm thought. "Helmut asked where we were going and I think

276

Elisabeth said 'To Wilhelm's house'."

Johann nodded. "And, no doubt, he thought that Elisabeth would be staying the night here with you. You heard the music because you were susceptible to it - but Helmut probably didn't know that. If Elisabeth had been here that night, she would have heard it too and would have been lured out, as she was last night. They must have wondered why their plan hadn't worked. But obviously they decided to try again - and this time she was here and the little rat that Helmut had given her made her susceptible to the music . . . and she went with them."

Wilhelm hid his face in his hands. The thought that They had got Elisabeth was terrible enough, but that they wanted her to join in their evil . . . that they might have methods by which to coerce her into doing so . . . He looked up at Johann. "What will they do with her?" he asked, not wanting to hear the answer.

"I don't know," replied Johann, "but I'll do everything in my power to stop them." He looked at his watch. "Shortly, I shall make some 'phone calls and then we must wait until it's time to go and find her."

"Why wait? Surely the sooner we go, the more likely we are to be able to get her back before they can harm her."

"No. I'm sure they'll do nothing until nightfall. They're nocturnal by nature. And there are preparations that we must make. Meanwhile, I want you to go and get some rest. You'll need all your strength tonight."

✳ ✳ ✳

"They'll do nothing until nightfall," Johann repeated firmly. "And it won't be safe for us to move until then."

"Why not?" shouted Wilhelm, standing up and thumping the kitchen table with his fist. He had been growing increasingly frustrated as the day wore on and Johann, his 'phone calls finished, showed no sign of making any move. "They've got Elisabeth. They've got her. You insisted that she come here - you said she'd be safer here - you promised. You told us to trust you and you've let us down. She's in their hands - alone, unprotected. It's all your fault!"

"No . . ." Marcus who had arrived a few minutes ago and was sitting with Johann at the table, started to rise to his feet but Johann put a hand on his arm and shook his head.

"In a way, Wilhelm is right," he said. "I did say that Elisabeth would be safer here. I'm sorry."

Wilhelm stared at Johann, rage and terror boiling inside him. He knew what They were capable of. He'd seen men worked to death, women and children Taken, healthy young women taken for breeding - and he knew now what breeding meant. And they'd got Elisabeth. And he was standing here in Magdalena's comfortable warm kitchen doing nothing.

Magdalena appeared at his side with a mug of herbal tea in her hand. "Drink this, Wilhelm," she said softly. "It'll help."

Wilhelm stared at her in disbelief, then knocked the mug out of her hand and onto the floor where it smashed, splashing its contents over their feet. For a moment there was silence then, without a word, Magdalena bent and started to pick up the broken pieces of pottery. Wilhelm stepped over her and ran down the hall, out of the front door and into the street.

Standing on the pavement, he suddenly realised the futility of his action. He didn't know where to go. He didn't know where the schloss was or how to get there. And even if he did, what would he do? Storm in at the front door and demand that They return Elisabeth? And if, as Johann said, They did have powerful forces at their disposal, how would he overcome them? He suddenly remembered something that had happened in the mines. There had been a fall of rock and three women had been trapped behind it. The man - the husband - of one of the women had rushed in, trying to free them, and had almost been killed by another rock slide. It was only when five men started to work together to lift the rocks that the women had been freed. And now he was rushing in like that man, to save his woman. He turned back to the house, common sense telling him that he must work together with his friends. When he got back to the kitchen, Magdalena had finished cleaning up the mess and was sitting with Marcus and Johann at the table. She looked as though she had been crying.

For a moment Wilhelm stood in the doorway, then he whispered "I'm sorry."

Magdalena got up and hurried over to him, smiling wanly and shaking her head. She took him in her arms. "It's all right," she said. "We understand."

She led him to the table and sat him down. "Tea?" she asked.

Wilhelm nodded, smiling ruefully, and she placed a mug in front of him.

Johann looked at his watch. "It's two thirty. We'll leave in two hours. Before that, we'll need to perform certain rituals to give ourselves added protection."

"Will any of your ... associates come with us?" asked Marcus.

Johann shook his head. "No. Just we three will go. But they'll be supporting us with rituals to generate power."

"Erika was distraught when I spoke to her," Marcus said. "She so wanted to come with us but, with six nurses off sick in the accident department, there was no one to cover for her."

"I know," said Johann. "But she'll still be giving us her support, simply by wearing the cord around her wrist. And she can join Magdalena and the others in the rituals when she comes off duty."

When they had finished their tea, they went upstairs and Magdalena produced four white robes. In turn they showered and changed and went into the meditation room. Johann, Marcus and Wilhelm knelt while Magdalena lit the candle and incense.

Turning towards them, she said "Let us invoke the light. Previously you have visualised it in your minds. But now you must see it in front of you. Fix your eyes on the candle and watch it arise."

Wilhelm stared at the candle, its flame burning clear and steady. He could feel the power already, a tingling in his hands and his face, a sense of something else - something greater than any of them - entering the room. And, as he watched, a column of white light started to grow up out of the candle, rising upwards to the ceiling, then spreading outwards until it filled the whole room.

He heard Magdalena's voice saying "Reach up with your mind and touch the Divine."

279

He could feel his mind stretching, lifting . . . Magdalena and Johann began to chant and, as before at the initiation, it seemed that other voices were joining theirs, until the sound of a great choir was filling the room with sound. Suddenly ribbons of glittering coloured light were snaking through the air. A ribbon of scarlet touched Wilhelm's arm and he gasped at the sense of exhilaration that it sparked. Ribbons of bright yellow and vivid blue, strident orange, cool violet and vibrant magenta, shimmering ribbons of gold and silver, rich indigo, warm crimson and deep sea green spun around them, chasing each other, faster and faster until the room became a swirling mass of colour and of pulsating energy.

After what seemed like hours, during which Wilhelm watched entranced, the chant diminished, then stopped and, slowly the colours subsided and the white light contracted until it was a single column stretching up above the candle. And then there was just the candle. Magdalena took a small crystal jug which stood beside it and poured the water it contained into a silver bowl. Dipping her hand into it, she went to each of them in turn and made a small cross over each of their chakras - the centres of energy in the body - on the crown of the head, the forehead, the throat, the heart, the solar plexus just below the ribs, and on the back at the level of the hip bones, and at the base of the spine. Then she knelt down with them and they remained in silence for several minutes.

In the candlelit room, with its flickering shadows and sweet-smelling incense, Wilhelm felt calmer than he had done all day and knew that in the calmness there was strength.

Suddenly Johann said "It's time to go," and stood up. Magdalena kissed each of the men on the mouth as they left the room to get changed. Then, dressed in jeans and thick sweaters, they went downstairs and out to Johann's car.

The schloss was in darkness when they got there. Johann parked the car some distance away and they walked quietly towards it. It was surrounded by a high wall into which was set a pair of huge wrought iron gates.

280

"How do we get in?" Marcus whispered.

Johann walked up to one of the gates and pushed. To   Wilhelm's surprise, it swung in, noiselessly.

"Do you think they're expecting us?" Marcus asked nervously.

"They're expecting someone," said Johann. "But I don't think it's us - I'm fairly sure they don't know we've located the schloss. Still, you can be sure that they're not going to make access easy for intruders. Keep close together."

They pushed through the gate and along the wide path leading to the house which loomed up at them out of the darkness, huge and threatening. No lights were visible but, although the schloss appeared to be deserted, ten or fifteen large cars were parked near the front door, starkly modern against the ancient stonework.

"As I suspected, he has guests," whispered Johann. "We can't hope to get into the house through a ground floor entrance. There'll be too many people about."

"So what do we do?" asked Marcus, looking up at the small inaccessible windows high above them.

"We look for some water."

"Water?" Wilhelm momentarily wondered whether this was all too much for Johann.

"Yes. In some ancient traditions the entrances to the hollow earth are said to be hidden at the bottom of wells or lakes. If we're lucky, we'll find something of the sort here that gives access to both the mines and the schloss."

Skirting round the side, keeping close to the wall, they found themselves on the topmost of three terraces running the breadth of the building. There were shallow stone steps leading down to the lower levels and they negotiated these slowly, treading carefully in the darkness. The third terrace stretched away into what seemed to be gardens full of dense bushes and low-hanging trees. An owl hooted, and Wilhelm shivered at the sound.

Suddenly Johann pointed. Over to the other side of the terrace was a shape which, as they drew closer, was clearly a well. They peered down into it but all they could see was blackness. From his pocket Johann produced a tiny flashlight and shone it into the shaft. There was a narrow iron ladder attached to the side. Johann climbed over the wall of the well and onto the ladder, surprising Wilhelm with his agility. "Follow me, but leave at least five steps clear between us," said Johann. "We don't want to run into each other in the dark." Once he had begun his descent, Wilhelm swung over the wall and started to go down after him. A few seconds later he was followed by Marcus.

It was very dark in the well but Wilhelm had spent most of his life in semi-darkness. As he descended the ladder, he wondered what it would feel like to be underground once more.

Suddenly, as he felt cautiously with his foot for the next rung, he heard Johann's voice just below him say "We're at the bottom." He looked down and saw by Johann's flashlight that they had reached the water. Johann said "It's not very deep - perhaps three feet. And I think I can see something underneath it, some kind of trapdoor."

"Can we open it?"

"It will need strength. The water will be holding it down."

"I'll try."

Wilhelm eased past him and dropped into the water. It was icy cold and came almost to his waist. He took off his sweater and shirt and handed them to Johann, then, taking a deep breath, he ducked beneath the surface. He could feel the door under his hands - it seemed to be circular and there was a handle in the centre. Grasping the handle with both hands he pulled. Nothing happened. He tried again. Still nothing. Gasping for air, he stood up. "I can't move it. . . Give me a minute and I'll try again . . . We've got to get in somehow."

"It may be protected," said Johann. "Are there any carvings on the surface?"

"I don't know. I'll have a feel."

Once more, Wilhelm took a lungful of air and plunged under the water. He ran his hands across the door. It wasn't smooth . . . there was some kind of pattern . . . very simple . . . Suddenly he realised what it was - it was a swastika. And the swastika, he knew, was a symbol of the solar system - a spinning symbol, spinning one way to promote goodness and well-being, spinning the other way to produce chaos and strife. Wilhelm lifted his head above the water, took another breath then, reaching down, grasped the handle and turned the door in the direction of its swastika, the direction of chaos. He felt it move and, exerting all his strength, he twisted it round and lifted it out of its setting. With a rush, the water started to drain away into whatever was below, leaving Wilhelm's wet jeans sticking unpleasantly to his legs, his shoes sodden.

He stood with the heavy metallic door in his hands, panting while the last of the water gurgled out of the well. "I should have brought a towel," he said, shivering, as he took his shirt and sweater from Johann and hurriedly put them on again. They felt rough and uncomfortable against his wet skin. Johann shone his torch into the hole that had been revealed at the bottom of the well. There was a flight of uneven stone steps leading down into the darkness.

Treading carefully, so as not to slip, they made their way down. At the foot of the stairs was a tunnel which seemed to have been cut out of the solid rock on which the schloss was built. The water from the well had pooled in places along the tunnel floor, reflecting the beam from Johann's torch. With Johann at their head, they started to move forward, stooping slightly because of the low roof. The walls looked greenish in the torchlight and there was a mustiness which spoke of eternal dampness. Wilhelm could hear Marcus's heavy breathing behind him and sensed his anxiety.

Slowly and cautiously they tramped onwards. The tunnel seemed to curve round and then turn back on itself so, before long, Wilhelm had lost all sense of direction. For all he knew, they might be going further away from the house rather than towards it. Suddenly he heard a harsh cough behind him. Looking over his shoulder, he saw Marcus, his hand over his mouth and nose, his eyes bulging.

"What is it?" asked Wilhelm, a shudder of alarm running through him.

"Gas," muttered Marcus through his hand. "Poison gas. I can smell it."

Johann had turned and was pushing past Wilhelm. Putting a hand on Marcus's arm he said in a calm voice "There is no gas. It's an illusion. I can't smell anything."

Marcus said nothing, Johann's flashlight reflecting onto his face which was now turning deep red as he tried not to breathe. Wilhelm stood by, feeling helpless, listening to his friend choke, wanting to do something but not knowing what. He could smell only the odour of the tunnel that had been there all along.

"The smell is just an illusion, Marcus," Johann said again. "We are perfectly safe."

Marcus, his eyes full of fear, shook his head.

"I'll prove it," said Johann quickly as Marcus sank to his knees, still clutching his mouth and nose. Putting his hand in his pocket, he drew out a box of matches. "Poison gas is combustible," he said and, before Marcus could stop him, he struck a match. It burned with a small yellow flame, then went out.

Marcus moaned and collapsed onto the floor, then turned his head and vomited. Johann squatted down beside him, offering a clean handkerchief. After a few moments, Marcus sat up and mopped his mouth, taking in great gulps of air.

"I'm sorry . . ." he said. "The smell was so strong . . . I was so sure."

"They will have surrounded themselves with all sorts of protective devices," said Johann, putting his arm round Marcus's shoulders in a gesture of reassurance. "This was probably just the first of many. We must make sure that we recognise them for what they are - illusions. It's fortunate that there are three of us. If you'd been by yourself, it would have had the desired effect. Either you'd have rushed back to the tunnel entrance and tried to escape up the well or, more likely, you'd have succumbed to the imaginary gas and your body would have reacted as though you really had been poisoned. This is why it's so important that we stay together."

Marcus nodded, his face now white, his breathing coming in gasps.

"I'm sorry," he said again.

"It's not your fault," Johann replied. "It could have happened to any of us. . . and it probably will."

"But why didn't either of you smell the gas?" asked Marcus. "Why just me?"

"These things work on our inner fears," said Johann. "I've had far longer to build up my defences than you have. And whereas Wilhelm may possibly have read about poison gas, it's obviously more of a reality to you."

Marcus nodded. "A patient some time ago, when I was still in America. He'd been a paramedic and he'd been called to the scene of a terrorist attack where they'd used poison gas. He'd helped to bring the bodies out - he'd seen what the gas had done to them. He described it all to me - it haunted him."

"And no doubt he told you what the gas smelled like," said Johann.

"Yes. Whiffs of it still clung to the bodies after they'd been brought out. I didn't realise it had made such a deep impression on me."

Marcus shook his head, then said "But why didn't it affect Wilhelm's subconscious, why didn't it bring out one of his deep rooted fears?"

"I think because, at present, Wilhelm has only one fear." Johann looked towards him and Wilhelm nodded.

"My only fear is for Elisabeth," he said.

"Think of this as an invisible barrier that we have just come through," said Johann. "It has probably been here for a long time - perhaps since the schloss was built. Its purpose is to stop any intruder - not just us - from getting any further. There would be no point in working on fears that would make the intruder more determined to get in - such as Wilhelm's fears for Elisabeth. And also, I think Wilhelm has very little fear of dying."

Once more Wilhelm nodded. "The knowledge that I might die very soon was something that I lived with for so many years that it isn't something that troubles me."

"We all have our own defences and our own vulnerabilities," said Johann. "They will attack us in every way that they can. We need to be on our guard all the time." He looked down at Marcus, whose breathing was returning to normal, and asked "Are you feeling well enough to go on?"

"Yes. I think so." Shakily, and with Wilhelm's help, Marcus stood up,

285

keeping one hand against the wall for support.

"As we continue into the tunnel," said Johann, "concentrate on a visualisation of a vajra. Try to see it suspended in mid-air, a few feet in front of you. See it glowing gold or white. Focus on it as strongly as you can."

He turned and led the way. They walked for a few minutes in silence. The floor was uneven and they were having to move slowly, putting a hand on the wall to steady themselves in some places. Wilhelm concentrated on the visualisation, finding that he could see the vajra clearly. He kept his eyes fixed on it, aware of Johann moving forward just in front of him. Suddenly, on the edge of his visual field, he saw a flicker. Something or someone had moved in the shadows. He glanced towards it, taking his eyes off the vajra. In an instant, the tunnel went completely black. He could see nothing. And then a glimmer of greyish light, growing, a metre or two in front of him. He looked at the light, conscious that someone was standing at its centre. As the light grew stronger he could see that it was a woman . . . a woman dressed in red and yellow . . . a Hundeiss woman . . . it was Lotte! Wilhelm gasped. He had thought Lotte was dead . . . and all the time she was here . . . He moved towards her, his arms outstretched, pushing past some obstacle in his way. She looked different from the way that he remembered her - her skin was clean, her hair washed and brushed, her clothes fresh and undamaged.

"Lotte?" It came out as a whisper.

She turned towards him, smiling. "Wilhelm."

Behind him, he could hear another voice but he couldn't make out who was speaking or what it was saying.

"Lotte, I thought you had been Taken."

She shook her head. "No. I'm still here. Come to me, Wilhelm."

As he moved closer, the other voice became louder, more insistent. He could feel something on his shoulder, holding him back. Awkwardly, he turned. Someone stood behind him, someone he didn't recognise . . . a man, dressed in dark clothes, with grey hair and a grey beard. He was speaking but the sound was distorted. He seemed to be trying to argue with

Wilhelm, holding onto his arm, pulling him back. Wilhelm stared at him, then clenched his fist and hit him full in the face. The man reeled back, letting go his grip and Wilhelm turned again towards the light. Lotte was still there, still smiling. She was beautiful. Wilhelm had never realised how beautiful she was. But even in her filthy and dishevelled state down in the mines he had loved her. Now, seeing her clean, in fresh clothes, smiling at him, he loved her more than ever. He was finding it hard to remember what he was doing here . . had he come here to meet Lotte? No, he couldn't have done - he had thought she was dead. But if not, then what . . . ? Behind him he could still hear the voice, louder now, speaking in a rhythmic way that seemed to claim his attention. But all he was interested in was Lotte. He took another step forward towards her outstretched arms. The rhythm of the speech behind him was distracting. He wished it would stop. He looked at Lotte.

"Pay no attention to the chanting," she said. "It has no meaning for you."

Somewhere in the back of Wilhelm's mind the word 'chanting' rang a bell. It seemed to have some significance, but he couldn't think what it was.

"Come to me," Lotte whispered. "Come to me, my darling."

He took another step towards her, then stopped. He couldn't remember her ever calling him 'my darling' before. And yet it sounded familiar. Was there someone else who called him 'my darling'? But Lotte was his woman. There was no one else . . .

"Come to me," Lotte said again. "No one else matters."

Behind him, the noise was increasing. Another voice was shouting now, in addition to the first. It was repeating two words, over and over again. He must stop the noise. Once again he turned. The grey bearded man was standing facing him again and, behind him, a younger man, shouting. Wilhelm looked at his mouth opening and closing, repeating the two words . . "Remember Elisabeth. Remember Elisabeth. Remember Elisabeth."

Elisabeth . . . he knew the name . . . why was it important? Elisabeth . .
.

287

He looked at Lotte. "Elisabeth. . . ?" he said.

"Elisabeth is dead," she replied. And then she smiled.

In that instant, Wilhelm knew that she wasn't Lotte. Lotte would never smile when speaking of the death of another human being.

Wilhelm shook his head. "No," he said, "It's Lotte who is dead."

As he looked at her, she seemed to change, her mouth becoming cruel and her eyes hard. Her top lip drew back and she hissed at him. Then the figure flickered and disappeared. Where it had been standing there was a deep crevasse in the tunnel floor, a crevasse wide enough for an unwary man, a distracted man, to fall down. Behind him, Wilhelm became aware that Johann was chanting and realised what it was that Marcus had been shouting. Slowly he turned. There was a trickle of blood on Johann's beard, coming from his lip which had been cut by Wilhelm's blow. Wilhelm gazed at him, unable to speak.

Johann put out a hand. "It's all right Wilhelm. No one is hurt, thank God."

Wilhelm looked past him at Marcus and said "Elisabeth. . . I saw Lotte and I couldn't remember Elisabeth." As he said the words, he felt something boiling up inside him and was uncertain whether it was rage or grief. His breathing quickened. The feeling became more intense. He wanted to scream, to tear his hair, to rid himself of the horror of that thought - that he had been unable to remember Elisabeth. Johann said urgently "Use that energy, Wilhelm. Use the energy that you're feeling. Don't waste it. Concentrate on it. Don't let it use you. You can convert it into a powerful protective force. Don't let it draw you into negative emotions. Concentrate on it. Use what you have learned in meditation."

Wilhelm shut his eyes and concentrated hard, aware that the nature of the energy was subtly changing, his breathing becoming slower and deeper, his muscles more relaxed. When he opened his eyes, he felt as though he were enveloped in a warm blanket. The chill that he had been feeling in his legs, from his still wet jeans, had disappeared. He smiled at Johann. "Thank you," he said. "And you, Marcus."

Johann nodded. "Let's move on," he said.

The tunnel, seemingly endless, continued to twist and turn. Wilhelm began to wonder whether it did, in fact, lead anywhere and, if it did have an exit at its far end, whether it would be anywhere near the schloss, the place that they were trying to get into, the place where Elisabeth was being held. Once they had started out for the schloss, after the frustrating day of waiting, his anxieties had begun to lessen, the knowledge that he was taking action giving him renewed strength. But now he was starting to worry again. What if they couldn't find Elisabeth? What if she wasn't here? What if . . . he felt sick at the very thought . . . what if she was already dead? No, he told himself, he would know. Even without the cord around her wrist to link them, he and Elisabeth were so close that he would know if she were dead. Memory reminded him that he hadn't known that Lotte was dead until he had been told by the other women. But then there had been the music, dulling his senses and his awareness. Now his mind was clear and not only the meditation practices but also the lovemaking that he and Elisabeth had shared had brought them closer together than he and Lotte had ever been. Even so, he hadn't woken when Elisabeth had been lured from her bed, lured out of the house. But Johann had explained that, explained why . . .   Caught up in these thoughts, for a moment his concentration slipped and the vajra, which he had seen travelling clearly in front of him, flickered and disappeared. As it did so, Wilhelm felt the ground beneath him tremble and heard a loud cracking sound which seemed to come from all around him. He knew what that meant. The roof was caving in. They would be trapped. With horror he looked about him but a dark dust cloud obscured his view and he could no longer see Johann or Marcus. He opened his mouth to call to them but found he could make no sound.   The floor was shaking violently now and the cracking sounds were almost deafening. Flinging his arms up to shield his head, Wilhelm fell to his knees and crouched, waiting for the end, waiting to be buried in tons of rock. As the roof caved in, his last thought was of Elisabeth.

Chapter Fifteen

When Wilhelm opened his eyes, he was still in the same crouching posture, but everything else had changed. All around him was a greyish mist which, every now and again, would part to allow him a glimpse of a bleak, colourless, alien landscape. Slowly, cautiously, he stood up, stretching his neck, his shoulders, his back, feeling for injury. There was none.

Bewildered, he looked around him. Although the light seemed natural, he could see no sky, no sun, just the greyness of the mist. He took a couple of steps forwards and the ground crunched beneath his feet. Glancing down, he saw a rough, white surface. He bent, peering through the mist that swirled around his feet, and found to his horror that he was walking on human bones. Instinctively, his eyes began searching for somewhere else to place his feet other than on the remains of living beings. The mist swirled, allowing only glimpses of what lay beyond the place where he was standing. But all of it seemed to be carpeted in the same stark whiteness.

He had no recollection of how he had arrived here. The last thing he could remember was being in the tunnel with Marcus and Johann and the roof caving in . . . He turned rapidly full circle to see whether he could glimpse anyone else moving in the mist. But there was nothing. He called their names, loudly, repeating them several times. But there was no reply. Apart from his voice, nothing. He remembered the time when, having escaped from the mines and from the music, and not knowing the word silence, he had thought of it as an emptiness of sound. He realised now that he had been wrong. That had been merely an absence of sound. What he was experiencing now was an emptiness of sound, as though all the sound in the world had been drained away, sucked out, leaving a vacuum. It was an emptiness in which there never could have been, never would be, any other living beings.

A shiver ran down his spine and he felt desperately alone. But the last thing that he recalled was that he had been with Marcus and Johann . . . so what had happened to them? Where had they gone? He wished he could remember . . . why could he remember nothing after the roof caving in? And how had he got out of there? How was it that he hadn't been injured? Maybe Marcus and Johann had been injured and that was why they were no longer with him . . . Maybe Marcus and Johann had been killed.

Wilhelm took a deep breath. He had no idea of what he was doing here in this barren place, nor of how to escape from it. But somewhere - somewhere - Elisabeth was in the hands of Them and, if the others were dead, then it was up to him alone to rescue her. But in which direction should he go? Through the mist it all looked the same . . . He must make a decision. He had never before felt so alone, even during his escape from the mines. Remembering that journey, he recalled how his instincts had taken him in the right direction. He would have to trust them to do so again. He must start walking because time was wasting, while Elisabeth was still a captive. But how much time had passed since they were in the tunnel? Perhaps it was already too late.

Trying to put that thought to the back of his mind, Wilhelm strode out into the mist, grimacing at the sound of bones splintering beneath his feet. Suddenly, to his left, the mist parted and he saw, in the distance, a tall stone tower, glowing red as though in the rays of the setting sun. But there was no sun, of that he was certain. And somehow the glow seemed to come from within the tower, as if a fierce red light was actually shining through the stone. There was something about the tower that made him want to keep away from it, some indefinable sense of menace. But on the other hand, it stood higher than its surroundings. If he could get to it, perhaps climb to the top of it, he might be able to get some sense of direction, some idea of where he was. Turning, he walked towards it, as the mist closed in again. After a few minutes, the mist became lighter and Wilhelm became aware of a reddish glow some distance away to his left. Turning his head, he saw the tower. He stopped, puzzled. He had been absolutely certain that he had been walking in a straight line. Apparently not. Once more, he turned and made for the tower and, once more, the mist closed in. For what seemed like hours, Wilhelm walked, every now and again catching a

291

glimpse of the tower, always in a different direction from that in which he was walking, never any nearer than the first time that he saw it. Was he walking in circles or was it the tower that was moving? He had no way of telling. As his anger and frustration grew, he found himself running. His foot slipped on the uneven surface and he fell, sliding over the thick accumulation of bones, feeling them scratch his hands and wrists as he slid along them.

Lying there, on the debris left by human beings long dead, Wilhelm gave way to his rage and despair, hammering on the bones with his hands, howling like an animal in pain. The sound seemed to echo back to him as off the walls of a cavern. But this was no cavern, he was sure of it. The light was like none he had ever encountered underground. But where was he and how had he got there and . . . The questions went round and round in his head, each generating more uncertainty. Wilhelm was finding it hard to think clearly now. His mind was muddled, his thoughts blurred. Perhaps, he thought, he was going mad.

A vague memory came back to him from when he was a patient in the hospital . . . a memory of a man who had been admitted to the ward, a man who had screamed and cried and howled, a man who had lost touch with reality, a man who was mad. Perhaps he, too, was mad. Perhaps all that he seemed to remember was just the product of his own disordered mind. Perhaps he had never left the hospital. How could he ever find out? He didn't know.

Lying stretched out on the bony surface, Wilhelm was aware of a feeling of exhaustion, both mental and physical. He was seized by an overwhelming desire just to stay where he was . . . to rest . . . to go to sleep . . . He shut his eyes, then realised what he was doing. How could he think about resting while Elisabeth was still in peril? Pushing himself up onto his feet, he staggered on. The mist closed in again, then parted to reveal a small area of rocky ground, grey and barren. As the mist continued to lift, he saw, a little way ahead of him, what seemed to be some white bundles on the ground.

Moving forward to investigate, Wilhelm noticed that each had some red markings on it. Suddenly he could see what they were and he drew back, a wave of nausea sweeping over him. Five tiny children, each dressed in a white robe, each with blood caked down the front of the chest from a horrific knife wound, each dead. Wilhelm knelt down, trembling with shock and with rage, and reverently touched the smooth cold faces and the tiny clenched fists and wondered who could do something like this, who could destroy tiny lives before they had even begun. He could feel the tears streaming down his face and he brushed them aside roughly with his left hand. His hand felt sticky and he looked down at it. It was covered in blood. But he had only touched their hands and faces. He hadn't touched their mutilated bodies, he hadn't touched the blood.

His heart pounding, he sprang to his feet, realising as he did so that he held something in his right hand. He knew what it was without looking. It was a knife. Opening his hand, he dropped it and watched the blood-caked blade as it hit the ground. There was a tight pain across his temples and he was finding it difficult to breathe. His mind was completely blank. Why had he been holding the knife? Had he killed these children? If so, he was indeed mad.

Turning away from the carnage, his eye was caught by something over to his right. Another bundle, larger this time, much larger. He stepped towards it and, shaking with fear, knelt beside it. It was the body of a woman. Even before he turned it over, he knew what he would see. Elisabeth's face stared up at him, her throat cut and gaping, the front of her white robe, like that of the children, caked in blood. Engulfed in pain, Wilhelm opened his mouth and a howl tore from his throat, seeming to come up from the very depth of his being and going on and on until he was oblivious to everything except the sound and Elisabeth's blank, dead eyes. Finally, exhausted, he fell on her body and sobbed.

He became aware of a shadow falling over him and, looking up, he saw a form that seemed familiar. It took him a moment or two to recognise the slim dark-haired man who stood there with a bloody knife in his hand. . . Marcus . . . with a knife in his hand. Wilhelm stared and his mind started to turn. Elisabeth was dead, her throat cut. Marcus was there with a knife in his hand. Marcus had killed Elisabeth.

Suddenly Wilhelm knew what he must do. He must kill Marcus. Getting to his feet, he reached out to pick up the knife that had killed the children, feeling the power of the anger and hatred that was rising inside him. But, as he turned towards Marcus, the knife held ready to plunge into his chest, he heard a strangely familiar voice in the back of his mind urging him to use the energy, not to waste it, not to let it use him, not to allow it to draw him into negative emotions. It seemed that he had heard these words recently. He paused and forced himself to concentrate. Suddenly into his mind came the memory of the mad man on the ward. When he had been brought in, he had attacked one of the nurses. No one had known why. The nurse had been trying to help him and the man had gone for her, tried to strangle her. For no reason other than that he was mad. Perhaps, thought Wilhelm, I am mad. But how can I know? How can I be sure? And from the back of his mind came the answer - the only thing that I can be sure of is that Marcus has always been my friend. Looking up at his impassive face, Wilhelm dropped the knife, stretched out his hands and whispered "Help me."

There was a subtle change in Marcus's face, his whole form seemed to be moving, altering. In a split second, where Marcus had been standing, Wilhelm saw another figure, a figure with black scaly skin, a figure with horns and long pointed teeth, a figure that reminded Wilhelm of something that he had seen in books on art, in paintings by Hieronymus Bosch. And then it disappeared and there was nothing there. It had been an illusion . . . An illusion! Suddenly Wilhelm found that his mind was functioning again. An illusion. That was what Johann had warned them against. Perhaps this whole thing was an illusion. Perhaps - please God, perhaps - the dead body of Elisabeth was an illusion.

As the thoughts tumbled through Wilhelm's mind, his wrist began to burn where the cord was tied around it. Yes, now he was becoming certain that this was all an illusion. He shut his eyes and, concentrating with all the energy he had left, he visualised the vajra, letting it grow until it shone strong and fierce. And, as he did so, he heard, from somewhere ahead of him, Johann's voice ringing out loud and clear, chanting something in a foreign tongue, the sound melodious and gentle, growing, echoing back, reassuring, comforting.

Wilhelm opened his eyes. The landscape, the mist, the carpet of bones, the bodies - all had disappeared. He was in total darkness. And then the darkness seemed to move and deepen and out of it he could see a monstrous figure growing - a huge figure that towered over him, a figure that held in its right hand a sword of fire.

Wilhelm fell to his knees in terror and, as he did so, saw the figure of Johann in front of him, also on his knees, prostrating himself in obeisance. Uncomprehending, Wilhelm looked up at the figure, expecting at any moment to see the fiery sword come crashing down on them. But instead of the demonic form that he had anticipated, he saw a face of such compassion, the eyes two deep wells of wisdom, that he knew without any doubt that this entity represented something pure and true and that it would protect them.

Following Johann's example, Wilhelm bent forward in a deep prostration, stretching his arms out before him, touching his face to the rock beneath him. When he raised his head again, the figure was gone and he was in the tunnel with Johann and Marcus, unharmed but shaking from head to foot.

For several moments they stayed where they were on the tunnel floor, saying nothing, all three breathing heavily as though they had been through some demanding physical ordeal. Then Wilhelm turned to Johann and asked "Was it all . . .?"

"All an illusion? Yes." Johann's voice shook slightly. "Whatever you may have thought to have happened was a falsehood. All that has really happened is that we have been walking through the tunnel and, from the strength of this last illusion, I think that we must be getting near the schloss."

"But the figure . . .?" asked Marcus. He was slumped back against the wall of the tunnel and, even in the dim light, Wilhelm could detect a haunted look in his eyes.

"The figure with the flaming sword? That was Manjusri, the Bodhisattva, or embodiment, of wisdom. His flaming sword cuts through delusion and illusion and he has given us his protection. In that last terrible illusion - and I have no reason to suppose that either of you had an experience less dreadful than mine - because we didn't succumb, because we fought to retain our humanity and wouldn't allow ourselves to be changed into animals, ruled only by our passions - because of that, the power of the illusion has rebounded on those who initiated it. That power is now on our side and has manifested as Manjusri."

"Manjusri," repeated Marcus in a whisper. "I remember the name from our initiation . . . the names of the aspects of God."

Johann nodded. "Manjusri is a great and powerful protector. We will see no more illusions while he is with us. And if we have to return through the tunnel, we need only to repeat his mantra to bring him to our side. But you need to know it too, in case anything should happen to me."

Johann spoke the mantra slowly and clearly, Marcus and Wilhelm repeating it after him several times, their voices becoming stronger as they did so. Johann joined in the chant and Wilhelm felt a warmth and a strength flowing through him, and the memories of the horrors that he had seen in the misty landscape began to recede. But he was growing increasingly anxious over the time they had spent in the tunnel. He didn't know whether it was hours or days since they had climbed down the well shaft. Even though the sight of Elisabeth with her throat cut had been an illusion, he had no way of knowing whether or not she was still alive. Even now they might be taking her . . . violating her . . . killing her.

Wilhelm jumped to his feet, breaking into the chanting. "We must go on," he said. "We've wasted so much time already."

To his surprise, Johann smiled and shook his head. Looking at his watch, he said "It's less than twenty minutes since we came into the tunnel. Time, too, can be illusory." He rose and put a hand on Wilhelm's arm. "We'll find her Wilhelm. We'll find her." Turning, he led the way into the darkness, shining the flashlight onto the rocky path.

To Wilhelm's relief, they met no more obstacles, no more terrors. The tunnel was just a tunnel and no one was in it except themselves. But suddenly it widened out and they saw that they were in a long low chamber. A single lamp on the far wall shed a faint yellowish light, emphasising the darkness all around it.

For a moment Wilhelm thought they had stumbled upon a zoo. The cages were similar to those that he had seen on that day with Elisabeth - the cages that had held monkeys and birds - but these were smaller . . . much smaller. In the corner of each was what appeared to be an animal, huddled against the damp and chill that emanated from the stone walls. Then one of them moved and Wilhelm realised that it was a human being.

He took a few steps towards the cages and, by the beam of the flashlight, saw that each of the occupants was dressed in a long loose garment which seemed, under the dirt, to be half red, half yellow. And he knew, with a sick feeling, that these were Hundeiss. He wanted to believe that this was another illusion, but he knew that it wasn't. He couldn't see any of the captives' faces clearly but wondered if they were people whom he had known in the mines, and thought it probable. The one who had moved stood up, showing itself to be a woman - little more than a girl, really - her body swollen in a way that Wilhelm now knew meant that she was pregnant. He looked into the other cages and saw that each contained a woman, some pregnant, some with babies in their arms or little children by their sides. This, then, was what happened to the strong young women who were taken for breeding. For a moment, he thought he was going to vomit. "We've got to get them out," he gasped.

"It may not be possible," said Johann, his voice shaking slightly. "They may have to wait until we can rescue all your people. The cages will be locked and . . ."

As he spoke, there was a sound from over to their left, footsteps coming closer, seemingly from another tunnel. The three men huddled back into the tunnel mouth. Suddenly, into the chamber came four figures. The two taller, dressed entirely in black and with close-fitting hoods covering their heads and faces, were carrying lanterns. Each was leading a thin, filthy creature with matted hair, dressed in blackened rags. The stench of unwashed flesh that they carried with them was overpowering, but Wilhelm's eyes were on the men. Hanging from their belts, each had a strong cord with a knot in it - a cord that was used to strangle their victims once they were of no further use to Them. Wilhelm felt a chill run down his spine. Even after all the terrors that he had gone through getting to this place, even after that, the Takers could still inspire fear in him.

The men set down their lanterns on the floor and pulled their prisoners roughly to the centre of the chamber. There seemed to be no resistance and Wilhelm remembered how no one had ever resisted - had ever thought of resisting - the Takers. The music had seen to that. One of the victims was pushed to the floor, then the men turned to the other and tore off its filthy rags, revealing the body of a young woman - a young woman chosen and brought up from the mines for breeding. One grabbed the woman's long hair and pulled it upwards. There was a flash of light on metal and for a second Wilhelm thought that she was about to be killed. But the implement was a pair of scissors and, roughly, the man cut off the girl's matted hair. They left her standing there, naked and shorn, in the middle of the dark cold chamber while they pulled the other girl to her feet and stripped her. Then, as with the first, her hair was pulled upwards, jerking her head so that Wilhelm could see her face. It was Marthe. With a cry of rage, he hurled himself towards the Taker, closely followed by Marcus. He was aware of the man, taken by surprise, standing stock still before he was knocked to the floor. Marcus had the second Taker round the throat and was brandishing the scissors, which he had torn from his grasp. Wilhelm ripped the hood off the man on whose chest he was sitting and looked into his eyes. He had wondered occasionally, since coming out of the mines, whether the Takers were Them or whether they, too were slaves. Now he could see that the man's eyes were glazed. So the Takers were subject to the music. They did as they were told and, outside the bounds of their own responsibilities, they could do nothing.

Marcus said "This one has got keys. We can let the women out."

Johann had come out of the tunnel now. "Thank God," he said. He reached for the keys hanging from the man's belt, but suddenly jumped back as though he had been stung. Falling to his knees, he clapped his hands to his ears.

"What's the matter?" Marcus' voice revealed his alarm.

"The music . . . I can hear the music. It's in the keys. Whatever you do, don't touch the keys. . . The music . . . it's very powerful . . . I don't think I can resist it . . . You must tell me what to do . . . tell me . . ."

Johann's voice tailed off and he knelt, unmoving, while Wilhelm and Marcus looked at him in horror. Then Wilhelm said "Johann . . ."

Johann's head turned towards him. "Johann, take the keys from that man's belt."

Johann got up and did as he was told.

"Now open these two cages."

Again Johann obeyed. Wilhelm turned and, in his own language, told the inhabitants of the cages to come out. They emerged slowly, their faces expressionless.

Wilhelm lifted the Taker to his feet and pushed him into one of the cages. Marcus put the second Taker into the other.

"Johann, lock these two cages," said Wilhelm.

Once the Takers were securely shut in, Wilhelm turned to the two girls, still standing naked and motionless, in the middle of the floor.

"Marthe," he said softly. She turned her head, no recognition in her face. "Marthe. It's me. It's Wilhelm . . . your adult."

Slowly her expression changed. "Wilhelm?" she said. "Wilhelm? We thought you were dead."

"No," he said, "not dead. Not dead."

Stripping off his sweater he dressed her in it. She looked down at the knitted wool and fingered it, then raised her eyes to meet his, a bemused expression on her face.

Wilhelm moved towards the Takers, sitting quietly in the cages. "What were you going to do with them?" he hissed, pointing to the two girls.

"Clean them. Then take them to the breeding rooms." The voice was a monotone.

Clean them, yes of course. They wouldn't wish to breed with

299

something that was unclean. Suddenly it struck Wilhelm that he must have been as filthy as this when he came out of the mines. No wonder that woman had set her dog on him. And poor Erika - having to put him in the shower. But she had done it so gently and with such compassion. . . As he thought of Erika, he felt a warm glow in his wrist and glanced down at the golden cord that encircled it. Yes, they were linked - he could feel the strength.

Wilhelm returned to Marcus, who had taken off his sweater and was gently putting it on the second girl. "Johann needs to be taken back to Magdalena," he said, "to be protected against the music. We'll let all the women out and you can take them with you."

Marcus frowned. "What do you mean 'you can take them'? What are you going to do?"

"I've got to find Elisabeth."

"You can't," said Marcus, in a horrified tone. "You remember what Johann said - we must stay together."

"That was before this happened." Wilhelm gesticulated at Johann who was standing motionless, awaiting instructions. "You've got to get him back. He can't continue with us - he'd be a liability. And he can't go back by himself. Someone's got to take him. But I've got to find Elisabeth. We're running out of time. If I were to come back with you we could lose any chance of ever finding her alive."

Marcus shook his head, his eyes worried. "Perhaps we can leave Johann here and come back for him . . ."

"No." Wilhelm was firm. "Suppose we have to make a run for it with Elisabeth. He could endanger all of us in this state."

Marcus said nothing for a moment, then "I suppose you're right. But I wish there was an alternative."

"Once you're out," said Wilhelm, "get the police or the army - you'll have the women with you as evidence - and get them to storm the schloss."

"We can't take the women with us," Marcus said. "Some of them are in an advanced state of pregnancy. They'd never be able to climb up the ladder in the well. And what about the children? Even with three of us I

300

don't think we could have done it. I'll take the two girls they've just brought. They're young and healthy and they'll be all right. But we'll have to come back for the others - and we'll bring the police or the army or both. I'm sorry, Wilhelm," he went on as Wilhelm opened his mouth to protest, "But you know I can't take them all - in the same way that I know you've got stay to look for Elisabeth."

"Yes. . . I suppose you're right. I'll tell Marthe and the other girl." Reverting once more to his own language, he quickly told them to follow Marcus and to obey everything that he told them to do. Then he grasped Marcus' hand and said "Take care of them."

"I will. And you take great care of yourself."

"I'll be all right," said Wilhelm. He looked down at his wrist. "I can feel the power of the group. They're all with us. It'll be all right."

✶ ✶ ✶

The great stone-flagged entrance hall of the schloss was deserted, its huge oak door, leading to the outside world, shut and bolted. Two life size full length portraits hung on the walls, both showing men - or perhaps the same man - dressed in sombre black clothes. Other, smaller, paintings were spaced around them but, in the dim light, their subjects were unidentifiable. A fine marble staircase curved round to Wilhelm's left, leading to the upper floor which was deep in shadow. At last he was in the house itself, after a trek which had taken him up steps and through passageways that had seemed, in his desperation to find Elisabeth, to go on for ever.

He stopped and looked around him, trying to sense which way to go next. He had thought that he would know instinctively where to find her, would sense her pulling him towards her. He tried to concentrate but couldn't feel her presence. A cold chill ran through him as the possibility arose in his mind that she was already dead. But he forced himself to dismiss it. They would have put her under the influence of the music, or drugged her. That was why he couldn't feel that mental bond that had grown up between them, that and his over-riding anxiety which was making concentration almost impossible. He would have to search for her - but where to start in this enormous place? Perhaps upstairs . . . He turned

301

and started to climb the staircase, carefully, ensuring that his shoes made no noise as he trod.

He was almost at the top when a man came out of the shadows ahead of him, a man in a dark business suit, silver haired, giving the impression of prosperity and authority. There was nowhere to hide. For what seemed like hours, Wilhelm and the man stood and looked at each other, saying nothing. Then the man, in a rough voice at odds with his appearance, asked "Who are you? What are you doing here?"

When Wilhelm made no answer, the man called, loudly, and two men came running out from a downstairs room. Similarly dressed to the first but younger and more powerfully built, they rushed up the stairs. In desperation, Wilhelm hurled himself at them, hoping to knock them off balance, but they caught him, grabbing him roughly by his arms. He struggled wildly, trying to evade their grasp but they were too strong for him and Wilhelm found himself being forced rapidly down the stairs, his feet slipping on the smooth marble. The door of the room out of which they had come was open and the light spilled out into the gloomy hall. Pushing him inside, they followed him in, shut the door and stood in front of it.

At first glance, the room was not unlike Johann's study, with a desk and books and leather upholstered chairs. But here there was no comfortable clutter, no feeling of welcome, no sense of pleasure in the sharing of knowledge. The room was cold, the light harsh, the surface of the desk clear except for an old fashioned bronze inkwell. On the wall hung a large metal swastika and, below it, something long and thin . . . something with a sharp metal head, something of immense age. Wilhelm stared at it and knew instinctively that it was the spear of Longinus . . . the spear that Hitler had craved . . . the spear that could conquer all.

Tearing his eyes from the spear, Wilhelm saw that there were two men in the room, both dressed, like the others he had seen, in expensive suits. One stood next to the window, his back to Wilhelm, apparently looking out into the night. The other sat at the desk. He seemed to be about fifty but Wilhelm had a strong impression that he was older. There was something about the eyes . . .

For a few moments, no one said anything. Then the man at the desk, who had been staring at Wilhelm with an expression of distaste on his face, asked, lightly "Who are you?"

Wilhelm said nothing, raging silently against himself, unable to believe his stupidity in getting caught . . . frantically trying to devise a means of escape.

The man laughed, a high pitched, mirthless laugh. "Oh, he wants to play the hero. How entertaining!"

His face contorted and he glared at Wilhelm. "Who are you?" he shouted. "Answer me!"

Still Wilhelm said nothing.

The man's face relaxed to its previously bland expression and, appearing to read Wilhelm's thoughts, he said "You can't escape, you know."

For a moment or two he examined his nails, then returned his gaze to Wilhelm.

"This is getting boring," he said. Then to the men by the door, "Tie him to a chair."

They dragged a strong wooden chair into the centre of the room. Together they pushed Wilhelm onto it and tied him to it with cords that cut into his flesh. His shirt had come undone in the struggle, revealing his amulet necklace, which one of the men now grabbed and pulled off. Wilhelm felt it tear his neck as the clasp gave way. To his surprise, they didn't cut the golden cord off his wrist, then he realised that it must be hidden under his shirt sleeve.

Almost lazily, the man who had been standing by the window turned . . . and, with horror, Wilhelm recognised him. It was Helmut. Elisabeth's friend Helmut . . . no, Elisabeth's lover Helmut. Wilhelm's stomach contracted as he realised the enormity of this man's betrayal.

As Wilhelm stared, Helmut began to smile.

"I know this man, Master," he said. "His name is Wilhelm Steiff."

Wilhelm fought to keep his face expressionless. So Johann had been right - they didn't know that he was Hundeiss . . . Of course, he should have

303

guessed that they would keep no tally of the names of those who toiled for them underground. To them, the Hundeiss were less than animals, expendable, nameless. When he disappeared from the mines, they wouldn't even have noticed.

"He has come for the woman," Helmut continued, still smiling. "He is her lover." The man at the desk nodded.

"It seems I must congratulate you, Herr Steiff, on finding your way into the schloss," he said. "How you did so, I confess, is a mystery . . . but it doesn't matter. You won't get out again. Nor, alas, can we allow you to take the woman away from us. You see, we are going to have an important ceremony here tonight. And the woman will be playing a central role."

A cold chill went down Wilhelm's spine.

"So," the man went on, "We know who you are. But I find your silence rather rude, you know. Fortunately, I have better manners than you and will introduce myself to you even though you have not asked my name. It is the polite thing to do since you are a guest in my home. My name is Pfeiffer, and I built this schloss."

Wilhelm's immediate thought was that the man was mad and his disbelief must have shown in his face because Pfeiffer smiled and said "Oh, yes. I built it . . . a long time ago - in 1282 to be exact. You see, I am much older than I look . . . much, much older. I was born in 1250 and in the years since then I have vanquished many enemies. You are the last of a line of puny, insignificant nobodies who have tried to prevent me from achieving my destiny. The last of a long line . . . The first were my parents who arranged for me to be ordained into the priesthood with its narrow minded notions of righteousness and sin. With all my talents! How I hated it and how I hated my parents. Once I had got myself excommunicated, I had the great good fortune to be taken up by an alchemist and a practitioner of the black arts whom I had met," he smiled at the recollection, "in a brothel. I became his apprentice and together we embarked on a search for the philosopher's stone."

Wilhelm gazed at him unblinking.

"You say nothing," said Pfeiffer. "Have you not heard of the

304

philosopher's stone?   Such ignorance . . . It has many powers but the greatest of these is to convey the gift of eternal life. And if you cannot die, cannot be killed, then you cannot be conquered, cannot be overcome. It soon became clear to me that I was a greater magician than my master.

"Once I was sure that he could be of no further use to me, I killed him and, with the money I inherited from him, I built this schloss. Here I could work without interruption or distraction. I needed diamonds for my work so I recruited some local people and . . . persuaded them to mine for me. Their descendants still continue to work for me . . . such loyalty!" He laughed again. "In 1302 I found the stone. I was 52 years old. And then I set about achieving my second ambition - to overcome the Church which I so hated, and the people who believed in its God. I started to recruit other men to my cause, promising them the gift of eternal life and supreme power in return for their allegiance. It was not hard to find such men. They came from throughout Germany, and from England, from Morocco, from Turkey and from Spain.

"Slowly our number grew and we grew in power. By the middle of the twentieth century, we were almost ready. But one had joined us who was greedy and who would not wait. He tried to take over - to take over our brotherhood and to take over the world. He persuaded our brothers to raise the power of conquest, but the result was disaster and defeat and that man died, realising at the last what he could have achieved if only he had waited. In the years since then, two more members have been recruited and now, tonight, our final brother joins us - our dear friend, Helmut Krohn."

Pfeiffer turned towards Helmut who, still smiling, gave a slight bow.

"Helmut will be the one who completes our number," Pfeiffer went on, "And the offering that he brings will be the final key to the power that we seek. I have been waiting for this night for over seven hundred years. And did you think that you could stop me?"

Pfeiffer fell silent, smiling to himself, his eyes unfocused. After a moment or two, he blinked and, looking at Wilhelm, began to speak again.

"The philosopher's stone . . . as our dear Helmut knows well . . . does not bestow life of itself, but it enables one to acquire life. The man who is in possession of the philosopher's stone but does not use it is no more immortal than any other. Imagine a number of vessels filled with a finite amount of water. If some receive more water, then others must have less. For water, read life. The philosopher's stone enables the man who possesses it to extract the life force from others. When he penetrates a woman, instead of ejaculating, he can draw life out of her. It is the most intense pleasure that can be experienced. . . the most intense." Again Pfeiffer smiled, and Wilhelm's stomach churned at the picture he had painted.

"And with the life of the woman," Pfeiffer continued, "come also her other attributes, so it is important that she be beautiful and clever because, in that way, the man will also become more attractive, more intelligent . . . Each brother when he joins our order brings with him an offering for all the brethren to share. He chooses that offering with care. But in the case of the final offering the woman must be exceptional. And Helmut searched long and hard and rejected many before he found one who was worthy - and then you came along and took her away from him." Pfeiffer shook his head.. "But no matter. We have her back. And she is a prize indeed. A beautiful woman with a fine body, strong, healthy and with an outstanding intellect. We shall enjoy her. . . After it is over she will, of course, not be quite the same. She will be like an orange after the juice has been extracted. But she may still be of use to our order – for entertainment."

Wilhelm's flesh was crawling. He felt cold and clammy and he wanted to vomit. He was frantic now, not for himself but for Elisabeth. He was not afraid to die - but he could not die, because if he died there would be no one to rescue Elisabeth, and Elisabeth had to be rescued. The ropes cut into his arms as he tried to move and, in despair, he knew that he deserved to die . . . he was Elisabeth's only hope and he had failed her. He was overwhelmed by his sense of failure.

Pfeiffer looked at his watch. "And now," he said "it is almost time. We must go and get ready for the ceremony. I've enjoyed our little talk."

He nodded amicably to Wilhelm and, getting up from his desk, said to the men who still stood by the door "Do something with him," and left the room, followed by Helmut.

Wilhelm braced himself, waiting for the blow on the head or the knife in the back which he was sure would follow Pfeiffer's command. But, to his surprise, it didn't come. One of the men knelt down in front of him and tied his ankles together, leaving a few inches of cord between them. The other man pulled his arms back and tied his wrists tightly together before loosening the rope that bound him to the chair. Then they hauled him to his feet. The way that his ankles were tied meant that he could only shuffle, but the men were in a hurry and pushed him out of the room, so that he would have fallen if they hadn't been holding him on either side.

They turned down the stone-flagged corridor by which he had reached the entrance hall, pushing him forwards until they came to a flight of steep stone stairs. The men picked Wilhelm up between them and carried him down. Setting him on his feet again at the foot of the stairs, they turned down a dim corridor. It looked like the one by which he had come in, the corridor leading to the cages where the women had been. What if he was being taken there? What if they discovered that the Takers had been put in a cage and that the two young women were gone? He thought of Johann and Marcus, wondering if they had had enough time to get away from the schloss, wondering if they had managed to get out unharmed, wondering if they had succeeded in persuading the police to raid the chateau, wondering if it would all be too late anyhow.

They walked on, still hurrying. The corridor twisted and turned . . . and then there were more stairs and more corridors. Eventually they stopped by a heavy oak door which had a large iron key in its lock. The men opened the door and pushed Wilhelm into the space beyond it. He fell heavily, bruising his knees and chest. Lying there, gasping for breath, he heard the door slam and the key being turned in the lock.

The room was lit by a single dim electric bulb, dangling from an ancient flex, which Wilhelm could just see by twisting his head around. He tried to get into a position that would allow him to stand up but, with his ankles and wrists tied, it was impossible. His arms were pulled tightly behind his back and he couldn't even roll over. He rested his head on the floor and tried to think.

He didn't know what Pfeiffer intended to do with him. Perhaps he would just leave him to die of starvation and thirst. Perhaps he would send someone to kill him. It hardly seemed to matter now. There was no way that he could escape. Nothing he could do. Hope . . . that wonderful feeling that he had discovered for the first time all those months ago when he had come out of the mines . . . hope had vanished. All that was left was despair.

Wilhelm clenched his jaw, feeling an almost irresistible urge to bang his head on the floor to punish himself for his inadequacies. So much had depended on him . . . and he had failed. He had let them all down . . . not just his beloved Elisabeth, but also Marcus and Erika, Johann and Magdalena and the Fellowship into which he and his friends had been admitted. He thought of all the hours he had spent in the meditation room, experiencing such wonderful spiritual energies. He was worthy of none of it. They would have done better to have left him out entirely, just taking Marcus, Elisabeth and Erika into the Fellowship. He was not worthy. He should never have left the mines. He should have stayed there and waited to be Taken.

Without warning, the self-loathing turned into rage . . . a fierce, burning hatred which threatened to overpower him . . . hatred for everything and for everyone that had brought him to this . . . hatred for Pfeiffer and for Helmut, hatred for Marcus and Erika and Johann and Magdalena and for the Fellowship and their useless God who had failed to protect Elisabeth. Most of all, hatred for himself. It boiled up inside him. He could feel its strength, its heat, its energy.

Suddenly something flashed through his brain. For a moment the hatred lost some of its power as he tried to retrieve the fleeting thought . . . And then he knew what it was. It was not just the golden cord around his wrist that linked him to Marcus and Erika and to Johann and Magdalena - he was linked to them by ties of love. To turn that love into hate was to lose everything. And with this realisation came the memory of Johann in the tunnel, saying "Use the energy, don't waste it."

With a superhuman effort, Wilhelm concentrated on the emotions boiling inside him and tried to focus them, trying to turn the hatred into love, trying to build something greater than either emotion. As he did so, he felt a warmth in his wrist, where his initiation cord still lay hidden under his shirt. The connection of love was still there. And as the turmoil in his mind started to subside, the memory of those words spoken in the tunnel sparked another memory . . . the memory of hearing Johann recite the mantra of Manjusri. For a few seconds, hope was rekindled as Wilhelm tried to bring it to mind. . But the words wouldn't come. Desperately he searched his memory but could not find it. And once again, he was overwhelmed by a sense of failure.

He could not bear to think what they might be doing to Elisabeth while he lay here. An image of her, terrified, calling his name, came into his mind and he felt tears of despair filling his eyes. There was nothing he could do for her. He could not save her. He knew that now. But if only there was something he could do to lessen her ordeal. Perhaps he could say a prayer. . . but how did you speak to God? And what did you say? God must be bombarded by millions of prayers . . . how did you make sure that yours was heard? Would the strength of his love be enough? And would God understand what it was he was feeling . . . what it was he was asking? God had never been in this position.

And then Wilhelm remembered a story that Elisabeth had told him about an ancient goddess, Isis, who had searched the whole world for the body of her dead husband Osiris, who had been killed by the evil god Seth. Isis would understand . . . but was she truly God? Suddenly into his mind came a phrase that he had heard at his initiation, and, at the time, had not fully understood . . . "You stand under the watchful eye of God in his many aspects . . ." God in his many aspects went by many names and would respond however he was called. Isis was an aspect of God, and she would understand.

It was then that Wilhelm remembered why Elisabeth had told him the story - and realised that he did know a prayer. Mozart had written an aria in *The Magic Flute* which was a prayer to Isis and Osiris - a prayer that asked

309

for blessing, for wisdom, for protection from danger for two people who loved each other. Wilhelm had listened to it so many times, he knew every note and every word. Softly at first, then growing steadily louder, he started to sing the only prayer he knew. He sang it fervently, keeping a picture of Elisabeth in his mind as he did so. By the end, he was exhausted from the physical and mental energy it had entailed.

But, other than that, nothing was different. He was still lying on the floor, with the coldness of the stone flags creeping into his body. His wrists and ankles were still tied, his body still painful from the position into which it had been forced. He didn't really know what he had expected . . . perhaps a manifestation of a spiritual being such as Manjusri. But, no, he didn't know the right words and God had not listened. In a fresh wave of self-loathing, Wilhelm acknowledged bitterly to himself that, while he could remember the words of an aria in an opera, he was unable to remember the mantra that could have protected them all.

He shut his eyes but opened them again after a few seconds, unable to bear the darkness of his own thoughts. As his eyes strayed towards the corner of the room, he thought he saw the shadows moving. It was as though the light was swinging. Twisting his head around, he looked upwards. But the bulb hung perfectly still. And then a slight rustling sound behind him told him he was correct. There was something in the room with him . . . perhaps his prayer had been answered after all. Perhaps he would see a god who would help him to escape and to rescue Elisabeth.

Shuffling with his feet, he managed to manoeuvre himself round slightly. Another movement in the shadows . . . And then Wilhelm saw what it was. A brown rat sat staring at him with little beady black eyes. Just a rat. Magdalena had shown him a picture of a rat when she had told him the story of the Rattenfaenger - the Pied Piper. According to the poem, the Rattenfaenger had taken the rats from the town of Hameln and led them into the river where all except one of them had drowned. And, after that, he had taken the children. Rats, like the Hundeiss, had suffered at the hands of Pfeiffer. And now, here they were, the Hundeiss man and the rat, locked into a cell, waiting to die.

Wilhelm closed his eyes again. He was overwhelmed by a sense of defeat. His prayer had done nothing. And that had been his last hope. He lay for a while, immersed in misery. And then he heard another sound . . . footsteps were coming along the corridor. Perhaps someone was coming to kill him. He hardly cared. There was a grating sound as the key was turned in the lock and he felt a draught of cold air as the door was pushed open. Someone moved round to stand in front of him. Wilhelm saw shoes and trousers of red and yellow . . . the colour of Hundeiss clothes. But these were not Hundeiss clothes . . . these were spotlessly clean - and, while one trouser leg and one pointed shoe were red, the other leg and shoe were yellow. Puzzled, Wilhelm raised his head. The man in front of him was dressed entirely in those two colours, with a red mask across his eyes and a tasselled hood on his head. And then Wilhelm remembered that these were the colours the Rattenfaenger wore in the poem. As Wilhelm stared up at him, the man took off his mask. It was Helmut.

"Well, Wilhelm," he said with a harsh laugh, "You thought you could beat us, did you? You thought that you could just come in here and walk out again with Elisabeth. Do you still believe in fairy tales, Wilhelm?" Again that laugh.

"Our ceremony will be starting soon, Wilhelm. It will be a magnificent event. Our entire brotherhood will be assembled to witness it and to take part. And Elisabeth will be at the centre of the ceremony. Of course, we can't allow you to watch, as you are not one of our number. But I thought you would like to hear what will happen . . . so that you can picture it in your mind."

Wilhelm stared at him with loathing and, once more, Helmut laughed.

"We shall all gather in the main hall . . . seventy two men, all dressed as I am dressed now. This is the sacred livery of our brotherhood. And each man has taken the name of a demon, as they are listed in the great books of magic. I, being the last of the brothers, will take the name of Andromalius, the mighty Earl of Hell, whose emblem you will see engraved on my athame."

He indicated to Wilhelm a knife that hung at his side, suspended by a

311

cord tied around his waist. Its black handle was engraved with a silver serpent, and its double sided blade gleamed dully in the dim light.

"My initiation will take place first," Helmut continued. "And when I have become Andromalius, Elisabeth will be brought into the circle. Then two of the brothers will strip her naked. A collar of diamonds will be put around her neck and a cuff of diamonds around each wrist and ankle. And then she will be led round the circle so that all the men can look at her . . . to whet their appetites, so to speak.

"Finally, she will be made to lie down on the altar at the top end of the hall. Her wrists and ankles will be tied to the corners of the altar so that she is ready to receive all those who will come to enjoy her. After some further ceremony in which we will invoke powerful spirits to support and aid us, Herr Pfeiffer will go up to the altar and insert the philosopher's stone into her. It is no bigger than a diamond . . . a large diamond . . . it will not interfere with our pleasure. But it is the catalyst . . . the thing that will enable each one of us to draw life from her . . . and to become invincible. And then Herr Pfeiffer will enter her. And when he has finished, each of the seventy one brothers will take his turn, to copulate with her, drawing out her life force through his phallus . . . You know what a phallus is, don't you, Wilhelm? It's what you have there." And he kicked Wilhelm savagely in the groin.

The pain was so intense that, for a minute or two, Wilhelm was totally unaware of anything else. Gradually it started to recede, and, as Wilhelm's eyes began to focus again, he saw that Helmut was crouching down beside him, smiling, enjoying his pain.

"Well, Wilhelm, I must go. I can't be late for the ceremony. I don't think anyone else will come to see you, so you can just lie here and think about . . ."

Helmut stopped in mid-sentence and leaped to his feet. For a moment, Wilhelm didn't understand why. And then he saw that the rat, whose presence he had forgotten, had climbed onto Helmut's red shoe and seemed to be gnawing at it.

Helmut lifted his foot and shook it vigorously but the rat hung on.

And then another rat ran out of the shadows and leapt up onto the yellow trouser leg. Helmut let out a yell and tried to swipe at the second rat, but only succeeded in getting his finger bitten. And now more rats were running across the floor . . . Wilhelm couldn't make out where they were coming from, but they all seemed to be heading for Helmut. There must have been twenty of them . . . climbing his trousers, burrowing under his red and yellow tunic, hanging onto his sleeves. Helmut was dancing madly in his attempt to dislodge them, but the rats held on. Suddenly, as though at a signal, they began to bite him. Helmut screamed as their sharp teeth dug into his skin, and he swung around the cell, banging himself against the walls in pain and terror. One rat had reached his shoulder and had sunk its teeth into his earlobe. Helmut grabbed the rat and wrenched it away from his ear, tearing the lobe with it. Blood poured down from the wound as Helmut hurled the rat into the farthest corner of the cell.

But the other rats were more tenacious and gradually the yellow of Helmut's costume became stained with red. Helmut sank to his knees, his mouth open, his eyes unseeing, his hands flailing around ineffectively. The largest of the rats had climbed onto his shoulder and Wilhelm, battling to control the terror rising inside him, saw it bite Helmut firmly in the neck. There was a sudden fountain of blood and Helmut fell to the floor. Within seconds he had stopped moving.

Wilhelm could hear his own breathing - rapid and rasping - over the scuffling and squealing of the rats. His heart was pounding and he felt sick. He had hated Helmut, but to see him die in that way . . . And what would the rats do now? Would they attack him, too? Lying tied up on the floor, he would be an easier target than Helmut. With rising panic, Wilhelm looked for any sign that the rats might be starting to move towards him. But, for the moment, they seemed to be engrossed in eating the man they had just killed.

There was a clunk and Wilhelm saw that one of the rats had gnawed through the cord around Helmut's waist, so that the knife that it had held now lay on the floor a few inches from the body. It looked sharp. If he could only get hold of it, it was possible that he might be able to cut through

313

the ropes that bound him.

Slowly, trying not to disturb the rats in their feast, Wilhelm managed to move himself onto his side so that his back was towards Helmut. Very carefully, he felt around . . . and his fingers found the stout wooden handle. Pulling it towards himself he tried to turn it so that he could rub the ropes along its blade. It was not easy but at last he managed to get it into the right position. But either the ropes were thicker than he had thought or else the knife was not as sharp as it looked and by the time he had cut through the last strand, he was aching from head to foot. He lay for a moment, too exhausted to move, then drawing his arms down to his sides, sat up. Cutting through the ropes that tied his ankles was much easier and within a minute or so he was cautiously standing up, testing out his muscles and joints, aware of rawness around his ankles and wrists where the ropes had cut him, and a heavy aching sensation where Helmut had kicked him.

For a few moments he could do no more than move to the side of the cell so that he could lean up against the wall. He tried not to look at the feasting rats. But he could not understand why they should have attacked Helmut as they did. Could it have been as a result of his prayer? Surely not. He had prayed for protection, not death and destruction. And it had not really been a prayer at all, but just an aria from an opera . . . Suddenly he remembered Johann saying that Mozart had written something into his music that would work against the power of Pfeiffer and his brotherhood. Wilhelm had not just recited the words . . . he had sung the aria. And he knew well how music could influence the mind. Could it be that the rats had heard something in the music that aroused an ancestral memory . . . passed down from that one rat who had escaped drowning . . . something that told them that a man dressed in a suit of red and yellow was their enemy and that by attacking him they would avenge all those rats he had killed so many centuries ago? Was it possible? Wilhelm would never know.

Feeling a little stronger, he stood upright and turned towards the open door. Time was short and he was unsure what to do. But the one thing he knew was that he had been given a second chance and he wasn't going to waste it. As he moved out into the corridor, he glanced back at the remains of Helmut. His clothes were in tatters, his body a mass of red, and half his face was gone.

Chapter Sixteen

The corridor was empty. But which way to go? Wilhelm had paid little attention when they had brought him here, had been too immersed in his own grief and anger. He thought they had come from the right, so he turned that way, walking swiftly and quietly. He wondered whether it was possible that Helmut's death would cause the ceremony to be postponed . . . cancelled, even. That there would be time for Marcus and Johann to bring the police to rescue Elisabeth. He wouldn't let himself dwell on the thought that, if the ceremony was not held, if Elisabeth was no longer needed, they would just kill her.

Wilhelm walked on, following the twists and turns of the corridor, praying that he was going in the right direction, back towards the house. But how he was going to overcome the seventy one men who still remained there, he had no idea. He needed help. He wished that Johann and Marcus were still with him, although he knew that it had been essential for Marcus to take the girls to safety and that Johann had been in no fit state to carry on.

A sudden thought made Wilhelm stop in his tracks. The Takers must have brought the two girls up from the mines into the room of cages. So the passageway from which they had appeared must lead to the mines. There were men in the mines . . . strong men . . . men with heavy tools . . . men who he used to know, who he used to work with . . . men who might come to his aid if he asked them to.

Wilhelm rested his back against the wall, his mind racing. How many men would he need? To overcome seventy one, he should have at least seventy. But were there seventy men in the mines? He tried to remember. He had never counted the Hundeiss in all the years that he had lived with them, but he thought it probable that there were only about fifty men, and fewer than forty women. And even if most of the men agreed to come, was it remotely possible that a group of exhausted slaves could overcome the men he had seen upstairs? It was a ridiculous plan. It could never work. But he didn't know what else he could do. If he returned to the schloss by himself, he would probably be recaptured, no matter how careful he was.

And, even if he remained free, Elisabeth was sure to be guarded . . . and how could he overcome the guards by himself? There was no alternative. He must try to find his way into the mines.

Once he had made the decision, a sense of urgency overtook him and he turned and almost ran back the way he had come. He was sure, now, that this was the passageway that led to the room with the cages. It must be beyond the cell in which he had been imprisoned. Within a couple of minutes he was passing his cell once more. Despite himself, he glanced in. The rats had gone. All that remained was a skeleton, still held together by gristle and tendons, all the flesh eaten away. Wilhelm felt sick, but the need for haste was more powerful and he moved on, putting the memory of Helmut behind him.

Down some more stairs, along another corridor, around a corner . . . and there it was. The room of cages. Seeing him, the women started to call to him. He had told them, before leaving, that someone would be back to let them out, to take them to safety. He realised that they thought that this was why he had come.

He shook his head. "No, not now." He looked round at their puzzled faces and went on "I must go to the mines first. I must get the men. We must find my woman who is . . ." He pointed back the way he had come. "And then we will take you out. You must be . . ." The Hundeiss had no word for 'patient'. He thought for a moment and said "You must wait. We will come for you."

And, with that, he moved down to the far end of the room and into the passageway along which the Takers had come with the two girls. It was cold in there and the walls seemed damp. There was very little light . . . just an occasional lamp hanging high up on the wall. Wilhelm walked quickly, aware that the floor was sloping downwards, hoping that he would soon come to the mine.

But the passageway ended in a flight of stairs . . . stairs that went round and round as they went down and down. Wilhelm knew that there was a word for such stairs . . . he had seen a staircase of this sort at the museum that Elisabeth had taken him to. But he couldn't remember what it was called. Well, he didn't need to know its name in order to use it. With a hand on the wall to steady himself, he began the descent.

As he went down, he counted the steps. Fifty . . . one hundred . . . one hundred and fifty . . . By the time he had got to four hundred and fifty, he was beginning to think that the stairs would go on for ever. It was very dark now, with just a single lamp every fifty steps or so. He was acutely aware of the pain in his joints and muscles, and the unevenness of some of the steps caused a jarring that reinforced the ache in his groin. His breath was coming in short spasms, partly from the exertion, partly from his anxiety about the lack of time.

When he reached the bottom of the staircase, it came almost as a surprise . . . he turned a corner and found himself in a short passage which ended at a heavy iron door. Wilhelm's heart sank. How could he have thought that he would just be able to walk into the mines. It was unlikely that any of the Hundeiss would ever have tried to escape . . . as he well remembered, they did not know that there was anywhere to escape to . . . but obviously They would take no chances. He realised that this was the first time since reaching the schloss that he had thought of Pfeiffer and his followers as 'Them'. If he defeated them, he would be doing it for the Hundeiss as well as for Elisabeth.

Wilhelm stared at the door. He cursed his own stupidity at not having thought that there would be locked doors . . . but then, if he had thought of it, what could he have done.? Hoping against hope, he tried the handle, but the door stood firm. It was large and heavy . . . impossible to break down without powerful tools.

But he had not come this far to be turned back now. He took a deep breath and tried to think, resting his hand against the wall as he did so. And something sharp scraped his palm. In the dingy light, he peered to see what it was, and was flabbergasted to see a key hanging on a hook. Could it really be as easy as that? But, as he thought about it, he realised that it was logical. The only people who would normally be this side of the door would be the Takers and the Carriers who were coming down to the mines from the schloss. So it seemed reasonable that the key would be left where they could use it. He almost laughed out loud at the simplicity of the arrangement.

Taking down the key, he put it into the lock and turned it. The door opened soundlessly . . . and the music hit him like a hammer blow. Reeling, he put his hands over his ears, knowing as he did so that it would make no difference, that the music was heard with the mind and not with the ears. But Wilhelm's mind was very different from how it had been when he was a slave in the mines. Johann and Magdalena had seen to that, teaching him to meditate, to concentrate, to focus, to lift his mind above the mundane. Slowly, he realised that he could consciously turn the music down. Of course, he could still hear it . . . nothing would make it go away completely . . . but it was less intrusive on his thoughts. He focused on breathing deeply and slowly, shutting his eyes for a few moments while he concentrated on what had to be done. Then, putting the key in his pocket, he went through the door and closed it behind him.

Here it was even darker and he had to feel his way along in places. Turning a corner, he saw ahead of him, faintly lit from the far side, an irregular archway and, going through it, found himself in the supply cavern at the head of the tunnels.

It was empty now but, even so, looked much smaller than he remembered it. Nevertheless, there were certain rock formations in its walls that served to identify it. He could find his way from here.

Leaving the cavern by the tunnel at the far end, he knew that he would shortly come to the living quarters . . . the dwelling caves . . . and, from there, it would be just a few steps into the cavern where the rocks were sorted and into the mines themselves. He could hear nothing other than the music and it occurred to him that, if the Hundeiss were at work, they could be scattered through the vast expanse of the mines and, although there would be women and children in the sorting cavern, it could take time to find any of the men. But as he came level with the first of the dwelling caves, the siren blasted out and suddenly there was the sound of people stirring.

Wilhelm could not believe his good fortune. This was the siren for the beginning of the working day. The men would be refreshed . . . or as refreshed as they could be . . . after their short period of sleep. But how many men would he need? And how many of them would agree to come with him?

A candle had been lit in the cave closest to him and Wilhelm went in. He had forgotten how tiny the dwelling caves were . . . The smell of urine, of sweat, and of burning tallow was overpowering. I used to smell like that, he thought.

A man was standing at the far end of the cave, urinating onto the floor. He turned and an expression of alarm entered his eyes. In the dim light of the candle, Wilhelm recognised him. It was a man he knew well, had worked with many times.

"Stephan?" he said.

"Yes, I am Stephan. What are you?"

"I am Wilhelm. Do you remember me?" It felt strange to be speaking his own language again after so long.

"Wilhelm?" Stephan's tone was incredulous. "I remember Wilhelm. I used to work with Wilhelm. But Wilhelm died. You have pale skin . . . and you have no beard. You cannot be Wilhelm."

"I am Wilhelm, Stephan. I didn't die. I . . . went to another place."

"What other place? We did not see you."

"I went out of the mines."

"I don't understand."

"No, I know you don't. But I need you to trust me. I need your help."

"Help?" Stephan sounded doubtful.

"Do you remember when we all worked together to move the rocks that had trapped Gertrude?"

"Yes."

"Well I need your help now. My woman has been trapped and I need to get her free."

"But Lotte was Taken."

"Not Lotte," said Wilhelm. "I have another woman. Her name is Elisabeth."

320

Stephan nodded. "I will help. How big is the rock fall?"

"It is not a rock fall. It is people who are holding her."

"People? Why would Hundeiss do that?"

"No, not Hundeiss. Other people."

"Other . . . " Even in the dim light, Wilhelm could see that Stephan looked stunned. "There are other people?"

"Yes. And I need you and some of the other men to come with me and help me to. . ." Wilhelm searched for the right word in the Hundeiss' limited vocabulary, "To overcome the other people . . . who are not good people . . . and to save Elisabeth."

"We can do that," said Stephan. "But what about the work? The siren has just gone."

"This is more important than the work. And if you help me against these people, you will have to do less work in the future."

"How can that be? I do not understand."

"Please Stephan. Just trust me."

Stephan nodded. "I will find the men," he said, and left the tiny cave.

Wilhelm followed him out into the tunnel and heard him calling to the other men, who were coming out of their caves, carrying their mining tools. Within a few moments, a crowd of thirty or more had gathered, and some of the women had joined them. Stephan spoke to them and they turned to look at Wilhelm, who had hung back at the top of the tunnel. One of the men stepped forward . . . little more than a boy, Wilhelm realised.

"Wilhelm?" he said.

Wilhelm recognised the voice, and his eyes filled with tears. "Konrad."

Konrad . . . the boy who Wilhelm and Lotte had raised in their tiny cave, the boy who Wilhelm had thought he would never see again.

"You are not dead?" asked Konrad.

"No. I am still alive."

"But you are pale like a young child and you have no beard."

"Yes."

"Marthe has been taken for breeding."

"Yes, I know. If you can help me, you may see her again soon."

Wilhelm turned to the men. "Will you help me?"

Slowly, they all nodded, although some still looked unsure.

"But what must we do?" asked one.

"Bring your tools and come with me."

And Wilhelm turned and led the band of Hundeiss men into the supply cavern.

✳ ✳ ✳

Once they were all in the cavern, Wilhelm turned to face them.

"We will go up here," he said, pointing towards the archway. "And then we will go through . . ." he stopped, realising that the Hundeiss dialect had no word for 'door'.

"We will go through an obstruction. On the other side of the obstruction, there is no music."

He was aware of the men muttering to each other and Stephan said "No music? How can there be no music. There is always music."

"Only here . . . only in the mines and the tunnels. There are other places where there is no music."

Some of the men were looking nervous.

"You talk of other places and other people," one of them said. "But we are Hundeiss and this is our place."

"You are Hundeiss, yes," replied Wilhelm, "But there are other places you can go . . . places where there is no music."

He saw a number of heads shaking and the man who had spoken - Wilhelm thought his name was Berthold - said "If there are other places, they are not for Hundeiss. We cannot go there."

"I am Hundeiss," Wilhelm reminded him, "And I have been there."

Still the men shook their heads. Wilhelm racked his brains for something to say that would convince them to go with him. He could not fail now, not when he was so close.

"I need your help," he said again, pleading. "My woman's life depends on it."

But still the men muttered among themselves.

"Stephan," said Wilhelm, "You were my . . . goodworker." It was the closest word the Hundeiss had to 'friend'. "I need your help."

"Yes," said Stephan slowly, "Yes, we were goodworkers together. Yes, Wilhelm, I will come."

"And I will too," came another voice. It was Konrad.

Wilhelm was all too aware of the time passing while he stood here. Perhaps it would be better to go now, with just Stephan and Konrad, rather than waste time trying to persuade the others.

"Very well," he said. "Follow me." And the three of them walked through the archway and into the tunnel beyond.

When they reached the door, Wilhelm said "There is no music beyond this point. It will come as a shock. But you will feel . . . better. Just walk forward." And he led the way through the door.

Even though he had managed to turn down the music in his head, Wilhelm felt a great sensation of relief when it stopped. He took in a large gulp of air, then, turning towards the other two who still stood on the far side of the door, he stretched out his hand to them. With a look of extreme trepidation, they stepped through. The effect was as intense as it had been on Wilhelm, when he had first stepped into the huge cavern with the rock teeth. They stood motionless, stunned expressions on their faces.

Konrad was the first to recover. "The music has stopped," he said quietly, "You spoke well." Stephan nodded his agreement.

"Yes," said Wilhelm. "This place that we are entering is quite different from our own. And I have lived here for . . . many, many days. This is where my woman is. And now we must move on, to free her."

He allowed the men a moment or two to get used to the change, then led the way towards the twisting staircase. At the foot of it, he stopped again and said "We must go up here."

Konrad and Stephan looked at the steps. "There are many," said Stephan.

"Many," agreed Wilhelm, starting to climb.

By the time they reached the top, all three were out of breath. Wilhelm allowed them a few seconds to recover. Both Stephan and Konrad were looking dazed.

"With no music," said Konrad, hesitantly, "My thoughts were . . ."

"Many . . . different," said Stephan. Konrad nodded.

"Yes," agreed Wilhelm. "The music stops many thoughts. That is what They want, so that the Hundeiss continue to work for them. But we do not have to work for them."

Both men looked at him with incomprehension in their eyes.

"But that is what Hundeiss do," whispered Konrad.

"When we have rescued my woman," said Wilhelm, "Hundeiss will do it no longer."

They walked on a short distance, then Wilhelm said "We will go through a cavern, now, where They keep the women who are taken for breeding. The women are trapped there . . . but when we have rescued my woman, we will come back and free these women."

Even though he had warned them, the sight of the cages was clearly a shock to the two men. The women called out to them and Wilhelm said "Soon . . . soon we will come back and you will be free."

They left the room of cages and continued on along the corridor, Wilhelm hurrying now, ever aware of the time that was passing, wondering what was happening in the schloss, whether they would be in time, whether three men with a handful of mining tools would be enough to rescue Elisabeth.

They passed the door in which the remains of Helmut's body lay and, telling the two Hundeiss to wait, Wilhelm went inside. Trying not to look at the corpse, he bent down and picked up Helmut's athame. Now he, too, had a weapon.

Suddenly it occurred to him that, since he had been imprisoned down here, this might be where they were keeping Elisabeth.

"We must look in every . . . cave," he told the men. "If we cannot open the . . . obstruction in front of it . . . we must bang on it and say 'Elisabeth?'"

But, although there were other cells along this corridor, similar to the one in which Wilhelm had been kept, they were all empty. They hurried along more corridors, up stairs, opening every door they came to. They found kitchens and store rooms, rooms piled high with furniture covered in white sheets, and many rooms empty of anything except dust and spiders' webs, but all were unlocked and Elisabeth was in none of them. By now, Wilhelm was getting desperate and the thought that they might not find her, that it was already too late, sent a shudder of fear through his body.

Eventually they found themselves in the corridor that led directly into the entrance hall of the schloss. All the doors leading off the hall were open, their interiors in darkness . . . all except one great pair of double doors which, Wilhelm was sure, led into the hall in which the ceremony was to be held. Or was it already being held? He could hear a murmur from behind the doors but it sounded more like conversation than any form of ritual. He prayed that he was right.

Cautiously, remembering his last assay to the upper floor, he led Konrad and Stephan up the great marble staircase. Urgently, they started to try the doors . . . finding bedrooms, sitting rooms . . . but all of them empty. Wilhelm started to feel sick at the thought that Elisabeth might already be in the great hall. And then he opened a door and found himself in a gallery that ran around the top of the hall itself. He beckoned the two men in, signalling them to crouch down, and they all peered through the intricately carved wooden railings at the men below. The hall was in semi-darkness, lit only by candles. But there was enough light to see what was happening. All the men were dressed in the same red and yellow costume that Helmut had worn. Only Pfeiffer could be distinguished from the rest, a great golden swastika hanging around his neck. And Wilhelm noticed that whereas all the men, like Helmut, had an athame hanging from a cord around their waists, Pfeiffer had instead what appeared to be a silver flute.

The men seemed jumpy, and although they stood conversing with each other in quiet voices, there was a general air of nervousness. Pfeiffer was striding up and down in the centre of the hall and it was clear that his followers were trying hard not to look at him. Suddenly he shouted "Enough!"

Everyone stopped talking and turned towards him. "Enough!" repeated Pfeiffer in a quieter voice. "I will not be stopped. Not now . . . not ever. Our erstwhile brother, Helmut, has not deigned to join us. He has evidently changed his mind . . . he has run, frightened by what he must do to achieve immortality. For not all are strong enough to accept that wonderful concept or to go through the ritual that proceeds it. Helmut has shown himself to be lacking by his fear . . . has shown himself to be as puny and insignificant as most of the human race." Pfeiffer was spitting out his words now, his growing rage becoming apparent. "I was deceived in his character," he went on, "But his failure will not stop us from reaching our conclusion . . . from attaining the power that I first glimpsed seven hundred years ago. I WILL NOT BE STOPPED!"

There was total silence in the hall. Then Pfeiffer went on "We do not need Helmut. I, Bael, can become Andromalius too. I shall be the first of the demons and the last of the demons. I shall be Alpha and Omega . . . for all eternity."

A cheer went up from the assembled men but Wilhelm was filled by panic. They would be continuing with the ceremony and he had not yet found Elisabeth. Where could she be? They had looked everywhere . . . everywhere they could find. He didn't know what to do.

Below him, Pfeiffer proclaimed "We shall begin. Cast the circles and bring in the woman!"

Six men stepped forward and started to pour a white powder onto the floor, tracing out a huge circle around the room, with a smaller circle at its centre. The powder sparkled, reflecting what little light there was, and Wilhelm wondered fleetingly whether it was made from diamonds. When the inner circle was complete, two of the men turned and disappeared through a small door at the far end of the hall

Urgently, Wilhelm beckoned to Konrad and Stephan and they crept out of the gallery and down the stairs. They were nearly at the bottom when they heard footsteps coming from the corridor through which they'd first come. There was nowhere they could hide and, not knowing what to do, Wilhelm instinctively crouched down, huddling up to the balustrade. But it was not men in red and yellow who came into the hall. It was a gaggle of some twenty men and women, with blackened skin and filthy clothes, and with mining tools in their hands. And at their head was Lotte's friend, Eva . . . the woman who had held her hand while she was Taken. They stood there in silence for a moment, looking around them, wide-eyed with astonishment. And then Wilhelm stood up and ran softly down to greet them.

Just in time, he stopped himself from smiling, amazed at how quickly he had forgotten the Hundeiss customs. He nodded to Eva and said "This is good." It was the nearest phrase the Hundeiss had to 'thank you'.

Eva lifted her head to look at him and said "Lotte was my goodworker. I do not want another woman of yours to be Taken, Wilhelm, if we can stop it."

One of the other women said "It was Eva whose talk made us come through to this place. She is a good woman."

"Yes," said Wilhelm. "She is a good woman."

From the great hall came the sound of chanting. They had already started their ceremony. Time was very short.

"The men who have Elisabeth are in there," he said, pointing to the double doors. "We must go in and get her out. The men are powerful and it may be hard to overcome them. But we must try as much as we can."

The Hundeiss followed him to the great double doors. Wilhelm put a hand to one of the doors and pushed, and it opened noiselessly. In the hall, the men were standing in the space between the two concentric circles, facing Pfeiffer who stood alone at the very centre. Wilhelm felt his skin crawling as he saw that two of the men were holding Elisabeth between them. She was still wearing the nightdress she had worn on the night she was taken, her feet were bare and she was clearly terrified. One of the men holding her had a knife . . . an athame . . . at her throat and she had twisted her head around in a pathetic attempt to protect herself.

The other men were ignoring her . . . she was not yet the focal point of the ceremony. Meanwhile, Pfeiffer was chanting. After a few moments, the other men joined in. It was not like the soothing, strengthening, reassuring chant that Wilhelm had heard at his initiation. This was harsh and rasping, giving the impression that the words being chanted had sharp edges to them. The hall was cold and getting colder and the glittering of the circle

327

seemed to be stretching upwards, like a shimmering transparent curtain.

No one seemed to have noticed the intruders, but Wilhelm thought it could not be long before someone caught sight of them. Elisabeth was on the far side of the circle . . . they would have to move around the hall in order to seize her . . . or charge straight across the circle. Beckoning to the others, Wilhelm crept through the shadows outside the shimmering curtain. Raising an arm as a signal, he lowered it and the Hundeiss moved forward.

It was like walking straight into freezing water. Wilhelm felt himself knocked back by the shock of it. Around him, the Hundeiss crouched or lay on the floor, shivering and gasping for breath. And in that instance, Wilhelm knew that Pfeiffer was aware of their presence . . . and that he was unconcerned. To the men within that circle, the attempts of Wilhelm and the others to enter it were as insignificant as the attempts of a fly to break through a plate glass window. And Wilhelm knew that, once the ritual was completed and Pfeiffer had the power he craved, he and the Hundeiss would be swatted like flies. And not just the Hundeiss. For perhaps the first time, he realised the significance of what Pfeiffer was trying to do . . . to raise an invincible power against the world itself.

Desperately, Wilhelm tried to lift himself up off the floor, where he had fallen, but he seemed to be immobilized by the cold. He was no longer touching the shimmering curtain but the icy feeling within him seemed to be increasing. Looking at the others, he could see that they were no longer shivering but seemed to be frozen like statues. Within the circle, though, the ritual was continuing. Pfeiffer raised his arms and, as the men continued to chant, a wisp of what seemed to be smoke arose from the floor at the very centre of the room. Within seconds, it had become a green-tinged column of mist . . . and then it started to take on human form. Or not quite human. For, while it had a head, body and four limbs like a man, it was curiously misshapen with strangely shaped excrescences growing from its skull and shoulders and back. And, as soon as the head was formed, it let out a deafening roar . . . and all the men in the circle knelt, the two who were holding the half-fainting Elisabeth pulling her down with them.

Pfeiffer faced the being and declared "Andromalius! I am Bael and I bid you enter me so that I am both the first and the last . . . Alpha and Omega."

The demon roared again. It was growing larger, taller, more solid, towering over Pfeiffer. Within his frozen body, Wilhelm was desperately trying to think. It could not end like this . . . he could not fail when he was within a few yards of Elisabeth. Surely the heat of his love should be enough to break down this wall of ice. As this thought entered his mind, he felt a slight tingling in his wrist. It was the golden cord. He had forgotten about it. Perhaps he could use it in some way . . . that golden cord which linked him to the people he loved. Again it tingled, slightly more this time. It felt almost as though it was warm . . . although Wilhelm was so frozen that his body was practically dead to all sensation.   Another   tingle and, this time, Wilhelm knew that the cord was getting warmer.   He focused on it, pouring out all his love for Elisabeth, for his friends, for the Hundeiss, for all those who were opposed to Pfeiffer and his followers. Now it was almost burning his wrist - and into his mind came the certainty that all members of the Fellowship were with him, that Johann and Marcus were safe, and that they were all using their spiritual energies to give him strength to achieve what, only seconds ago, had seemed unachievable. In his head, he could hear a single clear voice chanting . . . But no, it wasn't a chant . . . it was Mozart. Wilhelm recognised it as one of the arias sung by Tamino, the hero of *The Magic Flute*, when he looked at a portrait of Pamina and expressed his growing love for her. And it was love that would overcome Pfeiffer and his men . . . Wilhelm's love for Elisabeth, his love for his friends, his love for all that was good in this strange new world in which he now lived.

But he was too cold to sing. Taking as deep a breath as his frozen chest would allow, he started to hum. He could feel the music vibrating in his body. And gradually he became aware of a soft breeze . . . a warm breeze . . . blowing across his face. As he watched, the glittering powder that formed the circles started to move, as he had seen dead leaves move on a pavement when the wind blew. Wilhelm felt the warmth returning to his body, and his breathing became easier, his voice stronger.

Still the men in the circle seemed oblivious to what was happening. But then, as the powder twisted and turned, suddenly a small gap appeared in the line that formed the outer circle. A second later, the shimmering curtain collapsed. Pfeiffer turned and, as he did so, his foot moved against the inner circle, brushing a section of it away. With a roar, the demon, which was now almost the height of the hall itself, seemed to collapse in on itself and then disappeared. There was a shocked silence in the circle. Around Wilhelm, the Hundeiss were struggling to their feet. Grasping their tools, they rushed forward, cascading into the men who stood in their path. Suddenly there was chaos . . . people were fighting and shouting and, above all the noise, came Pfeiffer's voice screaming "Repair the circles! Repair the circles!" Wilhelm, surged across the circle towards Elisabeth. Her two captors seemed to cringe as he bore down on them brandishing, in one hand, Helmut's athame and, in the other, a pickaxe that one of the women had thrust into his hand. As he drew near, they let go of Elisabeth and turned to run . . . only to be concussed with heavy shovels wielded by two of the Hundeiss who had come up behind them.

Elisabeth fell into Wilhelm's arms, clutching at him and whimpering. He eyes were abnormally bright and she seemed close to fainting. Wilhelm held her tight, murmuring words of reassurance while, around them, the fight continued. It seemed that the Hundeiss, despite their smaller numbers, were winning. They were stronger than most of Pfeiffer's men and they were better armed . . . an athame was no match for a pickaxe or for a sledgehammer.

Elisabeth suddenly seemed to become aware of the mayhem going on all around them. She looked up at Wilhelm, a puzzled expression on her face. "Who . . . ?" she asked.

"Hundeiss."

Elisabeth smiled and closed her eyes. Wilhelm looked around the room, searching for a place where she could rest and be safe. With a shock, he realised that he could no longer see Pfeiffer. Urgently he looked for the identifying golden swastika medallion and the silver flute. But none of the men he could see had those insignia. And then Wilhelm thought he saw someone moving by the double doors.

Sensing his agitation, Elisabeth opened her eyes and said "What . . .?"

"Pfeiffer . . . I must find him. He is escaping."

Frantically he looked around . . . and saw Eva a few paces away. Grabbing her arm he said "Eva, this is my woman, Elisabeth. Look after her." And to Elisabeth, "She was Lotte's friend."

As the two women stepped towards each other, Wilhelm turned and raced across the hall, dodging between groups of fighting men and women. Reaching the far side, he charged through the great doors which led into the entrance hall. There was a light on in Pfeiffer's study.

Holding both pickaxe and athame firmly, Wilhelm moved into the room. Pfeiffer was standing behind the desk, taking the spear of Longinus down from the wall. He turned with it in his hands and, seeing Wilhelm, hissed like an angry cat. He advanced towards him, but Wilhelm stood his ground.

"I will kill you!" snarled Pfeiffer, and he lunged forward with the spear, aiming for the hand that held the pickaxe. Wilhelm, expecting the spear to be directed at his chest, was wrong-footed, and the spear scratched his hand as he dodged out of the way. But, although it was only a scratch, the pain was intense and he dropped the pickaxe which fell with a loud thud on the stone flags.

Pfeiffer smiled. "This is the spear of victory," he said, jabbing it towards Wilhelm, "And by this will I conquer!"

Wilhelm began to back away into the entrance hall, his eyes still watering from the pain in his hand. They started to circle around in the larger space, spear against athame, neither making contact with the other. But Pfeiffer had the advantage . . . the spear was longer than the athame . . . could reach further . . . and Wilhelm was being backed into the corner formed by the wall and the splendid marble staircase.

Suddenly out of the corner of his eye, Wilhelm saw two figures emerge through the double doors . . . Eva and Elisabeth . . . and he felt a surge of new energy flood through him. This was what he was fighting for . . . for the woman he loved, for his friends and for the freedom of his people. He was fighting with love in his heart, not hate. And with that realisation came the certainty that he could win . . . that he would win.

Sidestepping nimbly, he moved away from the corner to which Pfeiffer was pushing him and, as he did so, he heard a voice in his head. It was Johann's voice and it was reciting the Manjusri mantra. He knew then, without any doubt, that Johann and Marcus and the two girls were safe. Under his breath, he started to speak the mantra and, as he did so, heard many other voices joining in. Pfeiffer's head twitched swiftly from side to side and Wilhelm realised that he too could hear the voices, could hear the mantra getting louder and louder, ringing around the stone walls of the hall.

Wilhelm's whole body was tingling with the energy that the mantra was raising. He swung his arm to stab at Pfeiffer . . . and, with a gasp, found that he was no longer holding the athame but was wielding the flaming sword of Manjusri. Now it was he who had the advantage and he forced Pfeiffer back into the centre of the hall, slashing at him fiercely, although Pfeiffer continued to parry the sword blows with the spear.

But as he was forced backwards, the red and yellow shoes that Pfeiffer wore started to slip on the stone flags which had been worn smooth by the feet of many generations and, as he struggled to keep his balance, his concentration wavered. Seizing the opportunity, Wilhelm made a grab for the spear and, with a fierce jerk, pulled it out of Pfeiffer's grasp.

The hatred in Pfeiffer's eyes was now mixed with fear. He lunged towards Wilhelm, trying to reclaim his weapon but, once more, his shoes slipped and he fell forwards and then collapsed slowly onto the floor.

The head of the spear had gone right through him, but no blood flowed from the wound. As Wilhelm watched, Pfeiffer's body seemed to wrinkle, shrivel and crumble, falling into dust, leaving nothing but the yellow and red clothes, the swastika and the flute lying on the stone flags. The spear, too, was gone, and Wilhelm found that he was no longer holding the sword of Manjusri, but just a simple athame. He stood there, shaking with exhaustion and relief as the sound of the mantra dwindled and then disappeared. Hearing his name called, he turned to see Elisabeth running

332

towards him.

And, as he took her into his arms, deep, deep below them, in the mines and in the tunnels, suddenly, and with no warning, the music stopped.

THE END

AUTHOR'S NOTES

Although *And When the Music Stops* is a work of fiction, much of the information in it is factual.

The book on brainwashing referred to by Marcus Hellman is *Thought Reform and the Psychology of Totalism: a Study of 'Brainwashing' in China* by Robert Jay Lifton, published by Victor Gollancz, 1962.

Professor Jurgen Udolph's article, in which he linked the disappearance of the children from Hameln with the movement of people from Lower Saxony and Westphalia to the area between Berlin and the Baltic, appeared in the *Lower Saxony State History Yearbook* in 1997. The article was widely acclaimed. I have only read an abstract and, although for the purposes of my story, Johann Schultz found arguments against Professor Udolph's theory, there seems no reason to be believe that this is not, in fact, a feasible explanation of the legend.

Although Johann Schultz's knowledge of 'Pied Piper' legends in Morocco, Turkey and Spain is a product of my imagination, the other legends have actually been recorded. The story of the hurdy-gurdy player in Brandenburg comes from *Norddeutsche Sagen . . .* by A. Kuhn & W. Schwartz (Leipzig 1848); the story of the thousand children who danced and sang their way from Efurt to Arnstadt appears in *Sagenbuch des Preussischen Staats* by J. G. Th. Grasse (Glogau 1868); and the story of the abduction of the children on the Isle of Wight is in *Tales and Legends of the Isle of Wight* by Abraham Elder (London 1839).

The book mentioned by Johann Schultz in the discussion of the Holy Grail, in which the Grail is said to be the bloodline of Christ - the sang real - is *The Holy Blood and the Holy Grail* by Michael Baigent, Richard Leigh & Henry Lincoln (Jonathan Cape 1982).

The long closing passage spoken at the initiation, which Wilhelm finds so inspiring, is Psalm 91.

The pageant in Hameln takes place every Sunday during the summer months.

There are many legends connected with the spear of Longinus. Hitler is said to have first seen what purported to be the spear of Longinus in the Habsburg Treasure House in 1909.

Most of the information about Haushofer is correct although he did not, of course, visit any schloss belonging to a Herr Pfeiffer, since both schloss and Pfeiffer are my own invention. Similarly, most of the information about Robert Browning is factual. He did come through Germany on his way back from Italy in 1838, but I have no evidence that he stopped off to visit relatives. And the letters which Johann Schultz goes to California to see are purely imaginary.

Many theories have been put forward regarding the death of Mozart, and his murder by Freemasons is one of them. However, there has never - as far as I am aware - been any suggestion that he was involved in the occult. Again, this is my own invention. References to Freemasonry in *The Magic Flute* have been commented on by many writers, but the exact significance of such references remains obscure.